JOSIE BONHAM

The Duke's Bluestocking

First published by Pitcheroak Press 2022

First edition

ISBN: 978-1-913856-06-9

This book was professionally typeset on Reedsy.
Find out more at reedsy.com

Chapter One

Spring 1807 London

Angus Medley, the new Duke of Evesham, was well and truly lost. He must have turned off the main road too soon. London was so much bigger than he had expected. It had been foolhardy to refuse Captain McKay's offer of his London-born cabin boy's escort from the port to the orphanage. This area, with its shabby houses crammed tightly together, appeared none too salubrious. A sudden noise behind him made him turn on his heel.

A short, burly man, dressed in little more than rags, advanced towards him.

"Let's 'ave yer wallet, me fine dandy, and you can be on yer way."

Heart thumping, Angus stood his ground. He pressed the mechanism of the sword stick Luke had insisted on giving him. The sword shot out with a reassuring hiss and the would-be thief stared at it wide eyed. He backed off and scuttled away. Angus wiped his brow with the back of his hand and glanced all around. His best option was to retrace his steps and return to the main road.

He turned and set off at a furious pace, holding the sword stick in front of him as a shield against any more attempts to rob him. Within minutes he came to a fork in the road. Neither route looked familiar. He hesitated and then took the right-hand route when he saw a group of grubby urchins loitering in the shadows on the path going left. The rough, uneven cobbles underfoot hampered his progress. He retracted the sword, ready to use it as a walking stick to steady himself if he tripped, and picked up his pace. The sooner he was out of here the better.

Eyes seemed to be following him from behind grimy windows. Two men appeared as if from nowhere in front of him. They were more of a match for him in height than the first would-be thief and there were two of them. He dived down a side street to his left. The pavement was smoother and he ran to the end of the street and turned round. There was no sign of the two men behind him. He paused to catch his breath, still with the uncomfortable feeling of being watched. But then he stood out in a poor district like this. Should he go right or left?

The sun, already low in the sky, was coming from the right. The most important thing was to get out of this area before it got dark. If he turned towards the sun, that must take him westwards. Follow the sun and he should end up somewhere where he could hail a hackney carriage. The road bent to the right until the sun was to his left. He came to a fork in the road and turned left, onto the meanest street he had ever come across. Buildings clung together for support. An occasional flake of paint clung to wooden doors and windows that were grey with age and decay. There was nothing he could do but press on.

Angus shuddered. Edinburgh had its dark side, but nothing compared to this. Human waste rubbed shoulders with dead rats in an open drain which ran along the centre of the street.

His stomach churned and he held a handkerchief to his nose. Even this early in the year, the smell was vile. Heaven alone knew what it was like in the summer. No one should be forced to live in conditions like that. No wonder Luke's sister was keen to help as many orphans as she could.

The street was deserted. Even the thieves and pickpockets must steer clear. He breathed easier when he reached a crossroads. The road running across was much wider and cleaner, apart from an occasional pile of horse manure on it. Horses suggested it was used by merchants and travellers. There was no sign of any carts or carriages he could flag down. Still, it meant he must be close to a main route. If he followed the horse manure, he should find a way out to civilisation.

He took the road to the right. He had the sun to his left but there was another crossroads a bit further along. The houses he passed were in much better condition and there was no sign of anyone loitering. His breathing calmed. From the numbers of carriages, people and horses passing over the crossroads, he was coming to a major route. Where he might find someone to give him directions. Best not to pull out his pocket watch even here, but he was probably in time for his meeting with Miss Bamford. As long as he could find the orphanage soon. He quickened his pace and nearly knocked into a tiny, shabbily dressed woman who came out of a side road in front of him. He stopped.

"I'm sorry, I didn't see you."

She gave him a gap-toothed smile. "I am a long way down. No 'arm done, Sir."

A solitary, shrivelled orange rested in the basket on her arm. She looked him up and down and held the basket out towards him.

"One orange left. What will you give me for it, my fine lord?" She sounded weary.

"Nothing, but I'll pay you for directions to the Sunshine Orphanage in Arthur Street."

The harsh lines of the woman's face softened. "A good place that. You're nearly there. Turn left at the crossroads. It's not far along to the Orphanage. Big stone building. You can't miss it."

Could he trust her? He studied her face. His years as an advocate told him he could. A quick glance suggested there was no one else around. He pulled out half a guinea, the smallest coin he had on him, and slipped it into her basket.

"Thank you."

The orange seller smiled her thanks. "Bless you, my lord."

He raised his hat and carried on past a tall wall bordering the street. A rustling sound made him peer into the dark shadows along the base of the wall. The shadows seemed to dance. The muscles at the back of his neck tightened and he quickened his pace. It was probably rats; his lucky escape had left him jittery. He turned the corner and spotted a large stone building less than fifty yards away. That must be the orphanage.

He relaxed when he was close enough to read *Sunshine Orphanage* on the brass plaque to the left of the shiny, red front door. Without warning, a raggedly dressed man hurtled out of the shadows of a side street to the left of the orphanage and ran towards him. Angus dodged sideways and a flash of metal missed him by the narrowest of margins. The man snarled, showing the stumps of a few blackened teeth, and ran at Angus again. Angus dodged again and opened the swordstick. A pistol shot rang out. His assailant's knife clattered to the floor and the man ran off, clutching a bloodstained shoulder.

A vision in blue velvet climbed down from a smart town carriage which had pulled up. A groom jumped down from the seat next to the driver to join her.

Miss Blue Velvet pointed at the disappearing figure of Angus's attacker. "Jamie, try and follow him, his injuries will slow him down. Don't take any risks and stay clear if he has accomplices. I'll send you some help." There was a note of urgency in her well-modulated voice.

"Yes, Miss Bamford." The young groom set off in pursuit.

So, this was Luke's sister. She ran towards him, carrying a small pistol in her hand, and gently lifted his arm.

"Oh no, you're injured."

Angus glanced down to see a slit in the arm of his new coat with a trickle of blood seeping out. His head jerked back. "Good Lord, I am!"

Miss Bamford slipped her pistol into a large reticule hanging from her arm. "You need to have that cleaned and dressed immediately. Come with me." She turned back and addressed her coachman. "I'll send someone out to you. If we can catch this gentleman's attacker, we'll have to send for the magistrate."

Angus allowed himself to be led towards the door. His arm was starting to throb and he distracted himself by studying Miss Bamford. She had a strong look of Luke but much darker hair. If he had to get waylaid by a footpad on his first day out alone in London, at least he was being tended to in some style. A burly individual, whose misshapen ears suggested that he had once been a prize fighter, opened the door.

"I've sent my groom after a rogue who set upon this gentleman, Parker. He'll need help." Miss Bamford pointed in the direction they'd gone. "Down past the mews. You can follow the trail of blood, I managed to shoot the blighter."

Parker raced off and Miss Bamford directed two boys who appeared in the hallway to go and help the coachman with his horses. She turned her attention towards Angus. Her eyes were an interesting shade of hazel, with a ring of grey around the outer edges, set in a heart shaped face with eminently kissable lips. Tall and shapely, she radiated energy and was an impressive young woman. Angus's head started to swim. His arm was throbbing like the devil. Oh Lord, he wasn't going to disgrace himself by passing out, was he?

"Sit here and put your head down."

Miss Bamford's voice sounded distant against the roaring in his ears, but he managed to sit down without falling when she helped him to a wooden settle. She pushed him down with a hand on one shoulder, until his head was resting between his knees, and held the cut arm aloft.

"Don't worry, the bleeding is light. It's the shock that's made you feel not quite the thing."

Everything came back into focus and Angus tried to sit up. Miss Bamford kept a firm hand on his shoulder.

"Sit up very slowly. That's it. How do you feel now?"

"A lot better, thank you." Oh, the mortification. He felt his cheeks going pink.

Miss Bamford smiled at him. "You certainly have a lot more colour. Your face went whiter than one of Mrs Baker's starched aprons."

Angus grinned. "Who is Mrs Baker? She sounds a bit of a dragon."

"She's the orphanage's housekeeper and extraordinarily efficient, but quite lovely with it. Stay there a bit longer. If we can prop your arm up, I'll go and fetch some help."

Miss Bamford removed her hand from his shoulder and leaned forward to take the hand of the damaged arm she was holding aloft. The movement brought them so close that their bodies were almost touching. The smell of her perfume tickled his nose. A floral scent, reminiscent of summer, with strong overtones of lavender. She dipped her head to study his damaged arm. The tip of her tongue came out as she concentrated on the wound. The temptation to touch her cheek was so strong that Angus gripped his other hand between his knees.

"It's almost stopped bleeding, but let's rest it along the top of the settle to be safe."

Angus leaned back against the hard, wooden settle and allowed her to arrange his arm. She took a step away and he swept a glance over her shapely curves. The sound of footsteps came nearer. Angus dragged his eyes away from Miss Bamford to see a middle-aged lady, with a friendly expression, hurrying towards them.

"Ah, here is Mrs Baker now. We'll soon have that wound attended to."

"Some of the boys have been to tell me that a gentleman has been attacked outside our door." Mrs Baker gave Angus a reassuring smile. "What happened?"

Miss Bamford grimaced. "A footpad with a knife, Mrs Baker. This gentleman managed to dodge out of the way but he took a glancing blow. I don't think it's too deep though."

Miss Bamford stood back and Mrs Baker inspected his arm.

"I think you're right from the amount of bleeding, but we won't know for sure until we've got his coat off." She shook her head. "I see you're one of those fashionable gentlemen who wears his coat tight. I'm afraid we might have to cut it off, Sir."

Angus studied his smart, navy-blue coat and grimaced. "What a waste. It was only delivered this morning." He laughed. "I'm showing my frugal Scottish merchant blood here."

"We can get you attended to by a countryman then."

Miss Bamford smiled. "I take it you mean that Dr Jarvie is here, Mrs Baker. That's good."

"Yes indeed, Miss. He's nearly finished checking over the young people who are ready to start work."

"Any problems?"

"No. They all seem healthy so far. Let's see if we can get this gentleman along to my sitting room."

Angus stood, taking care not to move his head too quickly. "I seem to have recovered. I'm sure I can walk to your room, Mrs Baker."

"Follow me then, Sir."

Miss Bamford took his good arm and guided him along in the wake of Mrs Baker. She shepherded him into a cosy sitting room, with a blazing fire. Angus realised he was shivering. Miss Bamford led him to a worn, leather armchair next to the fire. Once he was settled, she hovered around him like a mother hen.

"Right Sir, I'll leave you with Miss Bamford and go and find Dr Jarvie." Mrs Baker bustled out.

Angus grinned at Miss Bamford. "There's no need to look so worried. I feel in perfect health now."

"In that case, why are you shivering?" She sat in a matching armchair on the other side of the fire.

"You must think me a poor fellow, going into shock for such a trifling incident."

Miss Bamford's clear, hazel eyes studied him. "Considering somebody made a serious attempt to kill you, I think you're remarkably calm."

"It was simply an attempt to rob me that went too far."

Miss Bamford shook her head so hard that the tendrils of dark curls framing either side of her face quivered. "I'm sure it wasn't."

"I hope you're wrong. I ought to introduce myself. I'm the Duke of Evesham, but I'm finding it difficult to think of myself as a duke." He frowned and pulled at his earlobe with his uninjured arm. "I still feel like plain Angus Medley."

Miss Bamford eyed him with interest. "Somehow, word has got out about your visit today. The children are so excited at the prospect of meeting a duke. Not that you will be up to that today after nearly being murdered."

"I'm sure he was just a thief. I got well and truly lost on my way here." Angus felt his cheeks flush. "I was grateful for the swordstick Luke gave me when I was set upon by one would be thief and I managed to outrun two more before I found my way here."

Miss Bamford frowned. "Luke said you would be coming from his man of business's office. It's not far."

"My appointment took much less time than I expected. I got a hackney cab down to the docks to see if my cousin's ship had arrived, with some belongings I wanted transported down to London. Stupidly, I refused an escort here and got lost. One of the thieves must have caught up with me."

"No. That man was waiting for you." Her brow furrowed. "I watched him from my coach. He kept popping out of the road that leads to our mews, as if he was waiting for someone. He looked so suspicious I had the window open and one of my pistols out before my carriage stopped. It's lucky for you I managed to hit him."

She stared at him, unblinking. "I have no doubt that he was trying to kill you."

Angus gasped and huffed out a breath. She was seriously worried. "Tarnation. Has all that nonsense in Edinburgh followed me down to London?"

Miss Bamford's eyes widened. "Has this happened before then?"

Angus shook his head. "Not actual attempts on my life, but threats have been made."

"Who by?"

"I'm not sure. I was an advocate in Edinburgh and made myself some dangerous enemies with my opposition to the treatment of the clans. I've also successfully defended many people who wouldn't have afforded an advocate's fees, to the fury of some influential people." Angus stroked his chin. "Even so I'm not convinced this was anything more than an attempted robbery."

Miss Bamford sighed and tapped a foot on the hard wooden floor. "He was definitely targeting you, my friend. He ignored a couple of elderly gentlemen who would have been much easier targets. The first time he lunged at you he was aiming that knife straight at your heart. If you hadn't changed direction, you would now be seriously injured, at the very least."

Angus pursed his lips but said nothing. She seemed a no-nonsense sort of female and not the sort to have flights of fancy. Even so, if someone was trying to kill him, why leave it until now? They must have had much better opportunities in Edinburgh.

Miss Bamford raised her eyebrows and leaned towards him. "What are you thinking?"

"That it would have been much easier to have murdered me in Edinburgh. I often used to walk home alone late at night."

"But much more suspicious perhaps?"

Grace Bamford was intelligent as well as practical it seemed. "That's a good point. I made a lot of friends as well as enemies and there would have been an outcry."

Miss Bamford nodded. "London used to be notorious for footpads and it's still a problem now, especially in poorer areas like this. Your friends would have thought it simply bad luck."

"Very likely." Angus rubbed at his forehead. "I could have done without this complication with so much to do to restore my estates."

"Since you and Luke are coming to dinner with us tonight, we may as well leave this discussion until then. Once Dr Jarvie and Mrs Baker have patched you up, I'll have you driven home in the carriage, with Parker to act as bodyguard."

Angus gritted his teeth and stared at the floor before throwing his head back. "I'm perfectly recovered, thank you. I won't trouble your people any further once my arm has been attended to."

"There is no need to poker up. If you want to walk home and risk the man having accomplices lying in wait, I can't stop you." Miss Bamford laughed. "On reflection, you will probably be quite safe. A smartly dressed gentleman with a blood-stained shirt showing through the slit arm of his jacket is bound to attract plenty of attention."

She rolled her eyes at him and Angus burst out laughing.

"Touché, Miss Bamford. I have no desire to be arrested for suspected duelling. I accept your offer of transport back to your brother's house."

"Sensible man. Dr Jarvie knows what he's about and Mrs Baker is a genius with her herbal remedies. You should suffer no ill effects."

Parker appeared in the doorway, holding a knife wrapped in a cloth. "No luck, Miss Bamford. The trail of blood disappeared after a cart went past me. I caught up with your groom. He says the man was pulled onto the cart by two other rough looking fellows."

"Thank you, Parker. Leave the knife in here, it may tell us something. I have a meeting of the orphanage patrons soon. Would you escort this gentleman home in my carriage once he's ready? He's staying with Viscount Enstone."

"Of course, Miss Bamford."

"Thank you. I'll leave you to sort out the arrangements. Make sure you and Jamie have something to drink after your exertions first."

Parker bowed and went out.

Miss Bamford scrunched up her nose. "Hmm. Do you still think you were attacked by a random footpad? It all sounds far too orchestrated to me. I'll see you tonight, Your Grace."

Chapter Two

Angus allowed Luke's valet to put the final touches to his neck cloth.

"That feels a bit too tight."

Luke laid a hand on his shoulder. "Nonsense it's perfect, even I can see that. Don't worry, you'll have a lovely evening."

Angus shuddered. "I've never been one for socialising and London high society is a far cry from the Edinburgh circles I'm used to."

"There will only be six of us. My Aunt Theo is a darling and the Duke and Duchess of Cathlay are always excellent company. I know my sister is an original but you've already met her."

Angus felt heat flooding his cheeks. "I forgot to mention that I nearly passed out after Miss Bamford rescued me and she had to guide me to a chair. She must think me a terrible weakling."

"I'm sure she won't blame you for a common reaction to injury." Luke grinned at him. "Come on. The carriage is waiting for us."

Angus allowed himself to be led out to the waiting coach. A smart affair with a coat of arms emblazoned on the gleaming yellow paintwork of the door. He suppressed a sigh. How was he going to deal with all this pomp and circumstance?

Miss Bamford's coach had been similar. The lady herself had seemed eminently practical. Was that frowned upon for the ladies of the Ton? Luke joined him in the coach and tapped the roof with the walking cane he was carrying. The coach set off.

"That spare swordstick you gave me came in useful today. Your sister is an excellent shot. Is that why you say she's an original?"

Luke chuckled. "Partly. It's not an accomplishment a lady would mention in public. Grace describes herself as a bluestocking, despite her love of fashion. Partially true though as she's a great scholar with a particular interest in Greek antiquities, as I know to my cost."

"Has she dragged you off to Greece then?"

"Oh no, much worse than that." Luke pulled a face. "If I'm in London she's always trying to get me to escort her to the British Museum, or some lecture or other. Anything to do with ancient history will do, it doesn't have to be Greece."

"You don't share her interest? You should, ancient civilisations are fascinating."

The coach slowed and turned into a road filled with large mansions. Angus stared out of the window as if he was studying them. Luke was watching him rather too closely for comfort. He had better be careful not to show any more interest in Miss Bamford or Luke would be pairing them off.

He had a great deal of work to do to set his newly inherited estates to rights and make proper provision for all the people depending on them. He couldn't afford to be distracted. When he was ready to search for a wife, he had no intention of marrying a society lady, even one as unusual as Miss Grace Bamford. Not after the way his father's family had scorned his mother because of her merchant origins.

"This is Cavendish Square," Luke said, "we're nearly there. Grace is what people call a managing female. She's involved in several charities besides her leading role in running the Sunshine Orphanage."

"I'm glad she is involved with the orphanage. It will take an army of people to put Medley House to rights, it hasn't been used for years." Angus's shoulders slumped.

"The thought of being a Duke terrifies me, my only consolation is the opportunity to provide good quality employment. If I can give some orphans their first jobs so much the better."

They pulled up in front of an impressive mansion, although it wasn't as big as Medley House. Angus followed Luke out of the coach. The sconces either side of the door were lit, creating a cosy impression. The inside of the house was just as inviting. A stately butler directed a footman to take their outdoor things.

The butler led them across a marbled hallway and threw open a set of double doors. "The Duke of Evesham and Viscount Enstone."

The doors closed behind them and Angus tried not to stare at the stylish interior of blue and gold furniture, gold-coloured walls and brightly coloured carpet which met him. He squared his shoulders and walked farther into the room, keeping pace with Luke.

"Allow me to introduce my aunt, Lady Grant."

A middle-aged lady with a lovely smile stood to greet him. "I'm delighted to make your acquaintance, Your Grace."

Angus relaxed. "I would much rather you called me Angus."

Before Lady Grant could answer, the door opened and Miss Bamford, this time dressed in ruby red silk, ran into the room. She threw her arms around Luke.

"Why on earth did Harvey announce you? Although I'm

glad he did. I don't want to miss a minute of your company tonight. How's Kitty? I'm so looking forward to being an aunt again soon. Sorry I missed you yesterday. We've been busy at the orphanage, setting up the new employment agency. I've hardly seen Aunt Theo in the last few days," she said, with a laugh in her voice.

"Woah there, Grace." Luke grinned and held her a little away from him. "Kitty is well except for feeling a little off in the mornings. Edward is spending his holiday with her at Enstone Court so she has company and I don't need to rush back. I've been busy myself, helping their newly discovered cousin settle into his new role." He nodded towards Angus.

Miss Bamford spun round until she was facing Angus and swept into a deep curtsy, with her eyes downcast. "Oh Lord, how rude of me to ignore you. My apologies, Your Grace."

Angus tugged at his neck-cloth. This was so awkward, but it was something he was going to have to get used to.

"Think nothing of it, Miss Bamford. It is but a small matter compared to the service you rendered me earlier today. Your brother has been singing your praises." He glanced at Luke, trying not to smile. "He tells me he's hoping you'll have time to fit in a visit to the British Museum before he returns home to Lady Enstone."

A musical laugh escaped Miss Bamford. "Now that's a plumper if ever I heard one. It makes me wonder exactly what Luke has been telling you."

Her eyes were dancing and Angus found himself relaxing. He couldn't stop his glance sweeping over her despite Luke's eyes on him.

"Indeed, Miss Bamford. Luke has warned me that you're partial to anything to do with antiquities. As someone who shares your passion, I told him he ought to make more effort."

Now why had he said that? Angus tried not to cringe. Luke was still watching him and talk of a shared passion was hardly what was needed to dampen any speculation about him and Miss Bamford.

Luke's eyebrows shot up. He snorted and gave Angus's good arm a playful tap. "I'll be happy to let you deputise for me. Although I find it hard to believe you're a student of antiquities. Not unless Scottish advocates spend a lot less time studying than English lawyers."

"I haven't had much time in recent years, it's true. My father was a great scholar of ancient history and I found his enthusiasm infectious."

Luke's glance flicked from him to Miss Bamford and back. He grinned at Angus. "In that case, I'm sure Grace will be happy to show you around the British Museum."

Angus looked at the ground to hide his hot cheeks. Would Miss Bamford think he had been angling for an invitation? "That would be most kind."

Miss Bamford stayed silent and Lady Grant took pity on him. "We're early, we might as well take a seat until the Cathlays arrive."

Luke joined his aunt on a sofa, leaving Angus to occupy one of a pair of armchairs opposite, after Miss Bamford settled in the other one.

Miss Bamford gave him a sympathetic glance. "How is your arm now?"

"Sore, but after Mrs Baker's treatment I don't think I'll have any problems."

Miss Bamford laughed. "She knows what she's doing, but some of her remedies do hurt."

"It certainly made my eyes water when she put the ointment on. There were some children waiting outside to be checked by the doctor, I hope I didn't whimper too loudly."

"Mrs Baker said you were stoical."

"I'm sure she was flattering me. I hope your friends aren't too fashionable. I couldn't get my new evening coat over the bandage. I'm wearing one of my old ones, which are much looser."

Miss Bamford ran her eyes over his dark green jacket. Angus felt his cheeks redden at her scrutiny.

"The Duchess of Cathlay is a noted society hostess, but I don't think she will find anything amiss with you."

"That's good, I wouldn't want to let Luke down after he's been so helpful."

"Are you planning to do much socialising now you're in London?"

Angus shook his head and grinned. "Not if I can help it. What about you? Are you too busy working for the orphanage to get out and about?"

"There isn't normally quite this much to do for the orphanage, although I am involved in some other charities." She lifted her chin and studied him through narrowed eyes. "I go to some events with Aunt Theo, but now I'm officially on the shelf I don't need to worry too much about that sort of thing."

Angus raised his eyebrows. "You don't look old enough to be on the shelf, an awful expression. I suppose studying ancient history keeps you busy."

"If you're implying that I'm a bluestocking," she smiled at him, "you wouldn't be far wide of the mark."

"I've never heard that expression until recently. I find it grossly unfair." Angus frowned. "Why shouldn't women enjoy scholarship?"

Miss Bamford's eyes opened wide. "That's a refreshing attitude coming from a man. Were you serious about being interested in ancient history?"

"Yes, I was. My father taught me a lot and I found it fascinating. I have a strong streak of my mother's practical merchant stock in me, though, and decided to study law."

The doors opened and the butler announced the Duke and Duchess of Cathlay. Lady Grant performed the introductions. She ushered them into the dining room, ladies first with the Duchess of Cathlay leading the way, at a signal from the butler. The dining room was much smaller than Angus had expected, with a round table. Lady Grant must have seen his puzzlement. She laid a hand on his arm.

"This is the family dining room, I thought we would be more comfortable in here as there are so few of us."

"I certainly feel more comfortable than I would in a large room." Angus looked around at golden damask wallpaper with a burgundy pattern and light-coloured wood work. A large chandelier suspended over the rosewood dining table created a cosy atmosphere. "This is an attractive room. I shall be asking for your advice when I come to redecorate Medley House."

"I should be happy to help, although Grace is much better at colour schemes than I am, if she ever has any free time."

Lady Grant locked glances with Luke, so briefly Angus could have almost thought he had imagined it. But he hadn't. He was going to have to be careful not to raise any expectations. The Duchess of Cathlay stopped near the table. "I have absolutely no idea which dukedom is the most senior."

After a moment's confusion enlightenment dawned. Angus remembered his father telling him of the ridiculous rules on seating precedence in the homes of the Ton. He bowed low.

"I confess I have no idea either. Let us assume that the house of Cathlay has that honour."

"Thank you, Your Grace," Lady Grant said. "That puts you on my left side with the Duchess next to you."

Angus took his place on the left-hand side of Lady Grant, wondering if he had just passed a test. The Duke of Cathlay was on Lady Grant's right-hand side, facing Angus, with the Duchess on Angus's left-hand side opposite to Miss Bamford, with Luke between them.

Once they were seated Lady Grant smiled at him. "We consider the Cathlays as family so we don't need to worry about precedence tonight, but at formal dinners the rules are followed strictly."

Angus bowed his head fleetingly. "I am aware."

"Of course, Your Grace." Lady Grant held his gaze, a smile playing at the edges of her mouth. It wasn't like him to be so touchy.

"Thank you for your help, Lady Grant. I was most ungracious." He gave a rueful smile. "My new role has left me feeling all at sea. My father was a distinguished scholar and uninterested in high society. My mother was brought up by her grandparents, Edinburgh merchants. The Medleys wanted nothing to do with us and I've always been close to my Edinburgh cousins. I'm very much aware people will be watching me and I don't want anyone to say that my mother didn't bring me up properly."

Lady Grant patted his hand. "I perfectly understand. A duke will be forgiven a lot so I wouldn't worry overmuch." She smiled up at him. "I shall be happy to advise you if you need a friend to talk to."

Angus felt his cheeks grow hot. "Thank you. It's not like me to bore on about myself."

"I'm used to drawing out young people. I raised four children of my own, besides Luke and Grace."

Angus nodded and his attention was claimed by the Duchess of Cathlay.

"Have you decided yet where you will make your principal home, Your Grace?"

"Not yet. I have so many properties to choose from." Angus laughed. "I am going to open up Medley House and have a London base."

The Duke of Cathlay looked up from his conversation with Lady Grant. He leaned forward and caught Angus's gaze.

"Since you intend to spend at least part of the year in London, will you take up your seat in the House of Lords?"

The Duchess of Cathlay laughed out loud. "I must warn you, Evesham, that Cathlay spends a lot of his time trying to persuade younger members of the family to take their seat in the House. It seems he's turned his attention to you."

Angus smiled at the Duke. "I don't need any persuasion, Your Grace. I fully intend to take my seat."

Angus studied the Duke with interest. The man was inscrutable. It was impossible to have any idea what he was thinking. He waited for few seconds until it was clear he had no intention of replying and suppressed a smile. The Duke was using the tactics of strategic silence he had himself perfected with potential clients. Often, they would rush into speech to fill the gap and reveal more than they meant to. Perhaps it was time to make his intentions known. It would be useful to discover whether the Duke of Cathlay was likely to be an enemy or an ally.

"I have a particular reason for wanting to take up my seat. I have spent the last ten years trying to stop the dreadful ways in which many of the Scottish people are being mistreated. I'm hoping I may be able to use my voice in Parliament to make a difference." Angus locked glances with the Duke and held his breath.

A huge smile spread across the Duke's rather stern face, making him seem much more approachable. "Rest assured that no person connected with any of my estates, no matter how lowly, has or will be treated in an unfair manner during my lifetime."

Angus relaxed against the back of his chair. "I'm delighted to hear that and happy to find I have an ally. I've heard that Parliament will soon be dissolved and so my first appearance in the House of Lords may have to wait a few weeks. I'm not at all sure of the formalities."

"I suggest you dine with me later in the week, perhaps at Brook's, and I can talk you through it. I'll be happy to put you up for membership of Brook's."

"Thank you. That would be much appreciated." Angus looked at Luke. "Are you a member of Brooks? I never thought to ask you"

Luke laughed. "I am, His Grace saw to that."

"Excellent. Now I have some political allies I can turn my attention to sorting out my estates. I know there have been five dukes of Evesham in the last three years but even so I cannot believe the mess they're in."

Miss Bamford gasped. "Five dukes in three years, what happened?"

Angus shook his head. "My grandfather died of natural causes first, followed by his eldest son. His son, my cousin,

Simon, had already been killed fighting in Europe. My grandfather's second son died before his father and left only daughters. My grandfather's third son was killed in a boating accident, along with his own son, less than a year after inheriting the dukedom. Grandfather's fourth son, my uncle Harry, died of fever within a few weeks of succeeding to the dukedom, only for his eldest son to break his neck on the hunting field six months later. His second son, William was killed in the army a few days after his brother died. If you count him, it's six, but he never formally inherited."

"What a dreadful sequence." Miss Bamford chewed at her lip, making it difficult for Angus to look away.

"You don't think that the attack on you this afternoon could be connected, do you?"

"Not for a minute. I have no truck with those people saying that the Medleys are cursed either."

Miss Bamford's face took on a mulish expression. "Humour me. Who is the next in line to the dukedom after you?"

Angus rubbed at his chin. "Probably a distant cousin called Ralph Medley. My cousin, William, the only member of the family we had contact with, met Ralph several times when he was at Horse Guards between postings."

Miss Bamford gave him a triumphant grin. "I expect it's Ralph then."

"I doubt that. As far as I know, he's still serving in the army."

Luke caught his eye. "Were they in the same regiment?"

"I don't think so, but William only mentioned him in passing."

"I've got some friends at Horse Guards. I might call in and say hello. Someone might know Ralph Medley." Luke grinned. "Purely to put Grace's mind at rest. She does love a mystery."

The Duke of Cathlay shook his head. "By all means do so, Enstone, but feelings are running high in the Highlands from what I've heard. Word of Evesham's campaign against what's happening has reached us landowners farther south. He will have made a lot of enemies."

Miss Bamford beamed around the table. "You agree with me that the Duke of Evesham is in danger then, Your Grace?" Her voice rose in pitch.

"Grace, you minx," Luke said. "Cathlay doesn't agree with your wild speculation, he's simply being cautious."

Angus studied the duke's grim expression. "I think he does, Enstone. I had better be careful."

Chapter Three

Grace descended the stairs as the huge, brass faced, grandfather clock in the corner struck two, humming to herself. The orphanage's new employment agency was ready. Besides the Duke of Evesham's visit later, they had their first interview of a potential employer. A lot was riding on this with so many young people needing work. She strode towards the front door but came to a halt when she heard voices coming from Aunt Theo's sitting room.

"Now we have Max married perhaps we should turn our attention to dear Grace."

That sounded like the Duchess of Cathlay. She ought to leave at this point but Grace found herself listening.

"I'm sure you're right, Augusta."

Aunt Theo agreed with the Duchess!

"Do I sense a 'but'?"

"I'm afraid so." Aunt Theo sounded distinctly worried. "Grace is determined never to marry, but her life would be so much more fulfilling with the right man by her side."

It was all Grace could do to stop herself exploding with wrath. She thought Aunt Theo, of all people, understood how she felt. Obviously, she was wrong. The last thing she needed was a man telling her what to do. She had a fulfilling life, especially with her work at the orphanage. She was about to slip away when she heard her aunt's voice again.

"The thing is, Augusta, Luke is convinced the Duke of Evesham is the perfect man for Grace. He's determined to push for a match."

Grace's mouth dropped open. She was tempted to march in and say her piece. The Duchess's voice stopped her.

"Enstone may be right. I had Evesham in mind too. He seems an interesting sort, with a genuine interest in helping the poor. Exactly the kind of man to appeal to Grace. If Enstone pushes her towards him any chance she might be interested will disappear through the nearest open window."

"Exactly. Luke is normally so sensible but he feels responsible for Grace's aversion to marriage. I'm afraid he's taken it into his head that Angus Medley is the man to change her mind and he's determined to see it happen."

Grace moved away from the drawing room door. Whatever they said in her hearing, her family wanted to marry her off like any other young debutante. It was a betrayal of the first order. She was seven and twenty years of age, a long way past the age of majority. What right did her brother have to meddle in her life? The worst part was the feeling, which she couldn't shake off, that Aunt Theo was more worried about Luke spoiling the Duke's chances with her than she was about Grace being pestered by such a nonsensical idea in the first place.

Aunt Theo had always supported her in the past. Was she growing tired of having a niece in permanent residence? Grace pulled her shoulders back. If she was, much as it would hurt, why not say something? Perhaps it was time to set up her own establishment in any case? The butler appeared in the hall and

Grace blinked back the tears that were threatening to spill.

"The coach has arrived for you, Miss Bamford."

"Thank you, Harvey. I believe I heard the Duchess of Cathlay's voice. I don't have time to stop. Would you convey my regards to her?"

Harvey bowed. "Of course, Miss Bamford." He glided to the front door and opened it for her.

She reached the pavement and a footman sprang forward to open the door of the family coach. Grace lifted her skirts slightly with one hand and climbed in, ignoring the footman's proffered hand. The coach set off and she sat back, watching the passing street scenes to distract her from what she had overheard. The route to the orphanage took them through the City of London. As always, Grace was fascinated by the sight of all the dark clad men, most of them probably clerks, scurrying about their business.

Why did they all have to wear black? Even the gentlemen of her acquaintance tended to wear dark colours. Being able to wear brightly coloured clothes was one advantage of being female. It was hard to think of any others. Indeed, when it came to dress, breeches seemed a much more sensible option for many activities. Although even Aunt Theo would be scandalised if she heard her voice such an opinion. Grace sniffed. It seemed that deep down Aunt Theo disapproved of her entire lifestyle.

Once they arrived at the orphanage, Grace tried to put her worries to one side and joined her friend and fellow volunteer, Lucy Vaughan, in the orphanage office. Lucy's blonde head was bent over a rosewood library table, topped with ink stained, green leather. She glanced up and smiled.

"It will soon be time to interview Mrs Craddock." Lucy

bounced in her chair and grinned. "She comes well recommended by a friend of my mother and is the wife of a successful lawyer."

Grace grinned back. Lucy's excitement was infectious. "I have to say, dear friend, I find lawyers boring. Which doesn't preclude them from being good employers. It turns out that the Duke of Evesham was the Scottish equivalent of a lawyer."

"Mrs Baker said he's coming later. Is he serious about employing some of our orphans?"

Grace fought to banish all thoughts of the conversation she had overheard and settled into the worn, but comfortable, brown leather armchair next to Lucy.

"I think so. He had dinner with us last night. He only has a skeleton staff at Medley House which he intends to open up. It could mean quite a few places. He needs grooms as well as inside servants."

Lucy's eyes shone. "Oh, that's famous! Mrs Baker took to him."

"I believe he is a good employer, but I'll leave the final decision to you. Now to Mrs Craddock. I hope she won't be intimidated by having two of us interview her."

Lucy tilted her head. "Would it be such a bad thing if she was? You often learn more about people when they're under a bit of pressure."

Grace burst out laughing. "Now I know why we picked you for this job. I do hope your mother won't take you off to the seaside for too long in the summer."

There was a knock at the door and Mrs Baker ushered in a well-dressed lady, probably in her late twenties. Both young ladies rose to their feet. Grace introduced them and left Lucy to take the lead, as the employment agency for their orphans was her idea.

"Thank you for coming, Mrs Craddock." Lucy offered the visitor the chair opposite to them. "It makes it much easier for us to introduce you to a selection of potential candidates."

Mrs Craddock raised her eyebrows. "If I pass inspection, of course."

Lucy stuttered something unintelligible and drew in a deep breath before starting again. "I hope we haven't offended you by asking for an interview."

"Not in the least. I'm a vicar's daughter and I appreciate what you're doing here."

Lucy seemed to be overcome with nerves. Grace smiled at Mrs Craddock. "Thank you. Would you like some tea before we start?"

"I need a parlour maid as well as a nursery maid, so perhaps we could leave it until after you've interviewed me and be served by your suggested candidate, assuming you approve me." Mrs Craddock gave them a smile that lit up her face.

"What a good idea." Grace studied Mrs Craddock. She was clearly intelligent and gave every sign of being of a good disposition. "We may as well be honest with you. This is the first time we've interviewed a prospective employer. I suspect you're more experienced at this sort of thing than we are. So, if you wouldn't mind, it would be helpful if you give us your opinion on our questions."

"I would be delighted. In fact, I'd like to offer my services if there is anything at all I can do to help."

Grace laughed. "I'm sure we can sign you up for something."

Lucy opened a brand-new ledger. A quarter of an hour later all their questions had been satisfactorily answered and the list improved upon with Mrs Craddock's suggestions. Grace exchanged a glance with Lucy who nodded.

"We are more than happy to put you on our books as an employer of our young people, Mrs Craddock," Grace said.

"Thank you."

"We have two young women who might be absolutely perfect for you. They are both fifteen and they're cousins. They want to take employment together. Mary loves children and has been marvellous with the little ones at the orphanage. She wants to be a nursery maid." Grace rang the little brass bell that sat on the table. "Esther is ambitious and the more confident of the two. She would like to rise to the position of housekeeper one day."

Mrs Baker entered so quickly she must have been waiting outside. Grace gave her a quick nod and the housekeeper broke into a broad smile.

"Would you be so good as to send Mary in please, Mrs Baker? Then ask Esther if she would bring in a tea tray for three people."

"Of course, Miss Bamford." Mrs Baker curtsied and bustled out.

A few moments later, Mary knocked on the door and entered, twisting her apron in her hands.

Mrs Craddock drew her into conversation and Mary visibly relaxed. Grace gave Lucy a little half smile. Mrs Craddock had a way with people and would be a good employer. Esther arrived a short while later. She placed a perfectly laid tea tray on the table in front of Grace and dropped a curtsy. She kept her eyes lowered but answered Mrs Craddock's questions sensibly and confidently.

"Miss Bamford, Miss Vaughan I have to say you've done a marvellous job with these two girls and they are absolutely perfect for the positions I have."

Mary and Esther looked at each other and grinned. Esther answered for both of them. "Thank you very much, Mrs Craddock. We won't let you down."

"We forgot to ask you when you would like the girls to start, Mrs Craddock," Lucy said.

Mrs Craddock glanced at the clock in the corner of the room. "My carriage will return in about half an hour. Would it be possible for them to start today?"

Grace nodded. "I don't see why not. It will give them less time to become nervous." She smiled at the girls. "Off you go and pack your things. Be down in the hall in half an hour please."

The girls curtsied and hurried out of the room.

Grace poured the tea. "After we have drunk this, would you like a tour of the orphanage, Mrs Craddock, whilst Lucy fills out the paperwork?"

"Thank you, I would enjoy that." She gestured to the tea tray. "I see Esther has been well taught. Are those gingerbread biscuits in the basket?"

"Yes, and all baked here."

Mrs Craddock bit into a biscuit. "Hmm. Delicious. I'll know where to come if my cook needs an assistant."

"We only employ instructors with a gift for teaching." Grace smiled. "It's rare that one of our young people doesn't give satisfaction. Once we've finished our tea, I'll show you some of the rooms we use here for education and vocational instruction."

Grace introduced Mrs Craddock to a good selection of orphans as she showed her around.

"The orphanage has grown apace in the last couple of years

and we have a lot of children ready to be placed. We have links with two country orphanages and schools. Quite a few of our boys go to the country to train as grooms, for instance. Although some of those will eventually take up positions in London."

"I see. Do you help the ambitious ones, like Esther, move on when they are ready?"

"Only informally so far, but that is part of our reason for wanting to set up a proper employment agency."

"That makes sense. I'm impressed with everything I've seen today. I would like to spend some time here in a week or two when I have settled Mary and Esther in. I might be able to help with the agency. After years of helping my father's parishioners I miss being busy."

Grace slipped a hand into the oversized reticule she always carried when she visited the orphanage and produced her card. "I'll be happy to show you around more fully, myself. Send me a message when you're ready."

The girls were already waiting in the hall when they reached it. Two tearful little girls had their arms around Mary.

Mrs Craddock bent down and put a hand on the shoulder of the most distressed girl. "Don't worry, my dear. Your friends will have a half day off every week and an extra full day once a month. You will see them regularly. Does that make you feel better?"

The girl nodded, keeping her eyes on the floor. Mrs Baker arrived and led them away.

A young boy ran in through the front door. "Your carriage is here, Missus."

Grace and Lucy waved the party off.

Lucy took Grace's arm and led her back to the office. "What's wrong, Grace? You seem subdued today. It can't be anything about Mrs Craddock from what I've seen of her."

Grace sighed. "No, indeed not. I'm sure she will be a good employer. All the children I introduced her to liked her and you know what good judges of character children can be."

"I agree, but what is bothering you? You've hidden it well but something is niggling at you."

Grace flopped into a chair. "Only that my brother is so taken with the new Duke of Evesham, who happens to be a distant cousin of his wife, that he wants to marry me off to the man."

"Surely, he was jesting?"

"I don't think so." A groan escaped her. She might feel better if she talked to Lucy about it. "I overheard something my aunt said to a friend as I was on my way out today, so don't mention it to anyone. Luke told her he is determined to push for a match. He can't make me marry but I don't want the bother of it all. Now I'm seven and twenty I thought I had escaped all that."

Lucy slipped into the seat by her and frowned. "It's horrible, isn't it? My mother keeps dropping broader and broader hints that it's time I made an effort to secure a husband. It's almost as if the poor dears are bales of cloth to be selected from a shelf."

Grace snorted. "What does that make us then? At least men have rights. We cease to exist in the legal sense on marriage. Don't worry. I'll come about, but I feel let down by my family. I thought they were more enlightened."

"I thought my mother understood too. I'm only two and twenty but she has changed her tune since her best friend became a grandmother."

Grace rested her elbows on the desk with her chin propped

up by her hands. "I'm considering setting up my own establishment. I have full control of my fortune." She sat up with a surge of energy. "That's it. Why don't we set up home together? I'm sure we can find an impecunious relative who would be happy to live with us to lend us countenance."

Lucy leaned towards her. "Oh, that would be famous." Her face fell. "I can't see my mother agreeing."

"You're of age, Lucy, there would be nothing your mother could do to stop you."

"I suppose not, but I would hate to fall out with her."

Grace smiled. "I agree it's a big step. Have a think about it and see how you feel when you've had time to consider the idea."

"I'll do that." Lucy's face lit up. "I trust Mrs Baker's judgment. If the Duke takes a lot of our children, we'll have room for more. Fancy him being attacked yesterday. What did you think of him?"

"He was perfectly pleasant." Grace sighed. "The sort of man I could imagine being friends with if it wasn't for Luke's fantasy of marrying him off to me. Luke thinks well of him and I'm satisfied he will be a good employer. It would be best if you looked after him."

Lucy grimaced. "Not a good idea. If my mother got wind of me helping a duke, she would be around here every day trying to push him into marrying me. She's not subtle like your family."

"I suppose not." Grace sighed. "Besides I'm sure someone is trying to kill him. That was no footpad yesterday. I need to keep an eye on him until he starts taking the threat seriously. He is Kitty's cousin after all."

Lucy's eyes opened wide. "Good Heavens. What makes you

think it was a murder attempt?"

They heard a commotion in the hallway and a low-pitched man's voice talking to Mrs Baker. Grace's head shot up.

"That's him now. I'll tell you all about it later." Grace stiffened at the sound of footsteps approaching, followed by a knock at the office door.

Parker thrust it open. "Your visitor, Miss Bamford."

The Duke strode into the room, every inch the confident nobleman for all his talk of feeling overwhelmed by his new position in society. Both women stood to greet him. Grace forced her features into a smile and waited until the door closed behind Parker.

"I'm glad you were able to come today, Your Grace. Allow me to introduce Miss Vaughan, who is leading our project to start our own employment agency."

The Duke bowed towards Lucy. "Good day to you, Miss Vaughan." He glanced around the room. "This is a lovely, light building with its large windows. I was a touch too shaken to notice much yesterday."

"Hardly surprising in the circumstances, Your Grace." Grace pointed to one of the armchairs opposite to them. "Do please take a seat."

"Thank you, Miss Bamford." The Duke waited until they were seated and took the proffered chair. "The light, coupled with the brightly coloured walls, make this much more welcoming than other orphanages I've been round. Still a far cry from growing up in a loving family home but it's good to see the effort you make here."

The wretched man was making it difficult to dislike him. "Thank you. We try our best."

"I've dressed in some of my old clothes today so the children don't think of me as anyone in particular. I don't want them to be nervous around me."

He gave a rueful smile and Grace looked away quickly. She really did not want to like this man.

Lucy rescued a pristine ledger, bound in red leather, from under a pile of papers. "I am not sure how much Miss Bamford has told you but, although our immediate aim is to place a large number of young people in their first positions, we are hoping to be here for them throughout their careers. We've already heard from a few who want to move on for promotion or family reasons. We don't have any senior staff looking for positions as yet, but we do have a lot of contacts and may be able to help you fill more senior roles."

"That would be most helpful, Miss Vaughan." The Duke of Evesham gave Lucy the benefit of a charming smile.

Grace closed her eyes briefly. The man was handsome and charming but so were a lot of men who proved to be awful husbands. A charming smile made no difference to the legal position of a wife either.

Lucy smiled back at him. "Where would you like to start?"

"Mrs Evans, the housekeeper at Medley House, is fairly young and seems very efficient. I plan to keep her on. Perhaps if we start with her list of the junior maids she will need." The Duke pulled a piece of paper out of his pocket and passed it to Lucy.

The door flew open and a small, thin boy ran in, his dark hair standing on end, closely followed by Parker.

Grace's heart skipped a beat. "What's wrong, Parker?"

"I'm sorry, Miss Bamford. I couldn't catch the little varmint." Parker put a hand on the boy's shoulder.

"Sam! It's you. I might have guessed. What possessed you

to run in here like that when we have a guest?" She gave him a rueful smile.

Sam twisted away from Parker and ran up to the big desk. He ignored Grace and stopped in front of the Duke.

"You're the cove who was nearly killed yesterday aren't you?"

Grace was about to order Sam out but she stopped when the Duke raised a hand.

"Yes, young man. I am. At least, I'm the man who was attacked by a footpad yesterday."

Sam shook his head. "I heard all about it from Jamie. He weren't no footpad. Jamie reckons he's a knife for hire."

Grace frowned at Sam. "That's doesn't explain why you're here. Jamie told me of his suspicions himself."

Sam grunted. "You don't understand. The gentleman needs me. I know how these gangs work."

Grace glanced at the Duke, they couldn't afford to have him think the children were ill disciplined and change his mind about employing some of them. He seemed amused rather than angry. Sam had been a street child for years. Perhaps he could tell them something useful.

"Which gangs, Sam?"

"There's lots of them, Miss. They'll do anything for the right money. I can spot one a mile off, I wouldn't be here now if I couldn't. He needs me to look after him." He grinned at the Duke." I could be your tiger. I want to work with horses but I've always lived in the city and they said I'd have to go and live in the country to train as a groom. I'm sure I could pick it up on the job, like." He held his breath and glanced at Grace, looking hopeful.

The Duke appeared to be fighting back laughter, but he

pulled himself together. "I like your reasoning, young man. I think I would be a disappointment to you though. You see I won't spend all my time in London. I might even want to travel to Edinburgh sometimes."

Sam frowned. "I might be able to manage a few weeks out of London every now and then, just to help you out you understand."

"That's a fair offer, Sam, but I never employ anyone under the age of fourteen."

Sam planted his legs wide and pulled back his shoulders. He stared at the Duke, his dark eyes pleading. "I might be small but I'm sixteen."

The Duke glanced at Grace. "Is there any proof of his age?" He smiled at Sam.

"The vicar who brought him here about a year ago, said he could be any age from twelve to sixteen. So, he could be sixteen, it's hard to say.

The Duke pursed his lips. "So, the chances are, Sam, that you are at least thirteen. What experience have you had with horses?"

Sam broke into a beaming smile. Grace couldn't help but smile herself. The little devil knew he was winning. He had a point though; he was certainly streetwise.

"I made good money holding horses for people when I was living on the streets." A shadow crossed his face and he stared at the floor. "Weren't so easy hiding it from the bigger boys. I learned though. I'm a quick learner, aren't I, Miss?"

The beseeching look he gave Grace left her close to tears. What sort of a life had this boy had?

"Yes, you are." Grace smiled at him and addressed the Duke. "He always tends to the horses for visitors and definitely has a way with horses. We were trying to persuade him to spend a few weeks in the country and learn how to drive a curricle. He is never going to be big and would make a good tiger."

Sam nodded in agreement. "There you are, Mister. I'm exactly what you need."

The Duke threw back his head and laughed. "I can see that and if you are at least thirteen I'm prepared to stretch a point, but I haven't had much experience of driving a curricle myself. I will have to consult with Lord Enstone to see if he can help. It might have to be those few weeks in the country young man."

"We could learn to drive together. If you're living in the country the gangs won't be able to get at you."

The Duke frowned. "True, but I've never been one to run away from a fight."

Sam shook his head. "You ain't never come across people like this before. I reckon I could keep you safe though."

"You're very persuasive, Sam. I'll talk it over with Miss Bamford and Miss Vaughan and let you know what we decide."

Sam looked as if he was about to argue. Grace shook her head at him.

"Off you go, Sam. We'll talk to you later."

"If you say so, Miss Bamford." Sam sighed and dawdled out of the room with his head hanging low.

Parker followed him and shut the door behind them. Grace jumped as the Duke fell into paroxysms of laughter. Lucy was in no better case and Grace found herself joining in.

The Duke recovered first. "I shouldn't laugh, that boy has had a terrible time, but I couldn't help it."

Grace looked away from him. Lord, the man was handsome, charming and compassionate but that still didn't mean she wanted to marry him.

Chapter Four

Angus sobered up quickly. "I would like to take Sam on, if we can find a way around his fear of leaving London."

"He does have the making of a good groom and he seems desperate to work for you." Miss Bamford chewed at her bottom lip.

Angus wrenched his gaze away from her. She was adorable. He had important things to do and this wasn't the time to waste energy being attracted to young ladies.

"Something's worrying you, Miss Bamford."

She was silent for a moment and then she shook her head and looked him square in the face. "I don't want Sam taking any dangerous risks. We had a job to get him to stay at the orphanage. Jamie was one of our boys before he started working for my aunt and he struck up a friendship with Sam. Somehow, he persuaded him to stay. Sam is now fiercely loyal to the orphanage."

"And you think he'll be as loyal to me. Which might lead him to take risks on my behalf."

Miss Bamford nodded. "Jamie spent several months in Kent being trained as a groom by Mr Bright, who works for one of Luke's friends. He was in army intelligence and always teaches the boys how to be alert for dangerous situations. I know Luke's not taking the threat to you very seriously, but Jamie is convinced something sinister is afoot."

"Believe it or not, far from not taking it seriously, Luke hasn't let me out of his sight until he dropped me off here today. A spell with your Mr Bright would be perfect for Sam but I honestly think he'd run away. He needs something or someone to be attached to and yes, you're right, that might put him at risk. At the same time if I leave him here until I've managed to get to the bottom of this, he'll think he's being rejected."

Miss Bamford frowned. Miss Vaughan put a hand on her arm.

"Grace, I think His Grace is probably correct." She smiled. "This is complicated with so many Graces."

Angus laughed. "If it was up to me, I'd have everybody call me Angus, but I have a feeling that would be frowned upon in society. I don't see why my friends shouldn't call me Angus in private though."

Miss Bamford pursed her lips. "What your male friends call you is up to you but it wouldn't be proper for female friends."

"I see." Not that he did really. She had been so natural with him when they first met, but a day later and she seemed determined to keep her distance.

"Luke is coming back for me when he's finished with his man of business. The best thing is to consult him about what to do with Sam." Angus shook his head and rolled his eyes. "He's on about finding me a bodyguard, would you believe."

Grace frowned and crossed her arms. "I suppose you're right. Luke can be so annoying but he was a good soldier. If you have a bodyguard, he should be able to keep Sam out of trouble. Aunt Theo might let you borrow Jamie as well. Now, perhaps we should get back to your list of maids."

"Mrs Evans suggested we take on two of each type of maid she's listed, on the understanding that they have to help with giving the house a thorough clean before they take up their proper positions. The place has been neglected for so long. Mrs Evans had only recently been taken on when I inherited it."

Miss Vaughan's eyes opened wide as she read the list. "If you take ten of our girls as maids that will make a dent in the number we have to place. In a way it's a pity we let Esther go to the lady we interviewed earlier, she is such a clever girl and a hard worker. I don't think her cousin would have settled without her though, and she's going to be a nursery maid. You're not likely to need one of those." Miss Vaughan went bright red. "At least I assume you're unmarried."

The poor girl went redder still and Angus took pity on her.

"No, I'm not married, Miss Vaughan. I have so much to do that's something I won't be considering for a long time." He smiled at her. "The last remaining male servants at Medley House have happily accepted a retirement pension, but there are a couple of maids who will stay on. They'll help Mrs Evans give your girls some initial training. I'll let you draw up standard terms of employment for them if that is acceptable."

The two ladies exchange glances.

Miss Vaughan extracted a loose sheet of paper from her ledger and handed it to him. "These are our suggested terms of employment. Where will the girls be accommodated?"

"Mrs Evans has started cleaning up the servants' quarters first. She says a few rooms are habitable without too much work."

"All our girls are well trained, but surely Mrs Evans will want to meet them before she takes them on? Could she come here?" Miss Bamford asked.

Angus thought quickly. He needed his own apartments put to rights as soon as possible and didn't want Mrs Evans to be distracted for too long. "I suppose she could, but perhaps it would be better if you two ladies came and inspected where they would be working and brought the girls with you."

Miss Bamford wrinkled her nose. "What do you think, Lucy?"

"It's probably a good idea. Then we can report back to the orphanage's patrons on their working conditions. Several of them were quite concerned about that sort of thing."

"True."

Angus relaxed. "It would be helpful if you could. Once Mrs Evans has some more pairs of hands to help she will be able to get a bedroom and a sitting room in a fit state for me. I don't want to impose on your brother for any longer than I have to, Miss Bamford."

She still seemed doubtful. Miss Vaughan looked at both of them and then smiled.

"I'm free tomorrow, if you are."

Miss Bamford sighed and gave Angus a challenging look. "So am I, as it happens. What time shall we arrange to arrive?"

"I can be available at whichever time suits you best."

Miss Bamford sat back and opened her eyes wide. "There is no need for you to be there, Your Grace. I'm sure we can sort it out with Mrs Evans."

That would be the sensible option but Angus couldn't resist teasing her. "I wouldn't dream of it, Miss Bamford. After all your help it's the least I can do to be there. Mrs Evans will need some senior maids too. If you know of anyone suitable, we can discuss that with her at the same time."

Footsteps sounded in the hall. The door opened and Luke strode in. "It sounds like you've found yourself a tiger then, Angus."

Angus grinned. "In theory yes, but there are certain complications."

Luke sat down and leaned back in his chair. "I've heard from my man, Fletcher. He's more of a steward these days than a groom but he was in the army. He's been down to see who Bright's been training lately and is bringing back a young man called Fallon to be your bodyguard. Fallon is also a trained groom but has the makings of filling a bigger role eventually, if you decide to take him on permanently."

"That's good news. If we get on, I'll be happy to keep him. I'm hoping to be able to move into Medley House in a few days' time. It will put your mind at rest if Fallon is with me then." He rubbed his chin. "That doesn't solve the problem of training Sam."

Luke leaned back at his ease, and looked from Angus to Grace with a satisfied gleam in his eyes. "I'll lend you Fletcher for a few days along with Fallon, once they arrive. In the meantime, why don't you ask Grace to teach you and Sam to drive her phaeton? It's not that much different from driving a curricle and Grace is an excellent whip. I'd offer myself but I have a lot of business to conduct before I can return to Kitty."

Oh Lord. He hadn't imagined Luke's intention to push Miss Bamford at him. Her face was a rigid mask and her eyes were shooting sparks at her brother. She must have realised too. What was Luke about to put them in this position? Neither of them could refuse without being rude. He damped down his anger and tried to think of a way out.

"Thank you, Luke. I appreciate all your help. It's hardly fair to expect Miss Bamford to give up her time, though. I know she has a lot to do at the orphanage."

Luke grinned. "Nonsense. Now you're finding jobs for so many of their orphans I'm sure Grace will have plenty of time and be pleased to help."

He could swear Miss Bamford flinched before she looked away from her brother to the floor. She let out a breath and moved her focus to Angus. He smiled at her.

She gave a little shake of her head. "It seems my brother is determined to organise our time for us, Your Grace. I'm at your disposal."

Angus rubbed at the back of his neck. Was there some scandal in Miss Bamford's past that had prevented her finding a husband? There must be some reason for Luke to be embarrassing her, and him, like this. At least he had tried to extricate them and Miss Bamford would know that whatever Luke was up to was not at his instigation.

"Perhaps we could discuss it tomorrow when you and Miss Vaughan join me at Medley House with your candidates for positions as maids? Would noon be suitable?" He smiled at her but Miss Bamford kept her eyes downcast.

"Certainly, Your Grace."

Luke sat back with a smile playing about his lips. "Good. That's settled then. Your new tiger is out in the hall, waiting to hear if he has a job. Shall we call him in?"

Miss Bamford snatched up the brass bell sitting on the desk and shook it so hard it was a wonder it didn't break. Angus swore under his breath. He needed her help to find good servants quickly but she was so angry with her brother he might lose it.

The door flew open and Sam ran in. "Are you going to take me on, Mister?"

"Yes, Sam. As long as you are happy with my terms. I won't be in London all the time."

Sam stared up at him, eyebrows raised and hands clasped in front of him. "I don't mind anything as long as I can stay in London some of the time."

"Good. I think we have an agreement."

Sam let out a loud breath and grinned at him.

Angus smiled back. "Lord Enstone has found me a senior groom who will take charge of you as soon as he arrives. I want you to join the group of girls from here going to Medley House tomorrow, to see what you think of the mews at the back of the house and the accommodation above it for grooms."

Sam jumped up and down, eyes shining. "Anything will do for me, Mister."

"Mr Fallon, my new senior groom, might be a bit choosier. We'll have a look around together and you can start cleaning the stables out. They haven't been used for years."

"I've got me bag packed. Can I move in tonight?"

Angus tried not to laugh. "Not until Mr Fallon arrives. Right off you go now. I'll see you tomorrow."

Sam grimaced. "If you say so, Sir." He bounced out of the room.

"Hmm. I'm not sure I won't live to regret taking Sam on but he deserves a chance. I hope he doesn't frighten off Mr Fallon!"

"I dare say Fallon will be able to manage him, Angus. Bright would have come himself but he says Fallon is the best student he has ever had and much fitter than he is these days. Have you got all the servants you need now?"

"We've made a start today but I will need a whole army of servants. You must come and see the place. Once my housekeeper has cleaned up the servant's quarters, with the help of the new maids from here, I will need pretty much every sort of servant. Even the cook wants to retire."

Luke beamed at them all. "I'm sure Grace and Miss Vaughan will be delighted to help you."

Angus groaned inwardly. Miss Bamford's expression was grim. "I am desperately hoping to trespass on their good nature for a while yet."

Miss Vaughan smiled at him. "We will certainly be able to help find some of them." She glanced at Miss Bamford and frowned.

He wasn't the only one to see how angry Miss Bamford was but Luke appeared oblivious. "Thank you, Miss Vaughan."

"You are helping us too." She glanced at her friend again and hurried on. "Have you seen our carpentry room? We take commissions for making and repairing furniture. Let me show you."

Miss Vaughan jumped up and left the room before he could answer. He followed her lead with alacrity but the hiss of Miss Bamford's furious voice had him pausing for a second before closing the door.

"Stay where you are, Luke. You are going nowhere until we've arranged a time for you to visit me at home. There are things we need to discuss in private."

Chapter Five

Grace strode up and down the library, barely noticing the shelves of leather-bound books. Luke had better come. She would explode if she couldn't have her say with him. She came to a halt by a side table and picked up her treasured copy of Mary Wollstonecraft's 'A vindication of the rights of woman'. She had her principles and she would stick to them. Just because she was a woman didn't mean she had to spend her entire life doing what men wanted her to do. She heard Harvey speaking in the hall and sat down at a desk by the window, trying to look calm. Luke sauntered in.

"Why all the secrecy, Grace?" Luke said in a bland accent.

Grace took a couple of calming breaths. If he thought she would be taken in by his innocent act he was well wide of the mark.

"There was no secrecy at all, dear brother. How could there be when you have made it plain what you are about."

Luke lowered himself into a leather armchair and smiled at her. Grace resisted the temptation to throw her book at him. It wasn't worth the risk of breaking its binding.

"Grace, what on earth are you on about?" Luke shrugged and held out his palms, a smile playing about his lips.

"That befuddled expression doesn't fool me, dear brother.

You're matchmaking!" Grace sat back and stared at him with her mouth pulled into a tight line.

"Don't tell me you're getting upset because I suggested you help Angus learn to drive a curricle. I thought you'd be more than happy to help him."

Grace sat very still. "Don't play the innocent with me, Luke. You're plotting to marry me off to him."

Luke looked away and studied the floor. "Now what on earth gave you that idea?"

"You made it so obvious today I would have guessed anyway, but I overheard Aunt Theo talking to the Duchess about your desire to marry me off to him."

Luke put his head in his hands and groaned. "Damnation. What were you doing listening at doors?"

Grace's cheeks grew hot. "I was on my way out and I overheard enough of their conversation, accidentally, to realise what it was about. You can hardly blame me if I stopped to listen after that. I'm seven and twenty years of age! What right have you to order my life?"

Luke got up and came across to her. He put a hand on her shoulder. "I would never make you do anything Grace. But you can't help me speculating. I like Angus a lot and he would be the perfect man for you. You're never going to find anyone else as acceptable to society and yet with unconventional views to match your own."

Grace pushed his hand away with such force that he staggered backwards.

"Let's get this straight. I do not want a man in my life. I want my independence and I want to be a real person in the eyes of the law."

Luke walked around the room for a few minutes "Oh, Grace

you aren't still on about that. I know it's not right, the position of women, but as long as your husband is a good man it doesn't matter. Kitty and I are really happy."

Grace slammed a hand down on the desk. She glared at her brother. "I'm very happy for you both, Luke. But I want to be valued for my own sake and not as some man's wife."

Luke threw his arms in the air. "If you want to dwindle into an old maid that's entirely your own affair. I hope you won't take it out on Angus. He has a lot to do to sort out his estates and I promised him as much help as he needs."

Why, oh why, couldn't Luke see her point of view?

"You made the promise to him. You help him."

"You're sounding petulant now."

Grace clenched her fists so hard her nails dug into her palms. "No, I'm not, I'm sounding angry, with good cause. I've said Lucy and I will help him find servants, which helps the orphanage too. You can give him driving lessons."

Luke crossed his arms and sighed. "It's only for a few days, Grace. I need to get in front with all my business affairs and get back to Kitty."

"Now you're resorting to blackmail." Grace shook her head and stared at him. "Why are you so desperate to get me married? He knew what you were up to. The poor man didn't know where to look."

"I'm sure he had no inkling. I was quite subtle."

Grace snorted. "About as subtle as a cavalry charge! You're not in the army now you know."

"I almost wish I was with you in this mood. Grow up, Grace. You'll never find someone like Angus again and I'm sure he's interested in you."

"Don't be ridiculous." Grace turned away to hide her hot

cheeks. "He hardly knows me."

Luke smirked at her. "What has that got to say to anything? He was trying to hide it but he was definitely giving you warm looks."

Grace stood and stalked around the room. Luke simply wasn't listening to her. Nothing would satisfy him except the Duke's ring on her finger. Why couldn't men, even intelligent ones like Luke, treat women as equals?

"You're impossible. I give you fair warning. Stop meddling in my affairs. You wouldn't go on like this if I was your brother instead of your sister. I will set up my own establishment as soon as this season is over and there is nothing you can do to stop me."

Luke strode across the room to her and tried to put an arm around her shoulders. Grace pushed him off and moved over to the desk holding her book. She hated falling out with him but this was too important for her to back down. She rested a hand on the book.

"I only want what's best for you." Luke threw up his arms and frowned.

Lud, why did he have to patronise her so?

"Let me be the judge of that. I wouldn't dream of telling you what to do, but then I'm a mere woman." The pitch of her voice rose and Grace fought to control her breathing.

The door opened and Aunt Theo came in. She looked from one to the other. "What seems to be the problem?" She sounded concerned.

Even Aunt Theo was against her and that hurt. Grace's control snapped.

"You can ask me that after you've been conspiring with Luke?"

"That's not true, Grace, my darling. Luke has talked to me about you but I haven't conspired with him. He feels it's his fault you don't want to marry and is trying, in his clumsy way, to make amends."

"Oh! That's the most ridiculous thing I've heard yet."

Luke shook his head. "No, it's not. I found a letter from Father and he asked me to look after you. He said he treated you like the son he was missing and realised, too late, that he hadn't done you any favours. I should have made more of an effort to get to know him as an adult."

"Are you saying that my father only valued me as he did because he saw me as a substitute son?"

Grace shook her head and strode out of the room, blinking back tears. Once she reached her bedroom, she dismissed her maid and threw herself on the bed. Not content to treat her in the manner of a child, Luke was throwing doubt on the strength of her relationship with Papa now. Why shouldn't Papa value her as much as he would a son? She had been brought up to think for herself and nothing would stop her doing that. Even if it meant falling out with the brother she had idolised when she was younger. A woman didn't need to be married to be a complete person, any more than a man did.

Chapter Six

Grace drew up in front of the orphanage, behind Lucy's family carriage. She handed the reins of her phaeton to Jamie, sitting beside her, without a pang. Her normal enjoyment at driving the phaeton, with her prized matched greys in harness, seemed to have deserted her. The door of the orphanage opened and Parker helped Grace to alight. Mrs Baker led out twelve excited girls. Sam sidled out behind them, seemingly trying to pretend they were nothing to do with him. His face lit up when he saw Grace's phaeton. Grace broke into a smile, the first time she'd smiled since her disastrous interview with Luke.

She walked up to Lucy's coach. "One of our carriage horses has a damaged leg. I've only been able to bring our big travelling carriage, which should take eight girls. Do you want to climb up with me, Lucy?"

"Why not, it's a beautiful day. Our coach should be big enough for the other girls and Mrs Baker. We can probably squeeze Sam in it as well."

Sam's face fell and Grace took pity on him. "He can climb up behind us. Jamie can sit with your coachman."

One of Grace's horses took exception to a passing cart. It was a few moments before Jamie had him under some semblance of control. Sam walked up to the horse and said something to it in a soothing voice. The horse quietened down immediately.

Lucy's eyes opened wide. "That boy certainly has a way with horses."

"Yes, he does. He should do a good job for the Duke."

Mrs Baker shepherded the girls into the waiting coaches. Sam scrambled up into the groom's seat at the back of the phaeton, grinning happily. Parker helped Lucy up into the seat next to Jamie and she took the reins from him, so he could jump down.

Grace did a final check on the occupants of both coaches and allowed Parker to help her climb into her phaeton. "Right, Jamie. You go and sit with the coachman in the first coach and then, if we get separated, I know you'll keep an eye on the girls."

Grace waited for a gap in the traffic and expertly pulled her horses out from behind the coaches. They set off at a smart trot and once they were past the other two coaches Grace glanced back.

"Off we go. Let's hope this is only the first batch we can place with the Duke. He has numerous estates."

"Definitely. Are you going to send Jamie back with the phaeton once we get there?"

"Possibly, although I'll get Jamie to check on the state of the mews at Medley House. If it's suitable, the horses can be left in there until we're ready to leave."

Grace was aware of Lucy giving her a sidelong glance. She was clearly agog to know what had happened between her and Luke, but far too diplomatic to say anything.

Grace lowered her voice so Sam wouldn't overhear, even though he was so engrossed in watching the street it was doubtful he would hear anything. "I had quite an argument with Luke last night. I think he will keep out of my affairs now. I was tempted to pull out of teaching Sam and the Duke to drive but when I thought about the number of young people who we have to place it seemed sensible to oblige him. It should only be for two or three days."

There was a fair bit of traffic and Grace used this as the excuse not to say any more. She would show Luke. Nobody was going to accuse her of being petulant. In what seemed far too short a time they pulled up in front of Medley House.

Grace stopped by the front door and Sam jumped down to go to the horses' heads without being asked.

The Duke appeared beside him. "Well done Sam. I can see I've made a good choice for my tiger."

Sam seemed to grow in height. There was no question that the Duke would be a good employer, but where on earth had he been hiding? As if reading her mind, he walked up to Grace.

"I've been around the corner to check the mews. The supplies of fodder and bedding I ordered have arrived."

The coaches appeared and pulled up behind them. Jamie jumped down and joined Sam by the phaeton.

Grace smiled at the Duke, but didn't meet his eyes. "My aunt has agreed that you can borrow Jamie for a while. He and Sam can make a start on cleaning out the mews if you think the horses will be all right in there for a few hours."

"The general condition is sound. They are perfectly dry. I'm sure Jamie and Sam can find somewhere to put the horses."

The Duke walked around and helped Lucy down. He called to Jamie to take her place. Once Jamie had scrambled up, the Duke returned to Grace and held up a hand. Grace hesitated for a moment and then put her hand in his. Her fingers seemed to tingle and a rush of heat burned her cheeks. She looked down as if watching where she put her feet and jumped to the ground. Her foot caught on a stone as she landed but the Duke held her upright. Grace blushed again. Luke's matchmaking had made her self-conscious with him, which was highly inconvenient.

"Thank you, Your Grace. I hope that's not your injured arm."

"Fortunately not, Miss Bamford. Although, my injury is healing so well I'm sure I would have managed with the other one."

Grace glanced at their hands, which were still joined. "I'm glad. Mrs Baker is a genius with her remedies."

"She is indeed." He let go of her hand. "Sam, can you run up and knock at the door. I'll leave the ladies with Mrs Evans and show you and Jamie the mews."

Mrs Evans opened the door to them herself. Wisps of hair peeped out from underneath her pristine white cap and her pink cheeks suggested she had been rushing. She broke into a smile when she saw them.

"Miss Bamford and Miss Vaughan, isn't it? I'm glad to see you. Bring your girls inside and we'll all go straight up to the servant's quarters so you can see what you think."

Grace left Lucy and Mrs Baker to usher the girls inside and walked across to the Duke. "I'll leave you to organise the stabling of my horses."

The Duke smiled at her. "Of course. They're a magnificent pair. I'll catch up with you a little later."

"Thank you."

Grace couldn't stop herself watching him disappear towards the phaeton. He had a splendid physique. She walked across to the two carriages.

"Could you return in about two hours?"

Both drivers agreed and Grace ran lightly up the steps to the front door to join Mrs Evans, who was waiting for her at the top.

"Your girls seem enthusiastic, Miss Bamford. I'm in desperate need of some servants." Mrs Evans laughed. "When I first came here it was so quiet that I thought I'd made a mistake. I'm not complaining about being busy now, but the sooner we can get a full complement of servants the better. His Grace is keen to move in as soon as may be."

They joined Lucy and Mrs Baker.

Lucy's expression shone with excitement. "Mrs Evans has offered to take some of our boys to train as footmen. Which has reminded me of the letter I had the other day from one of the group of boys we placed with Colonel Shepherd about two years ago. The old gentleman has died, leaving them a small legacy which will keep them for a while, but they're searching for new posts."

Mrs Evans's face lit up. "We have no menservants at all. I'll happily take them all." She gave Grace a considering look. "I assume there will be a short period during which I can change my mind if anyone doesn't fit in?"

Grace looked across at Lucy who nodded.

"Yes, that seems reasonable. How many young men are there Lucy?"

"Three footmen, including Hugh, that clever boy. He's been acting as butler for the Colonel, after his old one became too infirm."

Mrs Baker nodded. "It's a much smaller household than this one but, knowing Hugh, I think he would be worth a trial as butler here."

Mrs Evans hesitated.

"He writes that he would be happy to accept a job as a senior footman in a bigger establishment," Lucy said.

"That might be better. He must be quite young if he only left the orphanage two years ago."

Mrs Baker smiled at Mrs Evans. "Hugh must be at least twenty-five now. His widowed father, a clergyman, died suddenly when Hugh was barely seventeen. The family had to leave the rectory. Hugh came to London with his two much younger brothers to ask an uncle for help, which was refused. There was some money put by, but that was intended for the middle boy to train as a doctor. Hugh saw the orphanage when he was searching for cheap lodgings for the night and asked if we could help. He was well educated and we were about to advertise for a teacher. We took them in. He moved to the Colonel because he was offering to help fund the second boy's training."

Mrs Evans nodded. "That puts a different light on it. What if I was to take him on as acting butler?"

"That sounds sensible, Mrs Evans," Grace said. "I remember that Hugh was a good teacher. We have several boys at the orphanage who want positions as footmen, I'm sure he would be able to train them after two years in a gentleman's household."

Mrs Evans gave a beaming smile. "That will save me a lot of time. I'd rather have the experienced footmen first and decide how many of your boys to take once they have settled in. Whereabouts are they living at the moment?"

Lucy grinned happily. "They're in London, as luck would have it, not far from where I live. I could call by on my way home and ask them to report here whenever you want them."

"This afternoon would be wonderful. Let's go upstairs and

inspect the servant's quarters and you can see what you think. As soon we have enough rooms ready there's nothing to stop them all moving in."

"There is one other young man." Lucy said. "He's been acting as the Colonel's valet, but I don't know how much training he had."

Grace grimaced. "We will need to ask the Duke about him. It will be a shame if he can't go with his friends, but the Duke may need someone with more training in his position. It's far cry from looking after a retired military gentleman to looking after a duke."

Grace became aware of the murmur of voices from the girls waiting in the hallway. "Why don't we go and inspect the servants' quarters next. The girls are getting excited."

"Follow me, ladies," Mrs Evans said.

Grace and Lucy led the way behind Mrs Evans followed by the girls, with Mrs Baker bringing up the rear. It was a large building with several floors.

Grace exclaimed with delight when they reached the servants floor. "There's plenty of light in here, which always makes things more cheerful." She went into the first room she came to. Furniture was shrouded in Holland covers but there appeared to be four beds. It was a good size room with a fireplace.

"This could be made very comfortable. Are all the rooms this big?"

Mrs Baker stepped forward. "Some of them are but the more senior servants either share in pairs or have a room to themselves. I don't know, the place is full of cobwebs. I don't think anything could have been done to this place for years before I arrived. It's going to take some work to set these to rights."

Lucy looked around. "It seems fairly superficial to me. Our girls are hard workers, they will soon make a difference. Why don't we get them in?"

Mrs Baker ushered the girls into the room. Some of them hung at the back. One of the more adventurous ones strode right across the room.

"This is a good size and only four beds." She grinned happily.

There was a knock at the door and two maids entered, carrying a selection of brooms and dusters.

"These are all the brooms we could find, Mrs Evans," one said.

"You've done well. You've got more there than I thought you'd find. Do you want to take six girls each and make a start?"

The maids nodded. Mrs Baker quickly divided the girls into two groups.

"I've split them up into the groups I think will work best together."

Mrs Evans smiled. "Thank you, Mrs Baker."

Grace tapped Lucy on the arm. "Why don't we go and see if we can find the Duke. We can come back in a while and see how the girls are getting on."

Heavy footsteps sounded on the stairs and the Duke himself appeared.

"I see we've got some enthusiastic new maids here." He looked at Lucy and Grace in turn. "Thank you, ladies."

"Our pleasure," Grace said.

The Duke bowed. "Let's go back downstairs and you can tell me how we're getting on with finding servants."

"I'll stay up here for a few minutes if that's all right with you, Your Grace," Mrs Evans said.

"Certainly, Mrs Evans. You will find us in the library." The Duke turned to Mrs Baker. "I must thank you for attending to my damaged arm. It seems to be recovering quickly."

Mrs Baker beamed at him. "I'm so glad, Your Grace."

"Thank you. Do you want to stay with Mrs Evans for a while? Then you can tell her about the girls' strengths and weaknesses. Which will help her to decide where to place them all."

"Of course, Your Grace."

The Duke shivered. "It's cold for the time of year. If you have time, Mrs Evans don't be afraid to have some fires lit up here to give it an airing, and whenever you think the weather warrants it. I don't expect my servants to freeze."

He offered his arm to Lucy and they led the way down the stairs. Grace had a moment's pang of something that felt suspiciously like disappointment. If she wasn't careful, she would find herself falling for him, which would be seriously embarrassing after Luke's efforts to throw them together. Brothers.

The Duke led them into a library which had a fire burning. Grace looked around with interest, it was one of the largest private libraries she'd seen. Shelves stretched from floor to ceiling on three walls, with two more runs of shelves splitting the room into bays. There was still space for a huge writing desk and several armchairs in front of one of the windows. As they walked fully into the room, she could see that fires were lit at each end and one of them had a selection of armchairs gathered around it.

"What a fabulous library." Grace walked to the nearest shelf and sighed at the quality of the leather-bound books.

The Duke smiled at her. "Mrs Evans and her two maids managed to find time to dust this room for me. It's full of beautiful books, someone in the family must have collected them."

Grace put her head to one side. "You did say your father was a great scholar. Presumably it was whoever he inherited his love of scholarship from." She turned back to the books. "Look at these bindings. So beautiful, with the red and blue shown off by a light background and embellished with gold. This appears to be a set of several volumes."

"There are many such sets. At some point I will need to hire a librarian. It will have to wait for a while though. How many servants have you found me so far? Come, let's sit by the fire before you answer that."

Once they were settled, the Duke looked at them expectantly. Grace nodded at Lucy, who took a deep breath.

"Ten new maids, all of whom have had basic training at the orphanage. We've heard of three footmen, who used to be at the orphanage, searching for work after their employer has died. One of them was acting as the butler and there is also a fourth young man who was acting as a valet. Mrs Evans wants to meet the footmen. I'll call in and see if they're there on my way home."

The Duke scratched his head. "Won't the person who inherits the house want to keep them on?"

"It seems not. The house is to be sold and they would be pleased to find employment together. The eldest one used to teach at the orphanage. Mrs Evans hopes he'll be able to train some more footmen if we send him some boys from the orphanage."

"That sounds promising. Are these young men living far from here?"

Lucy shook her head. "Only a few streets away."

"I've asked Jamie and Sam to report back here once they've stabled the horses. We could send them around to see if any of these prospective footmen are in. Mrs Evans has so much to do it isn't fair to expect her and her two maids to keep answering the door. Did you say there was a valet as well?"

Grace frowned. "There is one who was acting as a valet, but looking after an elderly retired colonel is a far cry from dressing a duke."

"It might be easier in some ways. Luke's valet is a marvel and knows all there is to know about gentleman's fashion. If we had this young man spend a few days with him I'd soon be able to see if he was suitable."

The Duke went to one of the windows, which had a view of the street. "That was quick. Jamie and Sam are on the way here."

He strode out of the library and returned with them a few moments later. Sam looked so happy that Grace burst into a smile.

"I hope you've looked after my horses well, Sam."

Sam grinned at her. "Yes, Miss. They're a bang-up pair."

Grace turned to Jamie. "Do you think he has the makings of a good groom?"

"Yes, Miss Bamford. He loves the horses but I think they love him even more."

Mrs Evans came in. "I will take on all ten of the girls, if you're agreeable, Your Grace. They are hard workers." She eyed the boys. "May I borrow these two to carry up hot water? We'll soon have a room ready to scrub the floor."

The heat flew to Grace's cheeks when she noticed the Duke's attention was firmly fixed upon her as he walked across to join his housekeeper. "If you're happy with them Mrs Evans, that's good enough for me. I'll let you borrow Jamie but I've had an idea." He caught Grace's gaze and smiled. "I know you won't have time to give me formal driving lessons, Miss Bamford, but I have a favour to ask of you. Mrs Evans, I understand you're interested in taking on at least some of the ex-orphanage young men whose employer has recently died. If Miss Bamford would consent to drive me around there, I might be lucky enough to find them in and see what I think."

Lucy smiled at him. "That would be famous. If you take them on, how many trainee footmen will you be able to take from the orphanage?"

The Duke looked at Mrs Evans. "Four do you think?"

"Yes, that should be enough, Your Grace. We'll need several available to open the door to visitors once you move in." Mrs Baker tucked a stray lock of hair behind her ear and beamed at the Duke.

"That would be wonderful." Lucy's voice was close to a squeal and she bounced up and down in her chair. "I can think of four boys who want to be footmen and are more than ready to start work. I'm sure Grace won't mind driving you."

Grace gave Lucy a horrified glare. Which Lucy seemed determined to ignore. Not that she could blame her for concentrating on how many posts she could obtain for orphanage boys. Four pairs of eyes turned towards Grace. She knew when she was beaten.

"Of course, Your Grace, I would be happy to."

"Excellent. Right, Jamie, Sam, take off your jackets. We're going to carry hot water upstairs."

Grace's mouth dropped open as the Duke peeled off his own jacket.

"Don't look so surprised." He gave Grace a wicked grin. "I often helped my uncles in their businesses when I was a youth. It's lucky I'm still wearing my old jackets. I would never get out of my new ones on my own. We'll carry a good supply of hot water upstairs for Mrs Evans and then we'll leave Jamie to carry on. In the meantime, feel free to explore my library. Lead the way, Mrs Evans."

Grace found her eyes drawn to the Duke's disappearing back. His fine muslin shirt clung to him revealing broad shoulders and muscular arms.

Lucy gave her a rueful smile. "I'm sorry, Grace. I know you don't want to have too much interaction with His Grace but this is such an opportunity. A massive house like this will need so many servants and then there are all his other properties."

"I know. I understood your reasoning." Grace shook her head. "If only Luke had kept out of it, I could have worked quite happily with the Duke. Now I feel self-conscious every time we're in the same room. It will be even worse sitting together in a phaeton. I hope some of the young men are in when we get there."

"Just think of all those hopeful children at the orphanage. He's an unconventional sort of duke, but a considerate employer from what I've seen."

"Yes, I'm sure you're right. I'm going to have another look at these beautiful books."

Lucy smiled. "I'll go and see how the girls getting on."

Grace walked to the other end of the library and tried to study the bindings of the books. For the umpteenth time in the day her cheeks felt warm. The truth was the new Duke of Evesham was far too attractive for comfort. But even if he was interested in her, which seemed unlikely, the prospect of giving up her freedom was too terrifying to even consider. All in all, she would much rather keep well away from him. Particularly since Lucy knew her too well and had almost certainly noticed the effect the Duke was having on her.

Chapter Seven

It was a good while later when the library door opened and admitted the man himself. Grace couldn't help studying him the moment he entered the room. How on earth did he manage to have such an athletic physique when he had spent all his time in courtrooms?

"Your girls are working hard up there. I think they're keen to move in as soon as possible." The Duke shrugged himself into his jacket. "The boys will be here with the phaeton at any minute."

Grace closed her eyes for a moment and then walked away from the bookshelves towards him. "Let's hope we find someone at home. You certainly have a magnificent library here."

"Yes, I've made some interesting discoveries amongst the shelves."

Grace glanced out of the window. Unable to meet his gaze. "They're here,"

The Duke inclined his head. "Shall we join them?"

"Of course. Lucy has given me the address." Grace put her hand on the arm he held out for her. "I think you'll be pleased with Sam. He did well when we came here."

The Duke led her outside. "I'm impressed with Jamie too."

He grinned at her. "I don't suppose your aunt would let me have him permanently, would she?"

Grace laughed. "He's my groom, although my aunt is technically his employer, and no, you're not having him."

"Fair enough."

The Duke handed her up into the phaeton and she took the reins from Jamie. Jamie called to Sam to stay in the groom's seat and he jumped down and went to the horse's head whilst the Duke took his place.

"Thank you, Jamie." Grace settled into her seat, trying to ignore the solid presence next to her.

She grasped the whip, checked for traffic and set her horses to a trot. A quick glance behind showed Sam absorbed in studying the street. They turned a corner and the movement brought her and the Duke closer until she could feel his heat all along the length of her side and thigh. A surge of heat rushed to her cheeks. Her mind seemed to be blank, unable to come up with anything to say.

The Duke broke the silence. "I do appreciate you agreeing to drive me today. Luke has been so kind and I can see he's anxious to return home, although he hides it well. The sooner I can get the house into some sort of order the better. I've been lucky with Mrs Evans. She had only just been hired by the last Duke before he was killed."

"You have indeed been lucky. Lucy and I are impressed with her." Grace relaxed and was able to overtake a cart with ease.

"I can see that you're every bit as skilled with horses as your brother said." The Duke looked behind. He lowered his voice. "Sam is taking his duties as a Tiger seriously. He's concentrating so hard he will wear a permanent furrow in his brow."

Grace laughed. "He's determined to succeed. He was so happy after he and Jamie came back from stabling the horses."

The Duke had another quick glance behind. "I'm sure he can't hear us with the noise from the street as well."

He spoke quietly and so closely to Grace's ear that his breath tickled her neck. Her chest seemed to constrict and she forced herself to concentrate on the road.

"No, I don't think he can."

The Duke leaned in close yet again and Grace caught her breath.

"I have a proposition to put to you."

Grace gasped and her hands jerked at the reins, making the horses jink. She spoke soothingly to them and they quietened down. That was a surprise. What sort of man was he? His shoulder brushed against hers. She glanced at him quickly, he was shaking with silent laughter! Had he misspoken?

"Zooks. Why am I so clumsy? That didn't mean what you think it meant."

Grace found herself smiling. "I should hope not."

"Thank you for not taking offence. Is there any way we could have a private word at some point today?"

Grace frowned. What was this about? "Lucy is going to organise getting everyone back to the orphanage and once I've collected Jamie I shall go straight home. If you wish, you may come with me."

"Thank you. I shall be glad to pay my respects to your aunt if she is in."

"We're nearly there, Miss," Sam shouted from his perch at the back. "Next turn on the left and it's the fourth house along."

"Thank you, Sam." Grace turned her horses into the next

road on the left and pulled up in front of an elegant townhouse.

"It's well maintained. That's a good start," the Duke said.

"I remember Hugh Masters, the acting butler, well. Very organised young man." Grace turned towards Sam. "Jump down and knock the door for us, Sam."

Sam's knock was answered quickly by Hugh Masters himself.

"Miss Bamford, how lovely to see you." Hugh smiled. "Won't you come in?"

"Thank you, Mr Masters."

Sam ran to the horse's heads. The Duke climbed down and held up a hand to Grace. The feel of her hand engulfed in his sent shockwaves through Grace.

Hugh ushered them inside. "Won't you come into the drawing room?" He smiled. "I'm hoping you've come in response to the letter I wrote to Mrs Baker."

"Yes, indeed. This gentleman is opening up his London home and has some vacancies. Are you the only one in?"

"I am, but I'm expecting the others back quite soon. May I offer you some refreshment?"

"Thank you, but no. I don't want to leave my horses standing for too long." Grace looked at the Duke.

"I'm opening up a house that has been empty for quite some time. I'm interested in taking you all on, especially if you can start in the next few days."

"I think we would be happy with that, but I must consult with the others. We've signed on at one or two agencies but we would prefer to stay together." Hugh frowned. "Although I am hoping to find a different position than footman."

"My housekeeper has suggested taking you on as acting butler to see how that goes. You come well recommended by

Miss Bamford and Miss Vaughan."

Hugh looked at the floor. "I would certainly be happy to do that to help you out for a while."

The Duke studied him. "Are you hoping for a different occupation?"

Hugh nodded. "Now my brothers' futures are secure, my ambition is to find a post as a secretary to a busy man, or something of that nature." Hugh's eyes narrowed as he studied the Duke. "My father was a clergyman and I'm well educated. I spent several years at the orphanage teaching the children to read and write."

He looked away and his cheeks went pink.

The Duke smiled. "There is no need to be embarrassed. I don't blame you for trying to sell yourself. As it happens, I will be needing a secretary. However, would you be prepared to work as a butler for a few weeks until we can get the household organised?"

"Thank you, Sir. That would be most acceptable." Hugh's eyes shone. "The Colonel's butler taught me a lot. I should be able to help you to select a permanent butler."

Grace broke into a beaming smile. "I haven't introduced you, have I? Your Grace, allow me to introduce you to Mr Masters. Mr Masters this is the Duke of Evesham."

Hugh's mouth fell open but he recovered quickly and went into a deep bow. "I'm so sorry, Your Grace. I wouldn't have said anything if I'd realised."

"I know. That's why I was glad when Miss Bamford was sensible enough not to introduce us at the start. A permanent butler as quickly as possible would be a very good thing. Then you can take up the position as my secretary. I have a lot of paperwork to deal with, especially now I have a new man of business."

They heard the sound of the front door opening.

"That sounds like the others," Hugh said.

The duke smiled. "Bring them in here but don't tell them who I am."

Hugh went out and returned with a group of young men. "This is the gentleman. I believe he is offering us all work."

A sandy haired young man stepped forward, an anxious frown marring his open features. "Does that include me? I had been working as the Colonel's valet for nearly a year before he died."

The Duke stood and walked towards him. "Yes, it does. What's your name?"

"Peter Gillard, Sir."

"I'm staying with Miss Bamford's brother at the moment, Gillard. He has an experienced valet. I'm going to ask Viscount Enstone if his valet will give you some training."

"I'm sure my brother will agree," Grace said.

The Duke smiled. "So am I, but it will only be polite to ask him first. As soon as my housekeeper has some rooms ready for servants, I would like you all to move in. In the meantime," he looked at the sandy haired boy. "I'll send a message to you. Would you be able to move into Viscount Enstone's house as early as tomorrow?"

"I certainly would. I'm excited at the prospect. May I ask your name, Sir?"

Grace laughed. "Let me introduce you to the Duke of Evesham. His Grace didn't want you to know his rank until he had spoken to you, for fear of intimidating you. He is opening up Medley House in Mayfair. Mrs Evans, the housekeeper, will be delighted to welcome the rest of you in the daytime tomorrow to help preparing the servants' quarters if you are free."

Hugh answered for them. "I'm sure we'd all be happy to help."

The others nodded in stunned looking silence.

"Good, that's settled then." The Duke looked delighted. "Thank you, Miss Bamford for your hard work in arranging this. Now we had better get you home."

Hugh escorted them out. "Thank you for your faith in us, Your Grace. We look forward to working for you."

The Duke nodded in acknowledgement and held his hand out to Grace. She climbed into the phaeton and Sam handed her the reins. The Duke jumped up beside her. Grace gave the horses the office to start and they set off.

"Well, that was a successful meeting. I don't think there is time to drop Sam off at the orphanage, but I can always send a groom to escort him back. I haven't forgotten you want to come and pay your respects to my aunt."

Grace turned the horses towards home and gave them their heads. They broke into a smart trot. What on earth did the Duke want to talk to her about? Lord, he wasn't going to offer marriage, was he? Best not to think about it. She needed to concentrate with more traffic about at this time of day. She was preparing to move the horses out to pass a slow-moving vehicle when a shout from Sam stopped her.

"Pull them up, Miss Bamford."

Grace did as she was bid. Before they came to a halt a rider passed by them, close to their offside horse. The rider whipped up his horse and disappeared around the side of a large coach travelling towards them, on the opposite side of the road. Grace's horse reared in panic, upsetting his fellow. Grace called to them but it took all her strength to stop them from bolting. She felt the Duke move against her and realised he had managed to find one of her pistols in her reticule.

"I can't see anyone else around who looks like he might attack us but I'll put this in my pocket with your permission. I don't know what's been done to your horse but there's blood running down his shoulder."

An ashen faced Sam jumped down and ran to the stricken horse's head. "That cove stabbed at him. He followed us all the way from the orphanage and must have been lying in wait."

"You did well to spot him in time, Sam," Grace said. "If I had pulled out to overtake and the horses had bolted there would have been an almighty collision with the carriage coming the other way."

The Duke put a hand on her arm. "You did brilliantly to hold them. How far are we from your aunt's house?"

"Less than a mile. How much blood is the horse losing, Sam?"

"It's not too bad, Miss Bamford. I think the cove might have shoved something down his collar."

The Duke gave her arm squeeze. "I'll get down and check on him. Sam and I can lead the horses, to reduce the weight."

He jumped down and joined Sam by the injured horse. "Sam's right, it's fairly superficial but the poor animal is shaken up."

The horse tried to rear up and squealed. It took Sam and the Duke to calm it.

"I think you are right, Sam, there is something in its collar. Keep talking to the poor animal."

Grace watched as the Duke edged to the side of the horse and bent his head to inspect its collar.

"There's a piece of metal pushed inside. The more the horse struggles the more it will hurt." He pulled out a handkerchief. "This should help me get a good grip. It's covered in blood."

Sam crooned at the horse and Grace held her breath. The horse bucked when the Duke pulled at his collar but he withdrew his hand with a triumphant grin.

"I've got it. This coat is already ruined. I'll put it in my pocket and cushion the wound with my handkerchief."

It was swiftly done and Grace let out a sigh of relief.

"There, he's s easier already. Well done, Sam. If you hadn't spotted the rider, we probably wouldn't have realised he had pushed that in the horse's collar. You're the best with horses. You stay with this one and I'll walk with the other one. Shout if he starts struggling."

Grace walked them home at a crawl. The next twenty minutes seemed to take a lifetime.

They turned into Cavendish Square and Grace sighed with relief. "Here we are. We'll go straight round to the mews."

Jamie came out to greet them. His mouth opened in horror when he saw the blood-soaked handkerchief sticking out of the injured horse's collar.

"I'll go and get help." Jamie ran off.

Grace turned the horses to enter the mews and winced as the injured horse whinnied. They inched their way into the mews. Jamie came back with the head groom.

"Lordy, what's happened here, Miss Bamford?"

"We were set upon and the horse on the offside has been cut on the shoulder with a sharp piece of metal."

"Right. Don't you worry, Miss. We'll save him."

The Duke handed her down. Her legs were shaking so much she stumbled and was grateful for a steadying arm around her.

"Come on, let's get you inside. That poor horse is in good hands now, I can see."

"There's a door at the back of the house we can use to save going round to the street."

She didn't protest when the Duke kept his arm around her. The smell of his spicy cologne, coupled with warm male, helped to distract her from the horror of what had happened. They reached the door from the garden and the Duke opened it with one hand, keeping his other arm around her waist. They walked down the corridor which brought them into the back of the main hallway. Aunt Theo was coming out of her drawing room.

"Grace, dear, what on earth has happened? I've never seen you so pale."

"Let's go into the drawing room, Aunt Theo."

The Duke led her to the nearest seat which happened to be a sofa. He removed his arm but sat down next to her. Aunt Theo closed the door and came to join them.

Grace took a few calming breaths. "We decided to visit some ex-orphanage boys, who were looking for work, on our way back from Medley House. We were driving here when young Sam, the Duke's new Tiger, shouted at me to pull up. He'd spotted a rider, who he'd noticed following us from the orphanage, pull out of a side road and guessed something was up. The man stuffed a sharp piece of metal into the collar of my offside horse and rode off."

Aunt Theo stared at them. "Why would a rider want to hurt one of your horses?"

"That's the question, Lady Grant. If Sam hadn't noticed him, I doubt we would have known anything until the horse reacted to the pain of something cutting into his shoulder. There was a fair bit of traffic on the road and Miss Bamford was about to pull out into a gap to overtake a slow-moving cart. Sam shouted at her to stop and somehow, I don't know how, she managed to hold the horses and keep them from bolting. The carriage coming on the other side of the road was at a distance but, if the horses had bolted, anything could have happened."

"It seems that someone really is trying to kill you, Your Grace."

"I'm afraid so, Lady Grant. Young Sam said I needed him to keep me safe and he was right. I'm sorry to have put him and Miss Bamford at risk as well."

"Grace is extremely skilled with the ribbons. Few young women would be able to hold a terrified pair of horses. Next time you're out together you need to take armed grooms with you."

The Duke's jaw dropped. "You're as intrepid as your niece. Most ladies would be calling for the hartshorn now and never allowing their niece out in my company again."

"I don't see that you have any choice. The only way you're going to find out who is behind it is if you can catch someone in the attempt."

"I had better speak to Luke before going out in company with Miss Bamford again. I don't want him calling me out, especially if he's as good a shot as his sister."

He smiled at Grace and her insides somersaulted. "I ought to take exception to you thinking that Luke has anything to say to what I might decide to do but, in the circumstances, I can't blame you. He would be furious if he thought you were putting me in danger and yes, he is a good shot, better than me."

The Duke grinned at her. "In that case I must check on the

etiquette of duels. As a keen swordsman I would be better to select that medium if I could."

Grace laughed. She turned to face him and put a hand on his arm. "Luke isn't my keeper and I won't be intimidated out of helping you find servants, including some of our orphanage children."

The Duke shook his head. "I was going to ask you to help me sort out Medley House's restoration as well as find servants, but that's out of the question now."

"Surely that's my decision." Grace caught his gaze. "If you want my help, you shall have it."

The Duke jumped up and walked around the room. "It's your right to decide whether to offer me help if I ask for it. It's my right to decide whether to ask for that help. I can't reconcile it with my conscience to put you in danger. We could have all been killed today."

"Including Sam." Grace pursed her lips. "My life is no more important than that of your servants."

The Duke shook his head. "Of course not. Luke has found me a bodyguard. A young man called Fallon who is on his way to London. He has been trained by Luke's friend's man, a Mr Bright, who says he is very good. I can use him as a groom and not need to involve you or young Sam."

"What about a compromise?" Aunt Theo said. "Wait for Mr Bright's protégé to arrive and discuss security with him. I've a great deal of respect for Mr Bright. If he says Mr Fallon is good then he is."

"The Duke returned to his seat next to Grace. "What about if we discuss it with Mr Fallon and Luke?"

"We're getting back to asking permission from Luke again, aren't we?" Grace crossed her arms and glared at the Duke.

Aunt Theo laughed. "I want to have a quick word with Cook. I'll order some tea at the same time and leave you two to discuss this in private."

Aunt Theo went out leaving the door slightly ajar. The Duke gave Grace a smile that made her shiver. Was there a hint of citrus in that spicy cologne he was wearing? Oh help. She was becoming obsessed with the man.

"Miss Bamford, it's not a question of asking Luke's permission. He was a soldier and from what I hear a very good one. I'm sure he will have some useful advice on a situation like this."

Grace considered him and sighed. "I don't think that's entirely your reason but, in the spirit of Aunt Theo's suggestion of compromise, I'll accept it for now."

"Good. Now we have a minute alone I had better explain what my proposition was."

Grace looked away from him, her cheeks burning. "I would be interested to hear that."

Oh no. Why had she said that? Unlikely as it might seem, perhaps he was going to offer marriage? He might think she was encouraging him from that comment. She held her breath.

"It was partly to ask for your help as I said. I also wanted to clear the air." He hesitated. "You have treated me differently since that first day when you were quite at ease with me. I'm guessing that Luke's determination to play matchmaker has embarrassed you."

Grace's eyes flew to his face. "It certainly has. He couldn't even be subtle about it."

The Duke chuckled. "You have my sympathy. I had the same problem with one of my aunts a while back. She decided it was about time I married. In the end I had to have a word with my uncle to see if he could head her off."

"Did that work?"

"Up to a point. Not entirely, in fact, escaping that situation was one of the few positive aspects of inheriting the dukedom."

The smile he gave her made Grace catch her breath. "It wasn't something you relished but did you consider refusing to take up your inheritance?"

He shook his head. "No. I was happy with my law practice but there wasn't any way I could have refused the dukedom. Too many people would have been let down. Now I've seen the mess the estates are in, in a way I'm glad to be in charge of them. At least I can put things in order and provide more and better employment."

"That makes sense. What do you suggest we do about the Luke situation?"

"Become friends."

"What? Won't that make him worse?"

"Possibly, but I think us being friends would reassure him that I'm comfortably settled. He's keen to return home to Kitty and won't do so until he's sure of that." The Duke raised his eyebrows at her. "You seem sceptical. If you're worried that this is a ruse on my part, I can assure you I have far too much to do to even think about matrimony for at least a couple of years. You are quite safe with me. Women are badly treated in our society and I respect your determination to keep your independence. I would value your friendship."

Grace looked away. He seemed sincere and it would be churlish to refuse, even if too much time spent with him might test her resolve to stay single. He would have his pick of hundreds of suitable brides when he was ready. Why would he even be interested in trying to win a bluestocking of seven and twenty years in any case? He was right. She would be safe accepting his friendship and he was likely to be a big benefactor to the orphanage.

"I'm happy to be your friend as long as it does stop Luke being embarrassing. This threat to you might keep him here though."

The Duke frowned. "That is a worry but perhaps we can draw out the culprit quickly. They're taking a risk making two attempts so close together. The first one could have simply been a footpad but this one today was riskier. If they're that desperate to get at me it won't be long before they try again."

"Not all that risky. With the horse bucking and rearing he might have dislodged the metal eventually and we wouldn't have known what caused his injury. Not many grooms would be as alert as Sam. The rider might not even have noticed that he was seen. Also, whoever is behind this doesn't know that we were suspicious of the first attack."

The Duke rubbed at his chin. "I don't know what to think. I've written to the two men I gave my law practice to and asked them to set up an investigation into anyone they think might have a serious grudge against me. It might be a long list. Your aunt is right."

Aunt Theo returned, followed by a maid carrying a tea tray. The maid deposited the tray on a side table, dipped a curtsy and left.

Aunt Theo smiled. "What was I right about?"

"The only way I'll find out who is trying to harm me is to invite an attempt on my life, in a controlled situation, where we have a good chance of catching someone."

Aunt Theo poured the tea and handed it out. "That's a good

place to start, but whoever wishes you harm may hire someone without revealing their identity."

"But if we have people watching, I'm hoping they can trace whoever has been hired and keep a watch on them. That way we may get a lead to the principal."

Grace watched the Duke. He was calm for somebody who was under threat.

"What about our driving lessons? With any luck, today's attacker won't have noticed that he was spotted."

The Duke put down his cup. "Or won't admit it if he did notice. He was gone before I could see his face. I'll find out what Sam remembers. Although, I suspect whoever is behind this will use different people each time."

Grace nodded. "Very likely, but you may have been watched. Dispensing with Sam might arouse suspicion. Being with me again might make them think you are unaware of what's been happening."

"Perhaps, but let's see what the experts say."

His jaw was set and his hands were curled into fists. For all his easy manners the Duke of Evesham appeared to have a strong streak of determination. Another reason to resist his charms. They would be bound to clash.

Chapter Eight

Angus accepted the loan of Lady Grant's town carriage to take him back to Luke's house after resisting Miss Bamford's suggestion to summon Luke to join them. He wanted a chance to talk to Luke on his own. Grace's offer to carry on as normal was logical from the point of view of catching the perpetuator of these attacks, but he hated the thought of putting her in danger. Miss Bamford let him out of the back door to the garden.

"I know what you're up to you know." Miss Bamford smiled at him. "You want to talk to Luke first without me there."

"I won't insult your intelligence by denying it. I don't think there's anything we can do until Fallon gets here. Luke did say he could lend me his man Fletcher as well."

Miss Bamford nodded. "Fletcher used to be in the army. He had training from Mr Bright. Don't worry, we will get to the bottom of this."

Angus grinned at her. "You are taking equality seriously. It should be me who is reassuring you."

Miss Bamford crossed her arms and looked down her nose at him. Which was difficult considering she was nearly a head shorter, but quite tall for a woman. The perfect height for him. Lord, he must stop thinking like that. Perhaps marrying someone from an aristocratic background wouldn't be so bad after all. It seemed not all families were as stiff-rumped as the Medleys. But he had promised her they would just be friends. In truth, it was going to take a long time to sort all his estates out. Then there was the added complication of someone out to harm him.

"Hmm. You're as bad as Luke."

Angus caught his breath. The smell of lavender from her perfume was tickling his nose and making him painfully aware of her. He must try and avoid them being completely alone.

"Do you want to come down to the stables with me and question Sam?"

"Yes, that would be a good idea. That reminds me we need to get Sam back to the orphanage."

"I'm not sure that will be easy. He was so upset about your horse."

"Come on, let's see what he says."

Angus put a hand on her arm to detain her. She looked up at him with a puzzled expression.

"Since we going to be friends, couldn't you pretend I was an extra brother and call me Angus in private?"

She wrinkled up her nose. "It would be easier, as long as we remember to use full names when we're in public."

Angus forced himself to remove his hand from her arm. This wouldn't do. "Thank you. I'll feel much more comfortable. I'm not sure I'll ever become used to everyone calling me, Your Grace."

"Although now you will have to call me Grace." She laughed. "We must get on or I'll be late for dinner. I believe Aunt Theo and I have an engagement later."

They found Sam chatting away to Lady Grant's head groom.

"The horse is going to be all right, Duke. He's a bit upset still. Could I stay the night with him?" Sam sounded eager.

The head groom looked at Angus and laughed. "I've no objection if you haven't, Your Grace. The lad's a wonder with horses. Miss Bamford's grey is much happier when he's with him."

"What do you think, Miss Bamford? Since Sam is not officially in my employment yet, will the orphanage allow it?"

Grace shook her head. "What are we going to do with you?" She smiled at Sam. "I know, I'll send Jamie round to the orphanage with a message. I'm sure it will be acceptable."

Sam grinned at her. "Thank you, Miss Bamford."

"I must check on Nimbus to see how he's faring before I leave you."

Angus watched, fascinated, as she went up to Nimbus. He whinnied a greeting at her.

"Oh, you poor boy. You'll soon feel better with all this attention you're getting." Grace gave him one last pat and moved away.

"I think he'll be recovered enough to resume his duties in two or three days, Miss Bamford," the head groom said.

"Thank you. I'm sure Sam will be a great help in nursing him."

Angus watched as Sam seem to grow a fraction taller. Sam was as much under Grace's spell as he was himself.

Grace moved towards Angus. "If you ask Luke, he can probably find room for Sam in his stables after tonight, until the ones at Medley House are ready."

Sam gave him a beseeching look.

"I'll ask Lord Enstone if he can squeeze you in, Sam. Mr

Fallon should arrive soon and he can take charge of you. Before we go, can you describe what you saw of the rider who attacked Nimbus?"

Sam put his head on one side. "He was dressed in smart clothes, but he didn't look as if he belonged in them. His face was a bit pockmarked if you know what I mean. Oldish. Dark-haired going a bit grey. Don't think he was very tall. I can't think of anything else."

"Thank you, Sam. That's a useful description. Stay with Nimbus until you hear from me and mind you listen to what the grooms here tell you."

"Yes, Duke."

Grace said her goodbyes and strode into the garden. Angus watched her until she disappeared into the house.

"Right. I'll leave you to it then, Sam."

"Yes, Duke. You can rely on me." Sam saluted and went back to Nimbus's side.

Jamie joined them. "Miss Bamford said for me to go in the coach with you, Your Grace. Then it can take me to the orphanage after dropping you off."

The head groom had a quick word with Sam and then came across to them. "The carriage should be ready for you now, Your Grace."

Angus took one last look around the stables and then followed the head groom to where a smart town carriage, probably the one he'd seen Grace get out of on the first day, was waiting outside the mews.

He found Luke in the library when he arrived back. It was an inviting room. Smaller than the one at Medley House, the opened books and papers spread around gave it a homely air of being in regular use.

Luke put down his newspaper when Angus entered. "Did you manage to fit in a driving lesson?"

Angus laughed. "I'm afraid not, we've had a busy day."

"I've got some good news for you. Fletcher and Fallon have arrived."

Angus flopped into a brown leather armchair in front of a roaring fire. "Now that's the best piece of news I've had all day."

Luke poured two glasses of brandy and handed one Angus. "Drink this. It looks like you've had quite a day." He lowered himself into the seat next to him.

"It started off well. Grace and her friend, Miss Vaughan, have found me some experienced servants as well as some of their orphans already."

Luke grinned at him. "It sounds like you and Grace are getting on rather well."

"No thanks to you, Luke. Your sister was thoroughly embarrassed by your matchmaking." Luke looked so crestfallen that Angus couldn't help but laugh. "We've agreed on a truce and decided to use first names in private but not in public. Then I go and forget straightaway."

"First name terms?" Luke's brows shot up. "Perhaps I won't give up hope of pairing you two off just yet."

He ought to try and disabuse Luke of his obsession with a match between them but he probably wouldn't listen, or even take a protest as confirmation of there being something between him and Grace.

"Don't tell her I forgot, will you. I promised her that I wanted nothing more than friendship and I don't want to upset her. She's had a trying enough day today as it is and I need her help."

Luke sat up straight. "What happened?"

"Another attack. This time one of Grace's greys had a sharp piece of metal shoved down his collar. Sam shouted a warning but how she stopped her horses bolting I will never know." Angus sighed. "I need Grace's help but I'm not sure I ought to accept it. It's putting her in danger as well as me. I promised her I would consult with you, Fletcher and Fallon before I decided whether to accept her help or not."

Luke let out a long, low whistle. "I'll send for them now. No point you going over it all twice."

Luke put his head around the door and spoke to someone outside, presumably a footman. He must remember to ask him how many footmen a good-sized household needed.

"I've sent someone to fetch them. I found time to call in at Horse Guards between appointments today and was lucky enough to bump into an old army friend of mine who is in between postings. I'd trust him with anything so I hope you don't mind me talking to him."

"No, of course not. I trust your judgement. Did he have anything interesting to say?"

"He knows some of the Medleys."

Angus smiled. "At least you can say you've taken Grace's suggestion seriously."

"That's what I thought. In a situation like this it's best to take every suggestion seriously. You'll meet Ram, Major Ramsay that is, yourself later. I've invited him to come here for dinner when we can be private. He's a great gun and I thought you would find it interesting to talk to him since he knew William Medley. In fact, I'm sure he said he was in the same regiment as William."

"Yes, I'll look forward to meeting Major Ramsay." Angus sighed. "William visited friends in Edinburgh several times as a young man and always came to visit us. We got on well. I was so sad he was killed in battle. It was no more than a skirmish by all accounts and he was the only fatality that day."

There was a sharp rap at the door.

"Enter," Luke said.

The door opened to admit a middle-aged man with a military bearing and a fresh-faced young man with blonde hair, who looked little more than a youth but was probably in his twenties. The older man saluted and Luke grinned at him.

"Are we glad to see you, Fletcher! You will have guessed that this is the Duke of Evesham. There has been another attempt on his life today. Come on in, both of you, and take a seat. I appreciate you rushing back, would you like a drink?"

"I wouldn't say no to a drop of brandy, my lord." Fletcher smiled and nodded at the other man. "Young Fallon here is keen to get started. He loves a good mystery. Mr Bright says he's got all the brains of Bow Street put together."

Fallon blushed a vivid red and studied the floor, but not before Angus saw the excited gleam in his intelligent-looking grey eyes. These two seemed promising. Luke handed drinks to the two men and nodded at the brandy decanter.

"Another?"

Angus laughed. "Yes please. I need something after a day like today."

Luke poured himself a brandy and sat down. I'll let the Duke tell you what's been happening to him."

Angus quickly described the details of both attacks. "After the knife attack, I initially wondered if Miss Bamford was being a bit fanciful and it was nothing more than a robbery gone wrong. Now I know her better, I'm inclined to believe her analysis that my attacker was a hired killer. The second attack was quite bizarre. But very clever. Without young Sam shouting his warning and Miss Bamford already slowing her greys before the rider passed, the chance of avoiding a collision would have been small. The coach we avoided was much bigger than the phaeton and we would have almost certainly come off much the worst."

Fletcher rubbed his chin. "I've heard people mention Sam, he was a street boy, wasn't he? You've done well to employ him as your tiger. I'll happily train him in the finer points of becoming a groom. Have you kept the piece of metal that was used on the horse?"

Angus fished in his pocket and pulled out the bloodstained handkerchief. He passed it over to Fletcher. "It's inside this. I'd almost forgotten I still had it."

Fletcher placed the handkerchief on a side table and opened it out. "Hmm. That's interesting. I think it's part of a military spur which has been sharpened to give it more rough edges. It would have torn the horse to pieces if he'd managed to bolt." He passed it over to Fallon.

The young man blushed. "I think you're right. Nasty thing to do to a horse."

Angus sat back and studied both men. "I need to bring this to a head. There's a huge amount of work to do to put the estates I've inherited to rights and this is interfering with all my plans. What do you suggest?"

"Firstly," Fletcher said, "I think we would be as well to house Fallon somewhere else for the time being. And let him loose to investigate in his own way. He can report back after darkness."

Luke looked at Angus. "Are you happy with that? It will give him the freedom to investigate without being recognised."

"Yes of course. I'm entirely in your hands. What do you say, Fallon?"

"That suits me. The only problem is I don't know London all that well. How would it be if I took the street boy with me?"

Fletcher laughed. "That sounds like a good idea to me. Where is the boy at the moment?"

"Sam is still technically at the orphanage," Angus said. "But I've let him stay in the mews at Lady Grant's house tonight as he's developed a real rapport with the injured horse. We aren't sure how old he is but he must be at least thirteen. He says he's sixteen, but that was after I said I don't normally employ anyone under the age of fourteen. He's tiny and looks about ten at the most."

"That's even better." Fallon blushed again and glanced at Fletcher who nodded. "He could be inconspicuous anywhere by being one of those boys who always seem to be in the right place to hold someone's horses for a coin."

Angus laughed. "He'll have no difficulty with that part. That was what he was doing when a vicar rescued him and took him into the orphanage."

Luke grimaced. "Are you going to have enough manpower, Fletcher?"

"I've brought some more of your lordship's grooms back with me, including two lads who know London and can help me by acting as bodyguards. Fallon will need his own team to investigate."

Angus sat up. "Miss Bamford and Miss Vaughan have found me some young men who were brought up in the orphanage and have been working for an elderly colonel who recently died. They will know their way around London. The colonel's house is being sold up but they have the right to stay until they've found new employment. I'm going to take them all on but, as Medley House isn't ready yet, they're still there. "

Fallon's eyes lit up. "They're in control of their own time at the moment then."

"Yes, except I've asked them to help preparing rooms for themselves at Medley House. We can work around that. They seem an intelligent group of young men. Especially the one who's been acting as the butler. I can't remember his name but Miss Bamford knows him. Once Medley House is ready, he's going to be my secretary."

"That sounds perfect. No reason why they shouldn't carry on with working at Medley House when I don't need them. We could use them as messengers so I can avoid direct contact. Would they be able to fit me and Sam into the house do you think?"

"I don't see why not. One of them is going to be my valet. I had intended to ask Lord Enstone if his valet would give him some training."

Fallon thought for a moment. "It might be an idea to carry on with that. Mr Fletcher could give him some security training and a valet would be in a good position to keep an eye on you if you have to travel anywhere. I could have his room at the colonel's place. I don't mind sharing with Sam."

Angus sat back with his eyes closed. It felt like a weight was lifting off his shoulders. "I like the sound of that idea. Sam is as sharp as a butcher's knife but he will need watching." Angus burst out laughing. "He's quite a character. I've already told him that Mr Fallon will be in charge of him so he's expecting that."

Luke nodded enthusiastically. "If you need any more help, we will gladly find it for you but this is starting to sound like an excellent plan."

"It is, but I have a feeling you might well need to hire more people, Fallon." Angus grinned. "You might need to pay for some information too. I'll give you a letter of introduction to my new man of business and you can draw any funds for either from him."

Excitement shone from Fallon's eyes and he seemed much more self-assured. "Thank you. I'll make an appointment to talk to him if you don't mind. It's possible he may have come across things in your affairs that might be relevant."

"I have no objection. I give you a free hand. I'll make sure he knows to expect you."

"Thank you. Now we've sorted out the practical details, have you any idea who might wish to kill you, Your Grace?"

"It's a long list. It might be as well if I write it down for you if…." Angus drew in a sharp breath at Fallon's affronted expression, quickly hidden. The man had been offended by his assumption that he couldn't read.

Fallon smiled at him. "I was brought up in the orphanage on Lord Hargreaves's estate in Kent. I've been well schooled in reading and writing."

"Excellent. Tell me, why did you train as a groom then?"

"Mr Bright trained me. He used to work in army intelligence and suggested I might enjoy something like that. We decided I needed an occupation first. Since I've always liked horses, he also trained me as a groom. I thought about going into the army but Mr Bright suggested I might have a future doing investigations privately eventually."

"If you can solve the mystery and get me out of this mess,

I'd be happy to offer you employment."

Angus smiled at Fallon. It didn't sound as if he would be interested in a normal occupation but he looked a good man to know. "Or sponsor you to set up in business if that is your preference."

Fallon leaned forwards with his eyes glowing. "I'll solve it all right. Don't you fear. I can't wait to get started."

Chapter Nine

Grace woke up early the next morning after a night troubled by dreams of injured horses. The first rays of dawn sent pale fingers of light dancing around the edges of the drapes in the shape of prancing horses. Lord, it had been a close-run thing holding Nimbus. Her arms were still aching from the effort. She shuddered and pulled the covers over her head, in a vain attempt to blot out the terror of the moment when she saw the coach coming towards them. Her breath came in short pants. All that had stood between them and disaster had been her skill and strength. She had always been pleased that she was taller and stronger than most women, but never more so than in that moment as she wrestled with her terrified horses.

Grace rolled into a ball under the covers and breathed deeply. The sounds of Nimbus's screams in her ears. This would never do. No good ever came of stewing on things. She threw back the covers and forced herself out of bed. She rang the bell for her maid and wandered down to the breakfast room as soon as she was dressed. What would Angus's adversary try next? She had to stay calm or she would be no use to anyone. There was no way they were going to leave her out of this.

She worked her way, determinedly, through a hearty breakfast. Aunt Theo joined her as she was about to pour a final cup of coffee.

Grace smiled. "Coffee?"

"Yes please. What are your plans for today? You had an exciting time yesterday."

"I'm not sure I would use the word exciting." Grace shook her head and laughed. "It was certainly interesting. Someone is determined to rid the world of Angus."

Grace closed her eyes as she felt her cheeks heat up. "We've called a truce by the way and agreed to use first names in private."

Aunt Theo finished filling her plate and sat down next to her. She raised her eyebrows in surprise, but looked relieved.

"That's a sensible course of action, Grace. We're going to have to work together to try and sort this out. I wonder if Luke will call in today."

"He'd better. I'm determined not to let him stop me from helping with this. Why would anyone want to kill Angus?"

Aunt Theo put her head on one side. "That's the question, isn't it? There are landowners making a lot of money in Scotland by evicting crofters without a thought for what might happen to them. I suspect Angus is right and there's a nasty Scottish nobleman behind this."

Grace handed her aunt a cup of coffee. She sipped from her own cup.

"Perhaps, although it could be someone who has a grudge against him because of some sort of judgement they lost in court. Do you remember that magistrate who was beaten up in the local inn because he had annoyed someone by finding against them?"

"Yes, but that was in the heat of the moment. This is a

considered thing. Which is why I think money is at the root of it. How are you feeling? It must have been a scary moment when your horse tried to bolt."

"I've had better." There was no way she was going to admit that Angus had been obliged to support her for several minutes once they got back.

There were sounds of an arrival in the hall and Harvey ushered Angus in. Fletcher, Luke's steward and occasional groom, followed behind. Aunt Theo signalled to a footman who walked past.

"A fresh pot of coffee in here, please. Gentlemen won't you take a seat."

Fletcher seemed a little uncomfortable but followed Angus's lead and sat down opposite to them.

Grace pointed to the silver serving dishes arranged on a long sideboard. "Have you eaten? There's plenty of food left."

Angus grinned at her. "I had one breakfast early on but I won't say no to some more."

He filled two plates and handed one to Fletcher. "Being the intended victim of a murder plot seems to have given me an appetite."

Grace stared at him for a moment. He seemed entirely at his ease and ready for anything, when she felt drained. She had to admire his courage. "What are we going to do today?"

"Carry on as if we hadn't noticed anything yesterday. Fletcher has driven me here in Luke's spare curricle, behind his greys. To a casual observer Luke says they're not that much different to your horses."

Grace nodded. "He's right, they are fairly similar. I'm surprised he's let anyone else drive them."

"I'm sure Fletcher must have driven them before, but Luke

said there's no reason why you shouldn't drive them if you want to harness them up to your phaeton."

Grace gasped. Was this in the way of a peace offering from Luke? "I'll happily drive Luke's greys. I'm surprised he's letting me loose. I expected him to try and keep me away from the action."

"Luke is firmly of the opinion that we need to carry on as if nothing has happened, in the hope of drawing another attempt in the near future. Besides Fallon, who has been trained by Bright in intelligence gathering, Fletcher has brought some more of Luke's grooms with him and one followed us on horseback." Angus smiled. "I'm not sure how he's going to take it, but Sam has been allocated to help Fallon investigate as he's a stranger to London."

Grace laughed. "Sam needs a strong hand, but he knows London better than anybody."

Angus raised his eyebrows at Fletcher. "Fallon is extremely intelligent, what's he like at handling subordinates?"

"No need to worry on that score, Your Grace. The groom I brought today won't stand no nonsense either. He can escort Sam to that house you were on about on foot. He's a London lad originally. I'll take his horse later."

"Which house?" Grace asked.

Angus answered. "The one where Hugh Masters and his friends are currently living. We intend to get them to accommodate Fallon and Sam and provide Fallon with any assistance he needs."

Aunt Theo raised her eyebrows. "Luke's planning this out like a military operation by the sound of it. Where do you want Grace to drive you?"

"We were thinking in terms of a drive around Hyde Park at

the fashionable hour. Fletcher will follow on horseback."

"I'm more than happy to drive Luke's greys around Hyde Park but what are we going to do in the meantime?"

"I was hoping you would lend me a carriage to take me to see the Duke of Cathlay. I've had a message from him to say he's free to explain parliamentary procedure to me."

"The Cathlays are quite close. Why don't I take you there in the phaeton?"

Aunt Theo leaned forward. "We could all go and take a carriage if I wasn't engaged later, but I don't see any harm in it with Fletcher following you."

Angus looked at Fletcher. "Are you free to accompany us?"

"It won't take me long to question young Sam and I don't think there's much more I can find out here. The Duke of Cathlay is always a good man to have on your side. You should tell him about the latest incident."

"That's settled then," Grace said briskly. "Although we might be better riding in Hyde Park later. It's easier to avoid people on horseback. Can you ride?"

"Yes. I used to ride a lot, but I need a horse up to my weight."

Grace studied him and blinked at the feeling of warmth in her cheeks. "I doubt you are any heavier than Luke. If he hasn't got a spare horse, we have a couple of hacks here that he uses occasionally."

Aunt Theo nodded. "Grace is right. She has Jamie in the groom's seat at the back of the phaeton but wouldn't normally take a mounted groom in Hyde Park."

Fletcher rubbed at his chin. "I agree with Lady Grant. A mounted groom following a lady rider will merge into the background. I wonder if I could get away with bringing Jamie as another pair of eyes. He's only young and it would look as if I was training him."

"I'll leave you to decide that," Angus said. "I don't want all these young lads exposed to too much danger though."

"I'll make sure he's safe. I'll go down to the mews and wait for you there, Your Grace."

Angus nodded and waited for the door to close behind him before continuing, his expression pensive.

"Grace, do you remember your theory that it might be my heir behind all this? Luke found a friend at Horse Guards, Major Ramsay, and invited him to dinner yesterday. Ramsay is arranging an invitation for us to attend a ball at the home of someone called Colonel Gilbert this evening. He's sure that Ralph Medley will be there, even though he's not in the army any more. If you ladies are free, we'd like you to come too and see what you think of him."

A frisson of what could only be excitement ran through Grace. Surely it wasn't at the thought of a dance with Angus? Of course not. It was the thrill of investigating. That was all.

"I had planned a night at home and will be free. What about you, Aunt Theo?"

Aunt Theo laughed. "Fortunately, apart from my engagement shortly, I'm free for the rest of the day. Between us we should be able to get an idea of what this man is like."

"Thank you. Ramsay didn't know Ralph Medley well, but he said he seemed an innocuous sort of character. The more of us who get a look at him the better."

Aunt Theo nodded. "It's as well to be thorough. But, as I said earlier, Grace, I think some Scottish nobleman who doesn't want Angus ruining his chances of making a fortune is probably behind this."

"I'm inclined to agree with you Lady Grant. Cathlay hinted

in his note that my appearance in London as the Duke of Evesham has caused quite a stir amongst a group of Scottish peers."

"There are so many suspects. It's going to be tricky finding out who it is." Grace sighed. "Give me a quarter of an hour to change into a carriage gown and I'll escort you down to the stables. We can check on Nimbus and Misty whilst Luke's greys are harnessed up to my phaeton."

Grace ran upstairs and asked her maid to fetch the carriage gown which had recently been delivered. The cost had seemed exorbitant at the time but now she was glad. If she was going to help flush out a murderer, she might at least look smart while she was at it. The cream gown of cambric muslin, trimmed with a length of dark blue at the bottom, fitted beautifully. The high neck, which rose to a collar, had a touch of the military about it, besides being quite warm. The maid handed her a deep, russet-coloured, sarsenet mantle which fanned out into a broad cape.

"My word, this outfit is lovely on you, Miss Bamford." Her maid handed her a matching cream, chip hat trimmed with a russet ribbon.

Grace ran downstairs and re-joined Angus and Aunt Theo in the drawing room after a little over ten minutes.

Angus smiled at her. "I had a feeling you'd be the sort of female who made good on her promises to be ready quickly."

"I refuse to reply to that." Grace chuckled. "Come on. Let's leave Aunt Theo in peace."

They said their goodbyes and Grace led the way to the door that opened onto the path down through the garden. "I do hope Nimbus isn't too shaken up."

Angus grimaced. "I hope he doesn't take any lasting harm

from it. I will of course replace him if he does, but it wouldn't be the same."

"He's getting the best of attention. I can't see that being necessary."

They found Nimbus and Misty tethered together, with Sam and Jamie sitting by them.

"How are they, Jamie?" Grace walked up to Nimbus and stroked his neck. "You've certainly got him nice and calm."

"Sam stayed up with him all night, Miss Bamford. We re-dressed the wound and I don't think there will be too much scarring. Misty seems perfectly happy."

Fletcher joined them followed by a young groom. "Phillips will take Sam to Lord Enstone's house and then Sam can show Fallon the way to the house we want them to stay in."

Grace put her head on one side. "Should we perhaps warn Hugh Masters to expect them?"

"I thought of that," Angus said. "I've written a note and your aunt has sent a footman to deliver it."

Grace nodded. Jamie looked tired; he'd probably stayed up most of the night too. "Jamie, you go and have a few hours rest. You can accompany us on horseback to Hyde Park later."

"The phaeton is ready for you, Miss Bamford," Fletcher said.

Grace led the way outside and caught her breath when she saw Luke's horses harnessed up to her phaeton. They were similar to Nimbus and Misty but a little livelier. Never mind she shouldn't have too much trouble with them. Angus handed her into the phaeton and Fletcher disappeared to return mounted on a sturdy-looking hack. Angus jumped up beside her and Grace gave the horses the signal to start. Fletcher followed at a respectful distance.

"I'll take us a slightly longer way than normal to give me

time to get used to Luke's horses."

Grace soon settled the horses down. They turned a corner and the feel of Angus's thigh touching hers made her gasp under her breath. What was it about this man that stirred her senses so? She hurried into speech to hide her confusion.

"Thank you for not giving me away to Aunt Theo this morning."

"How do you mean?"

Now why had she said that? "By not letting on that I was so shaken after I got down from the phaeton yesterday that you had to hold me up for a few minutes."

Angus laughed. "I was simply returning the favour. If you remember I started shaking after the knife attack and you assured me it was a natural reaction to the shock. I'm sure this is just the same. Although, I'm not entirely happy about letting you take risks by accompanying me. After all it's me they want to murder."

Grace shook her head. "You're far too heedless of your own safety. There is no way I'm going to leave you free to take silly risks."

"I knew you would say that. If I'd thought there was any possibility of you agreeing to stay out of this, I would have tried harder to persuade you." Angus grinned at her. "My mother always said I was the most stubborn boy she had ever met. I rather think I've met someone who is even more stubborn than I am."

Grace turned away from him. "I'm not admitting to that."

"I rest my case."

Annoying man. Grace pressed her lips together and concentrated on the horses. Angus seemed to be humming under his breath. She risked a sideways glance and quickly looked away when he smiled at her. He was goading her like Luke.

"You've never said much about your family. I've gathered your parents are dead. Do you have a bevy of sisters tucked away up in Scotland?"

Angus burst out laughing. "Truce? I'm an only child but I do have several female cousins I'm very fond of. Fond enough to spend time teasing them."

Grace's cheeks went hot. Was he saying he was fond of her? "I thought you were goading me. I admit defeat. I can be stubborn but I'm not admitting to being more stubborn than you." She chuckled. "I have a feeling that might be difficult".

Angus laughed and rested a hand lightly on her shoulder for a moment. "I'm afraid you're right. If I think things are getting too dangerous, I won't hesitate to cut you out. I apologise in advance."

They pulled up in front of Cathlay House. Two grooms, who Grace recognised as being Luke's, were waiting to hold the horses. Angus jumped down and held a hand up to her. She grasped it and climbed down nimbly, carefully studying the floor as if she was afraid of falling. She didn't want to look at Angus. Just the touch of his hand set her on fire. Parts of her she hadn't known existed seemed to tingle. This would never do. One of the grooms took hold of the hack Fletcher was riding.

Fletcher transferred to the driver's seat of the phaeton. "I'll take these around to the mews, Your Grace. Then join you in the Duke of Cathlay's study."

The door was opened by a footman and Grace laid her hand on the arm Angus extended for her. She felt a little breathless as Angus escorted her into the house. Angus smiled down at her and his eyes danced, as if he knew what effect he was having on her.

"Will you join us in the Duke of Cathlay's study, or do you want to speak to the Duchess?"

The Duke himself came out into the hall. "Augusta sends her apologies but she had a prior engagement this morning. Won't you join us?"

Grace smiled at him. "Try and exclude me!"

"I rather thought that would be your response." The Duke of Cathlay's eyes danced.

The Duke led them to a selection of chairs and sofas set in front of a fire at one end of the library. "Can I get you some refreshment whilst we wait for Fletcher?"

Angus grinned. "A pot of coffee wouldn't go amiss. I was up early this morning."

The Duke went across and rang a bell which was answered by a stately butler. Grace found herself manoeuvred onto a leather sofa with Angus sitting next to her, before she could say anything. The butler disappeared on his errand and the Duke of Cathlay took an armchair set at an angle so that he could see both of them. There was a firm knock at the door and Fletcher entered at the Duke of Cathlay's invitation. The Duke waved him to a matching armchair the other side of the sofa.

Angus sat forward. "You've been busy, Fletcher. You must have sent those grooms on ahead."

"Yes indeed. Two more of Lord Enstone's grooms were following us. Mr Bright is a genius at training grooms to be capable of security work. Even though I knew they were behind us I never once saw them myself. You will be glad to know that they found no sign of anyone following you this morning."

Grace studied them. It seemed there was a lot going on that

Angus hadn't told her about. If she kept quiet perhaps more information would become apparent as they talked.

"I have a list here of peers known to be unhappy with you taking up a prominent position in the House of Lords." Cathlay handed Angus sheet of paper. "Most of those are probably no more than a touch disgruntled and are unlikely to bear you any strong grudge. The four names at the top definitely need watching. I've got several of my friends circulating around the clubs to see if they can hear any more."

"Thank you, Your Grace." Angus tapped the sheet of paper on his knee. "I've had dealings with three of these gentlemen in the past, but I've never come across the Earl of Hedburgh."

Cathlay sniffed. "I've crossed swords with him before now, it's a difficult thing to do. He's hard to pin down and tries to stir up trouble by using other people. I'm inclined to put him at the top of your list of suspects." He smiled at Grace. "Together with Evesham's heir of course."

Grace shook her head at him. "Are you serious about that or humouring me?"

"Difficult to say without meeting him."

"Ah, we've got some news on that." Grace glanced at Angus.

"Luke's friend, Major Ramsey, had dinner with Luke and I yesterday. It seems Ralph Medley is in London. Major Ramsay is getting the four of us, including Lady Grant and Luke, invited to a ball given by Major Gilbert tonight. Ralph Medley will almost certainly be present. Ramsay didn't know anything to his detriment but since he is in London..."

Cathlay's gaze focused on Angus. "He has to be on the list."

"Yes, I think so. Fletcher has brought some of Luke's security trained grooms with him, so we are well protected. Oh, that reminds me." Angus glanced at Grace. He fished in his pocket and pulled out her little muff pistol. "I forgot to give you this back."

Cathlay's eyes lit up. "With our eldest girl coming out next season I need a set of those for her. Do you think Enstone could teach her to shoot like you, Grace? I heard you winged the man who tried to stab Evesham here."

Grace laughed and replaced the pistol in her reticule. "If Luke can't, he will be able to provide a groom who can."

"I'll take a couple of your orphanage boys, after they've had Bright's training, if you can persuade someone to let me have a more experienced groom trained by him as well. Fiona takes after her mother. I will need someone to keep an eye on her."

Angus's shoulders shook. "Oh Lord. I'm mixing with a much more interesting set of aristocrats than my stuffy paternal relatives. I thought Grace was a one off."

The smile he gave Grace set her pulses racing. Her cheeks grew hot at the speculative gleam that came into Cathlay's eyes. They should never have agreed to use first names in private. It was so easy to forget in company. Angus was grinning at her, annoying man. She grimaced at him but that made him laugh out loud.

"You must admit, life is much more interesting with you around, Grace."

She raised her eyebrows at him. Was he goading her again by repeating his mistake?

A clock chimed twelve times in the distance. Cathlay sat up.

"I'm running out of time. Are you still available for dinner at Brook's the day after tomorrow, Evesham?"

"Yes, I've kept it free."

"Excellent. I'll introduce you to some useful and entertaining people and brief you on the procedure to take up your seat in the Lords."

"Thank you. I forgot to say Fletcher has also brought an investigator with him. I'll keep you informed of anything he finds out."

The door opened to admit the Duchess.

"I'm glad I managed to catch you, Grace. I've set up an afternoon salon with the wives of as many of the suspects on Cathlays list as I can invite without arousing suspicion. Theodosia seemed to think you were free tomorrow afternoon."

"Yes, I am." Grace chuckled. "Are you planning to ply them with alcoholic drinks and loosen a few tongues?"

"Something along those lines. Come to my sitting room and I'll give you a list of those I've invited." She put a hand on her husband's shoulder. "Don't forget you have to be at that business meeting in half an hour."

She turned and led Grace out of the library before Cathlay could respond.

"My word, Grace. That's a smart outfit."

They went into the Duchess's sitting room and Grace twirled around to display the cape better. "It's stylish, isn't it? It only came yesterday. I feel guilty about how much I spend on clothes sometimes, but it is my only weakness and I console myself with how much employment I'm providing."

The Duchess laughed. "This is very true and where would we all be without you to show us the way when it comes to fashion. Now where did I put that list?"

She walked across to a small desk and pulled out a sheet of paper. "Here it is. Cathlay has put the Earl of Hedburgh at the top. I can't say I like the man but I must warn you that Cathlay positively loathes him, so he may be biased."

Grace ran her eye over the list. "Ooh. There are some

interesting names here. Lady Curtis for instance. Her husband seems such an inoffensive sort of man. Although I suppose in a case like this people may not always be what they seem."

They heard voices out in the hall. Cathlay and Angus joined them.

"As you reminded me, my love," Cathlay's eyes twinkled, "I have to take my leave now. I'm sure I can rely on you to entertain Grace and Evesham." He saluted them all and withdrew.

The Duchess looked from Angus to Grace. "Do you have time for tea?"

"That's kind," Grace said, "but I have a feeling Evesham has several things he needs to do."

Angus gave a grateful looking smile. "At the risk of appearing rude, I would prefer to go now. I promise, once we've got to the bottom of this mystery, I'll invite you all to Medley House as soon as it's ready to return your hospitality."

The Duchess gave Angus a beaming smile. "I perfectly understand, Evesham."

Grace sighed inwardly. Even her old friend, the Duchess of Cathlay, was eyeing up Angus as a potential partner for her. She folded the list of names and put into her reticule.

"If you don't mind, I'll study this together with Aunt Theo and see what she thinks of these suggestions."

"Not at all, my dear. With three of us to circulate tomorrow afternoon, we may be able to turn something up."

Angus bowed. "Thank you, Your Grace. I appreciate your help."

They said their goodbyes and Angus followed Grace out into the hallway. The butler was waiting to open the front door for them.

"Your phaeton should be here in a moment, Miss Bamford. His Grace gave instructions for your horses to be harnessed up." His face was impassive.

Angus grinned at him. "Thank you. This is such an efficient household. I hope I can get Medley House organised to the same standard. This may sound a strange question, but how would I go about finding an experienced butler who was ready to take on a large household?"

The Cathlay's butler seemed taken aback but he soon recovered. "If it would be of help, Your Grace, I'm happy to listen out for any potential candidates. I have an afternoon off next week and I intend to meet up with some old friends. Would you object to me making discreet enquiries of them? I wouldn't say who was interested." His voice gave little away but he sounded interested.

"That would be very much appreciated."

The butler bowed and opened the door for them. Angus offered her his arm. Grace placed a hand on it and tried to suppress a shiver of pleasure that was becoming all too familiar when she was with Angus. They reached the pavement and she glanced up at him. Angus looked so pleased with himself that she was hard pressed not to laugh.

Angus smiled at her. "What's the Cathlay's butler's name?"

"Sayers. Incredibly efficient."

"I noticed. Do you think he'll find me a suitable butler?"

Grace wrinkled up her nose. "He offered to make enquiries straight away. I wouldn't be surprised if he has someone in mind. I'll ask our butler, Harvey, as well if you like."

"Yes please. I need Hugh Masters as my secretary as soon as it can be arranged." He squeezed her hand. "Speaking of which, let's go to the Colonel's house next."

Grace removed her hand. That sounded more like a command than a request, he did like to take charge.

"If you say so." She kept her voice calm and tried not to look too disgruntled.

"Thank you." Angus gave her a half smile. The wretched man knew he had annoyed her. "I want to check that Sam and Fallon have made it there safely and talk to the young man who is going to be my valet."

He handed her into the driving seat of the waiting phaeton. Grace accepted the reins from Fletcher, who jumped down and walked around to Angus. She could just about hear what they were saying.

"No sign of anyone following or lurking so far today, Your Grace."

"Good. We're driving around to the Colonel's house next. Miss Bamford knows the way."

"Right you are. I'll be close behind you but the rest of my men will follow on at a distance. You probably won't see them. I don't want anyone who might be lurking around that house because you were there yesterday to realise we're watching out for them."

Angus jumped up beside her. The groom holding the horses' heads let go and Grace guided her horses out into the road. She let out a sigh of pleasure.

"These are sweet goers. Nearly as good as Nimbus and Misty. I enjoy driving nearly as much as riding."

Angus laughed. "I prefer riding, largely because I've always found that easier. I tended to walk to a lot of places in Edinburgh. It sounds like Mr Bright trains a lot of your boys as grooms, with added training on security."

"Yes, he does. He works for the Overtons in Kent. He was Nat

Overton's batman in the army. They were involved in army intelligence quite a lot and Mr Bright enjoys training people. I think he's technically their steward but they give him a free range."

"It certainly sounds like the young men he's trained are in demand."

"They are. By employing some of the latest trainees you make more space for boys ready to leave the orphanage. If I were you, I'd talk to Fletcher, tell him what you need and let him sort you out."

"Yes, I will." Angus rubbed his hands together. "Things are starting to come together. If we can sort out the mystery of this attacker, I'll be able to concentrate on sorting out my estates."

Grace laughed. "You're enjoying this, aren't you? Do you miss your legal practice in Edinburgh?"

Angus sighed. "I do. But I can see this job will keep me occupied and I'm the only one who can fill the position. I've left the practice in good hands, with two of the best students I've ever had taking over."

Grace concentrated on the road as she overtook a cart. Angus seemed an adaptable sort of man with a strong sense of duty. If she was the marrying kind then she would definitely be interested. Her cheeks heated at the thought of what marriage to Angus might include. This would never do. She had met attractive men before but none of them had made her yearn for a physical relationship. They turned into a busier road and she was able to avoid making conversation on the pretext of concentrating. Admitting to herself that she longed to get closer to Angus physically was an unsettling thought.

Chapter Ten

It was a relief to pull up outside the Colonel's house. It was on the edge of a fashionable area of Town and few people were about. And certainly no one who appeared in the least bit nefarious. Which was just as well since she felt quite shaky driving again. Perhaps that was why Luke had suggested she drive his greys, so she wouldn't have too much time to think about it. The door opened immediately. Hugh Masters must have been watching out for them. Fletcher dismounted and Masters held his horse.

Hugh smiled up at Grace. "There's only me and Gillard here at the moment, Miss Bamford. Go on in and I'll show your man where to stable the horses."

Angus jumped down and Fletcher took his place. Grace handed over the reins and lifted her skirts with one hand ready to jump down unaided. Angus was too quick for her. He didn't wait to take her hand, simply placed his hands at her waist and lifted her down. Grace was too shocked to protest. Angus threaded her hand through his arm and whisked her inside.

Once they were inside Angus grinned down at her. "Don't look so furious. It seems to me that we need to assume that someone who wishes us ill is nearby at all times."

Grace was too breathless to say anything. Was he aware of

the effect he was having on her?

Sam exploded into the hallway his face alive with excitement.

Angus released Grace and put a hand on Sam's shoulder. "Not here. Let's go somewhere private."

Sam nodded and took them through a door which led into the servant's quarters. They heard voices coming from another room. Sam ushered them in to what proved to be the kitchen.

"Mr Fallon has told me and Fred all about what's going on. I'm glad you're letting me be an investigator."

Angus shook his head. "That's not quite the role I had in mind for you, Sam. I simply want you to make sure Mr Fallon can find his way around London."

Fallon stood as they entered. "Don't worry, Your Grace. I'll keep Sam under control. I threatened him with banishment to Kent if he disobeys orders."

Sam's shoulders slumped and he raised a woebegone face up to Mr Fallon. "I won't do nothing you don't tell me to. I don't want to go to Kent."

Grace was intrigued, the poor boy was shaking. "I know you prefer London, Sam, but I hadn't realised you actively disliked the thought of going to Kent."

Sam sniffed and wiped his nose on his sleeve. "The thing is, some old cove caught me once and tried to sell me to a chimney sweep, who was going to take me to Kent. I was lucky to escape. That's why I let that vicar take me to the orphanage." His voice shook.

Angus looked horrified. "We had better order a livery for you, Sam. As the Duke of Evesham's man no one will dare touch you, even in Kent."

"I would have told you that, Sam, if you'd been honest with

me." Fallon shook his head at him. "Never mind. I meant it when I said it's absolutely vital you obey every instruction that I give you."

The red-haired young man who Grace remembered from the day before put an arm around Sam's shoulders. "Don't you worry, Sam! You'll be safe with me around."

He had grown a lot but she could remember him at the orphanage. Didn't he have an interesting history?

The pinched expression on Sam's face disappeared. "I hadn't thought of that. Nobody would dare to tangle with Freddie Gillard."

Grace and Angus exchanged a glance. Angus looked at Gillard.

"Can I take it you have a bit of a reputation, Gillard?" Angus raised his brows and looked amused.

Gillard grinned. "Me Da was a prize fighter. When he died, I was left on my own. I soon learned to use every trick he had taught me."

Sam gazed at him in admiration. "It took three men to bring him into the orphanage, from what I heard. Even boys twice his size were too frightened to fight him."

Angus's lips twitched. "He does sound a useful man to have on your side."

"He is. I'm glad he'll be with us." Sam shook his head and let out a whimper.

"What's wrong, Sam?" Grace asked.

"I don't like all this. That was a nasty trick with your horses. I don't want anything to happen to the Duke. Mr Fletcher thinks it could be some Scottish Lord he's upset."

Gillard put a hand on Sam's shoulder. "Stop worrying, Sam. There's no way we're going to let anything happen to the

Duke." He grinned. "We're all happy to be working for him and determined to make sure it stays that way."

"Do I detect a bit of self-interest there?" Angus laughed. "I'm sure we'll find out who is behind it. There's no need for you to worry, Sam with Gillard moving in with me. You said yourself nobody would mess with him."

Sam nodded but stared at the floor. "I suppose not, but I wish I could go with you too."

"I need you to help Mr Fallon, but we'll all move into Medley House soon. We've borrowed Lord Enstone's greys today, Sam. Off you go and give a hand with them. You might get a chance to talk to Mr Fletcher."

"Yes, Duke." Sam gave a shaky laugh and scampered off.

Angus shook his head. "I think I've taken on a handful with Sam."

"He's a good lad underneath, Your Grace." Gillard flushed a fiery red. "You've no need to worry about me either, Hugh Masters put me on the right path." He wiped his hands on his waistcoat. "I hope what Sam has told you won't put you off employing me."

Angus smiled at him. "Considering the fix I'm in at the moment, a valet with your skills sounds perfect. Although I must insist you don't fight anyone within the household."

Gillard shook his head vigorously. "Of course, I won't."

"I can see Mr Masters has done a good job with you. Lord Enstone has agreed that you can move into his house from today so that his valet can give you some training."

Gillard's face lit up. "I can't wait. I loved looking after the Colonel, but he wasn't much interested in fashion."

Angus gave a rueful smile. "Neither am I, but I have a role to play as a duke and I have to live up to it. I'll need you to guide me, which will make me a more exacting master than a retired colonel I suspect."

"I'm a quick learner."

"I'm sure you are." Angus stroked his chin. "I would like Sam to have more training as a groom. Perhaps Mr Bright could be persuaded to give you both some security training if I sent you down to him together. It might be the only way to persuade Sam to go. We'll see. Off you go and pack. Enough for one or two nights will do for now. Lord Enstone's valet will be waiting for you. His name is Garner. Keep an eye out for anyone who might be following you."

Gillard nodded. "I'll go out a back way and circle around a bit to make sure I'm not followed."

Grace watched Gillard leave. He seemed to speak to someone in the little vestibule beyond the kitchen. The door opened and Hugh Masters entered. He seemed relaxed and enthusiastic. Angus certainly had a knack of gaining the loyalty of his staff quickly, even if the easy familiarity he had with them was unconventional. Perhaps the quick rapport was because of that? He was familiar up to a point but there was a strong element of command behind his easy way with them. Was he humouring her in the same way?

Angus addressed Fallon. "How are you settling down?"

"I'm being well looked after. Last night was interesting."

Angus pulled out a chair for Grace and signalled to Fallon and Masters to take the other two seats around the kitchen table. "I sense this is quite a long tale."

Fallon grinned at him and nodded. "The length of the list of deceased Medleys that Fletcher passed on is long enough to merit your heir, Mr Ralph Medley, being investigated."

"Definitely." Angus caught Grace's eye and laughed.

He was as bad as Luke for teasing her. She studiously avoided looking at him and concentrated on Fallon.

"Some of Lord Enstone's grooms invited me out with them last night. They're allowed a few hours off most evenings as long as a couple of grooms are available. One of them happened to mention that Mr Medley's staff sometimes drink in the Crown Inn, which is only about a quarter of an hour's walk from Lord Enstone's house. We went there." His eyes twinkled. "We were in luck."

Grace exchanged a glance with Angus. This did sound interesting. She laughed. "Don't leave us in suspense, what did you find out?"

"Nothing positive but we managed to get talking to a group of his servants, without being obvious. Mr Medley doesn't seem to be that popular an employer but that's largely because they find him pernickety and fussy. One did mention that the Medleys have been an unlucky family in recent years. There was something about one of Ralph Medley's cousins being killed in a hunting accident."

Grace leaned forward and raised her eyebrows. "Did they give any indication of finding it suspicious?"

"No. One of them pointed out that hunting accidents happen all the time. It was interesting though, because it suggests that Mr Medley has been following events with his cousins. Although from what I've been told there had been a string of unexpected deaths in the family, so it might be something anyone who moves in his circles would know."

Grace pursed her lips. "Possibly, although it's not always the case that servants would hear the same things. I suppose he might have mentioned it to someone, perhaps his valet."

"It does make you wonder, doesn't it?" Fallon said.

Angus frowned. "It does. I was sad about William Medley's death. William had friends in Edinburgh and I knew him quite well. I can't say I knew much about the string of Medley deaths. Interesting news usually filters up to Edinburgh and I often met up with English visitors."

Grace put her head on one side. "If Mr Medley is now a man of fashion, he would have a lot more time than you did and mix with people more likely to know the Medleys. It may not mean anything."

Angus laughed. "You're arguing against your own case for Ralph as the villain now."

Grace flapped a hand at him and wrinkled her nose. "I merely felt that your heir being the villain was a possibility that needed to be examined. As you very well know."

"Of course."

Angus turned away from her, but not in time to hide his wide grin. Annoying man.

"When the family lawyers contacted me, I was amazed. They insisted on explaining to me in great detail how the son of the fifth son of a duke had inherited the title. I was surprised that I had heard nothing about it before then. Which makes me think it wasn't something that was much talked about. I remember my father saying that the Medleys were always tight lipped about anything to do with the family."

Grace laughed. "You seem to be getting more interested in my theory. Has it occurred to you that Ralph Medley might have been friendly with his cousins, in which case he would be bound to know?"

Angus frowned in concentration. "It's a good while ago but I remember William Medley saying he barely knew Ralph Medley until he came across him in the army. He mentioned that Ralph seemed to know an awful lot more about the Medley family than he did. William didn't like the fellow above half. Said he was a toadeater, always making conversation about William's close relatives in order to ingratiate himself."

Fallon leaned forward. "We need to put Mr Ralph Medley on our list of serious suspects. I'm getting a picture of a rather sly individual."

"He's got a strong motive, hasn't he?" Grace rested her chin on the backs of her hands. "If it is him then he has a whole string of crimes to his name."

Angus stared at her. "Which would make him a dangerous man indeed. Perhaps we should cry off this ball tonight that Major Ramsay has got us invited to."

Oh Lord, he was going all protective again. "He's hardly going to attack us at a ball full of military men, is he? Luke is a force to be reckoned with."

"I suppose not, but I don't want you taking any risks. If someone introduces you to him, all well and good. What I don't want is you going out of your way to find opportunities to talk to him."

A stab of anger fizzed through Grace. Angus did like to take charge, didn't he?

"I expect Ralph Medley is perfectly harmless. We've all met these toadeater types far too often."

"You might have." Angus glared at her. "It's not something I've been troubled with overmuch. Although I have a horrible feeling that is about to change."

Grace looked down in an attempt to hide her hot cheeks. She shouldn't talk like that in front of servants. Was that enough to elicit such a strong reaction from Angus? He had told her he was brought up largely by his merchant relatives. Perhaps that had caused him problems in more than his family's relationship with the wider Medley clan?

Angus drummed his fingers on the table. "We'll go to the ball but not go out of our way to meet up with Ralph, if he's there."

"That's the cleverest course of action," Fallon said. "I've found it pays to be careful not to alert a suspect to your interest in them. You're more likely to get information. From a safety point of view, Mr Bright taught me to always assume the suspect is the guilty party until proved otherwise and act accordingly."

We'll remember that." Angus raised his eyebrows at Grace. "We'll get a report back to you."

Fallon nodded. "Lord Enstone's grooms are a sensible lot. I've asked them to keep their ears to the ground whenever they go to The Crown, but not to increase the frequency too much."

Angus nodded. "Good work Fallon. Major Ramsay is Lord Enstone's friend. He knew William Medley well. William died before he could inherit the title. Major Ramsay didn't think there could be anything suspicious about his death as he was killed in action."

"Did Major Ramsay know any of the other Medleys who died, Your Grace?"

"He met several of the Medleys through his friendship with William. My grandfather was old and Major Ramsay said my eldest uncle had been suffering health problems for years, so his early death was no surprise. He said the boating accident that killed my third uncle was a bit of a mystery but there was nothing that would suggest it was deliberate. He didn't know my Uncle Harry and couldn't comment on his death. Although, his son's death a few months later in the hunting field was the subject of discussion amongst some of Ramsay's friends, because he was known to be an excellent and careful rider. Ramsay still thinks his death was accidental."

Fallon gave a satisfied smile. "We're making a good start on Mr Ralph Medley. It might all be nothing. We'll see."

Angus pulled Cathlay's list of names out of his pocket. "The Duke of Cathlay has given me a list of peers known to be antagonistic towards me, because of my views on the treatment of the clans in the Scottish Highlands. Have you got pen and paper so we can make a copy?"

Masters jumped up. "I'll do that. I'll go and fetch what we need from the library."

Angus waved a hand to delay him. "That reminds me. I still need you to work as acting butler but I'll pay you as my secretary right from the start. We can sort out terms later in the week."

"Thank you, Your Grace." Masters almost ran out of the room looking pleased.

"The Duke is particularly suspicious of the man named at the top, the Earl of Hedburgh. It does sound as if he is particularly vocal," Angus said.

Grace laughed. "The Duchess warned me that the Duke of Cathlay dislikes the Earl of Hedburgh and that may have clouded his judgement. Although she agrees he is not a pleasant individual."

"The Duchess of Cathlay sounds like she would be good at my job." Fallon pursed his lips. "The villain in a case often is extraordinarily unpleasant but that's isn't always true. From what I've heard of the Duke of Cathlay we must still take his suggestion to put this man at the top of our list seriously."

Masters came back carrying a portable writing desk, which

he placed upon the table.

"The Colonel was infirm for the last years of his life. We took it in turns to carry him upstairs to bed at night. That's how we all got work with him. He pensioned off most of his elderly servants and wanted some strong young men. A friend gave him this so that he could still write his letters by placing it on his lap."

Angus handed him the list. "The Duke of Cathlay thinks the Earl of Hedburgh is the chief suspect on this list, but they are old enemies and his wife isn't sure."

Masters nodded. He opened the portable desk and extracted an ink pot and a selection of quills. "It shouldn't take long." He set to on copying the list.

"Grace, have I missed anyone from our list of suspects? We've got my heir and the Scottish peers."

"What about people bearing grudges connected to legal cases you've dealt with?" Grace suppressed a grimace. There was no mistaking the look that had passed between Fallon and Masters at the use of her first name. If she didn't know Angus better, she would think he was trying to force her into marriage.

"True but I don't think we can do anything about those until I've had a reply to a message I sent up to Edinburgh. If I spot anybody in London who jogs a memory of one of my cases, I'll pass his name onto Fallon. Although he has plenty of work to do with what we've already given him."

Fallon laughed. "There is certainly plenty here for me to make a start on but there are some capable lads available to help amongst Lord Enstone's grooms. Will you be going to many society events in London?"

Angus sat back. "I hadn't intended to go to any for the next few weeks. I've made an exception for tonight's ball since it's too good an opportunity to miss. I suppose you're thinking the more I socialise the more I might be able to spot anyone who could be a suspect."

"Yes, Your Grace."

"I'll see what I can do, but Lord Enstone will have to return home soon."

Grace avoided Angus's gaze. The only other people he knew in London were her and Aunt Theo. Did she want to spend time socialising with him, when the thought of it set her pulse racing? The silence stretched until Masters sat back with a triumphant smile.

"There, I've finished it." He handed both copies of the list to Angus.

"I'm glad to see you have such clear handwriting, Masters." Angus grinned at him. "I should have checked on that before I offered you the position as my secretary. Have you managed to get to know Mrs Evans, my housekeeper at Medley House, yet?"

"I went round early this morning. An excellent lady. I'm sure we can work well together."

"That's good." Angus nodded at Grace. "We are asking around for recommendations for a butler. I intend to leave the selection from amongst any suitable candidates put forward to you and Mrs Evans. Are you comfortable with that? "

Masters' eyes gleamed. "Certainly, Your Grace."

Angus drummed his fingers on the table. "Good. With you and Mrs Evans to organise the staff at Medley House that's one thing I don't have to worry about too much. Once you've selected a butler, he can help you fill any senior positions which are vacant. Mrs Evans will know what's needed. Miss

Vaughan may know of former orphanage people hoping for promotion."

Masters looked pleased at being given so much responsibility. Grace basked in a satisfied glow. Hugh Masters had put his own career on hold in order to get his brothers established and deserved this opportunity."

"I'm looking forward to the challenge already, Your Grace. What about stable staff?"

"Lord Enstone has offered me Mr Fletcher's help for as long as I need him. I'm going to ask him to see to setting up my stables as far as he can." Angus sat back. "There is so much to do without this silly problem of someone with a grudge against me."

Grace let out an unladylike snort. "Someone intent on murdering you is not what I would call a silly problem."

"It is when there is so much to do. Parts of the Medley holdings are in a terrible mess. The new man of business your brother introduced me to is helping in the search for new stewards and land agents. I believe he has one or two people in mind for me. Even so I need to visit all these estates and assess the problems for myself." Angus sighed. "If there's anything else you need, Fallon, let me know."

Fallon smiled. "Nothing at the moment. I'll be interested to hear your impressions of Ralph Medley if he is at the ball you are going to tonight. If anything needs your attention urgently, I'll send a messenger."

"Excellent. Now we must be going."

Masters opened the door for them. "Mr Fletcher suggested you go down to the mews to collect the phaeton. I'll show you the way."

They followed him out. Grace watched Angus on the way

through the garden. He appeared troubled. She ought to be angry with him for calling her by her first name in front of Masters and Fallon. They wouldn't be able to keep it to themselves. The servants would all end up convinced that she and Angus were about to make a match of it. Grace sighed. How could she be angry with a man who was trying so hard to appear strong but showing signs of struggling with the role he had been thrust into? A role that he couldn't refuse. No wonder he was frustrated at the added complication of someone trying to kill him.

For a moment, when he was talking to Fallon, he had looked so vulnerable her heart had gone out to him. There was no way she could desert a man in trouble, despite whatever embarrassments it led her into. The Cathlays would help, but she and Aunt Theo were going to have to let him escort them to social functions. No matter what speculation that might arouse. And if she was being honest, no matter how difficult it might be to damp down the physical desire she felt for him. Surely no man was worth giving up her independence for, the independence she had worked so hard to forge?

Chapter Eleven

Angus arrived back at Enstone House to find Gillard and Garner laying out his riding clothes. They were deep in conversation and Gillard's furrowed brow suggested he was concentrating hard. He was keen if nothing else.

A pair of leather breeches lay on the bed. Angus sighed. His new riding outfit must have arrived. Damn. His old clothes were much more comfortable. Garner looked up and smiled at him.

"Good day to you, Your Grace. It won't take long to train Gillard here. He's keen to learn. Doctor Jarvie will be here at any moment to re-dress your arm. If he uses a smaller bandage, we'll be able to get you into your new riding jacket."

Angus groaned. "I hope you're not suggesting it's going to take both of you to get me into it. I'm not keen on this fashion for tight jackets."

"Riding wear is cut a little bit looser, Your Grace." Garner smiled at him.

"Thank the Lord for that."

There was a knock at the door.

"Come in," Angus said.

A footman appeared and ushered in Doctor Jarvie, carrying

a black leather bag.

Garner nodded at Gillard, who stepped forward and helped Angus out of his jacket. The doctor walked into the room and the footman left, closing the door behind him.

Doctor Jarvie put his bag on a chair. "How have you been, Your Grace?"

"It's sore, as you can imagine, but between you and Mrs Baker it had excellent treatment. I'm sure it's healed well."

Angus was a full head taller than the doctor. Once Gillard had helped him out of his shirt, he took a seat so Doctor Jarvie could reach his arm more easily. He watched as the bandage was unravelled.

Doctor Jarvie gave a satisfied grunt. "Yes, this is healing well."

"Would it be possible to use less bandage this time?" Garner asked. "Some of His Grace's jackets wouldn't fit over the first one."

"I can certainly do that, but don't put him into anything too tight. We don't want the wound to open up again."

Angus laughed. "Garner assures me that riding clothes are cut a bit looser, but I'm not sure how we are going to manage getting me into an evening jacket later."

"I'll see what I can do with the bandage. If you feel the slightest pain or sensation of pulling then stop and find a looser jacket."

The doctor worked quickly. He stood back to study his handiwork.

"There. That should hold well but be careful."

"Thank you, Doctor Jarvie. You can be sure I'll make certain they don't put me in anything too tight."

The doctor laughed and allowed Garner to escort him downstairs.

Gillard held up Angus's new riding jacket. "This is beautifully cut and you can feel the quality of the wool."

Angus ran his hand over the fine wool of the olive-green jacket. "It's a lovely piece of cloth. Even my uncle, who is a cloth merchant in Edinburgh, would approve. How are you getting on with Garner?"

"Really well." Gillard smiled. "He's taught me a lot in half an hour. He said he's confident I'll be able to turn you out in proper style in no time at all."

"I never doubted it." It seemed he had found himself a competent valet.

Gillard laid the jacket down, next to the leather riding breeches. "I'll fetch you a clean shirt."

He disappeared into the dressing room and Angus sank into an armchair. It had been a busy day already, but a productive one. Angus sighed. He had embarrassed Grace by calling her by her first name in front of Fallon and Masters. The knowing look which had passed between them could have left her in no doubt that they had noticed. He should have realised he would forget in company if they started using first names.

Angus couldn't help but smile. Grace being Grace had swiftly progressed from embarrassment to anger. Her eyes had shot daggers at him. He felt so much more comfortable in Edinburgh, where most of his socialising was with his merchant relatives. Using first names like they all did was so soothing. He was not of Grace's world. The comment she made about toadeaters had proved that. The attentions of sycophants were something else he would have to deal with now he was a duke.

Grace's family weren't like most aristocrats. Even Cathlay,

who was more formal than them and was clearly held in some awe, was different and far more caring. Zounds, he would never forget the way his grandfather had humiliated his mother, when Papa had tried for a reconciliation. He'd been barely ten years old and he had never seen his mother so upset. They'd had to hold him back from punching the old man. It was ironical that he was now in his grandfather's shoes.

No, he didn't fit into this world but he understood the legal position only too well. No one else but him could be the current Duke of Evesham. If he tried to denounce the title it wouldn't help because he would still own the lands. It was his responsibility to look after all the people reliant on the dukedom. They would suffer years, possibly decades, of neglect and hardship under a caretaker administration until the next Duke inherited if he tried to step away. Somehow, he had to learn how to become part of this world. Thank goodness he had given in to the impulse to accept Kitty's invitation to visit the Enstones.

Perhaps it had been cowardice, putting off the inevitable moment of facing London. But curiosity had won out, fortunately. Heaven alone knew how he would have managed without Luke's help and now that of Grace and her aunt. He would have accepted the invitation anyway if he had been able to fit in a visit. It had been intriguing to learn he had two cousins he didn't know about in England, when their legal people had contacted him. He had been tempted to contact them at the time but decided against it, in case it seemed as if he was interested in the fortune they were about to inherit. It must have been the same legal firm which had passed on Kitty's invitation.

Garner returned. "We'll go through your evening coats later.

There are one or two of the ones you brought with you that should be adequate. Doctor Jarvie has impressed upon me the importance of not putting you in anything too tight."

Angus laughed out loud. "I like that man. Now I need to get ready for this ride in Hyde Park. Miss Bamford tells me the fashionable hour starts at five o'clock, but suggested we meet half an hour earlier. When the park is a bit quieter."

* * *

Angus and Fletcher arrived at the entrance to Hyde Park five minutes early, only to find Grace already there with Jamie in attendance. Both Fletcher and Jamie were wearing smart groom's liveries. That was something else he needed to sort out. All his servants would need liveries. There was so much to think about he was in danger of developing a permanent headache. Grace trotted up to them, riding a magnificent chestnut mare. The mare jinked at every gust of wind. Angus smiled. She was quite a handful but then had he really expected Grace to ride a docile animal?

Angus turned his attention to Grace and gasped. He blinked hard. She was stunning in her blue riding habit which showed to advantage against the chestnut horse. Its stylish, military cut showed off her trim but shapely figure and the bright colour suited her. She looked adorable with the matching blue, peaked hat nestled on top of her dark curls and the froth of cream lace at her throat. Angus took a deep breath and moved the horse he had borrowed from Luke alongside hers. The chestnut mare took exception, which gave Angus a moment to collect himself.

Angus smiled at Grace. "You look delightful, as usual."

Grace gave him an answering smile but with the hint of a puzzled frown furrowing her brow. He had surprised her with the compliment. He rushed into conversation.

"Before I forget, who is the best person to ask where to order liveries for my servants?"

"Aunt Theo changed the design of hers quite recently. I can't remember where the new ones were purchased from offhand. I'm sure her secretary will be able to help. It's something Hugh Masters will be able to organise for you, unless you want to wait until you have a permanent butler in place. Now, we had better move on."

Grace grimaced. "I've spotted one of the busiest gossips in London. People like that are the reason I suggested we ride. It's much easier to take evasive action on horseback. If she catches us, she will be discussing you all over London." Grace pointed her riding crop towards a stand of trees at some little distance. "Come on, let's go and hide behind those trees and take stock of who's around in the park."

Grace loosened her hold on the reins and the chestnut mare sprang forward. If she wasn't careful the mare would be galloping, something even he knew wasn't allowed in Hyde Park. Angus followed her at a more sedate pace. In no time at all Grace had reined the mare back into a slow canter. Was there no end to this woman's talents? She was a consummate horsewoman. He glanced around to see Jamie following at a respectful distance. There was no sign of Fletcher.

He scanned the area in front of them and caught sight of a rider disappearing behind the trees. As soon as he'd realised their destination Fletcher had obviously ridden on to check no one was lurking amongst the trees. It was reassuring to know that they were being protected by such well-trained servants.

They reached the trees and if it hadn't been for the jingle of harness Angus wouldn't have been able to tell that Fletcher was there at all. Jamie was in view behind them but he stayed well back. Grace slowed the chestnut mare to a walk.

Angus caught up with her. "What now?"

"If we ride round to the other side of the trees and position ourselves properly, we can watch people entering the park, without being seen ourselves. If there's anyone who I think would be useful for you to meet we can watch for a suitable moment to come up with them, hopefully with no one else nearby. I have this awful fear that a new Duke," Grace's lips twitched, "especially one as personable as you, will attract an amount of attention you won't be comfortable with."

Angus grinned. "I can't say I'm comfortable with much attention at all to be honest."

"I know." Grace signalled to him to pull up.

There was no sign of Fletcher, Jamie was barely visible behind the massive trunk of one of the trees separating them from the rest of the park. It felt almost as if they were alone. A surge of desire hit Angus. Grace was adorable but she had made it plain she was determined not to marry and he must respect her wishes. Lord that was a turnaround. He had been adamant that marriage was a long way from his mind when Luke and Kitty had teased him that taking a wife might be the only way to save himself from the attentions of all the matchmaking mothers in London.

That was before he met Grace. He had always intended to avoid marrying a woman from an aristocratic background after his grandfather's treatment of his mother but Grace was different. Her whole family were different. If they could ever get to the bottom of this mystery of his would-be murderer perhaps there might be some way to set about persuading her.

Grace laughed up at him. "You are so deep in thought I could be forgiven for thinking you find me boring."

"Nothing was farther from my mind."

Grace looked startled, as if she'd realised what he was hinting at. She was such an adorable mixture of worldly wisdom and innocence. He sighed inwardly. The chance of winning her seemed slim and there were other things he needed to concentrate on.

"I nearly didn't accept Luke and Kitty's invitation to visit them. I'm so glad I did. I knew stepping into the role of a duke would be difficult but nothing could have prepared me for how much there is to learn. I suppose if I had been bred to it then I would know most of these things already. I've run a small house since I was quite young but it's nothing compared to what I have to deal with now."

"Try not to worry about it." Grace's voice was soothing. "You're doing well. Already, you're collecting good people around you. In a few months' time I'm sure you'll feel much more comfortable. At least you will if we can find this would-be murderer."

She sounded so fierce that Angus grinned. "I appreciate your help and support, Grace."

Grace's chestnut mare seemed to have shaken off most of her fidgets and Angus edged his horse closer. On impulse, he took one of Grace's hands and raised it to his lips. Grace's cheeks went pink and her mouth flew open. How he wished he could do more than kiss her hand.

"Thank you, Miss Bamford. I'm sorry that I keep forgetting to call you that in public. You looked mortified when I called you Grace in front of Fallon and Masters."

Grace gave a rueful laugh. "I wasn't best pleased but there is nothing we can do about the conclusions they are likely to draw."

Angus felt heat rush to his face. "I know. Any disclaimers that we are nothing more than family friends would convince them we have some sort of understanding all the more."

Grace laughed and turned away from him. "Best not to explain yourself to people working for you. In fact..."

Angus's pulse raced at the sight of Grace's flushed face. Was she too wondering if she had been too hasty to rule out a match between them?"

"Don't take this the wrong way, I wonder if it would be as well to let people think there is an understanding between the two of us? An unattached duke with all his own teeth is bound to overexcite the matchmaking mamas."

Angus burst out laughing. Grace's mare threw back her head and pranced away from his horse. Grace soon had her back under control.

"You think I jest, my friend! Seriously, has it occurred to you that we could solve that problem, whilst we have so much else to worry about, by letting everyone think the same? Or at least that you are trying to fix your suit with me."

"It's not something I had thought about, but I can see the logic in the suggestion." Angus laughed. "We had better let Luke know what we're up to."

Grace snorted. "I don't see why. It would serve him right."

"I'm afraid he might call me out if he thinks I'm trifling with you."

"I wouldn't let him. Besides, Aunt Theo will guess straight away. It's impossible to keep anything from her. She'll keep him in check."

Grace turned her mare and rode out into the open. "We're in luck. That busybody I managed to evade earlier is still in the park. Come on."

"I'm still not sure this is a good idea."

"Someone is trying to kill you. You don't know which way to turn in your efforts to sort out your properties and estates. You don't want to battle all the mamas in London at the same time, do you?"

Angus sighed. "Put like that, I suppose not."

"That's settled then. Come on we don't want to miss her. She'll let more people know than any number of notices in The Times would."

"Zounds. You're not going to tell her we're betrothed, are you?"

"Don't be silly. That's something that would need a newspaper announcement. I'll be much more subtle. I want to give the impression that things haven't quite reached the betrothal stage yet, but your interest is entirely focused on me." Grace grinned at him and set the mare off at a smart trot towards the tangle of carriages in the distance.

Angus shook his head and sent his horse after her. When Grace put her mind to a task, she did it with overwhelming enthusiasm. He caught up with her and she threw him a saucy grin. His heart skipped a beat. What would it be like to court Grace for real?

"Remember to look like a lovesick swain, won't you. This has to be convincing or the matchmaking mamas will pursue you anyway."

Angus groaned. "You're enjoying this, aren't you, Grace dearest?"

The chestnut mare picked up speed when Fletcher's horse

overtook her.

Grace glanced over her shoulder and grinned at Angus. "That honey sweet tone will do nicely."

Grace slowed her horse to a trot and Angus rode up alongside her. He squinted at the swarms of people now thronging the park. Half of London seemed to be here. People were walking, riding or driving in carriages. It was a miracle how they all managed to avoid each other.

"So, this is the famous Rotten Row. I've been to London before but never had time to visit it. Is it always so busy?"

"It's hardly started. Within half an hour the carriages will be going at the walking pace of an aged chaperone. "

Grace looked up at him with her eyes sparkling and her cheeks pink from riding into the wind. Her lips were slightly parted, eminently kissable. Zounds, he must stop thinking like this. She was far too intelligent not to notice.

Grace leaned towards him and tapped him on the arm with her riding crop. "That landau coming round is our target." She pointed the crop at a smart equipage containing what appeared to be two matrons and two much younger ladies.

Grace eased her mare past three couples and two groups of young ladies walking and came up alongside the landau. Angus allowed his horse to drop behind her.

Grace nodded at the occupants of the landau. "Good day to you. May I introduce my sister's cousin, the Duke of Evesham," Grace nodded at the two older ladies, "Mrs Smythe, Mrs Winter," and then at the younger two, "Miss Smythe and Miss Winter."

Angus doffed his riding hat and bowed to the occupants of the carriage. "Delighted to meet you, ladies."

Mrs Smythe ordered her coachman to pull off the roadway. Grace and Angus followed them. The two young ladies simpered up at Angus in a way that underlined the merits of Grace's suggestion to pretend they had an understanding. Angus replaced his hat and gave Grace what he hoped looked like an adoring smile.

Mrs Smythe's own smile became strained. "What a pleasure to meet you, Your Grace. Will we have the pleasure of seeing you at some social events whilst you're in London?"

"I am escorting Miss Bamford and her aunt to Colonel Gilbert's ball tonight. I have no idea what they have planned for me after that." Angus looked down as he spotted Grace's lips twitching.

Mrs Winter raised her eyebrows at her daughter. "I believe that we may have an invitation to that, Your Grace. Isn't that so, Suki dearest?"

Her daughter's face brightened. "I believe so, Mama. I'm sure General Cox said we would be invited."

Mrs Smythe's face was a picture of chagrin. Clearly, she didn't know any generals. Miss Winter gave Miss Smythe a triumphant smile. He could swear Grace's shoulders were shaking.

"We will look forward to seeing you there," Grace said in a strangled voice. "We had better move on, it's becoming rather busy."

They trotted their horses back to the roadway. Angus couldn't resist a quick glance back at the landau. There seemed to be quite a heated conversation going on between Mrs Smythe and Mrs Winter. Once they were some distance away from them Grace gave a gurgle of laughter.

"You did that beautifully, Angus. I lay you anything you like that their landau will be disappearing from the park in short order. The question is, will Mrs Smythe prevail upon Mrs Winter to ask for invitations for all four of them. Failing which she'll be hoping that General Cox doesn't know the Gilberts well enough to get any of them invited. This is exactly what I thought you would be up against. We did a good job of arousing Mrs Smythe's suspicions of something between us. If they do manage to get to the ball tonight, we can work on that."

Angus burst out laughing. "Grace, you're a minx. I can see you're hoping that Mrs Smythe will then spread this information all around the Ton to explain why I didn't fall at the feet of her hideous daughter."

"Something like that. I can see some ladies approaching us. Do you feel like some more play acting?"

Angus groaned. He shook his head. "I'm not sure I'm capable of any more today."

"In that case, my friend, follow me. I'll get us out of the park before anyone can accost us."

She gave one rein a surreptitious tug. The mare jinked to the side and danced off the track and away from the press of people circulating. Angus followed with a shake of the head and pushed his horse to catch up with her in case her show of losing control of the mare came true. Not that it would, but he had better appear protective of her in case they were being watched. Zounds. What had he got himself into? The chestnut mare might be spirited but nothing to match Grace.

Chapter Twelve

Grace's eyes opened wide when Angus followed Luke into Aunt Theo's drawing room. Angus's evening coat was slightly looser than the current fashion, presumably one of his Scottish ones, but it suited him. The forest green coat, with buttons covered in the same cloth, was elegant and yet understated, like the man. His white quilted waistcoat was the height of fashion. She looked down at the floor, hoping Angus hadn't seen her staring. Aunt Theo rose to greet them and Grace moved so that she was slightly behind her.

Aunt Theo smiled. "Good evening, gentlemen. Do you have any idea of whether Ralph Medley will be there tonight?"

Luke shook his head. "None at all. I didn't want to make our interest obvious by checking on the guest list, although I was tempted. Whatever you do, ladies, be careful not to do or say anything to arouse suspicion."

Luke kept his gaze on Grace as he said it and she stalked towards him.

"What do you expect us to do? Walk around asking if anyone has seen Ralph Medley?" Grace couldn't keep the scorn out of her voice. "Of course, we'll be careful!"

Grace was aware of Angus's eyes on her and studied the deep

rose-pink silk of her evening gown. She brushed at the skirt as if to remove a speck of dust.

"I know you, Grace." Luke grimaced and shook his head. "You're not the most subtle person in the world."

Angus gave a smothered laugh. He looked away when Grace shot him a furious glance, but he wasn't quick enough to hide the amusement in his face.

She put her nose in the air and resisted the temptation to stamp a foot. "The carriage should be here for us at any moment. Why don't we go and wait for it before I lose my temper with you, Luke?"

"If you say so, Grace." Luke sighed and offered his arm to Aunt Theo.

Angus stopped Grace from following them with a hand on her arm. He had schooled his expression into a neutral one but his lips quirked up at the corners when he looked at her.

"I swear I didn't mention anything about your subtle methods in the park. It seems your brother knows you well." He smiled down at her. "If we are to go ahead with your plan of giving the impression of an imminent betrothal between the two of us, I insist we tell your aunt and brother."

This time Grace did stamp a foot. "We're both adults, I don't see why we should have to account to anyone for our actions."

"I can understand why Luke has annoyed you. However, I have a lot to be grateful to him for and would not feel comfortable deceiving him. I think your aunt deserves to know the truth too."

Grace sniffed. "Why do you have to be so reasonable?" And why did that smile, which he seemed to save for her, make her insides flutter?

"I'm close to one of my cousins who is two years older

than me and he has the same infuriating habit of stating the obvious. I've learned that it's better not to let it influence my actions one way or the other. I must make my own, considered, decisions. "He put a comforting arm around her shoulders. "What do you say, Grace?"

Grace surprised herself by resting her head against his shoulder for a moment rather than pushing him off. Something in his expression left her speechless. She pulled away with an effort and took a step back.

"Grace, you look troubled. What's wrong?" Angus sounded puzzled and concerned.

Nothing. That was the problem. It had felt so right to nestle into his embrace. "Why does life have to be so complicated? No don't answer that. We'd better go before they come searching for us. I know you're right and if we tell them in the carriage the dim light will spare our blushes."

Angus gave crack of laughter. "That's my girl."

"Humph. Now you're making fun of me."

"I could never do that, Grace. I wish we had met in less complicated circumstances."

Angus looked as if he wanted to say more but the door opened and Luke appeared.

"Come on, you two. What's keeping you?"

"We're discussing tactics, Luke. Grace has come up with a cunning plan which I have some reservations about."

Luke laughed. "I know that feeling well. We can talk about it in the coach."

Grace's arm tingled when Angus handed her into the carriage. What on earth was the matter with her? She was acting like a green debutante. Luke jumped in and took the seat next to Aunt Theo before she could. Angus sat down with a grin.

Had he guessed the effect he was having on her. It was no good chastising herself. He was an attractive man and she was an unattached woman of seven and twenty years. The only surprise was that she had never felt like this before. The coach moved off and Grace settled into her seat.

Luke sat back and smiled at her. "What's this cunning plan of yours then, Grace?"

Grace took a deep breath. "Angus was in danger of being swarmed in the Park this afternoon by all the matchmaking Mamas. I suggested we act as if we are close to an understanding between us to try and keep them at bay. I thought it would be more convincing if we didn't tell you, but Angus disagrees."

Luke's shoulders shook. "Come on, Grace. You wanted to punish me and you're cross that Angus is too much of a gentleman to go along with that. You've got a point about the matchmaking mamas though. Angus has enough to deal with without having to fight them off. What do you think, Aunt Theo?"

Even in the dim light of the carriage Grace could see her aunt smiling. Heavens, why had she started this?

"As long as we can avoid any damage to Grace's reputation, I see no harm in it. Any marriageable duke newly on the scene is bound to cause a deal of interest. With a young man like Angus there could be quite a rumpus."

They rounded a corner and Angus slid closer towards her. The feel of his thigh and hip pressed up against hers made her body ache with pleasure. He made no move to edge apart and Grace couldn't seem to make herself do so either.

Angus's hand briefly covered her own. "I have it on the best of authority that any marriageable duke with all his own teeth is guaranteed to overexcite all the doting mamas."

Grace joined in the general laughter which followed Angus's comment and that seemed to break the spell she was under. She moved away from him.

"We made a start in Hyde Park today. I have to say that Angus is quite good at play acting. I don't think it will be enough to keep the most determined matchmakers away from him but it should ease the situation."

Aunt Theo gasped and her hand shot to her mouth. "I've had a thought. Has it occurred to you that if your subterfuge is successful and Angus's would-be murderer is Ralph Medley, then the thought of an impending marriage is likely to spur him on to greater effort?"

"That's a point, Aunt Theo," Luke said. "Let's hope Mr Medley is there tonight. We can try and catch his expression if something makes him suspect that Angus and Grace are close to a betrothal. Not conclusive if he does seem bothered by it, I know, but people often give things away when they're surprised that they wouldn't normally."

Angus slapped his thigh. "There speaks the military strategist. Let's hope he's there and we can get some sort of indication as to whether he is involved. With so many potential suspects I can't see how we are ever going to unravel this. Unless we get a stroke of luck."

Grace sighed. "I don't think it will be that simple. I was impressed with your Mr Fallon. He seems thorough and he's already made a start."

She put a hand on Angus's arm without thinking and then quickly snatched it away. "Sooner or later this person will make a mistake and we will catch him, never you fear."

The coach slowed down and pulled up behind a line of coaches in front of the Gilberts' mansion.

"Even if Ralph Medley isn't here tonight, you'll have a good evening, Angus," Grace said. "Most of the guests will have a connection to the army and are far more sensible than nearly all of the society folk I know."

Luke laughed. "That isn't difficult. I always enjoy the Gilberts' events. I can guarantee to meet up with old friends. Ramsay will be there tonight, Angus."

"At least I will know someone then. I liked Major Ramsay very much."

The coach edged closer to the Gilberts' front door, illuminated with lanterns on either side, painfully slowly. Angus leaned forward as he chatted with Luke and his thigh brushed up against Grace again. She peered out of the window as if studying the people at the front alighting from their coaches and took a few steadying breaths. It was impossible to say if Angus had noticed their thighs were pushed together. The last thing she wanted to do was move away and have him giving that annoying little half smile again. Was he deliberately flirting with her?

At last, they reached the front of the queue. Grace was able to move away from Angus when the kerbside door opened, without making it obvious she had noticed the contact. She wasn't a green girl to be thrown into transports because a handsome young man appeared to be showing an interest in her. A footman helped her down and Angus jumped down beside her and offered his arm. Grace looked up at him and smiled. She had a part to play after all.

Aunt Theo joined them on the pavement, followed by Luke. Angus hung back and waited for Luke to lead them inside. Their progress was slow as Luke was hailed by friends on all sides.

Angus grinned down at Grace and lowered his mouth close to her ear. "I presume this is what Luke meant when he said it might be a crush tonight. I don't think I've ever seen so many people in one room."

The feel of his breath against her ear sent a shiver down Grace's spine. She ignored it and smiled back at him.

"I've been to busier events than this, but it is a crush. I would have thought Edinburgh assemblies would be busy."

Angus gave a rueful smile. "Too busy for me, but still nothing like this."

He sounded nervous but his expression was hard to decipher. His years of standing up in a courtroom must have set him in good stead when it came to hiding his feelings. No good lawyer could afford to show what he was thinking. Even so, the way he was standing, the rigidity of his back told her that he wasn't as relaxed as he was trying to pretend to be. It was probably imperceptible to anyone who didn't know him.

How could it be so obvious to her after such a short acquaintance? Grace sucked in a deep breath, fortunately none of her companions seem to notice. There was an intimacy between her and Angus that had crept up on her unawares. Angus wouldn't be the sort of man to show his vulnerable side lightly. Yet he had been open with her about his feelings of inadequacy for the task he had been landed with. What exactly did that mean?

Luke led them to join the line of people waiting to be presented to the Gilberts, at the entrance to the ballroom. Grace was glad of the distraction. Her mind shied away from the obvious conclusion that Angus was strongly drawn to her, whether he knew it or not. He was staying with her brother, perhaps he saw her as a sister figure?

She glanced at the floor and screwed up her eyes. How often had Luke admitted his insecurities to her? Never. Whatever Angus felt for her it wasn't brotherly. Her breath caught in her throat. That was a scary thought. She was temporarily bereft of speech. Thank goodness the hubbub around them was so great that conversation was close to impossible. Surely it wasn't possible to develop feelings for someone in so short a space of time?

They reached the front of the queue. The butler announced them and the ball room and stairway leading up to it fell silent. All eyes seemed to be pointing at Angus. Colonel and Mrs Gilbert smiled at them and the company came back to life with the noise level rising higher than it had been before.

Angus stepped forward. His cheeks were pink but that could simply be the heat.

He bowed towards Mrs Gilbert. "Thank you for including me in the invitation tonight."

Mrs Gilbert laughed up at him and placed a hand on his arm. "It is always a pleasure to welcome any friend of Lord Enstone. However, in this case we should be thanking you. I believe I am correct in saying that this is your first London ball as the Duke of Evesham. It's not often our balls are the height of fashion."

Angus joined in the general laughter but his expression soon became serious. "I am delighted to be of service."

Mrs Gilbert patted his arm then let her hand drop. She lowered her voice. "No need to look so concerned. The Ton will soon have someone else to talk about. Enjoy your evening."

Angus grinned at Grace. "How could I fail to do that when I have the most beautiful woman in the room on my arm? I am relying on Grace to stop me being fed to the lions."

Colonel Gilbert's eyes twinkled. "I can see you've been taking lessons on strategy from young Enstone. If anyone can keep you safe from the lions, in this case lionesses I imagine, it's Grace Bamford. I hope we have the opportunity for a proper conversation later. I would like to know more about your work in Edinburgh."

Angus bowed. "I shall look forward to that." He held out his arm to Grace and led them into the ballroom.

* * *

Angus strolled into the ballroom with a smile pinned to his face. At least he had the support of Grace. He felt the hand resting on his arm giving it a quick squeeze of support. His smile broadened. The eyes of everyone in the room were on them but Grace sailed in as if she was a queen and all this attention was her due. For his part, he now understood how all the people he had defended must have felt when they walked into the courtroom for the first time.

His collar felt tight but he kept talking and smiling and let Grace lead him. She steered a determined path for a group of older ladies occupying sofas in one corner of the room. He heard Luke address someone behind him and Lady Grant took his other arm. They came to a halt in front of the first sofa. Lady Grant introduced him to two older ladies who were both attended by a younger woman. He relaxed when he recognised one of them as Lucy Vaughan. He bowed politely to all the ladies.

Grace gave him a gentle nudge so he was standing in front of Lucy. "Lucy dances divinely, the perfect partner for your first dance."

Angus moved towards Lucy. "I would be delighted to lead you out for the first dance of the evening, Miss Vaughan, if you are free."

Lucy gave him a friendly smile and produced her dance card. "I certainly am, Your Grace. You will be my first entry."

"In that case, may I claim a second dance later on? I haven't had the opportunity to thank you for your help in finding me some servants."

They agreed on the second dance after the supper interval. Lucy's mama beamed at him.

Angus turned towards Grace. "I insist on reserving two dances with you, Miss Bamford, before your dance card is filled up."

Grace's lips parted as if she was about to protest and he raised his eyebrows at her. Her cheeks went a becoming shade of pink. Good. It felt like most of the room was still watching them and her high colour would be noted. Perfect for their plan. Was it possible that Grace might be attracted to him? The idea of a real match between them, if he could persuade her to give up her independence, was becoming more appealing by the day.

"I'd like to claim the supper dance, if I may, Miss Bamford."

Grace inclined her head. "I would be delighted, Your Grace. Perhaps the last dance of the evening for the second one?"

Angus accepted her card and wrote his name against the supper dance and the last dance of the evening. He bowed to Lucy and her mother. He moved on to the second young lady in the party and Grace whispered the word "two" in his ear. Angus briefly let his free hand rest on top of her hand to show he had heard. Two dances were quickly agreed.

Greedy glances were coming his way from several chaperones who were edging closer with their charges. Grace deftly whisked him around, at the same time carefully avoiding eye contact with any of them. Angus couldn't avoid a chuckle escaping him. Colonel Gilbert's description of the matchmaking mamas as lionesses was undeniably accurate. He followed Grace into an alcove and they were swiftly joined by Luke.

Luke clapped him on the back. "I can see you're a great success, Angus."

Angus looked around to make sure no one was in earshot. "I managed to book up six dances, two with Grace, two with Lucy Vaughan and two with Miss Carmichael. I'm hoping Grace can find me some more sensible ladies so I can avoid dancing with the charges of the lionesses."

"There are several young women from sensible families here tonight. There wasn't any need for you to claim two dances with anyone. You don't want to raise any expectations."

"I realised that when I saw the expression on her mama's face after I asked Lucy Vaughan to reserve two dances for me. I thought if I did the same with Grace and Miss Carmichael it wouldn't appear so particular." It also meant he had two dances with Grace but that wasn't something he wanted to share with Luke.

Grace smiled at him. "That was quick thinking, Angus."

Was there a hint of suspicion in that smile? He had better be careful not to reveal his growing interest in her or it might frighten her off.

Luke laughed. "Society is hard to navigate sometimes. At least you have Grace to guide you."

"I'd be lost in London society without Grace. I've claimed the supper dance with her in the hope of being able to slip into the supper room early and finding a quiet corner where we can't be accosted. I'll need a rest by then."

Luke nodded. "Good strategy but there's no need to cut your dance short. I'll keep the supper dance free and take Aunt Theo in with me and find us the perfect spot. I've found Major Ramsay, he's on his way over. Don't look round but he says Ralph Medley is here tonight."

Angus's mouth went dry. At last, they might get somewhere. The more he considered Grace's suspicions about the number of deaths of Medley heirs in such a short space of time, the more he wondered if there might be something in them. The light in the room seemed brighter and the noise seemed louder. This was the way he had always felt when he first walked into a courtroom for an important trial. He turned casually, as if about to address a remark to Grace and caught sight of a gentleman who seemed to be watching them.

Angus turned slowly back towards Luke. Major Ramsay had said Ralph bore a strong resemblance to William. The man wasn't as tall as William but that was Ralph alright from the cast of his countenance. He couldn't tell his eye colour, but his nose and the shape of his brows made him appear uncannily like William even from this distance.

"The man in the dark navy jacket with a gold and silver waistcoat, standing next to that matron with the hideous puce gown and ostrich feather headdress, looks so much like William Medley I'm sure he must be Ralph. I think he has spotted us, although I've never met him."

Luke laughed. "Are you sure? Perhaps he's been bewitched by the sight of Grace."

Grace tapped Luke on the arm with her fan. "Very funny. Everyone has been looking Angus's way ever since we were announced. It wouldn't take a genius to make a note of his appearance."

Angus gave a rueful grin. "If he hadn't happened to see me when we were introduced the rustic appearance of this looser jacket, which I've had over a year so it's not even the latest Edinburgh fashion, would give the game away."

Grace snorted. "Just about everyone in the room has been watching you, Angus. The jacket is a fashionable colour and it becomes you extraordinarily well. There are plenty of things, besides the jacket and your new title, that make you stand out so much."

"I suppose you're referring to my height? I know I'm taller than most men." Angus grinned at Grace and glanced over her shoulder. "I can see Major Ramsay approaching our man. I'm sure it's Ralph Medley. We'll meet him soon enough. This could be interesting."

What was even more interesting was the blush on Grace's cheeks. Had that been caused by her realising what a compliment she had given him? Could it be that she was less indifferent to him than she appeared?

Chapter Thirteen

Grace swallowed and looked at the floor. She moved closer to the alcove's window in the hope of finding a draught to cool her hot cheeks. Even the tips of her ears felt hot. What was she thinking? She had effectively admitted to Angus that she found him outstandingly attractive, with her own brother listening. She turned at the sound of footsteps, relieved not to have to say anything.

Major Ramsay stopped next to her and gave her a friendly smile. "Miss Bamford, Mr Ralph Medley. May I recommend Mr Medley as a suitable dance partner for you?"

Pushing her embarrassment to the back of her mind, Grace smiled at the newcomer. There was a definite resemblance to Angus around the eyes and nose but Mr Medley was a full head shorter, his hair was much lighter and his figure far less athletic. A pale shadow of Angus in fact.

Grace extracted her dance card. "I should be delighted to dance with you Mr Medley."

"Thank you. Am I being too optimistic to hope that you are free for the supper dance, Miss Bamford?" His voice was higher pitched than Angus's.

Mr Medley gave her a smile which didn't quite reach his eyes, or was that a trick of the light? Grace took care not to let him see the empty state of her dance card. He wasn't someone she wanted to dance more than once with. Her heart skipped a beat. Dancing twice with Angus was an entirely different matter.

"I'm afraid so. What about the dance after the supper interval?"

Mr Medley pursed his lips before smiling again. His mouth reached higher at the corners than before but this time Grace watched his eyes. There wasn't even a hint of a crinkle at the corners.

"Why not. That would be delightful, Miss Bamford." He stepped forward and raised her hand to his lips in an old-fashioned gesture.

It was as much as Grace could do not to recoil, especially when the heavy, sickly scent of his cologne reached her. She forced a smile and nodded at the same time, so he wouldn't see her eyes. It was probably her imagination coming into play but, for all his show of affability, there was something about this man that grated. He was fashionably and tastefully dressed, apart from his lurid taste in waistcoats and she'd seen far worse. His dark blonde hair was neatly cut if a little regimented for her taste. She preferred Angus's unruly mop with its tousled appearance. Mr Medley was altogether too manicured.

Major Ramsay stepped forward. "May I request a dance, Miss Bamford?"

"But of course. What about the second dance after the interval?"

This time Grace's smile was genuine. Luke had the knack of finding the best of people as friends. Major Ramsay was always good company, even if she had noticed the warm expression in his eyes when he looked at her of late. Luke getting married seemed to have put ideas into the heads of several of his friends. She wished she wasn't one of the women they were getting interested in. It must be an age thing. Indeed, wasn't Major Ramsay a little older than Luke? At least a year or two since he'd been at school with Max Lovell. A small voice niggled at her. She would be spared this sort of interest in her if she married Angus. She sighed.

Angus extracted himself from the conversation and drew Grace a little apart. "That was a big sigh."

"I suppose it was. I'm getting far too old for these sorts of events. I'd much rather sit out most of the dancing with Aunt Theo and watch the world go by."

Angus gave a bark of laughter. "It's not as bad as all that surely?"

Grace smiled at him and noticed Mr Medley watching them with pursed lips behind Angus's head.

Grace moved so that she was hidden from his view by Angus's tall figure. "Mr Medley seems to be studying us carefully." She spoke softly. "I won't say any more now but I think my initial suggestion needs careful consideration."

Angus leaned forward and whispered into her ear. "We might as well make him notice how close we are, just as we planned."

A shiver of something Grace couldn't quite identify shot through her at the feel of Angus's breath on her neck. There was something about him that drew her to him like a honeybee to a summer flower bed. Would marriage be so frightening if it was to a man like Angus with his sensible views of the world?

"The dancing will start soon. Let's go and find you those partners." Grace led him deeper into the room. "I've had a thought. We're down for the last dance of the evening. Why not change it to the third dance after supper and both try not to book any dances after that so we can leave early."

Angus raised his eyebrows. "If you like."

Lord, he looked perplexed. He hadn't wondered if she was propositioning him, had he? "I thought you and Luke could come back with us and discuss our next moves, if we can get away early enough. We'll be busy all day tomorrow with The Duchess of Cathlay's political salon."

Grace's cheeks felt unbearably hot. What a ninny she was. She might feel like propositioning him but there was nothing in what she had said to make him suspect that. She spotted a friend of Luke's with two of his sisters in tow. "The Rowberry girls, over there by the sofa where Aunt Theo is sitting, will be good partners for you. I'll introduce you."

The Rowberry sisters accepted Angus's invitations to dance with alacrity. Grace plotted a careful course around the room and in no time at all both of them had filled all the dances until the third dance after the interval. Grace spotted a Dowager Countess, with a nervous granddaughter in tow who didn't look older than sixteen, making a determined bid to catch up with them. She hooked her arm through Angus's and pulled him around at right angles. Luke was straight in front of them with a group of his friends. Grace twitched her eyebrows at Luke. He gave a nod of comprehension and organised his friends to pull them both into the centre of the circle, leaving a frustrated Dowager Countess stranded several yards away from her quarry.

Angus laughed. "I don't know what I would have done tonight without your sister, Luke. Thank you for being so quick to grasp the situation. That was a close call."

"Grace has done the same for me in the past, many a time. Let me introduce you to a few more of my friends."

They spent a few pleasant minutes with Luke and his friends until the orchestra started tuning up.

Grace looked at Angus. "I hope you memorised who all your partners are. I've never understood why they don't give the gentlemen dance cards as well."

Angus pulled a face. "I hope so, but if you see any horrified damsels who think I have snubbed them can you wave at me or something."

"I expect you'll remember when it comes to it. In case you do get stuck, I'll tell Aunt Theo who you are dancing with, so you can check with her if you can't see me."

"Thank you, Grace. It sounds like the orchestra is nearly ready to start the first dance. I can see Lucy not far away. I'm dreading this."

There wasn't time to say more with her own partner making his way towards her. This was a new version of Angus tonight. He seemed so confident in most situations. But then as an advocate in Edinburgh he probably hadn't had much time for events such as this. Grace had lined up a stream of unexceptional partners for them both and the orchestra were extremely good. She found she was enjoying herself. It seemed no time at all until Angus came to claim her for the last dance before the supper interval.

Angus pulled her little apart from the other couples waiting to dance. "I've been watching Ralph Medley. He doesn't seem to have danced much at all."

"I noticed that."

"At one stage I was convinced he had disappeared to the cardroom but then I spotted him. I think you may be right about him. I can't say I've taken to the man. Right, we're about to start." He walked them further onto the dancefloor.

"Is it always so hot in these places?" Angus waved a hand in front of his face.

Grace laughed. "What do you expect with so many people in one room. Why don't we forget about this dance and stand by the open doors to the terrace? There will be some breeze there, especially with the windows along that wall all open as well."

Angus put a hand under her elbow. Grace felt that now familiar little shiver run up her arm at his touch.

"Let's go one better and go outside for some air." Angus took her through the double doors to the terrace.

There were three couples standing by the balustrade near the door talking. Each pair a little apart. Grace didn't recognise anyone and they all appeared too engrossed in their partners to notice her and Angus. Angus put a hand at the small of her back and Grace caught her breath. It was a beautiful evening, despite the chill in the air. Stars twinkled down at them from a midnight blue sky. The sweet, spicy smell of an early flowering Syringa drifted up from the garden. It was the perfect place for a romantic tryst. Angus bent close and Grace held her breath.

The spell was broken when he whispered, "Let's go farther along. I saw Ralph talking to someone, who I suspect he knows well. They're by the last window opening out to the terrace, if I've calculated correctly. We might be able to overhear."

Grace nodded, too stunned by her reaction to Angus's nearness to protest. How could she have possibly thought he was about to kiss her with so many potential witnesses? They walked past the long row of open windows to the end of the terrace. A set of stone stairs, which led down to the gardens, was set at right angles. The branches of a tree hanging over the terrace partially obscured the last window, which was wide open. Angus drew Grace behind the branches so they were hidden from the ballroom and put a finger on her lips. He manoeuvred them until they were as close to the window as possible without being seen.

Someone laughed and Grace froze. That did sound like Ralph Medley and there was something about the laugh that caught her attention. It wasn't the sound of someone enjoying a joke. It was far too grating for that. She strained her ears. It was definitely Ralph Medley talking.

"He's much as I expected, Jack." Ralph's voice was a drawl Was he using that to disguise impatience?

"Handsome devil ain't he? Managed to break down the resistance of The Citadel too by the look of it."

"By which you mean the delectable Miss Bamford, I presume."

There was a harsh laugh. "She's delectable all right and tight, but I'm surprised you've noticed. Will he get the chit up to the mark I wonder? How would you like that, hey?"

"Really, Jack, your crudity offends me." Ralph's drawl was even more pronounced. Possibly uttered through clenched teeth. "This is my esteemed relative you're talking about and a most respectable young woman."

"Come off it, man. You must have had thoughts of inheriting with the Medley family's recent history. Not the most popular of men, our new duke, disliked in some rough quarters from what I've heard."

"You have the most lurid imagination. I wish him well with his pursuit of the lady. Her brother's only a viscount but still an excellent line and the family is well connected. She's a good choice for keeping up the family standing."

Jack gave a derisive snort. "Doing it too brown, old man. I hope you haven't borrowed against your expectations. You're dressed mighty fine in that rig for a poor relation."

"Another word from you, Jack, and I'll be asking you to name your seconds."

"See here now, I was only ribbing you. I'm not going up against a crack shot like you." A note of alarm sounded in Jack's voice.

"Is that so? You had better be careful what you say about me then. I'm not a poor relation. My mother's brother left me very well off if you must know. I don't want you spreading silly rumours about me."

"No of course not. I forgot about your connections to trade. Warm man your uncle by all accounts."

"I'm warning you, Jack." The drawl had disappeared to be replaced by the clipped tones of someone struggling to control their anger.

"No offence meant, old man. I'm off. You're in a strange mood tonight."

Angus put a hand on Grace's arm. "Come on. Let's hide in the garden. Ralph sounds angry enough to come out onto the terrace to cool off."

Grace allowed herself to be led down the stairs and along a garden path. "Aunt Theo said she would watch Mr Medley as much as she could when he wasn't looking. I hope she knows who this Jack is."

"Me too. It could be illuminating. That reference to me not being popular in some rough quarters was interesting." Angus checked behind them. "I don't think anyone has seen us but I'm right about Ralph. He's come out onto the terrace. Let's hide."

Angus found a minor path which went past a group of large bushes and finished in a clearing, dominated by a summerhouse.

Grace gasped. "It will be risky to hide in the summerhouse. We might be discovered."

"I don't intend to." Angus laughed gently. "You don't suspect me of trying to force you into marriage, do you? I was hoping we could hide in the bushes. I'm afraid of damaging your dress." He took her hand. "I'll go into that group of three bushes backwards and try and protect you. Ready?"

Grace heard footsteps coming closer. "Let's go."

Angus turned her so she had her back to him and put both arms around her waist. He backed into a small space between two bushes and pulled her after him. The bushes closed behind them just in time. Someone walked past their hiding place and stomped up the steps to the summerhouse. It had to be a man, no lady's dance slippers could make that noise, and an angry one at that.

Angus's breath tickled her ear. "It's lucky there's a full moon, even though it means us having to hide. It's Ralph. He's sitting on the bench outside the summerhouse, smoking a cigarillo."

Angus edged around so they were standing side-by-side, giving Grace a view of the summerhouse. One of Angus's arms stayed around her waist. A shiver of pleasure flooded through her body.

"You're cold. I hope we don't have to stay out here for too long. I'd give you my jacket but there isn't much room in here to take it off."

The arm around her waist tightened, leaving her in contact

with Angus all down one side. She was grateful for the warmth but his nearness made her shiver all the more. Her breathing quickened. She was glad of the support of his arm since her legs felt more like jelly than legs. The warm throbbing that ran through her to settle between her thighs had to be lust. She tried to concentrate on watching Ralph Medley. His face was in the shadows. He was leaning back against the wall of the summerhouse behind the stone bench, with his legs stretched out. At a quick glance he would appear relaxed but, even with several yards separating them, she could hear his free hand tapping restlessly against the seat beside him.

After what seemed a long time, but was probably no more than ten minutes, he stood and ran down the steps at the front of the summerhouse. He threw the end of his cigarillo into a bush and stalked back towards the house. They stayed quite still for a few more moments. Then Angus stirred. He parted the branches of the bushes with his free hand and led her out.

"Let's get you in the moonlight and check you over." He turned her around with his hands on her shoulders and ran his eyes over her.

Grace chewed at her lip. Did he like what he saw or was she simply Luke's little sister? Were all lawyers so difficult to read?

Angus released her shoulders and smiled at her. "I can't see any bits of twig on you what about me?"

Grace studied him, trying not to lift her eyes to his face. He might be inscrutable but she was all too aware that she had an expressive face. "I can see a few bits on your arm." She brushed his sleeves with her hand. "There, that's got rid of them. Turn round let's have a look at your back."

She removed bits of twig and leaf from his back. "I think

that's all of it but let's check your arms again."

Grace's heart beat at a furious rate as he turned to face her. She brushed away the last few remaining pieces of twig. His hand closed over hers on his arm.

"You're shivering again. We need to warm you up before we go back in or people will know we've been out here." Angus looked around. "I can't see anyone about but let's hide behind the summerhouse to be safe. There are no bushes on its other side."

Chapter Fourteen

Angus put an arm around Grace's shoulders and led her behind the summerhouse. He felt a shudder run through her. The moon came out from behind a cloud and the expression on her face was bewilderment. Her eyes seemed to sparkle in the moonlight. His mouth went dry and a surge of energy ran through him. Could it be that she too was feeling the attraction between them? Perhaps he hadn't imagined that moment on the terrace when he had felt sure she was expecting him to kiss her.

He shrugged out of his coat and put it around her. "My unfashionably loose coat has its advantages. It should soon warm you up. I can't get in or out of my new ones without help."

Grace looked up and their eyes met. "It might warm me up a lot quicker if you were still inside it," she said, voice husky.

It was hard to tell in the moonlight but her face seemed to have gone bright red. Angus ran a finger over her cheek and sure enough it was hot to the touch. She leaned towards him and he put his hands around her waist under the jacket.

"Are you sure, Grace?"

"Never more so." She reached up and kissed him briefly on the lips.

Angus hesitated. Grace was his friend's sister but she was also seven and twenty with a determined mind of her own. His body screamed at him to seize the moment. He pulled her close and she settled against him with a sigh. She felt so good in his arms, it was the most natural thing in the world to bend down and touch his lips to hers. Grace's lips opened on a gasp and Angus deepened the kiss. She responded with untutored enthusiasm. Grace might be seven and twenty but he would lay odds this was her first proper kiss. A gentleman would pull back at this point but it seemed he wasn't a true gentleman.

The last bit of tension seemed to leave Grace's body and she pressed closely against him, sliding her hands around his neck. Angus groaned inwardly. He didn't want to let her go but he couldn't endure this for long. His groin ached with his arousal. She must be able to feel the effect she was having on him. He tried to pull back but one of Grace's hands moved to stroke his neck and pull gently at his earlobe, sending another surge of desire through him. He deepened the kiss and she squirmed against him. Enough. He had to stop this before he ended up carrying her into the summerhouse with all the risk of being caught.

The thought sobered him up immediately. He put his hands on her shoulders and pushed her gently away. He didn't mind for himself, some parts of the Ton would never accept him because of his links with trade, despite his new rank as a duke. It wouldn't worry him if the rest of them decided he was beyond the pale. Grace was a different matter. She didn't deserve to have her reputation ruined. These were the people she had grown up with.

"I'm sorry, Grace. I shouldn't have taken advantage of you like that."

"You didn't. I agreed."

Angus lifted his head. He put a finger to her lips and lowered his mouth to her ear. "Hush, I think I heard something."

He kept his hands on her shoulders and listened hard. There was a rustle of footsteps through grass then the louder sound of footsteps on the path. They stood still until the footsteps were no longer audible.

"Whoever that was probably knows there was a couple out here." Angus kept his voice low. "Let's hope they don't work out it was us. I should never have started that."

Grace tossed her head back. "I don't see why not. I don't care what people think."

"You might say that now, but being ostracised would be hard for you. As a gentleman, albeit belatedly, I will of course offer you marriage if word of this does get out." Angus frowned as a thought hit him like a hammer blow. He sighed. "Knowing you I expect you would refuse, convinced I was trying to force you into marriage."

"There's no need to look so worried, Angus. There's no possibility of me agreeing to marry you. I'll not be forced into decisions about my future by anyone, you or society as a whole."

"How would you feel if Luke challenged me to a duel over my failure to do the decent thing?"

Grace snorted. "I'd inform the magistrate so you needn't worry about that."

"I believe you would. I'm not worried for me, you infuriating woman. You don't know what you're saying. Both Luke and your aunt would be heartbroken. Which is why I should have kept my urges under control. I have done you and them a great wrong."

"Oh, for goodness' sake! Stop trying to be noble." She gave him an enraged glare.

Moonlight lit up the planes of her face and Angus held his breath as he watched her expression soften. She turned her head away from him.

"I'm as much to blame as you," she said in a strangled voice. "I've wanted to kiss you all evening and I don't regret it one bit."

"You were worried about being caught in the summer house earlier."

Grace groaned. "Think, man. There is no point courting trouble. I wouldn't relish being ostracised but I would cope with it. Being found in the summerhouse would prove guilt, in the eyes of the Ton. A stroll around the gardens is a bit more open to interpretation."

"Grace, I would be more than happy to marry you rather than see you ostracised." That hadn't come out how he meant it, he was making a mull of this. "It would be far harder than you think. My mother suffered terribly because of the attitude of the Medleys towards her. I have to marry sometime and we're friends. That's more of a relationship than many couples have when they become engaged."

Angus ground to a halt. Grace was breathing heavily and her hands were clenched into fists. She looked ready to hit him! He ought to tell her that he wanted to be a lot more than a friend to her but the words wouldn't come.

"Oh, for heaven's sake, Angus. You know my views on marriage. I'll not compromise my principles to avoid a scandal that may never happen." Grace moved away from him and handed him his coat. "You stay here for a few minutes. I'll slip into the ballroom and go and hide in the ladies' withdrawing room. It won't do for us to suddenly appear together."

"I'm not letting you walk through the gardens on your own." Angus shrugged his coat back on. "You never know what disreputable men you might come across."

Grace shook her head at him and laughed. "I have a good idea. I'll let you escort me as far as the edge of the shrubbery. You can watch out for me from there."

Her hand grasped his and Angus felt a surge of emotion. It was going to be dashed tricky overcoming her reluctance but nothing other than marriage to her would make him happy, or keep her safe from herself.

"Lead the way, man. We can't stay out here forever."

Angus nodded and, keeping a hold of her hand, led her along the path. He stopped when he found a vantage point behind a bush that gave them a good view of the area of the garden next to the terrace. Besides a young couple, who appeared to be having an argument near the bottom of the steps, there was no one about. Grace moved as if to let go of his hand but he held her back.

"We need to watch for a few minutes to make sure no one is concealed in the garden, waiting to see who appears from that path."

"I suppose you're right," Grace said, in a grudging tone of voice.

Why was she so keen to get away from him? Was she embarrassed by his letting his feelings show? Or simply panicked by it? Her aversion to marriage ran deep it seemed. She shivered but he resisted the temptation to put his arm around her. His resistance was wearing thin by the time the warring young couple settled their differences and walked up the steps, along the terrace and back into the ballroom. Angus gave one last sweeping glance of the gardens.

He let go of Grace's hand. "I can't see anyone. Take care."

"With luck, if someone was watching in the garden, they'll think the couple they saw was those two." She ran up the path.

Angus watched until she disappeared into the ballroom. There was no sign of anyone else outside. He made a leisurely circuit of the garden as if taking the air. If they had been watched it must have been by a professional. A shiver ran up his spine. This whole business was devilish. He couldn't get on with sorting out any area of his life until he had found his enemy.

Angus sauntered into the ballroom a few minutes later. Most people had disappeared into the supper room and there was no sign of Grace. He stood irresolute until he felt a tap on his shoulder. Relief flooded through him as he turned to see Grace. She had taken the time to tidy her hair and clothing. She appeared perfectly composed, as if she hadn't set foot out of the ballroom all evening. A woman who was so calm under pressure would make a wonderful duchess. If only he could persuade her that he was worth changing her mind about marriage for.

Angus leaned close and kept his voice low. "You didn't take long to tidy up. No one would know you'd been outside."

"Thank goodness for that. Supper is nearly over and it wouldn't do for me to miss my dance with Ralph. If we're quick there might be enough time to at least get a drink, I'm parched."

The supper room was emptying when they went in. They found Aunt Theo and Luke sitting near to the door and collapsed into the vacant seats by them. Grace picked up a glass of lemonade Luke must have fetched and downed it in one go.

"That's better. We've overheard an interesting conversation, which we can talk about later. We're both engaged for the next three dances then we can leave." She drew a deep breath and sighed. "I must get back into the ballroom in time to dance with Ralph Medley. I'm not looking forward to it."

Grace had no sooner seen Aunt Theo settled with some friends amongst the chaperone's when Mr Medley sought her out.

"Our dance I believe, Miss Bamford." He gave her a bland smile and bowed.

His eyes seemed to bore into her. He couldn't have seen her and Angus in the garden, could he? She brightened. It might be a bonus if he had.

"It is indeed, Mr Medley."

He led her out onto the dance floor and once again his cloying cologne assailed her nostrils. She smiled at him in an attempt to hide her distaste. The orchestra struck up the introduction to a waltz. She had no idea what sort of dancer he was. It would be easier if he was a poor one and had to concentrate. There was far too much opportunity to converse during a waltz. It soon became apparent that he was a superb dancer, when he spun her in an impromptu turn to avoid an overenthusiastic young man who came close to knocking them over. A wave of apprehension swept over her. He was the sort of man it was easy to overlook, but it wouldn't do to underestimate him. He had been an army officer after all.

"You dance beautifully, Miss Bamford. Tell me, do you think Angus will make a good duke."

What a question. Grace considered her answer. "I'm sure he will be excellent. He's intelligent and Luke thinks a lot of him."

Mr Medley steered them into a quieter spot and Grace felt him study her, almost as if he was weighing up a horse.

"Lord Enstone's opinion is not one to ignore of course. What do you make of our new duke as a man?"

Grace felt herself flush, then remembered her role as Angus's suspected intended. "You put me to the blush, Mr Medley. What can a well brought up female reply to that?" She gave him an arch smile.

Lud, was she overdoing it a bit? She risked a glance at him and he smiled at her. This time it was a genuine smile.

"Yes, I think I can rest easy that the honour of the Medley family is in good hands. And the alliance with the Bamfords can only be a good thing."

Grace's face grew even hotter. Words failed her for once.

Mr Medley gave a soft chuckle, as if he was playing with her. "Angus is related to your brother's wife is he not?"

"Yes, Kitty is his cousin."

The music drew to a close and Grace concentrated on trying not to look relieved. Mr Medley returned her to Aunt Theo and bowed.

"Thank you, Miss Bamford. That was an excellent dance and a reassuring conversation."

Grace curtsied and watched his retreating back. She sat down next to Aunt Theo.

"Phew. I feel like I've passed some sort of test. At least I think I passed."

* * *

The music for the last of his booked dances petered out. Angus returned his partner to her family and dashed into the card room before he could be accosted by any hopeful mamas, with commonplace daughters in tow. Every woman in the room was insipid in comparison to Grace. Luke threw down his cards and admitted defeat at a table over at the back. He laughed and gestured to Angus.

"Let me introduce my friends, Evesham. Make sure to memorise them all so you can avoid getting drawn into their card games. They are far too good for us mere mortals."

Luke performed the introductions and then left the table, leading Angus out of the cardroom. "We had better go and find the ladies."

"I saw Lady Grant a few moments ago. Yes, there she is and Grace has joined her."

They collected Grace and Lady Grant and said their goodbyes to the Gilberts. Luke pointed towards the front door.

"I'll go and summon our coach. It's best if you stay with the ladies, Angus. Meet me by the door so that you can see it arrive. If you stay well back, you should be safe from attack. I'll have a quick check around outside for signs of trouble and Fletcher will be up on the box with our coachman."

Angus nodded and started a conversation with Major Ramsay, who had followed them out, whilst he waited for Grace and her aunt to fetch their cloaks.

Angus kept his voice low. "I can't explain now but I don't suppose you noticed Ralph Medley talking to someone called Jack, did you? Most likely someone he knew well."

Major Ramsay shook his head. "I can't say I did. Some of the fellows are meeting me at White's in a bit. Why don't you and Luke join us? We might be able to find out from one of them."

Luke strolled in. "Our coach will be here any moment.

Ramsay. Just the man I wanted to see."

"I've invited you and Evesham to join a few of us at White's. Meet you there in an hour say?"

Angus nodded when Luke glanced at him. "I'm happy to accept if you are, Luke."

"In that case we'll see you in an hour, Ram. I haven't been to White's in a while but I'm still a member."

"I'll watch out for you. Must go now. I can see my mother approaching. Promised to escort her home."

Lady Grant and Grace appeared. Luke stepped forward and offered an arm to his aunt. Angus smiled at Grace. For a moment he thought she was going to walk around and purloin her brother's other arm. She pursed her lips until Luke moved away and the moment passed. She unbent enough to slip her arm through his, but he could tell from the rigid line of her body that she was still angry with him.

He broke into a grin. It was just his luck that his interest had fixed upon a woman who was probably the only unattached, young, society lady, and a few not so young from the looks he had caught from one or two widows, not interested in marrying him. Lady Grant and Luke came to a halt near the door. Lady Grant introduced him to a friend of hers and Angus went through the motions of smiling in all the right places and saying all the right things. All the time his attention was fixed on Grace. He was so aware of her that it felt as if they were joined.

The carriage pulled up at the door and they extricated themselves. Luke waited for Angus to precede them with Grace. He helped Grace climb into the carriage and jumped in behind her.

"It doesn't feel right getting in before your aunt, but Luke has impressed upon me never to be out in the open for too long."

Grace sighed. "I suppose he's right. But it must irk you having to act so circumspectly."

They settled onto the backward facing seat and were soon joined by the others. He was going to have to at least admit to them that he and Grace had been onto the terrace. He waited, in case Grace wanted to take the lead but she seemed unusually silent.

"We went out onto the terrace after our first dance for some air. We overheard an interesting conversation between Ralph Medley and a gentleman called Jack. It sounded like he could have been an army colleague. Did either of you notice him talking to someone near the windows?"

Luke shook his head. "I saw him talking to any number of men tonight, many of whom I would wager had been in the army. None of them I recognised had the name of Jack."

"I didn't have a good view of the far side of the ballroom with the windows opening onto the terrace, from where I was sitting," Lady Grant said. "Like Luke, I noticed Mr Medley speak to several men of the sort of age to have been in the army with him. I couldn't put a name to any of them."

"That's a shame. I suppose it would have been far too simple if one of you had known who the mysterious Jack was."

Angus quickly recounted the conversation they had overheard.

"Have I missed anything out, Grace?"

"No, I don't think so." Her voice sounded abstracted. "I didn't take to Mr Medley at all, but I may have been prejudiced against him because of my suspicions. From what I saw of him we can't rule him out and we can't rule him in."

"You said he put you through something of an inquisition when you danced with him," Aunt Theo said.

Angus felt Grace stiffen next to him.

"I think he's taken the bait of thinking of Angus and I as a couple. I felt a bit like a horse in the sale ring. He wanted to know if I thought Angus would make a good duke too. I don't think we can rule him out at all. He sets great store by the honour of the Medleys and he's not as even tempered as he tries to appear. He got quite angry with Jack."

Luke tapped the floor of the coach with a foot. "This is so tricky. We're not making any progress. Let's hope you ladies do better at the Duchess of Cathlay's political salon tomorrow. Major Ramsay has invited us to join him at White's tonight. Perhaps he might have more idea who Jack is."

"I asked him if he did," Angus said. "We had the hallway to ourselves for a few moments. He had no idea but he said the friends who will be at White's might know."

Angus almost ground his teeth in frustration. It was important to trace this Jack and joining Ramsay and his friends in White's was a perfectly natural thing for them to do. It was too good a chance to miss. Even if no one knew Jack they might know more about Ralph Medley. He sighed loudly. It meant he would have no chance to talk to Grace on her own until the next day.

"Don't worry, Angus," Luke said. "We'll find your enemy, one way or another."

"I hope so, but I wish it didn't involve going to gambling clubs. I'm not much of a card player."

Luke laughed. "I don't mind the occasional game of cards but I'm not in form if tonight's performance at the Gilberts' was anything to go by. You've got deep pockets and I'll warn you if there is anyone you are better not to play. We can't have you dipping too deep."

"I'm not a bad player. I simply don't like taking money off people." Damn, why had he said that? It sounded so boastful. With luck, Luke would think it a joke. He would have to be careful not to play too well.

They pulled up in Cavendish Square.

"You stay in the coach, Angus. Fletcher and I will escort the ladies to the door. We had better get dropped off by Whites." Normally I would walk from here."

Angus groaned. "This is getting tedious." He squeezed Grace's hand under cover of the tails of his coat. "I'll try and visit you tomorrow, Grace, Lady Grant."

"We'll look forward to that, "Lady Grant said.

Grace stayed silent. He had a lot of work to do to persuade her he was interested in far more than a marriage of convenience. He was in love with the wretched woman! After his clumsy attempt at offering marriage to save her reputation, she would never believe that. Knowing Grace, nothing less than the prospect of a love match would make her even consider changing her mind about marriage.

Chapter Fifteen

The following day Grace woke up feeling listless. With Luke and Angus going on to White's after the ball there had been no time for any private conversation with Angus. Perhaps she had dismissed his suggestion of offering her marriage a little too hastily. After what she had experienced locked in his arms, could she settle for the life of a spinster? Her head ached. If he had mentioned love, she might have given him a different answer.

It was no good torturing herself with thoughts of a future with Angus. Better to turn her attention back to tracking down the mysterious, would-be murderer. Luke hadn't liked Ralph Medley any more than they had. None of them knew what to make of the conversation with Jack that she and Angus had overheard. She was fairly sure that Luke had a suspicion they had been dallying in the garden. He had probably been too busy wondering where they were to notice who Ralph Medley was talking to. Luke blundering into her affairs yet again was a complication she could do without.

At last, she and Aunt Theo set off to take luncheon with the Duchess of Cathlay, so as to be there before the guests arrived for the political salon. It was a relief to be away from home, instead of being bombarded with visits from gentlemen she had danced with. She had used up all her store of polite smiles. Especially since there had been no visit from the one man she did want to talk to.

The first guests arrived punctually at two o'clock and were soon joined by a steady stream of ladies in ones, twos and threes until every table in the Duchess's large, formal drawing room was taken. Grace smiled at everyone who arrived, making a mental note of anyone she didn't already know. She tried to avoid appearing too interested when the Countess of Hedburgh arrived. She was a mousy woman, who hung back in the shadows at the edge of the room, as if trying to blend into the background. Her clothes were an uninspiring shade of beige with little in the way of decoration. Grace had always considered her as one of a substantial minority who only attended these events at their husband's behest.

It was a lively afternoon and Grace enjoyed walking round the tables, taking part in various interesting conversations. The Duchess joined her on several occasions and squeezed her hand under the table as people were speaking, their prearranged signal to indicate anyone Augusta thought might be worth investigating. Conversations were about the state of Parliament in the main. There were several ladies Grace had never seen at one of the Duchess's salons before. Most of them had little to say or seemed nervous, but nothing that couldn't be accounted for by this being their first appearance. Invitations to the Duchess of Cathlay's political salons were much sought after.

Lady Hedburgh seemed quieter than normal, but she smiled in all the right places. Even so there was something about her that made Grace keep a careful watch when she could, without being obvious. The ladies on Aunt Theo's table said their goodbyes and Grace went to join her. Something about the posture of Lady Oulsnam, another new attendee who was sitting at a nearby table, caught Grace's attention. She was talking to two older ladies who were friends of the Duchess. She was quite animated and was leaning back in her chair, apparently at her ease. Even so the hunched set of her shoulders suggested that she was on high alert. Something was definitely troubling her, but whether it was connected to Angus's would-be murderer was doubtful. Even so Grace concentrated hard, searching for any visual clues. People and their motives could be fascinating.

Aunt Theo put a hand on her arm. "You seem distracted, Grace. Have you found out anything interesting?"

Grace smiled and shook her head. "Probably not, but Lady Oulsnam appears to be troubled by something and I would like to know what."

"I had the same feeling. She is trying desperately hard to appear relaxed but she's a bit too animated. At times I've noticed her chewing her bottom lip when she thought no one was looking. I don't suppose it's connected to our problem, but I'd like to know what troubles her just the same. I don't believe she had a specific invitation. I must check with Augusta. I noticed she came in with a close friend of Augusta's."

Grace nodded. "Now that is interesting. Why would you contrive to get an invitation to an event which made you nervous? Is she simply a social climber or is there someone here who she came to talk to?"

A rustle of silk alerted Grace to someone approaching them. She tried not to react when she realised it was the Countess of Hedburgh.

"Would you mind if I joined you, ladies?" Lady Hedburgh

gave them a nervous smile.

Aunt Theo pointed to the seat next to her. "We would be delighted."

Lady Hedburgh lowered herself onto the seat. She placed her reticule on the table in front of her and kept stroking the glass beads sewn onto the green and beige silk.

Aunt Theo gave her a beaming smile. "How are you keeping, my dear?"

"Very well thank you, Lady Grant." The Countess took a deep breath. "I understand the Duke of Evesham is staying with Lord Enstone, your nephew."

"Yes, he is. The Duke is related to Lord Enstone's wife." Aunt Theo raised her eyebrows at Lady Hedburgh. "Is there some particular reason why you ask that?"

The countess closed her eyes for a moment and then plunged into speech. "Being so friendly with the Duchess of Cathlay, you are bound to know that my husband has been making his disapproval of the Duke of Evesham common knowledge. There can't be many politicians he hasn't complained to about the Duke's support for the Scottish Highlanders."

Aunt Theo exchanged a quick glance with Grace before nodding. "We had heard about that, yes."

The Countess twisted in her chair and tightened her hold on her reticule. "Gervase isn't quite rational when it comes to the Scottish Highlanders. I've tried to persuade him to keep his opinions to himself, but he can't seem to let it go. I was hoping you would apologise to the Duke of Evesham for me for his behaviour."

Grace frowned. The poor woman appeared to be at the end of her tether. "We could, but why is your husband so critical of the Duke of Evesham?"

"Gervase's grandfather was killed fighting Bonnie Prince Charlie at the Battle of Culloden, which meant that his father inherited the title and estates at a ruinously early age. Gervase has spent his entire life trying to repair the damage his father did to the family fortunes. Thankfully, he has succeeded. It's been a dreadful struggle and his family's hatred of the people they held responsible for his grandfather's death has been magnified in him."

Grace pulled at her ear. "But that was so long ago and why focus on the Duke of Evesham?"

"Some of his Scottish friends have told him all about the Duke's efforts to support the Highlanders, when he was an advocate in Edinburgh." Lady Hedburgh stared at the ceiling and sighed.

"After the Duke of Evesham inherited the title and moved to London, Gervase was incensed when he saw him with the Duke of Cathlay. He's afraid that between them they may find a way to have the clearances banned. I've begged him to stop what he's doing, but he's obsessed with getting vengeance against people he sees as the enemy." Lady Hedburgh seemed close to tears.

Grace gasped. Aunt Theo looked as horrified as she felt. "That's hardly going to reassure the Duke of Evesham that Lord Hedburgh means no harm by his remarks. Besides, it sounds like it's the Scottish people your husband should be apologising to. No amount of handwringing is going to change that."

"I know, believe me, I know. Please, tell the Duke I will try and stop him being a nuisance and distract him from his plans for his Highland estates."

A stab of anger ran through Grace. Aunt Theo put a hand on

her arm and shook her head.

"Lady Hedburgh, thank you for being so open with us. My niece and I appreciate your efforts to persuade your husband to act reasonably. We will pass on what you have told us to the Duke of Evesham."

Grace watched Lady Hedburgh leave. Her shoulders were slumped, giving her a defeated air. Could her reassurances be relied upon?

"Well! I don't know what to think, Aunt Theo. Lord Hedburgh sounds unhinged and I have no confidence in his wife's ability to influence him."

"He does sound to be dangerously obsessive. Cathlay was concerned about him if you remember."

Grace nodded. "We had better put him at the top of our list."

"Agreed, but there is definitely something about Lady Oulsnam that worries me. She is still here on that last table. Why don't you join them? I'll go and have a word with Augusta."

Grace drifted over to the occupied table. She smiled at Mrs Dewar, a great friend of the Duchess, and took the seat next to Lady Oulsnam. That lady stared at her with an intensity that bordered on hostility. Her hands were resting on the table and they were so tightly clenched that the knuckles showed white. Grace gave her blandest smile. The talk seemed to be about the state of Parliament and Grace listened with interest, keeping a watchful eye on Lady Oulsnam. The Duchess and Aunt Theo came across to join them.

The Duchess sat next to Grace. "This is certainly an interesting year for politicians. How have you enjoyed your first political salon, Lady Oulsnam?"

Lady Oulsnam blinked several times. She unclenched her hands and they seemed to take on a life of their own with a series of jerky movements. "Very much, thank you, Your Grace. I'm glad my husband mentioned it."

Grace studied Lady Oulsnam. She looked anything but glad.

"Thank you for coming, Lady Oulsnam." The Duchess smiled at her. "We political wives must stick together."

Mrs Dewar laughed. "That is very true, Augusta. I too have had an interesting time today. I must be off now." She smiled at Grace. "Before I go, I wanted to ask you about your orphans. I need two junior maids who are used to London, but happy to move to the countryside for the summer months."

"We have plenty of girls ready to take up their first position at the moment."

"Excellent. Your young people are always so well trained." Mrs Dewar rose and signalled to Grace to follow her. Grace obeyed with a smile. She spotted Lady Oulsnam staring at her intensely again and looked away.

Mrs Dewar halted near to the door. "I'll call round and chat to Mrs Baker about suitable maids later in the week if you have no objection."

"Of course not. I'm always happy when we can place girls in twos and threes. I know they will be well treated with you."

Mrs Dewar lowered her voice. "Lady Oulsnam asked me to get her an invitation for today. I can't think why. Her husband rarely takes his seat in the House and she spent a lot of the time staring at you. Perhaps she was nervous, but I did wonder if you had done something to upset her."

Grace shook her head. "I noticed her staring at me too. As far as I know I've never met her before."

"Hmmm. Strange. Tell Augusta I will call on her tomorrow. Perhaps she knows more about Lady Oulsnam. Now I must be off. I'm sorry we haven't had more chance to chat. You're always welcome to call upon me, but of course you know that. I would love to hear more about your Duke of Evesham." Mrs Dewar patted Grace's hand and took her leave, before Grace could reply.

Angus didn't belong to her. A surge of heat went through her at the memory of Angus offering marriage when they were hiding in the garden of the Gilberts' house? He had seemed out of his depth, his usual air of confidence distinctly ruffled. Was he feeling guilty or was it possible that he had deeper feelings for her? If she ever succumbed to marriage, it would be for love and nothing less. Angus had aroused feelings in her that no respectable young lady could give voice to. Was she in love with him, or was that simply lust?

The other two ladies on the table decided it was time for them to leave. Grace and Aunt Theo walked with them to the door, where they thanked the Duchess for her hospitality. Lady Oulsnam followed and waited behind them. She looked back at Grace. For a moment Grace wondered if she was going to say something more. She smiled at her encouragingly. Lady Oulsnam gave a half smile, but her eyes darted all over the room. She took a deep breath, hunched her shoulders, opened her mouth then shut it quickly and scuttled out of the room. The Duchess watched open mouthed when she rushed past her without a word.

Grace waited until the sound of the last pair of footsteps disappeared. "There is something strange about Lady Oulsnam. It was as if she wanted to say something to me but was too frightened."

"Very odd. Let's go into my private sitting room."

The Duchess ordered a pot of tea from a passing footman and led them into her cosy, rose-coloured, private sitting room.

"Thank you for hosting that, Augusta." Aunt Theo said. "It was an interesting afternoon in more ways than one."

The Duchess laughed. "I intended to host a salon fairly soon in any case. I didn't expect it to be quite so illuminating from Grace's point of view. I wonder if Cathlay is right about Lord Hedburgh."

There was a knock at the door and the butler entered.

"Mr Lovell has called to see you, Your Grace. Shall I say you are not at home?"

The Duchess looked at Aunt Theo. "Bertie has been staying with Max. Do you mind if I invite him in?"

"Of course not, Augusta. We'll enjoy hearing his news."

"Show him in, Sayers. We will have four cups with the tea."

The butler withdrew and a few moments later Mr Bertie Lovell strode in. He bowed to the Duchess.

"Thank you for seeing me, Cousin Augusta." He nodded at Grace. "I've been searching everywhere for Miss Bamford." He stuttered to a halt. "I'm delighted to see you, of course."

The Duchess laughed. "That would be a first, but I won't tease you. Is your business with Miss Bamford connected with this little problem of the Duke of Evesham's, Bertie?"

Mr Lovell sat down on a nearby sofa, taking great care in arranging the tails of his impeccably cut coat. "I can't say I'd call some murderous swine sending cutthroats to finish him off a little problem. But, yes. It is about that. I've come from the orphanage, after a detour to Lady Grant's house, with a message from Lucy Vaughan."

Grace frowned. "A message from Lucy?"

"Yes. She had just had a visit from a lady called Mrs Craddock when I arrived. Apparently, she was there on the day of the knife attack on the Duke of Evesham. She said to let Miss

Bamford know that her husband had some information about someone with a serious grudge against Evesham. She's in tomorrow if Miss Bamford and the Duke would like to call."

Grace sat up straight. "That is interesting. Mrs Craddock is a sensible lady and her husband is a highly regarded lawyer. We'll certainly call tomorrow."

"Seeing as I've been to so much trouble to find you, it would only be fair for you to tell me everything that's been going on. Lucy, Miss Vaughan, said that Evesham has involved Fallon. He's the fly cove who got to the bottom of Max's little problem isn't he?"

Grace hesitated and the Duchess laughed. "Yes, it was Mr Fallon who helped Max and Georgie. Bertiehas matured a lot recently. I'm sure he can be relied upon. Believe it or not, there is a sharp mind behind all his bluster and Town polish."

Grace stared at Mr Lovell. His ears had gone pink at the compliment. From what she had heard of him he was something of a wastrel. Still, he must be a year or two younger than she was and men did mature later. The Duchess was rarely wrong about people. Grace glanced across at Aunt Theo.

"Mr Lovell knows a large part of the story already, Grace. I can't see any harm in involving him. He mixes with a younger set and may know people we don't. It won't hurt for us to remind ourselves of what we already know before we consider what we've learned today."

Grace nodded. "Very well. As soon as the tea has arrived, I'll go through all that's happened."

Sayers himself arrived with the tea tray. "Will there be anything else, your Grace?"

The Duchess pursed her lips. "I should have asked you if you would prefer something stronger, Bertie."

Mr Lovell smiled at her. "Not this early in the day, cousin. I'm a new man these days."

"That will be all then, Sayers."

The Duchess poured the tea and Grace gave a quick summary of everything that had happened.

Mr Lovell gasped when she mentioned the sharpened piece of military spur used on one of her greys. "That's nasty. There's somebody evil behind this."

Grace nodded. "There certainly is, although as far as I'm concerned the attempted knifing was pretty awful."

The Duchess laughed. "You can tell Bertie likes his horses. They would definitely rank above the Duke of Evesham in his eyes."

Grace laughed. "He does have a point, I suppose. My greys are beautiful. Anyway, today the wife of Cathlay's main suspect, the Earl of Hedburgh, made me an impassioned plea to apologise to the Duke of Evesham for her husband's having taken against him."

"Why has Hedburgh taken against Evesham?"

"It's all to do with the Earl of Hedburgh's grandfather being killed by the Scots at the Battle of Culloden and him resenting Evesham's opposition to the Highland clearances. The Earl sounds positively deranged. I think Cathlay may well be right to put him at the top of our list. Lady Hedburgh said that she would try and head her husband off from being a nuisance, but I don't place any confidence in her ability to do so."

"He's worth investigating." Mr Lovell stroked his chin and frowned. "He's a bit too obvious for my liking though."

Aunt Theo put her head on one side. "Perhaps, but sometimes the simplest solution is the correct one. We did have a question mark against another of today's guests. Augusta, what do you know about Lady Oulsnam?"

"Not a lot. She has a tenuous acquaintance with Mrs Dewar. Mrs Dewar is one of the select group of matrons I've got working on this. Otherwise, she would have tried to put Lady Oulsnam off when she angled for an invitation for today."

"She did well to bring her," Grace said. "Lady Oulsnam told me that her husband had suggested she attend the salon. Which seems strange, given that he rarely attends Parliament."

The Duchess pursed her lips. "From what Mrs Dewar said, the salon was discussed during a breakfast at Lady Sowerby's yesterday. She didn't think Lady Oulsnam had known anything about it beforehand from her arrested expression when it was first mentioned. Then nothing would do for the woman but to extract a promise to get her an invitation to the salon, so Mrs Dewar went along with it."

Mr Lovell whistled. "Very strange. It sounds as if the lady had a particular reason for wanting to attend."

Grace exchanged glances with Aunt Theo. She studied Mr Lovell with increased respect. "We both got the impression that she wanted to say something to me but lost her nerve."

"That would make sense." The Duchess nodded. "She suddenly scuttled past me at the door without taking her leave. Mr Ralph Medley is another suspect, Bertie, as Evesham's heir. There have been an unusual number of deaths in the Medley line of inheritance in recent years. Lady Grant and Miss Bamford met him last night at the Gilbert's ball."

Grace wrinkled up her nose. "I didn't know what to make of him. If he hadn't been in the army for years, I would have thought him too fastidious to go anywhere near something as sordid as murder."

"I know what you mean, Grace, although I found him a nondescript sort of man. The sort to merge into the background. Luke said the same."

Mr Lovell laughed. "Trying to hide in plain sight perhaps. I always keep an eye on quiet types. You never know what they're thinking."

Grace shuddered. "He made me think of a snake slithering through the grass. I wonder if he's the sort who like to collect gossip to use when it suits them." Could Ralph Medley have been the one spying on them in the Gilberts'garden? Angus had been convinced he had heard someone near their hiding place and Mr Medley had been out on the terrace.

"You didn't take to him, did you?" Aunt Theo tilted her head in thought. "I didn't like him at all, but if we had met him without these suspicions in the background, I suspect we would have found him quite unexceptional."

Mr Lovell slapped his thigh. "I bet he's your man. Exactly the sort of cove who slips by unnoticed and can get up to all manner of things without being suspected. He has to be on the list, with the motive of inheriting a dukedom, and vast estates from what I hear."

Mr Lovell downed the last of his tea and put his cup on the table by him. "I wish I could help but I'm only in Town for another day or so. I'm going up to an estate in Staffordshire I've inherited from my godfather."

"I heard about that from Max," the Duchess said. "I'm pleased for you. A great addition to your Devon holdings."

"It's much bigger. I may make it my main residence." Mr Lovell beamed at them. "Max has given me a lot of useful advice on estate management and I'm looking forward to going up there to see what I can improve."

"That's excellent news, Bertie. I'm so glad you and Max are friends now."

Mr Lovell laughed. "So am I. He and Georgie send their best wishes. Georgie said she will write to you soon. I'm about to call on a couple of friends who are in Town and would like to be of use to you today. How about I go and track down Fallon and pass on all this information, including the message from Mrs Craddock?"

"That would be useful, thank you, Mr Lovell," Grace said. "I wouldn't want to put you to too much trouble though."

Mr Lovell gave her an affable smile. "I've nothing else to do for the rest of the day than collect these two friends for an evening at my club. They live in different parts of London. If you tell me where I can find Fallon, or at least leave a message for him in safe hands, I'll happily try and track him down."

"If you're sure, that would be a good way to get information to him. Anybody who's been keeping watch won't have connected you to us. Lucy Vaughan's family are from Staffordshire, do you know them?"

"I was at school with her brother. My godfather's place is a short ride away from them and I used to spend quite a lot of my summer holidays there. I think of Lucy as a little sister."

Grace smiled. "If her brother is half as nice as Lucy, you must have had a good time."

"Oh, I did. It was also a good way to get away from Mama for a large part of the holiday. Right, I had better be going. Do you want to give me Fallon's address and I'll carry out that errand for you?"

Grace borrowed pen and paper from the Duchess and wrote down Fallon's direction.

"If Mr Fallon's not at home you can safely leave a message

with Hugh Masters. He's going to be the Duke of Evesham's secretary eventually."

"Right you are." Mr Lovell accepted the piece of paper and gave them a cheery wave before taking his leave.

Augusta watched him go with a smile on her face. "Bertie is a changed man. I always said he wasn't the rascal Max thought him. It will be interesting to hear what Mr Fallon makes of our news. I wonder what your Mrs Craddock has heard?"

Grace nodded slowly. "I'm intrigued. She's the lady who has volunteered to help with the orphanage employment agency. She struck me as very sensible. I have a feeling it might be something important."

Chapter Sixteen

Angus sat up in bed nursing a thick head, having drunk rather more than he was used to with Luke's friends the night before. It had been a convivial evening, and perhaps he had needed some time to relax, but they hadn't found out anything useful about Ralph Medley. Neither of the two men called Jack who Luke's friends had spotted at the Gilberts' ball were known to be friends of Ralph. In fact, Major Ramsay had mentioned that he hadn't been able to find anyone from Ralph's regiment who could name any real friends, let alone close associates, of his.

Perhaps that in itself was useful information? An army man with no close army friends was odd. All the soldiers he knew cherished the camaraderie of their fellow soldiers. It was that closeness that got them safely through battles. Ralph was an enigma. From what Ramsay had found out, he had been an exemplary officer, often mentioned in dispatches. His cleverness had turned around more than one battle. And yet, everything Ramsay had found out about him suggested he was a man who was respected rather than liked by his subordinates. It all pointed to a loner who might be capable of murder.

Angus groaned and threw off the covers. From the light seeping around the edges of the room's heavy, deep red, damask curtains the hour was quite advanced. What had he been thinking of staying out so late? There was a knock at the door. Gillard, his new valet, opened it with a nervous glance in his direction. Angus bit back a sharp retort at being disturbed. It wasn't the lad's fault that he had been out carousing until the small hours and felt like a bear with a sore head.

"I thought I had better wake you, Your Grace." Gillard looked at the floor, but not quickly enough to hide a wide grin. "I've ordered a pot of strong coffee."

Angus burst out laughing. "I think that's a good idea, Gillard. Let me reassure you that staying out so late is not my normal habit. What time is it?"

"Three o'clock, Your Grace."

"Tarnation! The best part of a day wasted." Angus leaned back against his pillows. Would Grace go home after the Duchess of Cathlay's political salon? He could use talking about that as an excuse to get her alone. Gillard was waiting patiently by the door.

"Could you see if cook can rustle me up something to eat as well as the coffee?" He ran a hand through his hair. "Once I've got myself together, I need to go out for a bit."

A little over an hour later, Angus stood up from the dining table, feeling a lot better after a substantial meal of ham and eggs. His best bet was to walk straight over to Lady Grant's house and wait for Grace there. She might even be back already. He went out into the hallway to find Gillard hovering near the front door.

"Mr Fletcher said he will be around in a moment, Your Grace."

Angus shook his head. "There's no need for that. I'm only going to Lady Grant's house. The walk will wake me up."

"Mr Fletcher said you need an escort. He's taking me as well, I'm handy with my bunch of fives." Gillard held up his fists and danced from foot to foot, looking proud.

Angus closed his eyes and took a deep breath. "I'm sure you are, but I don't think an escort is necessary."

Fletcher appeared through a door from the servants' quarters. "I can assure you it is, Your Grace."

Angus sighed. "I'm not going to waste time arguing about it. If you insist, you had better come with me."

Luke's butler helped him into a greatcoat. Was this nightmare ever going to end? He was going to be denied the quiet, solitary walk he craved to clear his head. They might as well take a carriage. He could make a detour and see if Fallon was at home, without wasting much time. Fallon might have learned something useful.

"On second thoughts, I'll take a carriage and call in to see Mr Fallon first."

Fletcher nodded. "Gillard, run down to the stables and ask for a town carriage to be brought around. As quickly as they can. We'll still take you with us."

Gillard scampered off. He was willing, as well as being a quick learner.

Angus raised his eyebrows at Fletcher. "Out with it, man."

"You've got to take this threat seriously, Your Grace." Fletcher grinned at him. "Lord Enstone hasn't long gone out. He was in nearly as bad a case as you. You need to be fully alert when someone's trying to kill you. I suggest you keep young Gillard with you at all times. His father was a prize-fighter and the lad is a dab hand at fisticuffs."

"Gillard said he was good with his bunch of fives. But that wouldn't help against somebody with a knife."

"He has other fighting skills, including how to kick out at the right moment and how to dance out of the range of a blade. The lad is needle witted and can handle a pistol well. I've checked him out thoroughly. A very intelligent young man. He knows to be looking out for trouble when he's with you. Given that Mr Fallon is too busy investigating to act as bodyguard, he's a great substitute."

The front door opened and Gillard appeared. "The carriage will be here any minute, Your Grace."

"We'll stay here, Gillard," Fletcher said. "You watch for the coach. Knock on the front door when it comes and climb up on the box with the coachman. I'll ride inside with the Duke."

Within minutes they were inside the coach. Angus relaxed against the squabs.

"Have you heard anything from Fallon?"

"I shared an ale with him last night." Fletcher shook his head. "He's got a lot of background information but nothing substantial yet. Except the feeling that whoever is behind this is a serious criminal. People are too frightened to talk."

Angus sighed. "This is so frustrating. I'll get a report from him and then go straight round to see Lady Grant and Miss Bamford. Let's hope the Duchess of Cathlay's political salon has thrown up some leads."

Hugh Masters ushered them inside a short while later. "You're in luck. Mr Fallon is here with a relative of the Duchess of Cathlay, who has information from Miss Bamford."

They left Gillard watching the street for any unusual activity and told the coachman to drive the coach around for a while.

Fallon stood to greet them as they entered the sunny breakfast room at the back of the house. "Take a seat, gentlemen." He turned towards an exquisitely turned out and exceedingly handsome young gentleman. "This is Mr Lovell, Your Grace. A cousin of the Duchess of Cathlay."

Mr Lovell stood and bowed towards him. "Delighted to meet you. I called round to see Augusta today. I arrived just after one of her salons with wives of political types. She and Grace Bamford have been telling me something about your difficulties."

Angus narrowed his eyes and studied Lovell. Was it safe to trust him? He must be on good terms with Grace if she had been prepared to talk to him about it. But then why shouldn't he be? He had probably known her all his life. English aristocrats seemed a tight knit group.

"Ah." Angus forced a smile. "Please take a seat Mr Lovell."

Mr Lovell beamed at him. "I offered to deliver a report to Mr Fallon from Grace, to help out. I'd love to do more but I have to travel north on business soon."

Angus damped down a spurt of an emotion he couldn't quite identify and smiled back. "Did the ladies find out anything useful?"

Lovell grimaced. "Possibly. It's difficult to tell. But, before I forget, the reason I called on Augusta was to pass on a message for Grace from a Mrs Craddock."

Angus sat forward in his chair. "I met Mrs Craddock at the orphanage Grace is involved with."

"That will be her. I called by the orphanage to say hello to Lucy Vaughan, her brother is a friend of mine. Mrs Craddock suggested that you and Grace call on her. She's in all day tomorrow. Her husband has some information that might be linked to whoever is out to get you."

Angus rubbed his chin. "She seemed eminently sensible. We had better accept her invitation. Thank you for letting us know.

Did the ladies find anything out at the Duchess of Cathlay's salon?"

"Possibly. Grace spoke to Lady Hedburgh, the wife of the Duke of Cathlay's main suspect. The Earl of Hedburgh is definitely an enemy of yours and could be the one behind these murder attempts. He sounds quite mad."

Lovell frowned. "Hedburgh seems too obvious for my money, but I'd put him above Ralph Medley. Let's face it, if anything was to happen to you, Medley would be the prime suspect after so many deaths in the line of succession."

"Yes. I can't say I took to Ralph, but I agree with you there. And one thing he's not short of is intelligence."

"The brother of a friend of mine served under him briefly. He's a clever cove all right and tight." Lovell tilted his head back and caught Angus's gaze. "A devious one too, I should say. Be wary of him, just in case."

Angus caught the shrewd gleam in Lovell's eyes. The man might dress like the dandy set and bumble around, but Ralph wasn't the only man with a sharp intelligence. He stiffened. Could he be a serious contender for Grace's hand? They seemed on excellent terms.

Lovell coughed. "No offence meant, old man. I'm sure you don't need me to tell you to be careful after at least two attempts on your life."

"Sorry, I was thinking. I agree with you on Ralph. I wonder if there could have been more than two attempts?" Angus glanced at Fallon.

"It's possible, Your Grace. Mr Fletcher has various members of Lord Enstone's staff watching you. Their presence, even though they will have been careful not to appear connected to you in any way, may have foiled potential attempts before they got started."

Lovell nodded in agreement. "I wouldn't be surprised. I can see how worried Grace is about you."

Angus grimaced and looked at the floor. Should he be pleased that Grace cared enough to worry about him, or nervous at this further evidence of the strength of the connection Lovell had with her?

"I wish Grace hadn't got embroiled in my affairs. I'll never forgive myself if she is harmed in any way."

"Oh, I shouldn't worry about Grace. I've known her a long time. Cleverest girl I've ever come across. Handy with those pistols of hers too."

Angus chuckled. "I found that out when she shot the first man who tried to kill me. I should be grateful she did get involved."

"You should. Back to this afternoon's meeting. Grace has got a hunch a cove called Lord Oulsnam might be involved after speaking to his wife. That said, neither she nor Lady Grant are ready to rule out Ralph Medley. Got the impression they didn't take to him at all."

Angus laughed. "I expect you're right. It's hard to explain why but I definitely didn't take to Ralph."

Lovell shook his head. "I don't envy you trying to get to the bottom of this lot. I'm engaged to meet some friends now so I'll take my leave."

Pleasantries were exchanged and Angus watched his departing back. Had he heard that name correctly? "Did he say Oulsnam?"

Fallon watched him intently. "Yes, Mr Lovell spelled the name out for me. O U L S NAM. Does the name mean anything to you?"

"It does, but I can't see that the Lord Oulsnam I'm thinking of has enough of a grievance to want to kill me." Angus dropped his head into his hands and groaned. "Tarnation! Unless my cousin was less than truthful with me. I had a feeling he was holding something back when I helped him out with a problem he had last autumn, with Oulsnam's Scottish man of business."

Fallon tapped the fingers of one hand on the top of the dining table he was sitting at to take notes. "What, exactly, happened?"

"I've never met Lord Oulsnam, but his Scottish agent is a bully and a cheat. I've come across him before in smaller cases. Last summer he tried to trick a hard-working young man out of his family business. When that didn't work, he tried to get young Hamish McClelland convicted of a theft he didn't commit, knowing his mother would have to sell the business for whatever she could get if Hamish went to prison."

"How would that help Oulsnam?"

"His man of business has a way of intimidating people out of bidding for anything he wants. We know it goes on but no one has been able to pin anything on him. People are too frightened to talk."

Fallon gave him a sharp look but nodded. "Go on."

"There was a lot of money at stake and the McClelland family couldn't afford an advocate. One of my assistants heard about it and we agreed to take on Hamish's case for free. We didn't just win, Oulsnam's man was laughed out of court."

"Meaning you cost Oulsnam a good deal of money. I've seen murders committed over money before now. But how was your cousin involved?"

"He lost money gambling. Someone bought up his vowels

and demanded immediate payment. They offered to take the business he had inherited from his father if he couldn't pay the debt. Fortunately, the lad, he wasn't much more, had the sense to come to me and I paid them off. The man who came to collect looked furious when I handed over the money in front of several trustworthy witnesses."

Fallon leaned closer and raised his eyebrows. "So now you suspect Oulsnam's agent was behind it and your cousin had been targeted because they wanted his business."

"I'm afraid so." Angus gave a heavy sigh. "I thought at the time that there was something that Rory, my cousin, wasn't telling me. I think he may know for sure who was involved. It may be that he was cheated in some way and didn't want to admit to being gulled."

Fallon laughed. "A case of needing your help but not wanting to accept it."

"Something like that. Rory came into his inheritance too young but the whole incident shook him up so much he grew up overnight. I don't think he will fall for any more tricks."

"Hmm. If what you say is true then Oulsnam has even more motive to dislike you. But I still don't see how he would profit from your death."

"Unless there is something about the business that makes him particularly want it and he thinks Rory would be easier to get around with me out of the way?"

"What sort of business is it?"

"Sea transport, import and export. The company has a sizeable fleet of top-quality ships."

Fallon let out a slow whistle. "Quite a prize then. Oulsnam is definitely worth investigating, but it's not clear that there is a link from him to Rory."

"I know. And yet my gut says there is. There is only one way to find out for sure. I'm going to send you up to Edinburgh to speak to my cousin and see what you can find out about Oulsnam's Scottish dealings."

Fletcher coughed. "Are you sure that's wise, Your Grace? Mr Fallon here is a good man to have around you. Couldn't you send a groom or someone to talk to your cousin?"

"No, I don't think that would be enough. Rory's problem had slipped from my mind with so much to distract me. Now I have thought about it, I'll feel a lot better having someone of Mr Fallon's calibre check whether he's had any more trouble and help him out if he has."

"I'm entirely at your disposal." Fallon pursed his lips. "Tell me, do you discount Oulsnam as your would-be murderer?"

"Not entirely. I think it's more likely to be him than the Earl of Hedburgh."

Fletcher leaned forward in his chair. "Clever man the Duke of Cathlay. We can't rule Hedburgh out."

"No indeed. It could be him, but Ralph Medley bothers me the most. There is something about Ralph that grates on me. He appears to have no close friends and is altogether too friendly towards me, considering how he talks to other people."

"He does have an obvious motive," Fallon said. He reddened. "Especially with you being seen with Miss Bamford so often.

Angus ran a hand through his hair. "I know what you're saying. I'm not sure what I should do about that at this point."

Instead of trying to court Grace, perhaps he should be distancing himself? An icy shiver ran down his spine.

"Do you think I'm putting her in danger by allowing her to be involved?"

Fallon tapped his fingers on the desk. "I don't think so, unless you were to marry her. That would be dangerous. Although she might be an incidental target when you're together."

"Like the attack on her carriage horse. That did worry me."

"Are you sure that I wouldn't be better staying here to keep an eye on you both."

"I don't know, but I am sure that Rory kept something from me. I need someone who can use his initiative to make certain he and his business are safe, whether Oulsnam is involved in the murder plot against me or not."

Fallon nodded. "Fair enough. You don't want to be distracted from staying safe! It might be best if I had a cover story, so as not to arouse any suspicion."

"I'll give you a letter of introduction to my Scottish Agent. McGregor looks after my Scottish financial affairs and organises a team of investigators which we use for our criminal cases. He can say he's taken you on as his assistant." Angus paused.

"It's a shame Rory's ship has gone back to Edinburgh. It's a long way by road. I sent a message for the captain to deliver to McGregor, when my luggage was collected. McGregor should already have the team investigating any cases I won which might leave the loser with a grudge against me by the time you arrive."

Angus turned to Fletcher. "This could take some time. It might be best to have the horses stabled here for a while."

Fletcher jumped up. "I'll see to it straight away."

Angus waited for the door to close behind him. He smiled at Fallon. "I think there's a chance that Oulsnam has something to do with this, but I am also a touch worried about young

Rory. Having you up in Edinburgh will ease my mind. You may turn something up and it's a good opportunity for you. Mr McGregor is more involved with the investigations than he is with my affairs. He has a business team for that. A spell working for him would give you a good grounding. I would love to take you onto my staff afterwards but I have a feeling you would rather work for yourself. Am I right?"

Fallon gave him a sheepish grin. "I would, yes."

"Spend a few months with McGregor. Once he thinks there is no more that he can teach you, I'll be happy to invest in your business and provide funds for you to get established."

Fallon's eyes shone. "A great opportunity for me, but I'm loath to desert you with this murderer on the loose."

"Mr Fletcher is right. The Duke of Cathlay is a formidable man. Lord Enstone and I are dining with him tonight. I'm going to ask him to hire the best of Bow Street for me. Now, let's go and see if Mrs Craddock can talk to us before you go up to Edinburgh, in case she knows any more about Oulsnam. I'll send Masters to buy you a ticket for the first mail coach out tomorrow."

"I had better stop Mr Fletcher stabling the horses."

Angus shook his head. "If we slip out of the mews entrance and hire a hackney, I'll be a lot less conspicuous than in the Enstone family coach. Before we go, I'll write that letter to McGregor for you.

Angus checked his pocket watch. There would be no time for him to seek out Grace now. Not with him and Luke engaged to dine at Brooks with Cathlay later. He had better take Gillard with them as it was, if he was going to be ready in time. He leaned his elbows on the table and rested his head in his hands. If he ever sorted out his tangled affairs it would be a miracle.

Fixing his interest with Grace would be even harder without the chance to talk to her alone. He had badly mishandled his proposal to her. The sooner he could put that right the better. Grace was the sort to stew on things and she was going to be hard enough to bring around to the idea of marriage as it was.

Chapter Seventeen

Grace woke up after a disturbed night, punctuated by dreams of a handsome Scotsman. Lord, she must have been drunk on the moonlight in the Gilberts' Garden. She had been so close to agreeing to marry Angus. And, if she was being honest, overwhelmed by the pull of attraction she felt between them. How fortunate he hadn't called around yesterday to see how they got on at the political salon. If he had asked her again, she might have given in to temptation.

It would never do. There were good reasons to stay single. Thank heavens she could see things more clearly after some time for sensible reflection. She damped down a spurt of anger that he had ignored her for a whole day with difficulty. It was harder still to quieten the voice urging her to explore her feelings for Angus more deeply. Emotions were dangerous things. She needed to get their relationship back on a professional footing, even though it would be difficult to ignore Angus's undeniable charm.

Her maid entered the bedroom. Grace endured her ministrations with barely a murmur. As soon as she was ready, she strode out of her room and ran down the stairs. Angus was bound to call today and she needed the fortification of a good breakfast. A few steps into the breakfast room she stopped. Angus, the man who had disturbed her sleep, was drinking coffee and chatting amiably to Aunt Theo. Her eyes were drawn to his face as he threw back his head and laughed at something Aunt Theo said. She forced herself to look away. She should have accepted her maid's offer of hot chocolate and toast in bed. It was too late to escape now.

Grace forced her features into a smile and walked across to the sideboard. "You sound cheerful for this early in the morning, Angus."

She filled a plate with ham, eggs and hot buttered toast. By standing at an angle to the other two, as she selected her food, Grace was able to hide her face from Angus. If she was going to persuade him that she was indifferent to him she needed time to school her countenance. She heard Angus laugh and resisted the temptation to look at him.

"I didn't feel nearly as cheerful when I finally dragged myself out of bed yesterday, I can assure you. I stayed out with Luke and his friends into the small hours after the Gilberts' ball. Fortunately, our dinner with the Duke of Cathlay last night finished much earlier and I went straight home to bed."

"You men. I expect the wine flowed freely." Grace took the seat next to Aunt Theo, who was sitting directly opposite Angus. Angus would be able to see at least her profile, but there wouldn't be any danger of them coming into physical contact.

Aunt Theo gave her a quizzical look and then smiled. "Angus managed to fit in a visit to Mr Fallon before his engagement with Cathlay."

Grace chewed on her breakfast for a few moments and accepted a cup of coffee from Aunt Theo.

"Thank you. You will have heard about Mr Lovell's visit to

the Duchess after her salon then."

Angus leaned back in his chair, completely at his ease. "I can go one better than that. Mr Lovell was there when I arrived."

"I see. Did he tell you all our findings from the salon?" Grace slipped delicately at her coffee.

She kept her gaze lowered. If Angus had been there early enough to see Mr Fallon, surely, he would have had time to come and pay them a quick visit. That he hadn't suggested she had read far too much into the events at the Gilberts' ball. A wave of irritation washed over her. She gave herself a mental shake. Heavens, since she wanted to restore a professional distance between them, she ought to be relieved.

"He did, in great detail. An interesting gentleman, Mr Lovell."

Grace glanced up to see Angus studying her intently. "I suppose he is. I've known him forever. He's the Marquess of Hargreaves cousin and heir." Grace smiled. "Although I suspect that may not be the case by the end of the year."

"I know what you mean, Grace." Aunt Theo laughed. "I'm sure Max would have stayed in town for the season, to show off his new bride, without a good reason not to. Augusta and I are convinced that he and Georgie are anticipating a happy event."

Despite Grace's best efforts, heat flooded her cheeks. "I had the same thought exactly. Not that Bertie will be worried. I don't think he was ever interested in inheriting the title. That was all down to his mother."

Angus raised his eyebrows. "Ah, he suffered from an ambitious mother, did he? I was inclined to write him off as of little account to start with, but I would say he's a young man of great intelligence."

"He certainly is," Aunt Theo said. "He had Max fooled with his wastrel act. I'm glad they are on much better terms now that Bertie's mother is leaving him alone, since she remarried. He would have told you about the invitation from Mrs Craddock. I wonder what information she has."

Angus studied the floor and fingered his cravat. Grace studied him. What was he hiding? He looked up and smiled at her as if reading her mind.

"I hope you won't be cross, but Fallon and I managed to fit in a quick visit to Mrs Craddock yesterday evening. Her information was about Lord Oulsnam. It's a long story, but what she told me suggests that it's my cousin, Rory he is targeting. Oulsnam's man of business in Edinburgh made an attempt last autumn to try and swindle Rory's business from him. It seems they haven't given up on trying to get hold of it."

Grace stared at him. "Why would Lord Oulsnam want to get your cousin's business?"

"It's a very successful shipping line, with some lucrative contracts and one of the biggest fleets of merchant ships in Scotland. I'm not sure why, specifically, they are targeting Rory. I do know that Lord Oulsnam has an extensive trading business, largely operated by his Edinburgh agent."

"And you think they want his business in order to expand their operations?"

Angus nodded. "Yes, I do. My legal team has had dealings helping people threatened by Oulsnam's empire before. The Edinburgh man is unethical. It seems even London lawyers are aware of his activities. Mrs Craddock was worried that I was being targeted, but after hearing all the information she had I'm confident it's my cousin who needs help."

Grace exchanged a glance with Aunt Theo. "Instinct tells me you have taken action to assist your cousin."

"I have indeed. I've sent Mr Fallon up to Edinburgh by mail coach, with a cover story, to keep Rory out of trouble until I can take a hand myself."

Aunt Theo gasped. "Do you think that is wise, Your Grace?"

"I needed to send someone of Mr Fallon's calibre. Otherwise, I would have been so distracted it could put me at risk the way things stand."

"I can understand that," Aunt Theo said, "but that leaves you without his investigative skills."

"Mr Fletcher, together with the Duke of Cathlay's steward, is spending the morning in Bow Street. Cathlay has arranged for them to be allocated the best Bow Street investigators available."

Grace crossed her arms. "That's all very well, but I'd wager none of them is as good as Mr Fallon from what I saw of him."

Angus gave a sheepish grin. "Probably not. However, they do know London well and I'm going to hire as many of them as I can get my hands on. I'm determined to get to the bottom of this so that I can get back to what I should be working on. There is so much to do to set the dukedom to rights."

"I still don't see why you couldn't have sent someone else to Edinburgh as well as hiring the Bow Street runners." Grace ground her teeth. "Surely your cousin could look after himself if someone went up to Edinburgh to warn him of the danger."

"Rory is young, barely one and twenty. His father died a year ago and I feel responsible for him."

Aunt Theo shook her head. "Angus has done what he thinks best, Grace. There's no point being cross with him."

"I suppose not." Grace turned towards Angus. "Are you

sure Mrs Craddock's intelligence does relate to Rory?"

"As sure as I can be. There are things that happened last summer that I shouldn't recount to anyone else. Given what happened then, I'm confident that the threat is to Rory and his business."

Grace sighed. "I suppose that's fair enough. I still think we need to leave Lord Oulsnam on the list of suspects though. You need to brief the Bow Street runners with what you know, they are too professional to give away any confidential information."

Grace studied Angus through narrowed eyes. Was he trying to shut her out of the investigation? He returned her gaze with a quizzical lift of his eyebrows. He was close enough for her to smell the citrus tang of his shaving soap. A wave of heat ran through her. The more she tried to suppress it the hotter she felt. She stared at the floor. A strong hand came to rest over hers. Her cheeks flamed hotter still. She forced herself to look at him.

Angus smiled at her. "I can see you think I'm being deliberately obtuse here. I suggest we both go and see Mrs Craddock again this morning."

"There doesn't seem much point if you've already had all the information she's got to give."

"If she tells you exactly what she told me, you can see if you come to the same conclusion. I'm not trying to keep things from you, Grace."

Aunt Theo coughed. "That might be a good idea. If you will excuse me, I need to go and consult with my housekeeper."

Grace watched her go open-mouthed. Never say Aunt Theo was playing matchmaker now. She snatched her hand from underneath Angus's and moved farther away from him. He seemed to stiffen but smiled at her and continued.

"Oulsnam never does anything without a specific purpose. My information is that he is very much involved in the management of his empire. To keep that from the Ton, a lot of it is run by his Scottish man of business. I can't see how murdering me would further his business interests."

Grace frowned. "Unless he thinks getting you out of the way would make it easier for him to get hold of your cousin's business."

"That's the only possibility I can think off. Hence, if I make sure he has no chance of getting Rory's business I effectively remove myself from being a target, in the unlikely event of Oulsnam being behind these murder attempts. They feel more personal to me. From what I know of Oulsnam, business is everything to him. "

Why did she have the feeling that Angus wasn't telling her everything? "Have you never had any personal dealings with Lord Oulsnam?"

"I did win a case against him for a businessman last year, or at least against his Scottish man of business."

"Perhaps he holds a grudge?"

Angus shook his head. "My team investigated him extensively. Nothing seems to matter to him but improving his business empire, apart from upholding his social position. I'd be surprised if he would risk trying to murder a peer of the realm. I doubt he could be directly implicated but

he wouldn't want even a breath of scandal. He goes to such lengths to keep his involvement hidden from the Ton. Besides, the young man I defended has been left alone since the case. If Oulsnam was the sort to hold a grudge he would have made another attempt to force him to sell his business cheaply."

Grace blinked. "He does seem to concentrate on trying to effectively steal businesses. You don't own anything else he might want do you?"

"Not as far as I know. That's one of the things I want Fallon to check, besides making sure Rory is free from further harassment. Why don't we keep Oulsnam on the list for now and wait for a report from Fallon? That's another reason for employing Bow Street. They may know more about the English side of Oulsnam's business interests."

"Do we have a choice, since you have already dispatched Fallon?"

"You're angry because I didn't consult you, aren't you? Time was of the essence last night. I couldn't be late for dinner with the Duke of Cathlay and there simply wasn't any opportunity to come and find you. It wasn't that I didn't want to."

Grace shook ahead and frowned. "If you and Luke hadn't stayed out late with his friends, you would have had plenty of time to come round and see me yesterday."

Angus raised his eyebrows at her and Grace looked away. For heaven's sake, what was wrong with her? Angus would think she was disappointed he hadn't been to see her now. Of course she had been disappointed, but also relieved. She glanced back at Angus in time to see a smug smile flit across his face. She studied the floor. It wasn't fair to lead him on. But how to make it plain that marriage definitely wasn't in her plans?

"Grace, look at me. I truly intended to see you but events overtook me. You and I need to have a good talk. Preferably today. Before that we must visit Mrs Craddock."

"I can't see any point in going to see Mrs Craddock now." Grace compressed her lips into a thin line and glowered at him.

"I was coming to that. Have you heard from Miss Vaughan?"

Grace shook her head. "I haven't spoken to Lucy since the Gilberts' ball."

"Miss Vaughan's father is insisting she and her mother retire to the country, immediately. She contacted Mrs Craddock, knowing you were distracted by this threat to me. Mrs Craddock and two of her friends have agreed to run the employment agency and help with the orphanage. Mrs Craddock met Miss Vaughan at the orphanage as there was a lot to discuss with Mrs Baker. She asked Miss Vaughan to get a message to you to call and mentioned she had important information for me. Mr Lovell arrived after Mrs Craddock left. It seems he is a friend of Miss Vaughan's brother and well known to her."

"Yes, he is. Lucy has always been friendly with him."

Angus nodded."

Mr Lovell said Miss Vaughan was in quite a taking but wouldn't tell him what was wrong. He offered to deliver Mrs Craddock's message and set off to find you at the Cathlay's house."

Grace's hand flew to her mouth. "Oh dear. I do hope they haven't had bad news. In that case I must go and see Mrs Craddock this morning and see what she knows."

"Exactly. Which is why I arranged to escort you. Mrs Craddock said that Miss Vaughan seemed upset and she and her mother were leaving for their country estate first thing this morning."

Grace chewed at her bottom lip. "That's worrying. I'm surprised Lucy didn't at least send me a note. She must have been upset."

"It does seem strange. Perhaps Mrs Craddock will have

enough information for you to work out what's happened."

"Hmm. Perhaps. But what about safety. You're still a target."

Angus grinned at her. "There's no need to worry. Fletcher suggested using Gillard, my new valet, as a bodyguard. He and Jamie will ride behind us, together with one of Luke's grooms. They will be as inconspicuous as possible. Sam will take the Tiger's seat."

Grace was momentarily distracted. She smiled. "Oh of course, I'd forgotten about Freddie Gillard being so fearsome when he wants to be. I'm not sure how much use his boxing skills are likely to be though."

"Fletcher says he's a good shot. All three of them will be armed and Luke's groom is an older man."

Grace frowned. "That's something I suppose. I'd feel happier if you stayed out of harm's way until your Bow Street men were in place."

"I absolutely refuse to cower away hidden from view. Besides, Mrs Craddock also said her cousin and son, from Edinburgh, are staying with them. She is arranging for the son to be available to meet me. He's the source of information about Lord Oulsnam. It will help us to hear from him directly."

Grace gave him a grudging smile and sighed. "I suppose we can't waste any opportunity to find out about our suspects. I wonder if my greys are both fit now."

"I consulted Sam this morning. The injured one has recovered well, but there is still a mark on his shoulder. Sam has arranged to have Luke's greys brought here. They should be hitching them up to your phaeton around now. There is one more thing before we go."

Angus leaned towards her and pressed his lips to hers. Grace gasped with surprise, allowing him to deepen the kiss. Logic told her to pull back instantly. Logic was no match for the hot spiral of longing his kiss ignited within her. She leaned into him and Angus put an arm around her and drew her close, until she was almost sitting on his lap. Grace closed her eyes and kissed him back. Her body didn't seem to belong to her. Her entire focus was on Angus and the way he made her feel. So much for not leading him on. She ought to stop this now. Instead, her treacherous arms wound their way around his neck.

Angus gave a satisfied sounding sigh. His arm around her waist hugged her tighter still and his free hand came up to caress her torso. Grace arched backwards and groaned. Angus's hand stilled until she relaxed against him and deepened the kiss. His thumb caressed the edge of her breast and waves of sensation ran through her. He took the whole of her breast in his hand and Grace caught her breath. If this feeling of heated expectation travelling down the length of her body was lust it explained so much. She was powerless to resist her own longing for more and wriggled across his thighs so she was seated completely in his lap. Angus groaned and pulled back from their kiss.

"You'll be the death of me, Grace." His voice sounded strained and he was breathing heavily. "We must stop now or someone will come in and you will have no option but to marry me. My offer still stands but I want it to be your freely given choice."

Grace licked lips that still tingled from his kiss. "I know, but I was enjoying that."

Angus grinned at her. "I didn't think you were indifferent to me."

Grace stiffened. "Just because I find you attractive it doesn't mean that I want to marry you."

"Why not?"

"You know why not. Like you, I value my freedom. Would you want to marry if it meant that you had to give up your claim to a legal identity of your own? My attraction to you simply proves that women have the same urges as men. And don't try and tell me that you wanted to marry every woman you have ever made love to!"

Chapter Eighteen.

There was a sound of an arrival in the hall. Angus rested a finger against Grace's lips. "Hush we'll talk about this later. That sounds like your brother."

Angus averted his gaze as Grace straightened her bodice. He tidied his cravat back into what he hoped was a reasonable resemblance to how it had started the day. There was time to take a few deep breaths before the door opened and Luke entered.

Luke sank into a chair and grinned. "I'm not sure I approve of the closed door."

Grace groaned. "Oh, for goodness's sake, Luke. Aunt Theo shut the door. It was nothing to do with us."

"I'll take your word for it. Where does this Mrs Craddock live? I thought I'd ride in that direction by a circular route and take up a hidden position before you arrive."

"That might be one of your better ideas, Luke." Grace rested her chin on her cupped hands, with her elbows on the table.

Angus glanced at Grace. Apart from a slightly flushed countenance there was nothing in her appearance to suggest what they had been about. It was fortunate he had resisted the urge to run his fingers through her hair. One thing was for sure, he didn't need to worry about Grace being physically attracted to him. On the other hand, her aversion to marriage was proving more intractable than he had imagined. There would be time to think about that later. He forced his mind to concentrate on the matter in hand and smiled at Luke.

"That's kind of you, Luke. Just be careful you don't fall over Jamie, Gillard and one of your grooms following us." Angus shook his head and sighed. "I can't believe all this is necessary on the streets of London. But I suppose there is every chance of yet another attack on me."

Luke snorted. "Another attack is a certainty if you ask me. I ought to try and persuade you to wait for Fletcher to come back with a few Bow Street runners. But I learned a long time ago that there's no point fighting a lost battle. I did a certain amount of intelligence work myself in the army, I'll keep a close watch, don't worry about me giving away the position of your other guards. You might be better to have one of them openly following you. Otherwise, it will make anyone watching you suspicious enough to look for hidden guards."

Angus nodded. "That's a fair point. Probably best if we have Jamie follow us openly. He may well have been seen with us before in his role as Grace's groom."

"I was going to suggest Jamie." Luke turned towards Grace. "Strange about Lucy Vaughan being summoned home at such short notice. What could be so vital that she and her mother have dashed back? Bertie Lovell seemed distinctly puzzled. Still, that's neither here nor there, your phaeton should be here soon."

"Yes. I'm concerned that Lucy's father may have been taken ill. Angus thinks she may have said more to Mrs Craddock. If not, perhaps I'll have a note delivered later that some hard-pressed groom has forgotten about. I had better run upstairs and change for a drive."

Angus suppressed a groan as Grace almost ran out of the room, avoiding her brother's gaze. Luke was too astute not to realise he had walked in on something. Sure enough, Luke rose and slapped a hand down on his shoulder.

"I was hoping I would be able to wish you happy when I saw Grace's flushed face when I came in. From her tumultuous expression as she ran out, I'm very much afraid that would be premature. I'm sure she is strongly attracted to you but father brought her up almost as a son."

Luke sighed heavily and hunched his shoulders, the picture of guilt. "Which was my fault for staying estranged from him. Grace is the one to suffer. Promise me you'll keep trying."

Angus grinned. "I might have guessed you would know exactly how things stand between us. Marriage was the last thing on my mind, but then I got to know Grace."

"These things have a habit of creeping up on a man. I hope you can change her mind about marriage."

"I'm determined to win her. I didn't help my cause by a clumsy proposal at the Gilberts' ball the other night, when I felt I might have compromised her. Her refusal did make me realise how strong my own feelings for her are." He banged a fist on the table. "If only I could find out who is trying to kill me, I might have more time to court her properly."

Luke squeezed his shoulder. "Don't worry, I'm sure we'll have them soon. One thing though. Don't you think you should have asked my permission before chasing my sister?"

Angus leaned back in his chair and roared with laughter. "Absolutely not if I'm to have any chance of winning Grace over to accepting my proposal!"

It was Luke's turn to laugh. "It sounds like you've got her

measure. You'll get there. And, for what it's worth, you have my blessing."

Angus drew in a deep breath. Was Luke as happy as he sounded? There was such a discrepancy between his and Grace's upbringings. "Are you sure about that? I've been brought up amongst a family of merchants, even though my father was the son of a duke. I'm not of your world."

"All to the good if you ask me. Kitty's fortune was made largely in insurance and her brother, Edward, is determined to make a career in business. He sees it as the future and I suspect he's right. Come on. Let's see if this phaeton is ready."

Out in the hallway the sounds of footsteps running down the main stairs made Angus look up. Grace raced down the last few steps to join them, wearing the blue velvet ensemble he had first seen her in. Her cloak billowed around her, revealing glimpses of the figure-hugging gown of the same colour underneath it. She had a figure that was well worth hugging. He banished the picture that thought conjured up. He ought to say something instead of standing there staring at her like a clodpole, but words were beyond him. He was dimly aware of Luke strolling out of the front door with a grin on his face. Grace came to a halt on the last stair, with their eyes on the same level.

She gave him a hard stare and chewed at her lower lip. "I still think you should wait until you have Fletcher available before you venture out. You seem to thrive on taking risks."

With the spell of enchantment broken, Angus glared at her. "Your brother might take exception to that. You said yourself that he's a brilliant shot. I'm taking a calculated risk. I absolutely refuse to cower away from whoever is pursuing me."

Grace descended the last stair and stamped a foot. "Men. You were going out with those untried boys and one older groom as your only guards, before Luke arrived."

"The only way we are going to find out who is my enemy is to draw them out." He raised his eyebrows at her. "I'd be prepared to hazard a tidy sum that you would be going out now if you were in my shoes. And before you say you are anyway, I was going to suggest that it might be safer for you to stay here this morning but you ran away before I could get a word in."

"I didn't run away. I simply didn't want to keep the horses waiting. Besides you haven't had any lessons in driving yet, apart from the fact that you have already spoken to Mrs Craddock."

"You've got me there. Truly, I was having second thoughts about driving out with you. I don't mind taking risks with my own safety but I'm not happy compromising yours."

Graces eyes flashed at him. "I see. It's perfectly acceptable for a man to risk his safety to catch a murderer but not for a woman to do the same."

Angus almost groaned aloud. He was getting into deep waters here. "That's not what I meant."

Graces voice rose. "What did you mean then?"

"Simply that this is my fight and it's not fair to keep drawing you into it."

"You're perfectly prepared to let Luke help you. Why not me?"

"Luke is trained for this sort of thing."

"I'm the woman who saved your life a few days ago. That's enough training as far as I'm concerned. I'm coming and that's all there is to it. What would Mrs Craddock think if you turned up without me?"

"There's no answer to that is there." It seemed he was well and truly beaten.

Angus pressed his lips together and since the butler was nowhere to be seen, walked to the door and held it open for her with a shake of his head. Grace marched out of the house, with her head in the air and her back rigidly straight. Angus ran a hand through his hair, he had upset her. There was nothing he could do about it. He felt so protective towards her it was impossible to hide it. And yet he could see her point. He hated to be fussed over himself, so why should it be any different simply because Grace was a woman?

He hurried to catch up with her. The phaeton was waiting. Angus managed to reach her side before Jamie could give her a hand up. The look she gave him would have frozen ice, but then she gave him a smile and put her hand in his. Only he was close enough to see that the smile didn't reach her eyes. His hand closed around hers and a blaze of excitement fizzed through him. No woman had ever had this effect on him. She climbed deftly into the phaeton, with very little help from him. He jumped up beside her. Sam handed her the reins and climbed into the tiger seat behind. He leaned forward until his head was almost between them.

"Lord Enstone said to carry on. He's gone on ahead," Sam whispered, so quietly that Angus had to strain to hear him.

Grace gave Sam a genuine smile. What did he have to do to have her smiling at him like that?

"Thank you, Sam. Jamie," Grace raised her voice, "I'll wait for you to mount up and then we'll be off."

"Yes, Miss." Jamie touched his cap and jumped into the saddle.

Grace turned to Angus with a beaming smile, as if they were

the best friends. "Are you ready, Your Grace?"

The scent of violets and lavender wafted across Angus and he caught his breath. "I am indeed."

The gazes locked for a brief second. Grace studied him quizzically before giving her horses the office to move. Lord, she hadn't guessed how much she aroused him had she? He looked around, pretending to be studying the passing scene, with his thoughts focused on Grace. He closed his eyes for a moment. He needed to concentrate. Someone who intended them harm could be lurking around any street corner. Not only would Grace be safer if she stayed at home but so would he, with her safely out of harm's way. At least then he might be able to concentrate fully.

He set his jaw and frowned. It was good to know that Luke was somewhere about, but Grace was right, he should have waited for the Bow Street runners. Gillard and Jamie were good lads and streetwise, but no substitute for hardened professionals. The thought pulled him out of his reverie. Now was not the time for self-indulgence. Concentrate he would, no matter how much effort it took.

Grace seemed disinclined to talk. The roads were fairly busy but, somehow, Angus didn't think that was the reason for her lack of conversation. He kept a smile pinned on his face and used the time to glance around as if taking in the view. There was no sign of Luke, which didn't surprise him. Apart from one brief glance of a young man who might be Freddie Gillard, the other two seemed to have blended into the background as well. As long as they hadn't lost them. He knew a moment's panic. They knew the route and would surely simply follow it if they had dropped back and lost sight of them.

They slowed to pass a cart and Angus looked back. He

spotted a horse and rider who could possibly be Ralph Medley. They were too far away to be sure. Grace negotiated the cart and took a left turn shortly afterwards. Angus waited for a few moments before leaning back in his seat, with an arm loosely around the seat behind Grace. He turned his head enough to check if the same horse and rider were still following them. He sat up straighter. There they were and the rider could be Ralph. He searched from side to side but there was no sign of Luke or the others. He slipped his free hand into the pocket of his coat and was reassured by the feel of cold metal. He had deliberately worn one of his old coats so that there was room to carry a pair of small pistols in the pockets without them being obvious. His arm tightened around Grace.

She glanced his way with a puzzled expression. "You're far too discreet to turn amorous out in the street, so why are you holding me so tightly?"

"It was an instinctive reaction to the knowledge that we are being followed by Ralph Medley. At some distance, but I'm pretty sure that it's him." Angus carefully slid his arm from around her and patted his second pocket. I'm carrying pistols. That said, I can't see any sign of Luke or the others."

"I'm sure they are somewhere around. This is far too busy a road for Ralph to try anything."

"At the moment he is too far away, if he intends us harm. The would-be murderer, or someone working for him, injured one of your horses with the hope of injuring us on a similar road to this."

There was a cough from Sam on the tiger's seat behind them. "There's a cove on a big dark horse been following us most of the way, Duke. Is that the man you mean?"

"It sounds like the same one, Sam. Can you watch without

him knowing?"

"Of course, Duke. I can sit a bit sideways on this seat if I want to. I'll let you know if he gets any closer."

Angus grimaced. Why hadn't he thought to involve Sam from the start?

"I don't suppose you've seen any sign of Lord Enstone or the others, have you?"

"Freddie isn't far behind." Sam laughed. "Freddie is dressed really rough like. Don't know where they got that horse he's riding from. It needs feeding up. He's quite close but don't look now. Not sure about the other man. Lord Enstone turned off a few minutes ago down a road that leads to another going the same way. He'll be waiting at the next junction."

Grace leaned closer to Angus, that perfume she was wearing was delectable.

She lowered her voice to a whisper. "It seems I under-estimated these boys. Although I expect Luke was behind Freddie's disguise. I hope he's going to take that poor horse in permanently and get him in better condition, if he's as rough as Sam says."

Angus rubbed the back of his neck. "That's generous of you to say. I apologise for my error of judgement. I shouldn't have put you, or Sam and Jamie, in harm's way like this."

"We're well protected, I've decided you were probably right. I wonder if it is Ralph Medley. We still haven't found the man he was talking to the other night."

"I'm hiring as many Bow Street Runners as Cathlay can secure for me. I'll have them tracing contacts of Ralph Medley."

Angus felt a tap on his shoulder and Sam's head appeared between them.

"If you ask me, Duke, you need a spy. I bet there is someone working for this Medley cove happy to do it for the right money."

"I'm sure you're right, Sam. I'll get the runners onto it."

Sam tapped his shoulder again. "Too slow, Duke. Why not ask Lord Enstone's grooms? I noticed grooms always seem to go to the same inns."

Grace gave a soft chuckle and Angus shook his head.

"I think there will come a time when we will need to train you for a better job than being my tiger, young man. That is an excellent suggestion."

"No thanks. There's no better job than being your tiger." Sam sat back on his seat. "The cove on the black horse is getting closer."

Angus risked a glance behind him. He turned back quickly. "Yes, it's definitely Ralph Medley. I have to say I'm surprised. At one stage I did suspect him, but despite that conversation we overheard I was reassured by meeting him. I'm not the judge of character I thought I was."

"Just because he's following us, doesn't mean Ralph Medley is our man," Grace said. "This is a busy route. It could be a coincidence."

Angus pulled out a pistol and held it on the seat between him and Grace. She must have felt the cold metal against her because she looked down.

"Angus, I hope you haven't cocked that pistol. One bump in the road and I'm going to get shot in the leg."

He laughed out loud. "Of course not. I may not have spent any time in the army but I do know how to handle a pistol. Although not as effectively as you can."

Angus felt another tap on his shoulder. He turned towards

Sam.

"He's still getting closer." Sam turned back. "I hope Lord Enstone appears soon. I don't care what Miss Bamford says, he's been following us for a long time."

"There's no need to be nervous, Sam if anything happens keep your head down."

Sam snorted. "What's the point of saving my own skin if anything happens to you? I'd lose my job."

Angus felt Grace shaking next to him. Remorse ran through him at putting her in such a dangerous situation that even Grace was scared, until he realised she was actually trying not to laugh.

"Don't worry, Sam," Grace said. "If anything happens to the Duke, I'll make sure you have a job."

A rider came out of a side turning on the left and pulled across them.

Grace slowed her horses slightly. "You can breathe again, Sam. I think my brother is about to intercept Mr Medley."

Sam gasped. "Well, I never. That horse His Lordship is riding is a tricksy one. How did they do that? They've turned right around until they're upsides Mr Medley. It looks like His Lordship is chatting with him."

"Keep watching, Sam, in case he has some people we'd rather not meet waiting for us," Grace said. "If he is our murderer, he's incredibly daring. It's obvious we will have protection when we're out and about."

Angus shrugged. "It does seem risky to be seen anywhere near us if we were to be attacked. I don't think it's him. He had a reputation for careful calculation and avoiding unnecessary risk in the army."

"Hmm. I wonder. Risky or clever? I'm not ready to rule out

Mr Medley just yet. There are some people who resent not being the one in a family with the title. I've seen it several times."

"If it had been possible to do it without leaving ownership of the estates in abeyance, he would have been welcome to the title."

"Couldn't you have given him the estates as well if you felt like that?"

"I believe that under English law I could have renounced the title but then I would have had no say about the estates." Angus spoke quietly so Sam wouldn't hear. "I saw no honourable option I could take to avoid shouldering the responsibility for the dukedom. So many people depend upon it for their living."

"It's as well it did come to you. Mr Medley doesn't seem the sort of man to have much interest in safeguarding the dukedom's estates."

"As it happens, he might have been better than me at it. My Scottish man of business told me that Ralph's father took over managing the estates for the Duke of Evesham years ago and was very efficient. Ralph is likely to have absorbed a lot of that knowledge."

Angus looked all around and could see no sign of Ralph or Luke. "Where did they go, Sam?"

"They turned off at the last junction, still talking. Don't worry. I can still see Freddie Gillard not far behind us. Jamie has caught up with us, not sure where he disappeared to, and that other groom is somewhere in front. I'll shout if I see anything odd."

"Good man."

Angus glanced at Grace. She seemed more relaxed but absorbed in her thoughts. At least she had stopped being angry with him for now.

"A penny for your thoughts, Grace."

She smiled at him. Was that the first time today?

"Mr Medley seems well off for a man whose father was an estate manager. Did one or other of the recent dukes leave his father money?" Grace said, in a soft voice.

"I don't think so. My Scottish man of business, McGregor, did say that Ralph was left a huge sum by a childless relative of his mother."

"That would explain his prosperous appearance then."

"And give him less motive to kill me."

"True."

"You still look puzzled."

"Oh, it's nothing."

"Nothing?"

"If you must know, I wondered why a lawyer would need a man of business. Then I remembered you said your father had received a generous inheritance."

Would Grace be put off if she knew the full extent of his links to trade? If she was, she wouldn't be the woman for him, regardless of how painful that would be. His jaw tightened. He had to tell her the truth.

"Yes, he did and he increased that at least tenfold. I don't know the half of his business interests. He loved investing in trading ventures and was very good at it. McGregor deals with all that for me." Angus grinned. "He sent regular reports to me in Edinburgh but I was always too busy to read them."

Grace laughed. "You'll have to mend your ways. I hope you've got some good managers in."

The mention of trade didn't seem to have worried her. That was something. Father was right and trade was the future. He was determined to keep investing.

"McGregor is superb. I've left him in charge of all my Scottish interests and simply employed the man Luke recommended for everything to do with the ducal estates. He's sorting out agents for me. I believe at least one has retired. If I have more than one son there will be something for the later ones to inherit."

A dull flush coloured Grace's cheeks. Angus closed his eyes and breathed deeply. She was a long way from indifferent to him if the mention of his potential offspring could have that effect on her. There was hope for him yet.

Chapter Nineteen

Grace kept her gaze fixed firmly on the road ahead. Heat flooded through her at the thought of what conceiving children with Angus would entail. She knew the theory of course, Aunt Theo had explained the mechanics of the process in meticulous detail, decrying the fashion for young women being sent to the marriage bed in complete ignorance. What she couldn't comprehend, and never would unless she changed her mind about marriage, was what the process felt like. Which had never troubled her overmuch until she had met Angus.

There had been men she found interesting who were interested in her, of course. She had always been quick to remove herself from the vicinity of anyone who might cut up her peace by becoming too interesting, as soon as she felt a tug of attraction to them. The threat to Angus's life had left her feeling honour bound to help, despite feeling drawn to him ever since they had met. He was related to Kitty after all. The problem was, the attraction she felt to Angus was a lot stronger than a tug. At times it felt like a tidal wave that she was powerless to resist.

Could she cope with being married? It would be hard to accept becoming the legal property of a husband, even one as sensible and enlightened as Angus. She loved her work for the orphanage and couldn't imagine not being able to study all the things that interested her as and when she wished. But loss of her independence had to be balanced against the dreadful sense of loss that she felt at the prospect of Angus having children with another woman. Surely that would fade quickly once the threat had been eliminated and she could distance herself from him?

After the way father had withdrawn from the world for years when Mama had died, Luke had been so badly damaged by the process it had nearly ruined his relationship with Kitty. There was the worry of how she would react if anything happened to a husband. Another reason not to marry, but if she gave up Angus now wouldn't that feel as bad? Perhaps not, since she had known him for such a short time. Once they had found Angus's enemy, Grace's usual tactic of keeping well away ought to work. Although, there would be the odd occasion when family events would throw them together.

Her head started to ache. This would never do. She needed to stay alert for any trouble. Worrying away at her dilemma would have to wait until she was alone later. She studied the road ahead. At last, they were close to the Craddocks' house.

Sam tapped her shoulder. "Is there much farther to go?"

Grace glanced back at him and smiled. "No, we're nearly there."

Sam rolled his eyes. "Thank the stars for that. All this watching for bad men is wearing me out."

"I thought you enjoyed a challenge, Sam," Angus said.

"Not when I need to stop you being killed. Where does Mrs Craddock live?"

Grace laughed. "You will soon be able to relax. The Craddocks have a house in Half Moon Street."

"Is that where all the lawyers live in London?" asked Angus.

"No, not at all. It's a fairly fashionable address. I believe that Mrs Craddock is well connected but her father was a clergyman and they weren't well off. Her husband has built up their fortune. Apart from getting a start from one of his wife's relatives, Mr Craddock is a self-made man. He's an attorney but a good one. I suspect he earns more than most of the best barristers."

Angus grinned. "I wouldn't be surprised. I pay the two advocates I left in charge of my Edinburgh law firm a regular salary, besides paying the fees for every young man they train. Criminal cases often don't pay well and I want them to be able to take on a proportion of worthy cases for a reduced fee, or free if necessary."

Jamie rode past them and touched his cap to Grace. "I'll have the door open before you pull up, Miss Bamford."

Grace watched him reach the junction with Piccadilly and turn left. Grace chewed at her bottom lip and glanced to her right, leaning forward slightly.

"Can you see movement in the bushes to our right?" Her voice rose in pitch. "We could be in the basket now if anyone is waiting to ambush us in Green Park. I should have taken a circular route to avoid Piccadilly."

Angus's arm brushed her side. "I can't see anyone rushing out of the park, but I have my pistols out." He sounded perfectly calm.

Grace's own heart was thudding. Two carriages coming towards them forced her to keep her eyes on the road. As the last one passed the tension in her neck was almost unbearable. A movement to her right drew her attention. Gillard and Luke's groom rode past and pulled up after the turn off into Half Moon Street. They wheeled their horses around, until one faced towards the park and the other back the way they had come. Grace gave a long sigh and relaxed into her seat. She turned her horses into Half Moon Street.

Jamie was waiting for them in front of a tall town house of pale, honey-coloured bricks. The black front door shone with fresh paint and the brass work gleamed. The door was opened when the phaeton pulled up. Freddie Gillard dismounted and took the reins from her. She felt Angus's weight shift. He jumped down and held out his hand to help her alight before the footman who had opened the door could reach them. Grace grasped his hand and closed her eyes for a moment. Her body seemed to hum with excitement at the slightest touch from him. This was getting wearing. She opened her eyes to see him smiling up at her.

"You're frozen with fear. You're quite safe now." Angus grinned.

Grace lifted her chin and marched to the door, without saying a word. He didn't need to know that it was his nearness that had held her spellbound. He had even changed his cologne. This one had the distinct tang of American cedar. The footman led them into a pleasant sitting room decorated in creams and blues. The window looked out onto a small city garden. Comfortable sofas were dotted about, interspersed with chairs. The Craddock family lived in good style. Mrs Craddock rose to greet them.

"Thank you for coming. I couldn't leave the children all morning and Miss Vaughan left a message for you, Miss Bamford. Do please take a seat. I'll ring for some tea."

Angus smiled at Mrs Craddock. "That would be most

welcome."

Grace headed towards a single chair but Angus put a hand on her elbow and guided her to the sofa opposite to where Mrs Craddock had been sitting. Grace resisted the urge to pull her elbow away and kept a smile on her face. She sank into the sofa as far away from Angus as she possibly could. He definitely had a grin on his face before he looked down. Grace ignored it and addressed Mrs Craddock.

"What did Lucy have to say, Mrs Craddock? She gave me no indication that she was planning a trip, I do hope there's no illness in the family."

"She gave me a rather cryptic message I'm hoping you'll understand it. Something about being summoned by her father who is entertaining unexpectedly. He insisted that Miss Vaughan and her mother return home immediately. There was no mention of any illness but Lucy seemed quite agitated. Not her usual calm self at all."

Grace wrinkled her nose. "How strange. I perhaps shouldn't say this, but Mr and Mrs Vaughan lead separate lives as a rule, they don't get on at all. I think that's one of the reasons Lucy is determined never to marry. Her parents have not been a good example. At least no one is ill. I'm sure Lucy will write to me as soon as she can."

Grace thought hard. There was a lot to do with the orphanage and then there was Angus to help. Hadn't something been said about Mrs Craddock offering to help with the new employment agency?

Mrs Craddock laughed. "Miss Vaughan clearly wasn't happy about having to see her father, I can see there's no love lost between them. I told her not to worry about the orphanage. I have two sensible friends who have offered to help with what needs doing there. Between the three of us I'm sure we can work with Mrs Baker to organise the new employment exchange for you. And, indeed, anything else that needs doing. I can see you are tied up helping His Grace at the moment."

"Thank you, Mrs Craddock. That would be extremely helpful." Grace studied the Aubusson carpet on the floor and rubbed at the back of her neck. Being coupled with Angus in this way was inevitably going to lead to speculation about their relationship. She was going to have to make a decision soon. For now, she would do well to concentrate on the matter in hand.

"We have no idea how long it will take to find out who wishes me ill," Angus said. "Thank you for taking on the role at the orphanage. Will it need to be ratified by the rest of your committee, Grace?"

"I had already notified them that Mrs Craddock was going to help, I think it can wait until our next committee meeting to explain that she is taking over the project, at least for now."

"That's good. We've already made a start. Now the other thing I wanted to talk to you about was Lord Oulsnam's intentions. My cousin's son will be here soon. His mother married a Scot. He has recently finished a degree at Edinburgh University in law and was about to start training as an advocate. Now his father has died and my cousin would like to return to England. They're staying with us at the moment."

Angus's eyes gleamed and he smiled at Grace. "This is the young man who is the source of Mrs Craddock's information on Lord Oulsnam."

"Yes. Duncan should be here at any moment so you can speak to him yourself. We only have one son, Andrew, the rest of our children are girls. Andrew is an outdoor type and his godfather has recently made him his heir. He will have a sizeable estate one day." Mrs Craddock smiled, happily.

Grace smiled back. Who could blame her for being so pleased for her son?

"Mr Craddock's partner has no sons to follow in the business. They have both taken to young Duncan since he arrived yesterday. They're giving him a trial in the business, with a view to taking it over one day if it goes well. He seems an intelligent young man."

There was a knock at the door and Esther came in carrying a tea tray. She gave Grace a quick grin before laying the tea tray on the side table next to Mrs Craddock. Mrs Craddock smiled at her.

"Esther is doing very well indeed for me. In fact, my housekeeper has suggested we train her to take over when she retires in a few years' time."

"All our girls are well trained, but I can honestly say Esther is the most quick-witted we've ever had. I'm not surprised you're so pleased with her."

Esther bobbed a curtsy. "Thank you, Miss Bamford. I appreciate everything the orphanage has done for me."

"I'm delighted to see you doing so well, Esther."

Mrs Craddock laughed. "So am I. It's hard to find good people. Duncan and his mother are having this house soon, if Duncan takes the position in my husband's firm. We're moving to something much bigger. Esther will be housekeeper of a good-sized establishment one day."

Angus smiled at Esther. "I hope the young people I'm taking on from the orphanage will do as well as you."

"Thank you, Your Grace." Esther gave him a fleeting smile. "I hope you don't think me impertinent, but there's something

I've heard I believe I ought to tell you about."

"If you think it important then I would like to hear it."

"The thing is," Esther studied the floor and shuffled her feet.

"His Grace won't be cross with you whatever you want to tell him," Grace said. "There is no need to be nervous."

Esther nodded and squared her shoulders. "An elderly society lady lives next door and I've become friendly with Jemima, her lady's maid, ever since we bumped in to each other after being sent to the same shop to collect things."

Grace watched as Angus waited patiently. He showed every sign of being a good employer and knew how to handle young people.

Esther took a deep breath and continued. "The lady is sociable and is always out and about despite her age. She came back the other evening from a ball and told Jemima that there was trouble brewing for the new duke. That must be you, mustn't it?"

"I would imagine so." He glanced at Grace.

"Yes. It must be you. There are no other new dukes this season to my knowledge. If there was another one in London, we would have been bound to hear about him."

Angus nodded. "Did Jemima give you any more information?"

Esther looked at Mrs Craddock. "I don't want you to think I spend all my time gossiping."

"I'm sure you don't, Esther. You were right to find out more since you know His Grace is a particular friend of Miss Bamford. Tell us everything you know."

Grace lowered her head to hide her face, in case she was blushing at being linked with Angus.

"The old lady is acquainted with the Countess of Hedburgh. Lady Hedburgh told her that she fears her husband is losing his reason. The Earl has some sort of grudge against the Duke. He's been away for a few days and she was hoping he had calmed down. Then someone mentioned the Duke of Evesham in his hearing and he got so angry she thought he might have an apoplexy. He marched off, swearing revenge. Jemima didn't know what his grudge is."

Angus huffed out a breath. "Now that is interesting. You were at the orphanage that day I was attacked outside, so you must know we're worried someone is targeting me. I'll have my people investigate the Earl, without mentioning any names. Thank you for telling me."

"Yes. You did the right thing, Esther," Mrs Craddock said. "When Mr Mackay arrives send him in here, please."

"Yes, Mrs Craddock." Esther bobbed a curtsy and withdrew.

She returned a few minutes later with a tall young man. "Mr Mackay, to see His Grace, the Duke of Evesham."

Esther slipped out of the room and Duncan Mackay bowed towards Angus. His face flamed red, emphasising the auburn highlights in his brown hair.

"Delighted to meet you, Your Grace."

Angus appeared decidedly uncomfortable at Mr Mackay's formality. Grace shook her head slightly. He was going to have to get used to that sort of reaction. His modesty was one of the things she liked about him.

Angus stood and shook the young man's hand. "There is no need to stand on ceremony. I believe we've already met at least once in Edinburgh."

Mr Mackay's face flamed even redder. "Yes, Your Grace. Two of my university friends have joined your old firm. We met before you left Edinburgh."

"I remember now. I hope they're both enjoying their new positions." Angus waved him to the chair next to Mrs Craddock and sat back down next to Grace.

"Absolutely, Your Grace. They're very happy there."

Angus laughed. "You wouldn't tell me if they weren't! Are they the source of your information?"

Mackay nodded and his expression sobered. "Yes, they are. Lord Oulsnam has been making threats to your cousin. He wants his shipping firm and what Lord Oulsnam wants he usually gets. Fortunately, we don't see him personally in Edinburgh, only his agent." Mackay scowled. "Not a man I would trust to act honourably."

"Mrs Craddock told me as much yesterday. Do you have any more details?"

"Not really, but I can tell you that your cousin is standing firm with the backing of your man of business. He doesn't seem the sort to be intimidated."

"I'm glad he's consulted Mr McGregor."

Mackay flushed again and fished in his pocket. "Mr McGregor asked me to deliver a note to you as soon as you arrived. I would have delivered it sooner but it slipped my mind, with the excitement of being met with the offer of a trial in Mr Craddock's business."

Mrs Craddock smiled at him and patted his arm. "It's not your fault Duncan, what with Mr Craddock taking you off straight away to meet his partner." She turned to Angus. "Duncan rushed back to tell me about the note yesterday as soon as he could. The bulk of his luggage didn't arrive until this morning and the note was with it. Which is why I thought it best if you called today, hoping we could give you the note in person."

Angus quickly read through the note. "It doesn't tell us much more but Mr McGregor is asking for us to send someone not known in Edinburgh to help. My instinct to send Fallon up was right it seems."

Grace frowned. "Could Lord Oulsnam be your enemy do you think?"

"Perhaps, but I don't see what his motive could be. His quarrel is with Rory."

"It's such a puzzle." Grace glanced at Angus with a grimace.

"I know. Thank you for bringing the message from Edinburgh, Mr Mackay."

Mackay inclined his head. "It was my pleasure, Your Grace." He looked at his cousin. "I promised to get back to Mr Craddock as soon as possible."

"Of course, Duncan. I'll see you at dinner."

Mackay flushed. "I don't mean to be rude, Miss Bamford."

Grace smiled at him. "We appreciate you taking the time to see us Mr Mackay."

The men shook hands and Mackay bowed his way out.

Angus sat down and rubbed at the back of his neck. "An estimable young man, Mrs Craddock. I am very grateful indeed for his assistance and I'm sure I can rely on his discretion." He grinned. "I can't get used to people being overawed by my presence. I'm still the same man I was before I inherited the title."

"You'll notice it less as time goes on, Your Grace. We have all been careful to say nothing of your current difficulties to outsiders and I impressed that on Duncan last night. He assured me that he hadn't mentioned the note, or the conversation he had with his friends about your cousin, to anyone but us. He can be relied upon to keep his own counsel."

"I don't doubt it, Mrs Craddock. I suppose we had better be going now, Grace?"

Grace nodded. "Thank you so much for your help, Mrs Craddock. At least you have put my mind at rest about Lucy. It's good of you to step in to help at the orphanage."

"We're looking forward to it, Miss Bamford."

"I'm happy for you to consult me at any time. I'd like to meet your friends as soon as I can. Once His Grace's problem is resolved I'll be able to turn my attention back to the orphanage."

"Thank you, Miss Bamford."

Mrs Craddock didn't quite meet her gaze and a smile played about her lips. Grace closed her eyes for a second. Not only was Mrs Craddock mentally pairing her off with Angus, she had them marked down for the altar it seemed. The sooner this was all sorted and she could distance herself from Angus the happier she would be. Once she was away from him, she would soon forget the physical response he elicited in her.

Chapter Twenty

Angus tucked the note into his pocket and escorted Grace out to the waiting phaeton. She pulled away from him and accepted a hand up into the phaeton from Jamie, who looked at him for approval. He gave a small nod. Grace was definitely trying to avoid him. It was no good speculating what maggot had got into her head. All he could do was obey his instinct to give her time to work her feelings out without pressing her. He climbed in beside her. For now, he needed to concentrate on keeping her safe on the drive home. It wouldn't help his cause with Grace, but it was time to work with Luke and avoid being in her company too much. It was the best way to lessen the risk to her.

There was no sign of Luke, but Gillard and Luke's groom were mounted by the phaeton. Jamie's horse was tied to the back, whilst he held the greys still. Sam tapped Angus on the shoulder.

"Jamie's worked out a different route that wanders around a bit. He didn't want us going past the park again. We're to follow him, Duke," Sam said in a conspiratorial tone.

Grace turned to glance at Sam. "That's a good idea."

Sam jumped down and went to the horses' heads.

Grace held the horses steady until Jamie had mounted and

Sam had regained his perch behind them. She loosened the reins and called to them to move on. The carriage set off at a spanking trot. Grace controlled the high-spirited pair better than anyone Angus knew. He felt in his pocket for a pistol and his hand closed on the note. A glance at Grace showed her stony faced, staring straight ahead. His best course of action was to act normally. Oulsnam was a puzzle.

Angus leaned closer to her. "I'm worried about my cousin. Mr McGregor never panics and he says in his note that Lord Oulsnam is a serious threat to Rory's business. He must want a shipping company for something nefarious. I wish he had chosen a different one to chase."

"Smuggling do you think? Wouldn't an English company be better for that?"

"Not necessarily. A Scottish company might give him better cover for free-trading. Rory's company is doing so well his ships often do trips down to London." Angus laughed." I still can't believe I managed to get lost walking from the docks to the orphanage."

A ghost of a smile flitted across Grace's face. That was encouraging.

"Hmm. If you're right then Lord Oulsnam is nothing more than a crooked business man. I expect his wife simply wanted to warn you that your cousin's business was a target for one of his murky deals." Grace sighed. "Which leaves us no farther forward."

"It's all coming back to Ralph, isn't it?"

"That's true. I wonder what's happened to him. I expect Luke will have trailed him somewhere."

"Luke said to wait for him at your aunt's house."

Grace nodded and her spine stiffened. She seemed angry

about him going in with her. She would probably disappear to her room to change and stay there to avoid him. Winning Grace over was not going to be easy. Still, that would give him a chance to talk to Luke without her. Things were getting too dangerous to have Grace so involved. Not that he wanted Luke taking too many risks on his behalf.

Angus concentrated on scanning both sides of the road looking out for ambushes. By the time they pulled up in Cavendish Square a niggly pain behind the bridge of his nose was threatening to turn into a full-blown headache. At least they had arrived safely. Fletcher appeared from somewhere. That was a relief. He could get the Runners involved in tracking Ralph and leave Luke out of it as much as possible.

Once again, Grace had alighted from the carriage before Angus could hand her down. He left the phaeton with Jamie and asked Gillard and Sam to wait for him in the staff quarters, once the horses had been seen to. Luke was waiting for him in the hallway and pulled him into the library, shutting the door behind them.

"I don't know what to make of Ralph Medley." Luke dropped into a high backed, leather armchair. "He said he was on the way to visit a friend and sounded quite convincing."

"But you're not convinced?"

"Hard to say. He's invited us to dine at his club tonight, with him and the friend he was visiting." Luke's eyes shone.

"Not the infamous Jack?"

"Could be. His name is Jack Letherby."

"You accepted of course."

Luke grinned. "How could I resist such an invitation? I was sure you would want to take every opportunity to get to know your cousin better. Come on. There's a Bow Street Runner hiding in the stables who wants to talk to you."

"I'd rather we didn't tell Grace. I don't want her put in any more danger."

Luke grinned at him. "I thought you would feel like that."

"I don't want you taking risks either, Luke. What would I say to Kitty if anything happened to you?"

"No need to worry about me. I can take care of myself."

"Perhaps." Angus glowered at Luke. "Whoever Jack is, the other night he said that I was unpopular with some rough people."

Luke's eyebrows shot up. "I don't give a fig for that. Interesting though. Hard to know which way to take it. Was Jack fishing in the hope of working out if Ralph was behind the people targeting you? Or does that mean that Ralph is definitely not our man?"

"Hard to say. Either way, let Fletcher and the Runners deal with it, Luke."

Luke grinned at him and kept quiet.

Angus sighed. "Nothing I can say is going to stop you getting involved, is it?"

Luke shook his head and led the way out of the library. Angus followed. There was no way he could keep tonight's engagement with Ralph without Luke. He needed a private word with Fletcher. If he was happy with the quality of the Runners it was time to cut Luke and Grace out of the investigation. He could do with keeping Jamie for now, though. The way the lad had taken the lead over the route home was impressive.

They reached the stables and Luke ushered him into the tack room. Fletcher had Jamie with him. Hugh Masters was there too, towering over a short, stocky, roughly dressed individual, nearly as wide as he was tall, who must be the Bow Street Runner.

Fletcher saluted them. "This is Mr Spratt who is in charge of the Bow Street Runners you've hired."

Angus hid a grin. He wouldn't forget a surname that fitted its owner so well.

"Good to meet you, Mr Spratt. I'm sorry I had to send Mr Fallon away, on another vital errand, before he had time to pass on what he has found out so far."

Mr Spratt took Angus's outstretched hand in such a hearty grip that Angus winced.

"Don't you worry, Your Grace. Your secretary has made me a copy of the notes he had for you from Mr Fallon." Spratt hooked his thumbs into the lapels of his coat and rocked backwards and forwards between his heels and the balls of his feet." Impressive, very impressive indeed."

"Angus's eyebrows shot up. He looked at Hugh. "How did Fallon have time to do that?"

"He didn't, Your Grace. I had been copying his notes out every day for him to pass on to you. Fortunately, I had finished for the day when he was called away."

"Ah, I see. Impressive from both of you, Hugh. What did you find of particular interest, Mr Spratt?"

"Plenty, but I'll start with Lord Hedburgh. The Duke of Cathlay is suspicious of him. Fallon had struggled to find him but it turned out he has been away at one of his estates. He's back now though." Spratt pulled out a notebook. "He's been seen at White's and he's known to have accepted some society invitations for this next week."

"We've been invited to White's tonight by Ralph Medley," Luke said.

Spratt did some more rocking. "Very good. Very, very good. I'll have some men following you. With luck we might see both of them later."

"Which of the two do you think is the most likely suspect?" Angus asked.

Spratt stroked his chin. "I'm not sure it's either of them. Mr Masters told me about Lord Oulsnam. Now there's a rum customer if ever I saw one. His name comes up in all sorts of bad situations, but no one can ever prove he did whatever he is accused of."

Angus shook his head. "I can't see what motive he could have for trying to kill me. He's currently busy trying to get his hands on my cousin's shipping business. I wonder if he is involved in smuggling."

"Very, very likely. Still, you never know. Now, Mr Medley's motive could be the title. Mr Fallon had started investigating all the deaths in the family recently. I've already sent a couple of good men to work on that."

"What about the Earl of Hedburgh? Miss Bamford and I heard just now that he is threatening revenge on me publicly."

"Ah. The Duke of Cathlay's had problems with him too, over this business of clearing out the Scottish crofters in revenge for the uprising. The Earl lost his grandfather at Culloden." Spratt grimaced. "Seems a bit unlikely to be enough for him to commit murder to me. He's annoyed the Duke, but not threatened him."

"Our information, from a sensible source, is that Lady Hedburgh believes her husband is becoming unhinged over the issue. He might think that with my legal connections in Edinburgh I pose a serious threat to what so many Scottish landowners are doing. Especially in concert with Cathlay."

"Hmm. There is that. It all seems a bit calculated for a madman though. I'll have him followed as well, to be safe."

Angus exchanged glances with Luke. "I'm sorry to say that my cousin must be our chief suspect. Do you know anything about a man called Jack Letherby? He's joining us at White's this evening."

Mr Spratt rocked so far back on his heels that it was a wonder he didn't fall over.

"Well, I never! Jack Letherby, hey? Now that is interesting. There's a Jack Letherby who has connections with the War Office. If it's the same man, having him as a friend would make me wonder if Mr Medley is innocent after all. Unless the War Office have an interest in Medley for some reason. Very clever cove, Letherby."

"I can see why Angus is tearing his hair out over this problem," Luke said. "As soon as you think you might be getting somewhere another piece of information comes to light. If it is the same man, I wonder how long he and Ralph Medley have been friends."

"Wouldn't Cathlay know if the War Office had an interest in Ralph?" Angus asked.

"Cathlay might not tell us if he did. He's an old stager who never reveals anything unless it's essential. He did humour Grace when she voiced suspicions about Medley." Luke's eyes gleamed, even in the subdued light of the tack room. "Things are heating up nicely."

Angus groaned inwardly. "Do you have to look so gleeful? I would happily settle for a quiet life. We'll need to be on our guard with those two tonight."

* * *

Angus settled back against the squabs of Luke's town coach and closed his eyes. He was going to need all his wits in first class order for tonight's ordeal. Thinking about Grace avoiding him completely after their visit to Mrs Craddock was not going to help. At all. All too soon the coach slowed down and came to a halt in Saint James's Street. He leaned forward to open the door of the coach. Luke put a hand on his arm and pulled him back.

"Wait until Jamie opens the door. He will have checked it's safe."

"Sorry, I keep forgetting."

"I know it's hard, but you must concentrate now. This is serious stuff. Let me get out first."

The door opened and Luke jumped down. He signalled to Angus to follow. Angus landed on the pavement and studied the light-coloured stone building in front of them. It was solid looking but not as inspiring as he had expected for the famous White's club. He copied Luke in having a quick glance around and ran lightly up stone steps to the front door behind him. The best way to deal with this dinner was to treat it like a difficult and important court case. Every word he said needed to be carefully considered. They were ushered into a lounge where Ralph Medley was waiting for them.

He rose from his chair. "Good to see you, Angus and in such good time. I see Viscount Enstone's precise military ways are rubbing off on you."

Angus studied Ralph from the shadows so his face would be partially obscured. Had Ralph watched them leave the coach and look around, from the window behind him? He moved forward and gave an easy smile.

"Very likely. Luke hates to be late for anything."

"Jack isn't here yet. As another military man that's a touch unusual. Why don't you take a seat here while we wait?"

They settled into leather armchairs, which were functional but nowhere near as comfortable as the ones in Luke's library. So, Jack had been in the army.

"You must have served with Jack then, Ralph," Angus said.

Ralph shook his head. "As it happens, we never did serve together. Did I tell you my father was the Duke's steward for many years? He preferred to live in the most northerly property, near the Scottish border. He saw to all the northern estates himself and kept a close eye on the English land steward the Duke employed. Jack's family own the estate that runs next to what is now one of your properties. We grew up together. We even went to the same school."

A tall, dark-haired man walked up to them and Ralph rose to greet him. What a shame he hadn't taken a few more minutes. Ralph had never been quite so informative about himself before.

"Good to see you, Jack. Your Grace, Viscount Enstone allow me to present Mr Jack Letherby."

Mr Letherby's eyes narrowed as if assessing them.

"I'm delighted to meet you, gentlemen. Apologies for my tardy arrival."

"We've only just arrived ourselves," Luke said.

"My apologies. I was detained on some business and got away as quickly as I could." Mr Letherby smiled at them.

The voice sounded right for the man they had overheard. Angus kept his expression neutral. They all shook hands and made their way to the dining room. Apart from his height there was nothing remarkable about him and yet he had presence. There were depths to Mr Letherby. He must be the one with links to the War office. The clenched muscles at the back of Angus's neck tightened a bit more. Annoyingly, Luke appeared to be in his element.

The two men proved to be convivial company and the meal passed pleasantly enough, with no more than general social chitchat. Angus relaxed and the headache which had been troubling him all day eased. He sat back and sipped at his port.

"Do you spend much time in London, Mr Letherby?" Angus asked.

"A fair bit. I saw you at Colonel Gilbert's ball the other evening, but we hadn't been introduced." Mr Letherby smiled. "I knew it was you because you were with Miss Bamford."

Angus stiffened. Luke blinked at him a few times. Was that a warning to be careful? Knowing Luke, it probably was.

"Yes, I did spend quite a bit of time with Miss Bamford. I'm grateful to her and Luke for helping me become familiar with London."

Luke was still sporting a lazy smile but it didn't reach his eyes. He stayed silent. No one spoke for a moment. Letherby appeared to be watching Ralph. Now that was interesting. Had that pointed comment been aimed at Ralph rather than himself? Luke must have thought so since he leaned back in his chair, looking more relaxed.

It was Ralph who broke the silence. "I believe you're related to Lady Enstone."

"Yes, we're second cousins on my mother's side. Even so, it's good of the family to give me so much help."

Ralph looked down; his expression hidden. "I'm grateful to them as well. They are far more able to help ease you into society than I am."

"You never were much interested in polite society were you,

Ralph?" Letherby said.

"No, indeed. I attend a few balls when I'm in London, mostly military families. For the most part, I'm happy to socialize with friends and family. My mother's family." He sighed. "The only Medley who had time for me was William. Not that we were particular friends, you understand, but he did recognize me. A lot of the Medleys would walk past me in the street. Stiff-rumped lot. They didn't like my mother's family being in trade."

Angus felt a surge of sympathy. "My father had the same problem, but like you he was happy to socialise with my mother's family. Such an outdated attitude in my opinion. Trade is the future. It should be valued and nurtured."

Ralph's face lit up. "I do agree with you. I was sorry when William died, he would have made a good duke, honourable without being arrogant. However, you're a worthy successor."

Luke gave one of his lazy smiles which always seemed to mean he was thinking hard. "Have you never wished it was you inheriting the title, Mr Medley?"

Ralph's face became a mask of horror. "Good Lord, no. I should hate it. I'm glad to see the family in safe hands but I wouldn't want those hands to be mine."

Letherby smiled. "It can't be much fun having all the doting mamas hunting a man."

"Horrific." Ralph shuddered. "Perhaps our new duke has already solved that problem. Let's change the subject. How are you finding Town?"

Angus glanced at Luke, who was twirling his glass in the light of the chandelier over their table. His concentration seemed to be firmly fixed on the patterns in the ruby-coloured liquid. The white knuckles of the hand holding his glass gave away his unease. Grace's reputation would be in shreds if he didn't persuade her to marry him.

"So far it's been very interesting" Angus forced a smile. "I'm not sure I would want to spend more than a few weeks of the year in London though."

Letherby appeared surprised. "I thought you were brought up in Edinburgh and are used to city life."

"I am in a way, I suppose. It was different in Edinburgh as I was always busy with my legal career. I've always enjoyed staying in the country whenever I've had the time. I miss my legal work but I think living more in the country will be quite a consolation. I'm looking forward to learning more about estate management when my new land stewards have bedded in."

Ralph's eyes widened. "Have you divided the position in two for southern England then?"

"No. The southern steward wanted to retire and the northern one objected to my decision to demote him to the northern estates only. We agreed to part ways. My new man of business," he nodded towards Luke, "recommended by Lord Enstone, is arranging replacements."

Ralph clenched his hands into fists before lowering them under the table. "Why do that? The arrangement worked well in my father's time. His assistant took over when Father died and I heard he was doing very well indeed."

Angus caught his breath. How to explain the decision tactfully? It was to Ralph's credit that he was so obviously concerned for a former employee of his father.

"Don't worry, I provided a generous payment, more than enough for a comfortable retirement. Our agreement was amicable."

"I see. That does relieve my mind." Ralph stared at the table. "Time passes so quickly. It's years since Father died. I suppose you wanted a younger man?"

"Not especially. I've put overall control of the ducal estates in the hands of my new English Man of Business. Although I intend to take a keen interest myself. I've kept my Scottish man on to manage all my Scottish business interests as before."

"A sound plan." Ralph stared at the ground and sighed. "It's not my place to comment. I grew up with my father having oversight of all the Medley Estates. It's easy to forget that times have changed sometimes."

"You need have no fear for the Medley estates, Ralph. My new man is the son of the Duke of Cathlay's man. He will ensure the estates are all well managed. I intend to give the new land stewards all the working capital they need to improve things where needed. I'd like to see newly discovered farming methods introduced where they think it will be of benefit."

Letherby laughed. "No need to look so dismal, Ralph. I'm sure the new Duke of Evesham will do a splendid job. The new Medley land agents will have an easier time than your father had."

"I don't doubt it. Father had a difficult time more often than not. I try not to dwell on the past, but I can't help but think about him sometimes." Ralph grimaced. "Angus sounds far more conscientious than any duke he worked for."

"I promise I will do my upmost to ensure the estates are well managed and all employees and tenants are treated fairly. I like everything to be done right."

"I've heard you're a man of straight dealing." Ralph twisted a heavy, oval shaped gold ring around on the index finger of his left hand. "More so even than William Medley. The estates are in good hands."

Luke grinned. "There you are, Angus, a family seal of approval." He nodded at Ralph's hand. "Is that a signet ring?"

Ralph lowered his hand until the ring was hidden by the table. "Yes, it is. My father left it to me. It has his initials engraved on it. He used it for estate business, a lot of country folk preferred a seal to a signature on legal documents. It's purely decorative now of course."

The group broke up shortly after. Luke pressed a cane into Angus's hand as the door of White's closed behind them. His free hand was resting in his pocket and his eyes were everywhere. Their town coach pulled up, driven by Fletcher. Jamie jumped down from the interior to hold the door open for them. Luke urged Angus to get in quickly and jumped up behind him. Jamie ran forward, presumably to join Fletcher on the box. Angus glanced to the rear through the coach window and caught a glimpse of two men on horseback, who he recognised as Luke's grooms.

Angus threw himself back against the squabs. "Lord, I'm so tired of all the security and I don't think we are any closer to getting to the truth after tonight."

"I don't know about that. I'd love to see what's on Ralph's signet ring. I'd lay you odds his father added his own initials to the Medley family crest. Not unknown for a land agent to have one, especially if he worked for a peer who had little interest in the land, still unusual though. Are you sure that Ralph, possibly like his father before him, doesn't hanker after the title?"

"I can't see it, Luke. His horror at the thought of being the duke looked genuine to me. He would have to be a seriously good actor to fake that. If you must know, I have a lot of sympathy with him. I know trade is still looked down upon in some quarters. The Medleys were almost vicious about it. They upset my mother more than once. My father cut them out in the end. I can't help thinking I might have ended up as bitter as Ralph if Father's fortune hadn't been enough for him to be independent. I expect Ralph's father had no choice. It's hard to get a position without contacts. But it can't have been ideal for Ralph being brought up on one of the Medley estates."

"That's my point exactly. Could Ralph's upbringing have bred enough resentment for him to have murdered all the people in his way of getting the dukedom himself?"

Angus shook his head. "I can't see it. He seemed sad rather than angry."

"You may be right. What about Jack Letherby? Is he the man you overheard that evening do you think?"

I only got a glimpse of him through the window but the height and colouring seem right. I think it's the same voice. He sounded a touch more cultured tonight. It was a private conversation at the ball and friends from childhood, may well rib each other in a rougher manner than they would normally use. Yes, I'm sure it's him. And, if he's the man who works at the War Office, that would explain him having heard things about me that would give him an inkling of my problems. He would want to warn Ralph of potential danger."

"That makes sense. I think we have to keep Ralph on our list but put him lower down."

"Agreed. I didn't like Letherby's references to Grace. He seems much more a man of the world than Ralph. If I can't persuade her to marry me, the damage to Grace's reputation from spending so much time in my company, without an engagement, might be irreparable."

"I'm not worried on that score. She can't hide her attraction for you when she thinks you're alone. She'll come round." Luke smiled happily at him.

Angus froze and swallowed hard. "I owe you the truth but I hope you won't call me out. Yes, Grace is physically attracted to me. We have kissed and she enjoyed it. However, ever since I offered her marriage, she has kept me at a distance."

Luke surprised him by bursting out laughing.

"I don't blame you for kissing her. Grace is stubborn. She's insisted she's going to avoid marriage for so long she will be reluctant to admit she's changed her mind."

"It's no good, Luke. I made an almighty mess of proposing marriage to her. It didn't come out the way I meant it. Now she thinks I'm only interested in saving my reputation, when nothing could be further from the truth. I don't care about me, but I don't want Grace to suffer for helping me out. I believe her aversion to marriage is far more deep-seated than you think."

Luke sighed. "My mother died when Grace was born and my father largely withdrew from society and family. He and I became estranged, I was so hurt by his lack of interest in me when I was young. Later, he treated Grace as a substitute son. They discussed the newspapers together and studied the classics. Once Grace comes to terms with being female, I don't see how she'll be able to resist you." He sounded annoyingly optimistic.

Angus put his head in his hands. "Oh no, it's far more complicated than that. I warn you now, I'm not sure I'm going to win her around no matter how hard I try. If only we could solve this wretched attempted murder mystery, I might be able to concentrate on trying."

Luke clapped him on the shoulder. "You'll come about, man. I made a mull of my proposal to Kitty, but we got there in the end."

"I hope you're right, Luke. I don't know what I'm going to do if Grace won't have me."

"We haven't got any engagements until a ball at the end of the week. Take my advice and keep away from Grace until then to give her time to come round."

Angus grunted. "I could, but there is a lot to do on Medley House in the next few days. Hugh Masters is moving all the staff from the old colonel's house in tomorrow. He has a potential butler coming for an interview the day after and wants me there. Mrs Craddock, with help from Mrs Baker has found a cook who left the orphanage a few years ago to interview."

He ran a hand through his hair. "And Fletcher says some trained grooms he's had Mr Bright pick out for me are arriving soon."

"Perfect! Let Grace see what she's missing by not being involved with all that."

"She's more likely to be angry with me."

"Even better, she won't be able to complain after trying so hard to push you away."

Angus leaned forward. "Oh Lord. Has that been obvious to you too?"

"I'm afraid so. Grace has an expressive face. Let her see what she's missing out on and she will be keen to change her mind. She always was a touch on the contrary side."

"I wish I had your confidence." Angus threw himself back

against the squabs. "I've never suffered from an excess of sensibility until now. What with all this watching out for murderous attacks and Grace becoming so cold towards me, I feel like I've been through a mill with Mendoza himself."

Chapter Twenty One

Grace awoke early to the sound of a maid lighting her bedroom fire. She threw back the curtains around her bed. The maid, kneeling in front of the fire, jumped and dropped back onto her heels.

"You're awake early, Miss Bamford. I've nearly finished this. Is there anything you'd like me to fetch for you?"

Grace rarely ate breakfast in bed and opened her mouth to say no. She closed it again with a snap. Why not have breakfast in bed?

"Hot chocolate and buttered toast please, Jenny."

"Of course, Miss Bamford."

Jenny watched the fire until the flames took hold and crackled merrily up the chimney. She gave a satisfied nod and jumped up.

She bobbed a curtsy. "I'll be back presently."

Grace frowned. Even the fire was out of step with her mood. A day with nothing but her own company was what she needed. Aunt Theo never pried but she would certainly be aware of her changed attitude to Angus and wouldn't be able to hide her curiosity. She felt so raw that even Aunt Theo's sympathy would be enough to overset her. Her subconscious mind had let her down in daring to imagine that she could be happy giving up her single status. No matter how attracted she was to Angus, she simply couldn't do it.

If she had realised that straightaway, she would have saved herself a lot of pain. And not just herself. Even if Angus's feelings weren't as thoroughly engaged as her own, it was obvious he had grown accustomed to the idea of marrying her once his present difficulties were over. Someone like her would be the perfect helpmate for him, with her extensive knowledge of the Ton and what would be expected of him as a duke. He was bound to be disappointed and quite possibly rather put out.

It was best not to think about Angus. She ought to visit the orphanage in case they needed any help. A wave of weariness washed over her. Even that was too much effort. Mrs Craddock was very capable and she seemed to have amassed a team to help her. It wouldn't hurt to keep out of the way for a few days and give her time to settle down. Heaven alone knew what had happened to Lucy. No doubt she would hear about it in good time. She could hardly stay in her bedroom all day. The new book on Roman history, delivered the other day, might be her salvation. She could hide away in the library and start reading it.

Jenny arrived with her breakfast.

"Thank you, Jenny. Send my maid to me in a quarter of an hour please and make sure the fires are lit in the library."

"Yes, Miss Bamford." Jenny bustled out of the room.

Half an hour later, dressed in a drab grey gown she rarely wore, Grace made her way to the library. She stopped a footman in the hallway.

"I'm going to be studying today. Please make sure I'm not disturbed."

She marched into the library and closed the door behind her, without stopping to hear the footman's response. The fires at either end of the library burned as merrily as the one in her bedroom. Had they no consideration for her mood? The green, leather-bound history book nestled amongst some others on a side table. Grace picked it up and stroked the gilt edges of the pages. She held it close. Oh, the smell of a new book was bliss. Studying was what she was meant to do.

She glanced down at the grey dress. If she was going to be taken seriously in bluestocking quarters, she had better stifle her love of fashion. She could still keep her dressmakers in work but simply order plainer dresses in dark colours. Although there seemed little point in having too many dark coloured clothes as they tended to all look alike. She stifled a pang for her blue velvet outfit.

It was tempting to think she could start a trend for wearing blue velvet in female scholarly circles. She couldn't see it happening amongst the ladies who referred to themselves as bluestockings she had met at lectures and suchlike. They wore dark coloured, plain clothes most of the time. The only thing she had in common with them was her delight in scholarship.

And then there were her beautiful evening dresses. The red one which seemed to have captivated Angus would cause seriously raised eyebrows amongst these women. She would still have to accompany Aunt Theo to some society events, it wouldn't be fair to desert her. Perhaps she should keep the evening gowns. Indeed, there were plenty of male scholars who were also fashionable so why should she give up all of the clothes she loved? Why indeed. It could be her life's work to turn scholarship into an acceptable occupation for a lady.

With this comforting thought she picked up the book again.

Excellent as it was, with its descriptions of places she could only dream about, it failed to hold her attention for long. What would it be like to see some of these sights for herself? She had never travelled abroad and Italy sounded fascinating. Perhaps she could persuade Aunt Theo to go on a visit with her.

Grace put the book down and cupped her chin in her hand. If she was a man she could travel on her own. She ground her teeth. If she was a man she wouldn't be in this predicament. They could travel wherever they wished, as long as they had sufficient funds. Most women simply accepted their inferior position in society. It was so unfair, why should they have to? Grace threw the book onto the side table and jumped up. She paced the room.

Most women had little choice but to accept their lot. They needed to marry to survive very often. Men had little trouble in finding a wife, unless they were truly awful. Or poor. For the poor had even less control over their lives than rich young women from good, kind families like her own. All she had to do was stop yearning for Angus and concentrate on staying in charge of her own life. She was not giving up her principles simply because a handsome man had kissed her.

She was lucky that she had money of her own and didn't have to live with society's expectations of women. A day or two to wallow was what she needed to recover her equilibrium, but she must visit the orphanage soon and throw her energies into helping the children forge better futures. With a deep sigh she turned her attention back to the book. After her mind wandering a few times, she managed to lose herself in its pages. It was a surprise when the door opened and Aunt Theo entered.

"You'll need spectacles soon with all this reading, Grace. Will you join me for luncheon in the morning room?"

Grace lowered the book and gave her back a stretch. "I believe I will. I hadn't noticed how hungry I am, I was so engrossed in this book. Thank you."

Aunt Theo smiled at her and raised her eyebrows. "Is there anything you would like to talk about, whilst we're on our own?"

Grace sighed and shook her head. "Not today, perhaps tomorrow."

"I'm here whenever you're ready."

* * *

Angus had no sooner finished breakfast than the butler informed him some paperwork had arrived from his new English man of business, accompanied by a messenger. The butler escorted him to a small side room near to the tradesmen's entrance, where a young, plainly but neatly dressed, messenger waited patiently. He held out a note.

"I'm to wait for a response, Your Grace."

The lad sounded keen. Angus waved him to a seat. "Thank you. I'll return in a few moments."

He took the note and the papers into the library and smoothed it out on the mahogany writing desk to reveal beautifully executed English Round Hand writing. Ah ha. That was quick work. The first of his new ducal land agents cum stewards was available to meet him, at his earliest convenience, for final approval. Good. That would give him something useful to do with the day. Luke entered and approached the desk.

"My man gets on with the job, doesn't he?" He pointed at the stack of papers. "Looks like you'll be busy today."

"He does indeed. I'm in your debt. The first of my new land agents is in London awaiting my final approval of his appointment." Angus studied the note. "Mr Robert Croft. Do we have to go anywhere today or may I invite him here for interview?"

"Or course. Today is free for you, which is what I came to tell you. I have to go out. I could track down Mr Spratt and ask him to call here and give you a progress report later."

"Yes please. I need a rest from all the constant security every time I go out."

"I thought we could dine here tonight."

"Now that would be restful."

Luke laughed. "Why not ask Mr Croft to stay to dinner, assuming you are happy you can work with him? I'll be amazed if you can find any fault with his abilities."

Angus glanced at the letter. "He comes well recommended with an aptitude for mathematics, as well as solid experience of dealing with tenants on a smaller estate. Why mention Croft's skill at mathematics?"

"Ah. Our man is known for his new ideas about how to study figures and compare them to previous years and so on to see how things are progressing. He has quite a reputation for it. It will have weighed strongly with him to find someone for you with good mathematical skills."

"That will give us something to talk about at the interview. I trust his judgement. I hope Croft's free to stay to dinner. I'm confident he will suit and it will be a good opportunity to get to know him."

Luke shook his head at him. "He'll make sure he's free. He's not going to refuse an invitation from a duke."

"I hate all this fawning over me because I'm a duke."

"Surely you took men on for your advocacy team."

"True, of course. I must stop feeling sorry for myself and be glad I'm not one of the men who might feel the need to fawn over an employer. I would have offered a new man a choice of dates."

A grin spread over Luke's face. "I propose we dine at home tomorrow as well and you can give him two dates."

Angus grinned back. "Hoping Grace will miss me?"

"Now would I be so devious?"

"Yes!"

"You know me too well. I have a few other ideas about how to make her take note of how much you have shared. By the by, will you confide in Croft about your would-be murderer?"

"I believe I must in case there is any risk to him. Which seems unlikely, but he needs to understand the nature of the job and its problems."

"I suppose you're right. I might try and persuade Mr Spratt to come for dinner tonight. Depending on whether he has anything new to report. Let's hope Croft is free."

"If he is, I'll invite Hugh Masters to join us. As my secretary, he needs to meet my new land agent. I wonder if the candidate he has found for the post of butler at Medley House will be suitable. I hope to be able to move in soon. I'm grateful for your hospitality, but I'm sure you will want to get back to Kitty as soon as you can."

"No need to rush to move into a house in uproar from having so much work done to it. Aunt Theo has offered to accommodate you once we've caught the villain who is after you and I've finished all I need to in London."

Angus frowned. "I don't think Grace would be impressed by that. She seems determined to avoid me since my clumsy proposal and moving in with them might push her even farther away. Once we've got to the bottom of this mystery, I'll be happy to move into Medley House."

Luke gave him a sympathetic smile. "As bad as that, eh?"

"I'm afraid so." Angus shrugged. "I'll concentrate on solving the mystery alone for now. So far, I've gone out of my way to invite another attack in the hope of catching someone. I have enough things to work on for me to stay hidden for a few days, which may result in the villain becoming impatient."

Luke stroked his chin. "And making a mistake? Enabling us to catch them."

"That's what I'm hoping for. In the meantime, I might hear from Fallon with more information on Lord Oulsnam."

"Oulsnam sounds a rum customer. The more we know about him the better." Luke's eyes crinkled at the corners. "And Grace might appreciate you more after a few days without your company."

Angus smiled but avoided Luke's gaze. As much as he loved Grace, and love her he did, could he afford to take a wife who was so temperamental? He had the responsibility for the livelihoods of so many people in his hands. In many ways Grace was the perfect wife for him, but her self-obsession reminded him of his father's family. His shoulders slumped.

It was true that she had a strong grievance about the legal position of married women. He couldn't blame her for being angry. However, could he be sure she wouldn't be as obstinate on other issues if he succeeded in persuading her to marry him? She had been brought up in an aristocratic family after all. From things Luke had said their father sounded as starchy as some of the Medleys and Grace had spent a lot more time with him than Luke had. At the same time, his feelings for

Grace were so strong it would be a long time before he could even contemplate marrying any other woman.

Chapter Twenty Two

A week later, after days of solitary study, Grace was ready for company. Aunt Theo had been out a lot and they hadn't seen Luke and Angus at all. Not even for dinner. She sent a message down to the stables for Jamie to organise a coach to take her to the orphanage and changed into her blue velvet travelling outfit. She would keep wearing her normal clothes for now at least. To do otherwise would trigger the sort of surprised comments she wasn't up to facing for the time being.

She waited in the library for the coach to arrive. By which time, she had read a whole chapter of a book on Rome she had found on one of the history shelves and was about to check if her message had been passed on. She allowed the footman who had acted as messenger to hand her into the coach, taking little notice of the street scene. She settled into her seat. The coach moved off and she tried to enjoy the journey. She needed something to distract her from thoughts of a certain Scotsman.

The carriage pulled up in front of the orphanage. Jamie jumped down from the seat next to the coach driver and ran around to open the door for her. He lowered the steps and helped her onto the street. Two of Luke's grooms halted their horses behind the coach. She must have been distracted not to have noticed them before they set off. Jamie walked her to the door. Angus's doing no doubt. What gave him the right to interfere with her arrangements like this?

"Who organised this, Jamie?"

"I did, Miss Bamford." Jamie grinned at her, looking pleased with himself. "Mr Fletcher is around somewhere with another armed groom. I sent a message round soon as you ordered the coach."

Grace marched to the door. "It's not necessary, Jamie. Not when I'm on my own."

"I have my orders, Miss Bamford."

Grace stopped walking. "What do you mean? You work for me."

Jamie blushed, but stood his ground. "Express orders from His Grace, Miss Bamford."

Fletcher arrived and dismounted behind the coach, handing his reins to one of the grooms. Grace threw her head in the air.

"I'll talk to you later, Jamie."

The door opened and she strode inside to find Mrs Baker waiting for her.

"Why, Miss Bamford. We weren't expecting you today. One of the boys insisted you had arrived so I thought I'd better come and check."

Grace gulped in a breath and forced a smile. "I've neglected you for far too long, Mrs Baker. I thought it was time I put that right."

"But..." Mrs Baker twisted her apron in both hands and frowned.

An awful suspicion entered Grace's head. "Why don't we go along to your sitting room?"

Mrs Baker gave her a worried look and scurried down the

corridor towards her sitting room. She held the door for Grace to enter.

"Would you like some tea, Miss Bamford?"

Grace fought to keep her voice steady. "Perhaps later, Mrs Baker."

Mrs Baker ushered her to a chair. "Mrs Craddock and her group of ladies are proving to be a real asset, Miss Bamford. Mrs Craddock has visited several times and made an effort to get to know the children who are ready for their first positions. She's picked out three of the boys for the Duke of Evesham to take on as junior footmen. She and her friends have found good places for several of the girls and they have a waiting list for our boys training as grooms with Mr Bright. The agency is coming along nicely too. She's taken a couple of our former girls, now experienced maids, to Medley House today for the Duke of Evesham to meet. I thought..."

Grace blinked hard a few times. "I see. I'm glad Mrs Craddock is coping so well. We need to take every opportunity to find employment for our children. I've been rather busy, but I intend to spend more time here from now on."

Mrs Baker looked so uncomfortable that Grace decided to take pity on her. After all it wasn't Mrs Baker's fault if Angus had decided to take care of his own affairs from now on. If it was anybody's fault, it was her own. She had no right to expect to be invited to help after turning down his proposal. At the same time, it would have been polite for him to at least have kept her informed of what was happening with the orphanage young people.

"Perhaps we could have that cup of tea now, Mrs Baker. And then you can tell me how many orphans you think have been placed since the last time I visited."

Grace jumped up and walked to the window as soon as Mrs Baker left the room. She stared out at the well organised gardens behind the orphanage and blinked back her tears. Leaving Angus was going to be much harder than she had anticipated. She paced around the tidy, but rather Spartan sitting room. Was Mrs Baker someone else who had assumed she and Angus were a couple?

Their act to try and flush out a murderer had been far too successful. Mrs Baker must think her the biggest of fools. She did another circuit of the room. The problem was it had started to feel like a lot more than an act. She should have recognised it sooner and spared herself some of this pain.

Grace had managed to compose herself by the time Mrs Baker re-appeared with the tea tray. She settled down for a cosy chat. Mrs Baker soon relaxed and it was obvious she had taken to Mrs Craddock. Another thing to be grateful for. The orphanage could use all the help it could get.

"I'm glad to hear that so many young people have been found places, Mrs Baker. Have we had many new children being taken in?"

"It's been quite quiet. We've had a couple of little girls dumped on the doorstep but no other children. I think that's about to change though. One of the churches is bringing us a group of children in the next few days."

"In that case, will you need me to top up the funds to pay for Doctor Jarvie to check them over?"

"There is no need unless you want to, Miss Bamford. The Duke of Evesham has been most generous."

Grace sat back and closed her eyes. What was Angus up to? Was he deliberately trying to embarrass her?

Mrs Baker smiled. "I forgot to tell you about the two

boys who have been placed with Doctor Jarvie as his new apprentices."

"How is the good doctor going to afford that? I know he never charges half his patients."

Mrs Baker's rosy cheeks became redder than ever and she avoided Grace's gaze. "His Grace has made some sort of arrangement with Doctor Jarvie. I believe he is also giving him a regular contribution to cover the fees for some of the patients who can't afford to pay him."

His Grace was, was he! Grace gritted her teeth. "I'm delighted of course. Which boys has Doctor Jarvie taken on?"

The youngest Masters boy and that quiet lad with the red hair, Peter Brown. He hasn't been with us for long and came from a good background. The one who had the misfortune to lose both parents quickly and was lucky enough to be brought here by his local vicar."

"Oh yes, I remember him. A quiet but kindly boy. It will do him good working with Doctor Jarvie and I'm sure he'll make a good doctor one day."

Grace made a show of checking the grandfather clock near the window. She needed to escape before Mrs Baker told her about any more of Angus's doings.

"I must be getting on. Could you have one of the boys send for my coach please?"

It was a few minutes before the message came that Grace's coach was ready for her. Jamie had once again amassed an impressive array of bodyguards. Grace shook her head and accepted Jamie's hand to climb into the coach, without saying a word. She threw herself back against the squabs and closed her eyes. The coach moved off and her stomach lurched. She had turned Angus down so it was no surprise that he had rejected her help. At the same time, it stung. It didn't help that he also seemed to be usurping her place as the effective leader of the orphanage.

She massaged her temple. They had been acquainted for such a short length of time, but he had become a huge part of her life. It was no wonder she was feeling bereft. She had managed without him for seven and twenty years and would soon learn to do so again. Her hands tightened into fists. Her throat ached with the effort of holding back the tears and she forced herself to breathe slowly and deeply.

* * *

Angus reached the hallway of Luke's house to find Luke waiting for him. He accepted his evening cloak from the butler and joined Luke at the door. Luke smiled at him. "How did you get on at Medley House? Have you got enough servants now?"

"I've got enough to open up the house and Hugh Masters has found me an excellent butler. His previous employer died and his widow has gone to live with her daughter, which means the man is free to start straightaway."

"It's all coming together well."

Angus nodded. "Mrs Craddock has been a huge help, but I feel guilty excluding Grace. She was enjoying helping me find servants from amongst her orphans."

Luke rested a hand on his shoulder. "That girl's had things too much her own way up to now. It's time she had a check. Ahh! I think that's the carriage drawing up." He went across to the window. "It is. Come on, we don't want to be late for dinner."

The butler open the door and they ran lightly downstairs. Fletcher was on the pavement watching and Angus was sure he spotted several more of Luke's grooms. Lord, he would be glad when this was all sorted. Luke waited for him to climb in first. He appeared to be carrying a pistol under his evening cloak. Sure enough, Luke sat down next to him and put a pistol on the seat between them.

"I'm not quite sure how to break it to Grace about Mrs Craddock's help today." Angus laughed. "I admit to being a coward. I would much rather have met Grace again on neutral territory."

"Knowing Grace, she probably already knows. Anyway, we can fill her in with what we've found out which should placate her."

The carriage pulled up in Cavendish Square. Luke alighted first. He had a good look round and then signalled to Angus to follow.

Harvey opened the door for them himself. "The ladies are in the rose drawing room, my lord," he said to Luke.

"Thank you, Harvey."

Luke handed over his cloak and his pistol. Harvey didn't so much as blink in surprise, he must be used to Luke.

Luke strode across the hall and Angus trailed after him into the rose drawing room. Lady Grant was sitting near to the fire, but there was no sign of Grace. Angus's hunched shoulders dropped down from their position almost underneath his ears. He could breathe for now. Lady Grant rose to greet them and Angus settled into the chair she indicated next to hers.

Lady Grant gave him a warm smile. "I'm delighted to see you, Your Grace."

Angus smiled back. "I would rather you called me Angus."

"Hmm. That might not be politic at the moment." She raised an eyebrow at him. "I take it that all is not going well between you and Grace?"

Luke gave a shout of laughter. "That's something of an understatement. Angus has been like a bear with a sore head for the last week or more."

Angus started to protest but Lady Grant put a hand on his arm.

"Don't mind Luke. He did his best to spoil his own relationship with Kitty. The Bamfords always seem to make these things difficult for their partners."

Angus wrinkled his nose and shook his head. "I think Grace is determined never to marry. I have no idea what to do about it."

"Things are certainly difficult at the moment. Grace has spent most of the last few days hidden away in the library." She laughed. "Let's be grateful we don't live in medieval times."

Angus frowned. "Why?"

"If we did, I'm confident that Grace would have taken herself off to a convent by now!"

Luke shot upright in his chair. "Good Lord, Aunt Theo. Is it as bad as that?"

"I'm afraid so. Grace even mentioned that perhaps she ought to suppress her love of fashion and wear much plainer clothes so she is more obviously a bluestocking. I was relieved when she went off to the orphanage first thing in that lovely blue velvet ensemble."

Angus shifted uncomfortably. "Oh dear. She won't be pleased I excluded her from Mrs Craddock's visit to Medley House today. I thought Luke's advice to keep my distance for a few days might work. Now I'm not so sure."

"Hmm. She was even quieter than she has been when she came back. I wouldn't fret over what you've done though. I believe we were bound to hit this point with her." Lady Grant frowned with concern.

Angus winced. "I made a complete mull of offering her my hand."

"Ah, so that's what brought on her current mood." Lady Grant caught his gaze. "I believe Grace has been too busy falling in love with you to think about the future. A proposal would have woken her up from her dreamlike state."

Luke jumped up and walked across to drop a hand on to Angus's shoulder. "See, Aunt Theo agrees with me that Grace is in love with you. It's only a matter of time until she comes around to the idea of marrying you."

Lady Grant grimaced. "I'm not so sure."

"Neither am I." Angus's voice shook. "I'm not sure Grace will ever accept marriage for herself with anyone, let alone a clumsy blockhead like me."

He rubbed the back of his neck. Luke was keen to marry him off to Grace and was naturally optimistic. Lady Grant seemed to share his own worries. Grace had strong principles. Who was he to try and persuade her into giving them up?

"It will be Grace's decision. I'll ask her again when she has had time to think and after we have caught my enemy. I won't put any pressure on her."

Footsteps sounded in the hall. Luke moved away and dropped back into his seat. The door flew open and Grace glided in with her features arranged into a serene expression, although the purple smudges under her eyes told a different story. Angus bit back a gasp. The last thing he wanted was to cause her distress. She was wearing a dark grey dress of plain cut. Her gait was missing its normal energy. The aura of happy joy in life that he had noticed around her from the first time they met, had been replaced by a genteel lethargy. Lady Grant was right. It was easy to imagine Grace taking sanctuary in a nunnery in an earlier age. Was the possibility of marrying him so awful?

Common sense quickly reasserted itself. Grace's disturbed state was no reflection on him. She simply couldn't accept the role marriage would thrust upon her in present day law. It was a stance she had long since adhered to and she had her pride, as demonstrated by her determination to appear unmoved by her dilemma. If anything, her distress, so obvious to him, reinforced Lady Grant's assertion that Grace had fallen in love with him but not fully realised it until he had proposed.

Angus closed his eyes for a moment. The kindest thing he could do for her was to pretend he had noticed nothing for now. Whatever happened he must keep his promise to Luke and Lady Grant and avoid putting any more pressure on her to change her mind. Even if it meant him remaining unwed. So much for wondering if Grace was too aristocratic for him. It was agonisingly obvious, from the strength of his feelings for her, that no other woman could ever match up to Grace in his eyes.

Grace lowered herself into the chair nearest to the door and farthest away from Angus. "You two are early. What have you been up to for the past few days?"

Angus swallowed hard. Luke's idea of excluding Grace from their plans for a while didn't seem so sensible now. She would know about his dealings with the orphanage. He might as well own up to everything that had happened.

"Mrs Craddock has been most helpful and I have enough

servants to open up Medley House as soon as it is safe to do so."

Grace lifted her chin and skewered him with a hard stare. She was in high dudgeon with him. "Yes, I've been to the orphanage and had a lovely chat with Mrs Baker."

Perhaps deflection would help to soften her. "Is there any more news on Miss Vaughan?"

"Nothing at all. Tell me about your scheme to fund medical training with Dr Jarvie."

Angus clenched his fists to stop his fingers from loosening his suddenly too tight neckcloth. He had infuriated her by setting up the scheme without her.

"Dr Jarvie called in to Medley House to see a sick footman. Hugh Masters had mentioned that he was going to spend most of his wages on funding his brother to work with the good doctor. That didn't seem fair so I offered to fund Hugh's brother and another orphanage boy. They will work with Dr Jarvie and attend university courses. A similar arrangement to the legal one I've set up in Edinburgh, but on a smaller scale."

An idea hit him. Perhaps it wasn't too late to get Grace involved in the project. "Dr Jarvie had another boy in mind as well as the Masters boy. If you could identify some more suitable candidates..."

"Mrs Baker did mention that he's also taken on Peter Brown from the orphanage." Grace's eyes flashed blue ice at him.

Angus grimaced. This wasn't going well. "I was about to say that the good doctor has two friends who have space for an apprentice each."

Grace tilted her chin even higher. "I'm sure Mrs Baker and Mrs Craddock will be able to advise you." Her voice dripped with scorn.

"Possibly, but I have rather depleted the supply of your orphans who are ready for work. I believe you're friendly with several ladies who have village schools and such like. Ladies who might know of boys desperate for such a chance. So many young people are held back by lack of resources, don't you think?"

Grace glanced at the ceiling, appearing deep in thought. Angus rubbed the back of his neck. Perhaps she would thaw a bit now.

"Hmm. You could ask Kitty," Grace wrinkled her nose, "or Eliza Overton might be able to help. Why don't you ask Luke to put you in touch with her and Nat?"

"Thank you. I'll do that."

Conversation stalled and Angus breathed easier when Harvey announced that dinner was ready. Grace almost skipped out of the room in Harvey's wake.

Lady Grant shook her head and gave him a wry smile. "She didn't give you any opportunity to escort her, did she? I'll see if I can find a way to get her to talk to me, but I don't promise anything."

Angus nodded his thanks. "We're planning to attend Lady Coulson's dinner and ball later this week. It seems that both Lord Oulsnam and the Earl of Hedburgh have been out of town but are due back at any time. Both have been invited."

"We have an invitation for that." Lady Grant laughed. "How on earth have you found out that those two are on the guest list?"

"Luke's secretary is a close friend of Lord Coulson's secretary. Luke and I don't think that Ralph Medley is my would-be assassin. There have been no attempts on my life whilst Hedburgh and Oulsnam have been away."

Lady Grant frowned. "Which makes it all the more likely it's one of them."

"Agreed. We were going to offer to escort you both to the ball, in the hope of having a chance to observe them both. Perhaps we should go without you with Grace in this mood."

Luke shook his head. "We'll have no chance of getting anywhere if Grace isn't there. It would appear so odd, now people are used to seeing you together. If it is one of them, we don't want to put them on their guard."

"I suppose you're right. Let's see what she says and then decide." Angus offered Lady Grant his arm. "We had better follow Grace before she gets angry, thinking we're talking about her."

Chapter Twenty Three

The coach bowled along, taking the four of them to the Coulson's ball. Despite Grace's best efforts, Angus had managed to take the seat next to her. He made no attempt to move closer to her, for which she was grateful. She hugged herself, partly from a sense of resignation, but largely to reduce the chance of any accidental touching of shoulders whenever the coach went round a corner. They had finally included her in their latest moves, only because they needed her. Not that she expected the evening to yield any clues.

They couldn't even be sure that any of the suspects would be attending. Still, it was presumably all part of the act of showing her and Angus as a couple. Not that it mattered so much now that Ralph Medley had dropped to the bottom of the list. Or had he? The Earl of Hedburgh had a motive of sorts. Was it enough? How could Lord Oulsnam's business affairs be enough for him to want Angus dead? It made no sense. Grace relaxed as she puzzled over everything they knew. If only there hadn't been this huge spark of attraction between her and Angus, cutting up her peace, she would be enjoying herself now.

The coach pulled up and Fletcher opened the door nearest to the Coulson's mansion. Angus jumped down and held up his hand to help her alight. Grace almost jumped when she reluctantly accepted his hand and an even stronger wave of energy than usual ran through her at his touch. Thankfully the dark would hide her reaction. She pinned a smile on her face when they walked into the light from the sconces burning at either side of the front door. Aunt Theo and Luke were deep in conversation behind them.

Once inside, they took their place in the receiving line. Grace followed Angus's lead in making conversation as best she could. She would swear he was affected by her as much as she was by him, and yet, somehow, he managed to hide it better. Lady Coulson was a noted hostess and the party showed every sign of becoming a fashionable squeeze. They shuffled forward and Angus lowered his head towards her. The feel of his breath caressing her ear made her shiver.

"Don't look now, but the Earl of Hedburgh keeps glaring in our direction." Angus raised his head.

Grace smiled up at him as if they had been exchanging pleasantries. All eyes seemed to be on them. Their charade had been far too successful. They would have to go their separate ways soon or Angus's reputation would be in shreds. Not that that would stop plenty of mothers throwing their daughters at him.

At last, they reached the head of the queue. Grace went through the motions of introductions and social chitchat as if in a dream.

"Thank you so much for coming." Lady Coulson said. "Tonight's bidding fair to become the squeeze of the season." She dimpled up at Angus. "You're a brave man, facing all the ambitious mamas, Your Grace. If I were you, I would fix my interest with Miss Bamford here as soon as may be."

Angus laughed. "I've never been one to shirk my duty, Lady Coulson." He glanced through the double doors into the ballroom. "What a delightful ball."

Lady Coulson tapped him across the knuckles with her fan. "You're not going to deflect me that easily. I was hoping we could crown the evening with an interesting announcement, Your Grace. I suppose it was too much to hope for. The dancing is about to begin. Off you go and enjoy yourselves."

Angus laughed and bowed low. "Lady Coulson."

He led Grace into the ballroom as the orchestra struck up the first notes of a well-known country dance. He glanced down at Grace, amusement in his eyes.

"As soon as we find out who is behind all this, there is no way you'll get me in a ballroom again for a hundred years. Certainly not in London in any event. The Society Hostesses here seem to be competing with each other for the best spectacle." His expression hardened. "But it's not going to be me."

Grace studied his flushed face. "Most of the time I find it amusing, but it can be too much. Oh no! Someone I don't want to speak to is heading towards me."

Angus gave her hand a squeeze. "In that case, Miss Bamford, would you do me the honour of dancing with me?"

Before Grace could answer, he swept her out onto the floor of the ballroom and took the last available place in a nearby set. His tactics and execution were admirable. And yet, was this even more evidence of a managing nature? Grace sighed and gave herself up to the movements of the dance. She distracted herself from her inevitable reaction every time the dance brought her back to Angus by watching the other dancers. Especially the other women, whenever it was their turn to partner Angus.

It was no surprise they were all fawning over him. A handsome young Duke with easy manners and a carefree smile was not something you saw very often in the ballrooms of London, or anywhere else. If these girls knew she had turned down an offer from him, and intended to turn down another, they would think she was mad. Perhaps she was. The dance came to an end and Angus steered her towards an alcove next to an open window.

"Lord, Grace. I think I know what a fox feels like when it's being hunted. It's hot in here. There's a balcony, or more likely a terrace, a bit further along through those open doors. I expect it leads to the gardens. Could we hide out there for a while?"

Grace glanced around, but there was no one in earshot. "We could, although I suspect we'll be followed."

"Let's risk it. If we can position ourselves by a window, we can have a good look round the ballroom and see what Hedburgh is up to and if Oulsnam turns up. As far as we know, Oulsnam is back in London. It would be good to have it confirmed."

"I don't know Lord Oulsnam well. From what I've seen of him, I don't think I would want to. He has a perpetual sneer on his face as if he's looking down on everyone around him."

Angus grimaced. "Something of a bully from what I've seen of him. I'm not sure he would have any time for balls."

"I've seen him at these sorts of events quite often and he nearly always gravitates to the card room."

"We might be lucky and spot him then." Angus shook his head." I hope we haven't missed whoever is behind this off our list."

He pulled her arm closer into his side and Grace almost

missed her step. The scent of citrus spices and something a bit deeper hit her. Angus loved his colognes. It was fortunate his taste in tailoring was so severe, or he would have been taken for a dandy. Angus paused before they reached the open double doors to the terrace and shrugged his shoulders as if to loosen them. He stared at the increasingly packed ballroom.

"Difficult to find anyone in this crowd."

Grace followed his gaze. Luke came into view and Angus visibly relaxed. His shoulders dropping and a smile spreading across his face.

"Good, Luke is watching us. He would have let us know if it wasn't safe to go outside. He's so anxious not to let me out of his sight that it's making me nervous. I have the feeling we are drawing close to a conclusion to all this. I hope so."

Grace pursed her lips. Luke, she was sure, would do anything to push her towards Angus. Heaven alone knew why. They hadn't set this up between them to give Angus another chance to propose to her in a romantic spot, had they?

Angus smiled down at her and led the way out onto the terrace. Grace's stomach tried to turn somersaults at the heat in his gaze. This was madness. They needed to concentrate on solving the mystery.

"Angus, something has been bothering me. What if we've missed the real culprit off our list?"

Angus frowned. "That thought has been exercising me too. There could be a lot more than our three potential murderers. More likely only two now. Luke has investigated Ralph a bit more. It's true that Ralph and his friend, Jack Letherby, have been best of friends since childhood. Which they mentioned when we dined with them. Luke has spoken to a friend at the War Office. Letherby is well thought of there and holds a senior position. Luke's friend has worked with him and vouches for his good character."

Grace looked out over the garden and enjoyed the feel of the cool night air on her face. Angus seemed firmly focussed on the mystery now. Her imagination, and dread of marriage, must have coloured her judgement tonight. She could relax on the seduction front. For now. For all his upstanding reputation and honourable actions so far, could she trust Angus not to try and seduce her once this was over? She suppressed the little voice that suggested she might want to be seduced as firmly as she could.

"That is reassuring. I've heard Luke say, more than once, that you can usually judge a man by his friends."

"Exactly. Ralph didn't seem to have any close friends in the army and that worried us. Luke's found out that he was promoted quickly and he's confident that Ralph's lack of close friends was simply force of circumstance."

"What about that conversation between Ralph and Jack we overheard, out on the Colonel's terrace?"

"That was the sort of friendly banter between them we noticed the evening we dined with them."

Angus hesitated and stared at the ground. Was he remembering the passionate embrace they had shared that night at Colonel Gilbert's ball? The embrace which had shaken her more than anything else she could remember. Or were such things two a penny to him?

Angus raised his head and shook it. "I don't think it's Ralph. In fact, I'm confident it's not Ralph."

Grace chewed at her lip. "The Medley run of bad luck still bothers me, but after years of defending people in court you must have a good instinct for whether people are innocent or not."

"I like to think so, but it's not infallible. Now Hedburgh is a possibility. We'll have to go back into that ballroom soon, even if it is hotter than my mother's succession house at our country estate used to be. Let's try and get closer to him and see how he interacts with people. The Runners have failed to find out where he disappeared to this last couple of weeks."

Grace wrinkled her nose. "Then there is Lord Oulsnam. Do you know where he went?"

"Up to Scotland to meet with his Scottish Man of Business. The Runners say that's something he does regularly."

"It's a coincidence there were no attacks while those two were away." She grimaced. "I can't see how being angry at a few business deals going the wrong way would give Oulsnam enough motive for murder."

"That's another reason why I was so keen to send Fallon up to Edinburgh. I never took much interest in all my father's businesses. I've got complete faith in McGregor and I've left the overseeing of them to him. I don't even know what some of the businesses are. McGregor might know of something connected to one of them that would give Oulsnam a stronger motive to remove me."

"It seems unlikely."

"By all accounts Oulsnam is obsessive about expanding his business interests and none too ethical in his methods at times. It's worth investigating."

Grace nodded. "I suppose so. It's quite a journey up to Edinburgh. I wonder how long it will be before you hear from Fallon?"

"I suppose it depends on what he finds. The journey itself is going to take up some time."

Two other couples emerged out onto the terrace. They walked past darting little glances towards them, as if fascinated by them but too nervous to look directly. Grace waited until they were out of earshot.

"We seem to be causing a lot of interest. I'm sure those couples were trying to overhear what we were saying."

"I suppose we'll have to go in soon." Angus sighed and released her arm. He walked across the paved terrace until he reached the stone balustrade guarding the drop down to the garden below. He leaned forward and rested his elbows on the stone, staring downwards.

He straightened and turned towards her. "Grace, we need to talk. I can't seem to get any time alone with you lately. I'm in love with you and it's eating me up. I'm more disturbed by the distance between us than the prospect of a madman managing to kill me."

Grace's heart hammered. This was neither the time nor the place for such a declaration. She spun around, wildly scanning the terrace and the sweet-smelling garden. There was no one in sight. In all her seven and twenty years she had never met anyone who could even remotely match Angus Medley, but that didn't mean she wanted to marry him. She didn't want to marry anyone. She was terrified at the thought of marriage. What was she going to do?

She loved him so much the thought of the danger he was in if he didn't regain his composure terrified her. All the strength seemed to have drained from her limbs. She tried to walk towards him and stumbled. He jumped forward and caught her elbow to steady her. Her breath came in short gasps at her reaction to the nearness of him. The heady scents of spring flowers faded and the figures walking through the garden below disappeared into the distance. She stood there unable to move.

The sound of voices coming closer pulled her back into the moment. How could she have thought that their owners were moving farther away? This distraction from reality was dangerous.

"Angus, we can't talk here." She lowered her voice to a whisper. "Come back tonight and we'll talk then. For now, forget about me and concentrate. I'll never forgive myself if I become the death of you."

Angus gave a half-hearted shrug. "Thank you. I know we need to keep clear heads. Come on. Let's go back in and see if we can find Luke."

He strode towards the double doors leading back into the ballroom. Grace struggled to catch up with him until he halted before entering and held out an arm to her. She breathed deeply and slid her hand inside the crook of his elbow. This was going to be a long evening. Relief washed over her when she spotted Aunt Theo chatting to Luke on a nearby sofa, arranged against the wall of the ballroom. She needed some time away from Angus to compose herself.

Grace pulled away from Angus. Before she could join Aunt Theo on the sofa, the sound of increasingly loud whispers made her come to a halt. The crush of people in front of them parted and the stocky figure of the Earl of Hedburgh found its way towards her.

A large hand landed on her shoulder and the Earl shook her. "Keep away from him you..."

His words were drowned out by a roar from Angus. The Earl dropped the hand from Grace's shoulder and she took a step backwards.

Angus stepped in front of her. "I'll thank you to leave the lady alone." A visible pulse throbbed in his temple but he sounded admirably calm.

The Earl sneered. "She's no lady to associate with you."

Grace grabbed Angus's arm and stood on tiptoe to whisper in his ear. "This could be a ploy. He's trying to force you into fighting a duel."

Angus gave a curt nod. He glared at Hedburgh. "I suggest you go home and sober up, my lord."

Hedburgh moved towards him. "You misbegotten son of ..."

Luke pulled Hedburgh back with a hand on his shoulder. "You forget yourself, my lord. Apologise to the lady and move on."

"Why-should-I?" Hedburgh stabbed a stubby finger into Luke's chest with every word. He turned back towards Grace.

"Seduced by the chance to be a duchess are you? More fool you. How could a misbegotten cur like that be a peer? He's a disgrace to his family name." Hedburgh's voice became louder until he was almost shouting. "Standing up for Scottish thugs. They need to be put in their place. People like him caused my grandfather's death. I won't rest until I see him disinherited."

Grace shivered. Had they found their culprit? An ashen faced young man pushed his way through the crowds towards them. He raised anxious eyes towards Angus and gestured for him to move away from the crowd, which Luke was trying to disperse. A distracted looking Lady Hedburgh, wisps of white hair protruding from her lace cap and her bosom heaving under her puce satin evening dress, took Lord Hedburgh's arm. He tried to shake her off but she hung on grimly.

The young man lowered his voice, so much that Grace had to struggle to hear. "Your Grace. My father isn't well. Is there any way we can remove him from the ballroom without him making more of a disturbance than he already has?"

Grace caught Angus's eye and pointed to the open doors to the terrace. "There will be a way out through the gardens."

The matron threw Grace a grateful glance. Two young women joined them. The taller of the two caught Lord Hedburgh's other arm.

"Hush, Papa."

The Earl quietened down, but carried on muttering to himself. Angus said something to Luke who nodded and slipped out of the ballroom, by dint of keeping to the edges of the room.

Angus rejoined the group around Hedburgh and addressed the matron. "Lady Hedburgh, I imagine."

"Yes, Your Grace. I'm so sorry for the disturbance."

Angus nodded. "Lord Enstone has gone to fetch his grooms. Let's get your husband onto the terrace. They will join us there and help you get him out to your carriage via the gardens."

The anxious expression on Lady Hedburgh's's face relaxed slightly. "Thank you, Your Grace."

Her son mopped his brow with a handkerchief and drew Angus away from his parents. "Let me add my thanks to my mother's, Your Grace. My father's not himself. I was so worried he would call..."

Angus swiftly cut him off. "We can talk about that later." He frowned. "For now, we need to be clear that your father has been taken ill."

The young man nodded and glanced at his sisters. "Indeed. Thank you once again." He moved forward to take his mother's place in holding onto his father's arm.

Grace took a few deep breaths. Aunt Theo had enlisted their

hostess's support in ushering people away from the fraught little group. She had best join them. Angus was right. Sudden illness was the line to take. Those poor girls didn't deserve to have their futures blighted by their father's outrageous behaviour. The people nearest to them would dispute it but, from what Cathlay had said, the Earl was known for outbursts that bordered on the unhinged.

If the Earl of Hedburgh was mad, was he still capable of hiring assassins? Very possibly. If he wasn't mad then his behaviour had been an attempt to force Angus to call him out. As a peer of the realm, the Earl couldn't be tried for murder if Angus suffered a fatal injury. There would have been a scandal, but it would have died down eventually. Without doubt plenty of peers shared the Earl's antipathy to Angus's attempts to help the Highlanders.

She waited as Angus ushered the family out on to the terrace. The Earl drooped between his son and one of his daughters, giving out what sounded like strangled cries. His wife followed behind them, wringing her hands and sobbing quietly. The second daughter divided her time between talking in a soothing voice to her mother and watching her father's progress. It shouldn't be too difficult to persuade most people that Lord Hedburgh had been taken ill. For once, Grace was glad to leave things in the hands of the menfolk.

Chapter Twenty Four

Angus had seen the looks of disgust the Earl of Hedburgh had given his son when his wife and daughters arrived. He kept well behind the family group as they went out on the terrace so he could watch them carefully. Sure enough, as soon as they were away from the ballroom the Earl shook his daughter off so violently her sister had to stop her from falling over. He tried to do the same with his son but the young man stood firm.

"What are you doing letting your mother and sisters interfere, you idiot?" The Earl jabbed a finger into his son's chest. His spittle reached the young man's jacket. "If the cur calls me out, I can get rid of him once and for all. I can't do that in front of your mother and sisters."

Lady Hedburgh's wailing drowned out her son's reply. Luke, Fletcher and several burly young grooms appeared from the top of the steps leading up from the garden.

"You're just in time Luke," Angus said. We need to get Hedburgh out of here quickly." He grinned. "We have found our man."

Luke nodded and rushed forward motioning to two grooms to grab Hedburgh's free arm. He and Fletcher replaced the son holding his other arm. The Earl planted his feet and tried to resist them. In response, he was lifted off the ground and bundled down the steps in short order. Luke must have been a formidable army officer.

Angus took Lady Hedburgh's arm. "Hush, my lady. I can see your husband is not himself. I won't be drawn in to any duels. Let's get you home."

Once they were down in the garden, the Earl's son tapped Angus's arm. "What are you going to do with my father?"

"I'm not sure. I've known for a while that someone was trying to kill me and I have involved the Bow Street Runners. I could call them off. I will need assurances that your father will be confined somewhere where he can't approach me or order any more attempts on my life.

The young man gasped. "You are saying he has tried this before?"

"Not trying to force a duel on me, no. He hasn't come out into the open before, but I've suffered knife attacks and attempts to have me thrown from a moving carriage. I've spent a lot of money on investigators. Besides the Runners, I've even sent someone up to Edinburgh to check for potential assassins amongst connections of the business assets my father left me. I can't tell you how relieved I am to finally find out who is behind it all. Come on, let's get you home. Lord Enstone will send one of his men for the Runners."

* * *

It was a couple of hours later, with the family restored to their home and Lord Hedburgh confined to the attics with several guards, supervised by two Bow Street Runners, before Angus and Luke could return to Cavendish Square. Angus skipped over the ground lightly. At last, with his enemy found, he could have a serious discussion with Grace about the future. It was lucky it was too dark for Luke to see his face; he must be grinning from ear to ear. Which was utter madness. Getting to the bottom of what was holding Grace back, when he was sure her feelings for him were as strong as his were for her, was not going to be easy. But at least now he could give it his full attention. There must be some way to help her past her difficulties over marriage.

They reached Lady Grant's home and Angus slowed down. "Grace agreed to have a talk with me tonight. I'm wishing that we hadn't arranged it and I could have had more time to think of what to say."

Luke stopped when they reached the steps to the front door and slapped a hand on his shoulder. "It's best this way. She'll be so relieved you're safe now, she will be much more receptive."

"I hope you're right."

Luke laughed and ran up the steps. "Believe me, the anticipation is always the worst part before any battle."

Angus gave a shout of laughter. "You're not doing anything for my confidence."

"I know my sister. My father treated her like a son and she's convinced herself she would be better off as a bluestocking rather than a wife. But apart from her love of anything ancient and her partiality for blue-coloured clothes, I don't know anybody less like a bluestocking. She loves all bright colours and her fashion sense is followed by half the ladies in the ton. If anybody can tempt her to let go of her doubts, Angus, it's you. Come on. We'll all be happier when she has agreed to marry you."

Harvey himself opened the door at Luke's knock. Angus followed Luke inside. He gave Harvey the fancy walking stick, with the hidden sword, which Luke always insisted he carry when out on foot. His mind whirred as he removed his evening cloak and gloves. Grace was an intelligent woman, would an approach based on logic be best? Perhaps not. Luke had mentioned his father treating Grace more like a son than a daughter before. Something about her relationship with her father might have left her with a more emotional reaction to the thought of marriage.

A cough from Harvey disturbed his deliberations. He handed over the gloves and cloak, followed by his hat. Harvey discreetly withdrew when Lady Grant came into the hallway to greet them.

Luke smiled at his aunt. "The Earl of Hedburgh admitted, in Angus's hearing out on the terrace, that he was trying to force him into a duel so he could kill him. We have finally found our man."

Lady Grant's eyes shone. "Oh, that's wonderful. All this must have been such a strain for you, Angus."

"I would have been lost without the help of you three. Even tonight. I don't know the etiquette around duels and Grace's warning of what he was trying to do stopped me from saying the wrong thing and making things worse. I hope, for his family's sake, your efforts to persuade people he had been taken ill will avert a scandal."

"There will be talk." Lady Grant sighed. "You must know by now that the Ton have nothing better to do than gossip. Hopefully, not for long. What have you done with the Earl? The poor man seemed quite insane to me."

Angus nodded. "The Earl of Hedburgh has lost his reason

from what I can see. At the moment he's being guarded by, amongst others, two Bow Street Runners. I don't know how the family are going to manage him, but that's their problem."

"At least we know who's behind all of this at last." Lady Grant blinked hard and then smiled. "Such a relief for all of us. Grace tells me she's agreed to have a private word with you, Angus. I think she was quite shocked by the Earl's actions tonight. Let's hope, now we've got you safe, she'll see things in a different light and realise what she has so nearly lost. I wish you good fortune. You're the perfect partner for Grace. Let her talk herself out and then quietly make your case. She's in the rose drawing room."

Angus ran a hand through his hair. "Thank you. With your permission I will join her immediately. Before I lose my nerve."

Lady Grant waved him on with a smile and Luke grinned at him.

"Off you go, old man."

Angus strode into the drawing room. Grace didn't appear to notice him. She was standing by the garden window, drumming her fingers on a side table. She was so agitated all he wanted to do was to throw his arms around her and comfort her. But this was Grace. He was going to have to feel his way as carefully as if he was defending someone in a tricky case.

Grace looked up when he walked into the room, clutching her hands in front of her as if to ward him off.

"Grace, I want to thank you for all the help you've given me and not just for tracking down my would-be assassin."

Grace sat down on a sofa near to the window. She rose a little as if to change to another seat.

Angus laughed. "I promise you won't need to fight me off."

Grace blushed a fiery red. Lord, she must have seen the hunger in his gaze.

"I want to thank you for helping me find staff for Medley House as well. My new butler is excellent and I'm already relying heavily on Hugh."

Grace tossed a stray curl over her shoulder. "I hope you're not suggesting that you need me to run your households."

"That is a consideration of course." Angus grinned at her. "Grace, I want to marry you because I love you, it's a simple as that. I understand and agree with your views on the status of women. Don't you trust me to treat you fairly?"

Grace studied her clasped hands lying in her lap. "I know you're much fairer than most men, but that doesn't mean I want to give up my identity. I decided when I was young that I would always stay single. You are the first man who has ever tempted me."

Angus huffed out a breath. "That's something at least. Are you sure there's not more behind this? Is there something else you're afraid off?"

Grace shook her head but her hands trembled in her lap.

Angus fiddled with his signet ring. "Your mother died giving birth to you. You're not afraid of childbirth, are you?"

"No more than any other woman. It's the thought of giving up my identity. I enjoyed my father's company, in his last years, in a way I'm sure I wouldn't have been able to if he had treated me more like a girl. Women don't matter in the same way men do." She shook her head. "That sounds so selfish. I'm not explaining it very well."

Grace's hands fluttered and Angus put a hand over them and squeezed. That wasn't the right thing to do either. Grace had to come to him, he couldn't force her. This overwhelming urge to protect someone who wasn't a close relative was a new experience for him.

"I promise that, if you agree to marry me, I will always treat you as an equal. I may not always agree with you, but I will always value your opinions. I won't try to control you in any way. You'll be free to carry on your charity work, visit friends, stay with your aunt, whatever you want to do."

Grace smiled at him. "Now you're being hopelessly unrealistic. When you live with someone there has to be compromise."

"Very true. But I certainly wouldn't put any more constraints on you than your aunt would."

Grace jumped up and took a turn about the room. "That's my point though. Much as I love Aunt Theo, my plan has always been to set up my own establishment and have my freedom."

"In a different world, you would have had the chance to do that for a while. I have and I've enjoyed my time as a bachelor. I'm sorry that, as a woman, you haven't been able to have that experience."

Grace shook her head until another lock of hair fell loose against her shoulder. "I can if I have my own establishment."

"But that sort of freedom can't last forever, for anyone, unless we want to lead a lonely life. Besides, it wouldn't be the same, Grace."

"Why not?"

The stubborn tilt of her chin meant he was losing the argument. He ran a hand through his hair.

"Unmarried women are not treated well in High Society. You would have to invite some impecunious relative to live with you, unless you wanted to be ostracised. There would still be compromise in your life. You would have more freedom as my wife."

"Only if you allow me to. I want my freedom as of right."

"I want to spend the rest of my life with you. I'm asking you to trust me, Grace."

"You're the most trustworthy man I know. You're still a man."

He was being too logical. Emotions! Appeal to her emotions! "Think what you will be giving up if you don't marry me. You can't deny the spark there has been between us right from that first meeting."

Grace sighed. "I know. I'm so tired I can't think straight."

"I'm the one being selfish, pressing you for a positive answer. Why don't you take some time to think it all over?"

"Thank you. When do you want your answer?"

"Luke is going home tomorrow and needs Fletcher with him. I shall be busy settling in to Medley House. He's persuaded me to stay at home until he returns, in case any of Hedburgh's henchmen are still around. Fletcher is sending some grooms for me, all trained by Mr Bright on Lord Overton's estate. I'll have a message delivered to you when Luke is back. Then it's for you to decide when to give me your answer."

A smile hovered about Grace's lips. "That was a tactful answer."

Angus grinned at her. "It was, wasn't it? Would you like me to give you a taste of what you would be missing without me before I go?"

"Perhaps a quick kiss. No more!" Grace ran her tongue over her lips, making then glisten.

His pulse quickened. What had possessed him to suggest this? She had already admitted she desired him. He had nothing to gain, except a bittersweet experience, and everything to lose. He must take things gently and let her lead.

He stood. "One kiss and then I will leave you in peace."

Grace's eyes opened wide. She too rose, but stood well away from him. Angus lifted his eyebrows and she moved closer, staring up at him with her lips parted. Her scent of summer flowers teased his nose. His breathing quickened. He placed his hands on her shoulders. His arms quivered; it was so hard to resist the urge to pull her to him. Instead, he leaned forward. Their lips were so close her breath warmed his face. She touched her lips to his, briefly. He closed the distance between them and kissed her back, gently.

Grace gave a little sigh. She threw her arms around him, so tightly he could scarcely breathe, and deepened the kiss. His body responded. His head swam with the feel of her pressed up against him, their lips moving as one, warmth flooding his body. She moaned and pulled a little away, gasping for breath.

"Are you alright, Grace?"

She grimaced and stepped away from him. "I don't know."

Angus lowered his arms to his side and studied her flushed face. "What's bothering you?"

"I can't say. I'm so confused. I'll leave you now and give you my answer when Luke comes back."

She gave her head a little shake and ran out of the room, without a backward glance.

Chapter Twenty Five

Angus put his book down on the table next to the soft leather armchair in his newly refurbished library and stretched. He had never been good at waiting for things. These last few days had been a sore trial. Especially since he had given Hugh Masters some time off, leaving him alone apart from the servants. He sighed. Why had there been no word from Luke? It was strange without him, although he anticipated Luke's return with a certain amount of dread, since then he would learn whether Grace would have him or not. Their last meeting had left him more worried that she would refuse him than at any time before.

His new butler, Arnold, put his head around the open library door. "A messenger has arrived, Your Grace." He walked in, carrying a folded sheet of paper on a silver salver. "He's waiting in the kitchens in case there is a reply."

Angus accepted the note, inwardly wincing at the salver. Arnold was an excellent butler even if he had old fashioned ideas about the ceremony due to a duke. It was best to humour him.

The outside of the note was blank. Could it be from Grace? He unfolded it, impatience making him clumsy. It was signed by Ralph Medley. Oh. Not Grace! Angus sank into his chair, gulping in a breath. What could Ralph want? He forced himself to read the note. Ah, Jack Letherby was due back in Town and Ralph invited him to join them for dinner at his club that evening. He thought for a moment. Why not accept? It would be a change from his own company and what harm could he come to with his new town coach to transport him, complete with grooms and a coachman to protect him?

Angus checked his pocket watch. It still wanted ten minutes until noon. Plenty of time to give notice to the cook that he would be dining out. He dashed off a note of acceptance and handed it to the waiting Arnold.

"I'll be joining some friends at White's this evening, Arnold. Could you inform Cook and let my stable staff know I will be requiring the town coach later."

Arnold bowed so deeply it was a wonder he didn't topple over. Angus fought back a grin as he watched. The prospect of company had raised his mood for him to notice.

* * *

Angus's coach slowed up outside the Portland stone exterior of White's and came to a halt next to the stairs into the building. Angus jumped out and ran lightly up the steps. Ralph was waiting for him. He led him upstairs and into the members' dining room. They settled down at a table near the back of the room.

"Bad news, dear boy," Ralph said in a soft voice. "Jack has sent a message to say he will be delayed and to dine without him. Affairs of State have him in their toil, I'm afraid. He hopes to be in time to join us for a drink afterwards."

"Let's hope he is." Angus smiled to hide his disappointment.

Jack was livelier than Ralph. "Thank you for inviting me. I find myself rather bored with my own company at the moment. Even my secretary is away visiting his brother before the young man starts his medical training."

"Yes, I heard about that. I'm glad you're making an effort to give some deserving young men a chance in life. I would be happy to subscribe to the project if you need more patrons."

"That's good of you, Ralph. Everyone deserves a chance in life."

Ralph smiled. "That's what my uncle said when he paid for my schooling. I don't mind if my contribution is used for medical training or legal training, as long as my name stays hidden."

"A Mrs Craddock is organising the scheme for me. She's the wife of a prominent lawyer and the daughter of a clergyman. Very discreet. Would you mind her being involved? She has friends helping find placements but patrons' names will only be known to her, unless they make their involvement public themselves."

Ralph steepled his fingers together and pursed his lips for a moment. "Yes, I'll agree to that." He smiled at Angus. "I trust your judgement."

"Good. That makes it easier. I'll put you in touch with her."

"Excellent, dear boy. Now won't you try some of the superb claret I had here yesterday?" Ralph summoned a passing servant.

Angus sipped his wine when it arrived. "This is good, Ralph. Luke and some of his friends have offered to sponsor boys from impoverished but genteel backgrounds by buying them their colours to join the army. Would that interest you as an army man?"

Ralph waved a beautifully manicured hand. "I'll give Mrs Craddock a regular donation and leave her to apply it wherever it's needed."

"That's very generous."

The meal was reasonable but not up to the standard of Angus's new cook. The leek and ham soup was rather bland, and the beefsteaks were a touch overcooked for his taste. Although the tasty buttered asparagus, coupled with the excellent and free flowing claret were good compensation. He finished with raspberry cake and sat back sipping at the glass of port Ralph poured for him.

What was it about gentlemen's clubs? If he wasn't careful, he would end up with as bad a headache in the morning as after that night with Ramsay and Luke's other friends.

"This is a cosy dining room, Ralph. The dining room at Medley House is a bit like a mausoleum." A shout of laughter came from a nearby table and Angus grinned. "Especially when there is only me in it. The first time I dined with Hugh Masters there, his place was laid out at the opposite end of the enormous table. We would have needed to shout to be heard. I soon had him moved next to me."

Ralph inclined his head. "I'm glad to hear you are bringing more modern manners to Medley House. On the odd occasion I was taken there as a boy, under the old Duke, I found it quite terrifying. Mind you the old Duke himself was enough to terrify anyone."

Angus laughed. "I hope you feel more comfortable with me."

Ralph studied him, eyes narrowed, until a slow smile spread across his face. "I do indeed."

A servant approached them carrying a message. Ralph

pressed his lips together and shifted in his chair as he accepted the folded note.

"Oh dear, that could be a problem," Ralph said almost under his breath. He raised his voice. "Jack won't be back until tomorrow now."

Angus raised his eyebrows. What was making him look so worried? "What is it, Ralph?"

"I can't say here." His gaze flitted about the room. "I recognize some acquaintances over there. Come back with me and I'll explain."

Angus pulled out his pocket watch. "My carriage will be here soon. Come to Medley House with me."

Ralph said little on the journey to Medley House. Arnold took their outdoor clothes from them himself. Ralph gave the butler a cursory nod. He did seem pre-occupied.

Angus took his arm. "There will still be a fire in the library. Let's go in there. It's the cosiest room in the house."

Angus pulled a side table next to a chair for Ralph and poured him a generous measure of brandy. "What's troubling you?"

"This is rather embarrassing." Ralph accepted the drink and drummed his fingers on the glossy, mahogany surface of the table. "I had better tell you the whole. I hope you won't judge me too harshly. I dined at White's yesterday evening and arrived early to leave some time for me to read the newspapers. I had barely settled down with 'The Times' before I was accosted, there is no other word for it, by an old acquaintance. He made some very rude remarks about the Medley family. I am sorry to say I lost my temper." Ralph paused.

"I can't blame you for that. All families have their faults. You don't want other people pointing them out." Angus felt a surge of sympathy, remembering how he had felt as a youngster overhearing his grandfather criticizing his mother's family.

"Quite. In this case I ended up being drawn into a duel. Now Jack is out of Town and there is no one else who I can ask to be my second." He raised his eyebrows and sent a questioning gaze in Angus's direction. "I don't suppose you would help me out?

Angus frowned. "I can't say I approve of duelling, but I can see how you were unable to refuse. I don't know a thing about the etiquette or the role of a second."

Ralph waved a hand. "There's no need to worry about that, I've made all the necessary arrangements. It's with pistols. All I need you to do is come with me to Hyde Park early tomorrow morning. I will arrange everything else, including bringing a set of duelling pistols. You simply need to be there to make sure there is no foul play."

Angus wrinkled his forehead in thought. Luke wouldn't approve, but Ralph was in a fix and all in defence of the Medley name. He sighed heavily.

"What time shall I meet you and whereabouts? It's a large park."

"I'll pick you up in my carriage at six in the morning. We'll need a carriage to make a quick getaway. We can go back to my house for breakfast afterwards, so as not to disturb your household."

Angus laughed. "Agreed. It wouldn't look good for the new Duke of Evesham to be arrested for officiating at a duel."

* * *

Angus settled back against the squabs of Ralph's smart town

carriage, as they pulled away. He pointed at the wooden box resting on the opposite seat, next to Ralph.

"The duelling pistols, I presume."

"Indeed. A present from my father when I first joined the army. They're a splendid pair. He had them specially made, believing that officers regularly fought duels. This is the first time I've had need of them. Although duelling isn't unknown amongst army officers."

"You never said who the other duellist is."

"Ah. This is a little complicated," Ralph said in honeyed tones.

Ralph's gaze darted around the carriage, as if to avoid looking at him. Angus sat up straight with a jerk. He hadn't walked into a trap, had he? "What exactly do you mean by that?"

Ralph laughed. "There is no need to be alarmed, dear boy. Believe me, if I had been behind the recent attacks on you they would have succeeded."

Angus suppressed a shiver, in the pale light of the dawn filtering through the carriage window it was impossible to see if Ralph was smiling or grimacing. "Would you care to elaborate?"

"It's a long story, but rest assured you will be well protected."

Angus's hands tightened into fists. "I'm your second, why do I need to be protected?"

"I'm sorry for it, but I had to trick you. You are the principal and I am your second. I gambled that, having been brought up in a family of merchants, you would have no knowledge of duelling etiquette. I'm not quite sure how I would have persuaded you had you realised a man's second always, without exception, makes the arrangements with his opponent's second."

"I see. Who is this opponent of mine?" Angus said in clipped tones. His hands formed into fists as he fought down his anger. How dare Ralph trick him like this and what was he up to?

Ralph leaned forward. "Ah, good! You are as cool as I expected you to be. Can't you guess, dear boy?" He raised his eyebrows, looking pleased with himself.

"I'm afraid not. Won't you enlighten me?" Angus glanced through the window at the street scene spinning past them. They were going far too quickly for him to risk jumping out.

"Really, Angus. You disappoint me. Lord Oulsnam of course. You don't believe that madman, Hedburgh, would be capable of hiring killers, do you? It's well known his son has been running the family's affairs ever since he left university."

Angus gasped. "Why would you want me to fight a duel with Lord Oulsnam? Don't tell me that the dukedom is what's behind this. Grace has always thought it strange how many Medley dukes and heirs have died in such a short space of time."

"Such a clever young woman. The perfect mother to improve the Medley blood. A bad lot most of them, although I was fond of William. Excessively fond. His death was a sad loss. He would have made a good duke, although no better than you, I'll wager. I don't want the dukedom and never have." He shuddered. "If you play your part well, I'll be spared that."

"Good Lord, are you setting me up to kill Lord Oulsnam?"

"Perhaps. That would be my preference, but I expect it will be taken out of my hands. Don't worry. If you kill your man, it will be well hushed up. I have excellent contacts."

"Absolutely not. I won't be involved in this."

"Don't be silly, dear boy. It will be self-defence. Make no mistake, Oulsnam doesn't just want you dead, he's a dead man himself if he doesn't get you killed."

"Why?"

"Jack will explain it all to you. Briefly, Lord Oulsnam is working for the French. He needs that Scottish shipping company or he won't be able to deliver what he's promised."

Angus darted a glance at Ralph and grimaced. Was he dealing with a madman?

"Which shipping company? The only one I know anything about belongs to my cousin. You're not making sense."

They turned into a road of elegant, well-proportioned houses. Several people, including a well-dressed man climbing into a smart coach, were already about. Angus knocked on the carriage roof with his walking stick. If the coach slowed down, he might find a way to escape. Ralph wouldn't want to shoot him here.

"The driver has strict instructions not to stop, in any circumstances, until we reach our destination."

Angus felt for the sword mechanism on his walking stick. Ralph was too quick for him, knocking it out of his hand with a sharp blow to his wrist.

"Know this." Ralph's voice was harsh. "I want you to come out of this alive, but if it's the only way to save my father's reputation I will kill you myself, as well as Oulsnam."

"What is this all about, Ralph? I'm beginning to wonder about your sanity."

"There's no time now. I'll explain more fully when we have breakfast afterwards. All you need to know, for now, is that Oulsnam thinks I've tricked you to get you to the duelling field."

Angus spluttered. "You have!"

"I know, but I've also warned you. You're a lot cleverer than Oulsnam thinks and I wasn't sure I could keep things under control if I didn't. I don't want you killed."

"Do you expect me to believe that?"

"You have no choice, my boy." Ralph shuddered and mopped his brow with a handkerchief. "The thought of being the duke and all that entails is almost too much for me. Trust me and you will be safe."

"But not Lord Oulsnam?" Angus narrowed his eyes and peered at Ralph through the gloom. "Does he know something about your father you want to keep quiet?"

Ralph sighed. "That's part of it. I told Jack you were uncommonly sharp. We're nearly at Hyde Park. Remember to act surprised when you're told you're a principal in this affair. Make a fuss but, whatever you do, don't get between me and Oulsnam."

Ralph patted his pocket. "I've a muff pistol in both pockets. Miss Bamford's heroics gave me the idea. Jack's men will be all over the place, but if Oulsnam does try any tricks I'll keep you covered."

"What's Jack got to do with this?"

"A lot. Our coachman is one of his men. Patience. You need to concentrate on staying alive for now."

Angus frowned and peered out of the window. The coach barely slowed as it turned into a wooded park, narrowly missing the gate post. This must be a minor entrance to Hyde Park. What had he got himself into? Reassuring that Jack was involved, with him working for the British Government. Luke had been impressed with the man. All he could do was go along with this charade of a duel and hope to come out of it unscathed.

Chapter Twenty Six

More than a week of indecision had taken its toll on Grace. After lying awake for hours, she was in a deep sleep when she came to with a start, to find a maid shaking her shoulder.

"Miss Bamford! Miss Bamford."

"What is it? Is the house on fire?"

"Nothing like that, but young Sam dashed in when I was laying a fire in the breakfast room, Miss. He was in such a state, it was a wonder he didn't rouse the household. He says he needs to speak to you. But he didn't know which room you're in. If he had, I think he would have come to find you himself."

Fully awake now, Grace sat up. Sally, the parlour maid, was a sensible girl if ever there was one. "Spit it out, what's got Sam in such a worry?"

"I'm not rightly sure, Miss. He's gabbling on about something to do with the Duke of Evesham going off in a carriage with someone."

"Perhaps it's my brother."

The maid shook her head. "That wouldn't have Sam so bothered. Clever little chap he is. I think you ought to speak to him."

Grace jumped out of bed. "Quick hand me my wrap. I'll go down to him."

"I'll go and fetch him, Miss. Why don't you find some warm clothes? Sam said he's sent Jamie to get your curricle ready." Sally ran out of the room.

Why on earth would Angus go out with anyone at all, let alone at this time in the morning, when Luke had told him to stay in Medley House until he was back? Was it some sort of trick? She pushed her feet into her slippers. If she rang for her own maid, it would wake the household. The door opened and her maid ran in with her mob cap hanging at a crazy angle.

"I don't know what it's all about, Miss Bamford, but I've never seen Sally in such a pucker. Let's get you dressed for a carriage ride."

"Something warm but dark coloured. I have a feeling I'll need to merge into the background. I had better take my muff pistols with me."

Grace was fully dressed when Sam charged into the room. His hair was standing on end and his eyes were too big for his face.

"What is it, Sam?"

"Miss, Miss, the Duke's gone and run off with that Medley cove. He crept out. I don't like it. Me gut's telling me something's wrong." Sam jumped up and down, his eyes fixed on her face.

Grace's stomach turned over. It was never wise to ignore one of Sam's hunches. Was Ralph the killer after all? Icy fingers ran down her spine.

"Take a deep breath, Sam. Have you any idea where they've gone to?"

"I crept round, so the driver and the guard couldn't see me.

They were talking about breakfast back at the Medley cove's house once they'd finished in Hyde Park. I made sure Medley or the Duke didn't see me neither."

"Well done, Sam. Let me think."

Grace closed her eyes, heart thundering. Had Angus managed to get himself embroiled in a duel or something? This was no time to panic. She needed to keep calm.

"Sally said Jamie is getting the curricle ready?"

Sam nodded vigorously, rubbing his eyes with his knuckles.

Grace squeezed his shoulder. "Come on then, let's get after them. I think I know where they're heading. We'll find them before any mischief can be done."

Sam gave her a lopsided smile. "If you say so, Miss Bamford, I won't worry anymore. Let's go."

Grace hurried out after Sam, her heart racing, fighting to stay calm. If she could restore her own confidence as quickly as Sam's her head might clear. She must think clearly to have any hope of saving Angus if Ralph Medley intended to kill him. Could Angus have enlisted Ralph's help instead of hers for some reason? If he had, she would kill him herself for putting her through this agony of fear for him.

Jamie was waiting for them with her greys harnessed to the phaeton ready to go.

"Let me drive, Miss Bamford. You know what to look out for better than me."

"That's true."

Sam ran to the horse's heads. Grace allowed herself to be helped up into the passenger side. Jamie climbed up beside her and had the horses turning onto the road as soon as Sam had jumped up into the seat behind them.

"Hyde Park Sam said, Miss Bamford. It's a big place."

"The Duke must be involved in a duel, Jamie. Lord Enstone once took me on a tour of Hyde Park and showed me where the most likely duelling sites are. We don't want to be seen. They'll be in front of us and they should already be in the park. We'll go in from the northern end."

It was so early the streets were quiet. The clip clop of the horses' hooves as they raced along sounded so loud that Grace half expected people to come out of their houses to see what was happening. A cart on its way to market slowed them up, but Jamie barely checked the horses as he swung out round it. Grace tried to remember everything Luke had told her about duels in Hyde Park. Fear fizzed through her. He'd said as many as a fifth of duellists didn't survive and a lot more were seriously injured. She forced her mind back to watching the route, not far to go now. Could they risk driving through the park to find them? If they didn't, they would be too late anyway.

"Not far now, Miss Bamford," Jamie said. "I wonder how long it'll take them to get themselves organized?"

"I was thinking the same. We'll have to drive around. I think I can remember the most likely spots. There's a lane that goes right through to the south."

They reached the park. Grace turned round. Sam's eyes were everywhere and his face was pinched.

"I've got a job for you, Sam. We are looking for any sign of a vehicle." Grace shivered. "They may well have a doctor with them. His carriage might be easier to spot."

Sam nodded and his gaze became more focused.

The early morning gloom was giving way to the dull light of a cloudy day. Which might make her greys harder to see and give them a bit more time if they spotted the duelling party.

Sam tapped her on the shoulder. "Over there, there's something hiding in the trees."

Jamie slowed the phaeton. "He's right, Miss Bamford. See that shabby, dark coloured coach parked by the lodge cottage?"

Grace watched as they drew closer. "He is. Pull up, Jamie. Do you think we can hide the phaeton in that stand of trees just off the road?"

Jamie's face glowed with excitement. "I'll see what I can do."

He eased the horses off the road and into the stand of trees and bushes. Grace jumped down as soon as they came to a halt.

"Sam, stay with the horses. Jamie come with me."

Sam's protests went unheeded. Grace ran through the edge of the trees, closely followed by Jamie.

There were several men milling about in the garden of the cottage, fists up. A strange place for a fight. Grace pulled Jamie deeper into the trees.

"This could be connected, but I don't understand why they would have so many men. Let's skirt round the cottage. The duellists will be out in the open somewhere, unless we're too late." She wiped a shaky hand across her brow.

They managed to slip past the cottage without alerting anyone to their presence. Grace's heart thundered in her ears. Would they be in time?

Jamie tapped her arm and whispered in her ear. "There they are, Miss. Down closer to the lake. See, there's two carriages waiting nearby."

They halted at the edge of the trees. Grace peered out.

"That's the Duke. I'd know his walk anywhere. They're getting the pistols ready!"

Grace gathered her skirts in one hand and ran towards Angus at full pelt. Perhaps she could shame them into stopping. What was it Luke had said? As many as a fifth of the men involved in duels got killed every year. Somehow, she increased her pace even more. A tall man looked up at their approach. Lord Oulsnam! He pulled a pistol from his pocket and aimed it at Angus. Sam shot out from behind a bush and hurled himself at Lord Oulsnam's knees. Oulsnam fell to the ground as his finger squeezed the trigger. His shot caught Ralph Medley who still managed to fire his own pistol at the sprawling figure of Lord Oulsnam.

Grace stared at a set of duelling pistols lying on the ground in an open box, unused. Jamie raced past Grace, in pursuit of a group of men running towards a distant stand of trees.

"Come back, Jamie," Grace shouted. "I don't want you getting hurt."

Angus joined her. "Jamie, here now!"

Jamie, finally, pulled up and Angus ran towards Ralph.

Ralph flapped a bloodstained hand at him. I'll survive. I've had worse." He clamped his hand back on to his wounded shoulder. "Make sure Oulsnam is no longer a threat."

Sam reached Oulsnam before Angus and pulled a second pistol from Oulsnam's other pocket. "He won't trouble you, Duke. He looks dead to me."

Ralph gave a harsh laugh and nodded at the small pistol in Sam's hand. "Oulsnam had the same idea as me, hiding ladies' muff pistols."

Angus bent over Ralph." We need to get you patched up. I thought you said Jack's men would be all around to cover us."

"They should be. I hope Jack hasn't been ambushed." Ralph's gaze flittered all around them. "Be careful in case any of Oulsnam's men are lurking in the carriages. I can't see any sign of the two men Jack sent with us. They should be watching from my carriage."

Angus gripped Grace's shoulder and thrust her roughly behind him as he scanned the ground around them.

"I can't see anyone at all. Something must have happened to delay Jack and his men." Angus shook his head. "Grace, I don't know how you found us here, but I'm glad you did." He picked up Oulsnam's pistol from the ground and accepted the second one from Sam.

Grace stamped her foot. "What were you thinking of, getting involved in a duel. There are a lot of men in the grounds of the cottage by the lodge, fighting. We made sure they didn't see us."

Ralph groaned. "Jack must have a traitor in his team. Be careful. If it's the two with us you're still in danger, Angus."

"Grace, Sam, lie on the floor around Ralph. I'll take this muff pistol and creep around to see if anyone is in those carriages."

Grace grabbed his arm and held on tight. "Stop, you'll be an easy target then. Where's Jamie?"

"I saw him creep around the back of those carriages, Miss." Sam jumped up. "I can't see him." There was panic in his voice. "I'll wriggle through the long grass over there and see if I can find him."

"Stop, young man." Ralph ground out the words, beads of sweat on his forehead. "Is that your friend climbing onto the box of my carriage?"

Grace spun round, still hanging on to Angus's arm. "Yes, that's Jamie."

Jamie waved and drove the carriage towards them. He pulled the horses up a few feet away.

"The men in this carriage went after some others who ran from the lodge. The other carriage is empty."

Grace slumped against Angus, who put a steadying arm around her. She pulled herself up straight with an effort.

"Well done, Jamie. We need to get Mr Medley to a Doctor as soon as we can."

Angus hugged her to his side, so tightly it was hard to breathe. Not that she wanted to complain. Her legs felt as if they belonged to someone else.

Grace sucked in a huge breath. "We're not far from Dr Jarvie's house. Let's take him there. I'll hold the horses while you get him into the carriage."

Angus threw off his jacket and handed it to Sam. He bent down and scooped Ralph up. He staggered a couple of times but got him to the coach. Sam yanked the door open, Grace held onto the horses' harness and Jamie jumped down. He helped Angus lift the now semi-conscious man into the coach and lay him flat on the forward-facing seat.

Angus pushed his rolled-up coat under Ralph's head. Covered him with his greatcoat, which had been left in the carriage, and jumped down.

"Sam, make sure Mr Medley doesn't roll off the seat." He pulled out a handkerchief from his waistcoat. "Keep this pressed to his shoulder where it's bleeding. Grace, get your pistols out and keep a watch out for anyone following us. I'll cover us from the box with Jamie driving."

Grace opened her mouth to protest, but a groan from Ralph stopped her. He needed attention as soon as possible.

Jamie drove at a steady trot but it wasn't many minutes before they pulled up outside the shining black door of a sprawling, brick-built townhouse. A brass plaque to the side of it bore Dr Jarvie's name. Grace held her breath as Angus rapped on the door. It was a few minutes before a grumbling manservant opened it.

"Why can't folk learn to get sick at civilised hours?"

"Never mind that, man, this is an emergency," Angus said. "A gentleman has been set upon and shot in the shoulder."

The manservant snorted. "Duelling more like. We gets it all the time with being so close to Hyde Park."

Doctor Jarvie's voice rang out. "Quick man, let's get him inside."

The manservant gave another snort, but lumbered out to the coach. Dr Jarvie, still in his shirt sleeves, followed behind. He called into the depths of the hallway.

"Isaac, bring that board."

Grace watched as Ralph was carefully loaded onto a board and carried into a back room. The complaining manservant knew his job and had thrown off his irritation, taking the lead in making sure Ralph was transported with the least amount of jarring.

Dr Jarvie waved them into a sitting room. "Get yourselves warm. The fire is lit. I'll call you if I need you."

Grace stopped to tell Jamie and Sam to walk the horses around the block.

"Lord, we've left the greys in Hyde Park."

Sam grinned at her. "Don't worry, Miss Bamford, I tied 'em up tight."

Grace accepted Angus's arm and they trailed into the waiting room. She collapsed into a well-worn leather armchair and closed her eyes. The grandfather clock out in the hall chimed seven times, making her start. She opened her eyes to find Angus smiling at her from an adjacent armchair, his expression soft.

Grace shook her head at him. "What a day, and it's still only seven o'clock. I don't know what you have to smile about. I ought to be angry with you for putting me through that, but I haven't the energy."

"I was smiling at you. You looked so adorable with your eyes closed and your head nodding. A pity the clock woke you. I hope Ralph makes it."

"Hmph! After putting you in so much danger. What possessed you to agree to a duel?"

"I'd like to say I was doing my bit for king and country. The truth is I was tricked. Ralph told me he had been forced into a duel, defending the Medley honour, and he needed a second. He had a message to say Jack couldn't get back to town in time and he asked me. Like a fool, I agreed. I trusted him."

"Then you found yourself as the principal?"

"He warned me in the coach. I'm not sure if I believe him about Jack being behind the plan. At least not entirely." Angus frowned.

Grace studied Angus's face. Something was worrying him. "What is it you're troubled about? I can see from your expression that it's something serious," she said softly.

Angus leaned towards her and spoke so quietly she had to strain to hear. "When Luke and I had dinner with Ralph he was on good form. Until, that is, the conversation got around to details about my new English land agents. It was when I mentioned they will be overseen by my London man of business who Luke introduced me to. Ralph's father used to handle the northern estates and had overall control of the rest."

"Ah. I see. You suspect Ralph's father wasn't always entirely honest in his book keeping."

"Yes. Luke's man of business took me on as a special favour to Luke, he has as many clients as he can handle. Anyone employed by him will be first rate. If there is anything to find the new man will find it, even if not straight away." Angus sighed. "If Ralph survives, I'll get the truth out of him."

Grace frowned "I'm not sure I trust Ralph. If he knew Lord Oulsnam was the one trying to kill you, why didn't he warn you?"

"Which is what makes me wonder whether Jack being behind today is true. Ralph told me Oulsnam was working for the French and Jack has been investigating him for a while."

They lapsed into an exhausted silence. Grace woke up with a start when Doctor Jarvie entered.

"I've removed the bullet. Mr Medley is a lot more comfortable now. I wanted to give him more laudanum, but he insists he needs to talk to you first."

Angus stood. "Did he say what about?"

"No, Your Grace. We'll keep him here for a day or two. Make sure the wound doesn't get infected." The doctor laughed. "It will also keep him away from prying eyes. Why you young men will get involved in duels I have no idea."

"I can't believe I let Ralph talk me into becoming involved. I'd better go and see what he wants."

Grace jumped up. "I'm coming with you. After all the trouble we've had I want to hear anything Ralph has to say."

"He's in the next room. Isaac will show you the way. I'll leave you now, I've got some urgent patients to see."

Grace moved towards the door and Angus put a hand on her arm.

"I'm not sure it's a good idea for you to come."

"Why ever not? You've cut me out of the investigation for the last few weeks, but I've been a part of this. I deserve to know everything there is to know." A tremor ran through her. She looked at the floor. "Besides, I thought I'd lost you and for the time being I can't bear to let you out of my sight."

Angus put a hand on both shoulders and turned her to face him, a huge grin on his face. "Does that mean you've changed your mind?"

Grace nodded and raised her eyes to his. "It means I've made my mind up, more of that later."

Angus kissed her on the forehead and dropped his hands. "Let's go and find out what Ralph wants to say then."

A manservant was waiting for them in the hall. "Follow me."

Ralph was propped up against several pillows, his arm and shoulder bandaged.

"Apologies for my appearance. My valet will be here soon with some fresh clothes for me." He hesitated and chewed at his lip.

"What is it you want to talk to me about, Ralph," Angus said.

"Have you heard from your new man of business yet?"

Angus pulled up two stools next to the bed and took the one nearest to Ralph. "Only an interim report on the current state of my finances. It will be some time before they get round to studying the historical figures but I think I know what you're about to tell me."

Ralph plucked at the covers with his uninjured arm, his hand trembling. "Jack said you were a downy one. Oulsnam was so well protected that Jack wanted to wait a bit longer to reel him in. After we had dinner with you that evening, we both knew that any agent hired by your new man of business would soon find out what my father had done."

"What exactly did your father do, Ralph?" Angus's voice was stern.

Ralph started trembling and Grace laid a hand on Angus's arm. "Try and relax, Mr Medley. Angus is not the man to visit your father's sins on you."

"I know that." The pitch of Ralph's voice rose considerably and he appeared to be in some distress.

"Are you sure you wouldn't like to leave this until you are feeling stronger, Mr Medley?"

Ralph shook his head. "His Grace needs to know what happened. I want a promise it will stay between us. The Medley name is an old one and doesn't deserve to be besmirched. You have to understand that my father would not have done what he did if he had been treated fairly by the old Duke."

Ralph's good hand opened and closed convulsively. Angus placed his own hand over it. "I've no more wish than you, Ralph, to air any family secrets in public. I do need to know exactly what's involved."

"The old Duke was as tight-fisted as they come. He didn't even offer to pay my school fees, like most men in his position would have. My mother's brother paid them instead. My family wanted me to have the same sort of education as my cousins. Then my father found out that, although he was working incredibly hard, he was being paid less than half of what most men in his position were getting. When he brought it up the old Duke got angry.

Family was important to my father so he put up with it. Then he decided to pay himself the extra and hide it in the accounts. He used that money to invest in some of my uncle's projects. He became quite wealthy, but not as wealthy as my uncle. Everything was left to me. I'll understand if you want some of the money repaid. All I ask is that you protect my father's memory by making sure that none of this comes out."

"I thought it was something like that. Don't worry, his secret is safe. Now tell me, if you knew all along that Oulsnam was trying to kill me why wasn't I warned?"

Ralph laid back against his pillows.

"That was Jack. He had men watching you and Miss Bamford as well as Viscount Enstone and his men. We knew you'd be safe." He gave a laugh that turned into a cough.

"When you and Miss Bamford seemed to fall out, I was disappointed." Ralph smiled at Grace. "I can see you are reconciled, my dear. For which I'm extremely grateful. You're exactly what the Medley family needs."

He plucked at the covers. "I wonder what's happened to Jack, I hope he's all right."

Angus put a hand on Ralph's good shoulder. "You should rest now. If Jack contacts us, I'll let you know and tell him where you are."

They slipped out of the room and back into the waiting room. Angus put an arm around Grace's shoulders.

"Let's get you back to Cavendish Square. Where you can give me a formal answer to my proposal. I'm sure Jack will be in contact when he's ready. "

Grace came to a halt. "Angus, I will marry you. I felt so torn, afraid of losing my identity. Then this morning when it dawned on me you were fighting a duel, I was so frightened. I knew I would say yes if you survived. I don't know how I'll manage but I know I can't manage without you. Come on, let's go and put Aunt Theo's mind at rest."

Grace allowed herself to be led out into the hallway. A

manservant went out to summon their carriage before they could ask. Within minutes, Jamie and Sam drew up in Grace's phaeton.

Sam grinned at them. "Jamie drove us straight back to Hyde Park so I could tend to the greys. Then he came back and left Medley's carriage here and walked back so he could drive us to pick you up."

Grace exchanged glances with Angus. "I'll forgive you for disobeying orders this once. What's happened to Mr Medley's carriage?"

Jamie answered. "His valet came in another carriage and the groom with the coachman has driven it back."

Sam tugged at Angus's sleeve.

"Not now, Sam. You've both done well."

"But Duke, I need to tell you. I've decided I need to drive, so I'll go and get trained by Mr Bright."

"That's excellent, Sam. We'll talk about it later."

Angus picked Grace up and lifted her into the phaeton. The feel of his hands at her waist made her gasp. She took a few calming breaths.

Angus climbed up beside her. "Do you feel up to driving us back, or shall we try and squeeze Jamie in beside us?"

Grace put her hands up in mock horror. "Stop trying to wrap me up with caring or I might change my mind about wedding you. Of course, I'll be able to drive us back."

Jamie handed up the reins.

Angus leaned over the side of the phaeton. "Can you find your way home on foot? At least Jamie's home. Sam, you go along with him and we'll see you in Cavendish Square."

"Yes, Your Grace," Jamie said. He grinned at Sam and took his arm as they ran off."

Grace wrinkled her nose up. "Jamie heard me mention marriage. Those two will run all the way back and tell all the servants before I can speak to Aunt Theo if we aren't careful."

Grace let her horses go and soon had them at a fast trot. They turned a corner and Angus's arm found its way around her waist. Rather than being stifling, it felt right, comforting even. She laughed up at him.

"I'm sorry I put you through so much uncertainty, but I had to work it all out for myself."

Angus gave a shout of laughter. "It was worth being half scared to death to win your hand in marriage. I even contemplated jumping out of Ralph's carriage but it was going too fast."

Chapter Twenty Seven

They arrived back in Cavendish Square to find Luke shouting directions for the town carriage to be made ready. Reluctantly, Angus removed his arm from Grace's waist and jumped down from the phaeton.

"Luke, there is no need for that. Here we are safe and well."

Luke's mouth fell open. "Thank the Lord for that. Aunt Theo was convinced you were about to be killed in a duel."

"I'm untouched, Ralph's injured, but not badly and Lord Oulsnam is dead. Come inside and we'll fill you in on the details." Angus diverted one of the grooms with Luke and sent him over to take the reins from Grace.

He lifted Grace down and swung her around before putting her back on her feet. "That was some good driving. Looks like we beat Jamie and Sam back. Come on, let's go and find Aunt Theo. Explanations can wait until she's heard our news."

Angus linked arms with Grace and they ran into the house. They found Aunt Theo pacing the floor in the rose drawing room. Her face broke into a beaming smile before they could say anything.

"Thank goodness you're both safe. Is there anything you want to tell me?"

Grace freed her arm and went over to hug her aunt. "Thank

you for putting up with me these last few weeks. I've finally agreed to marry Angus. When I thought he might be killed, I was so scared. I knew it had to be marriage if he survived."

"I'm so glad. You two are made for each other. Now tell me what's been going on?"

They heard the sound of a commotion in the hall and Luke entered followed by Fallon and another man.

"Fallon. You're back sooner than I expected," Angus said.

The man behind Fallon came into view. "I brought him back by ship and we had good sailing winds."

"Rory! It's good to see you, what brings you to London?" Angus ran over and slapped his cousin on the back.

"Fallon here is convinced that Lord Oulsnam is the man trying to kill you." Rory's face became nearly as red as his hair. "Sailing down was the quickest way to get here to warn you."

"You're right. As I found out today. Come and meet my future wife and my future aunt, before we go into that."

Angus ushered a red-faced Rory over to Grace. Why was he looking so embarrassed? He must make time to find out later. Rory was far too confident to be intimidated by his surroundings.

"Lady Grant, Grace, this is my cousin, Rory Brodie. Rory meet Lady Grant and Miss Grace Bamford."

Grace smiled at Rory. "I'm so pleased to meet a relative of Angus's, Mr Brodie."

"I'm happy to meet you, Miss Bamford. The aunts will be delighted Angus has finally found himself a wife"

Angus smiled at everyone, swept up on a wave of happiness. He had finally secured the woman of his dreams. He guided them all to chairs. This time Grace sat on a sofa and he took the seat next to her.

Luke stood, with his elbow resting on a windowsill. "Before we start, Angus, why did you ignore my express instruction to stay at home until further notice?"

Angus sighed. "It's a long story. I was bored with my own company, even Hugh Masters was away, and Ralph invited me to dine at his club with him and Jack. I saw no harm in it. When we arrived, there was a message from Jack to say he was out of town on the King's business and wouldn't be back in time to dine with us. Ralph told me he'd been challenged to a duel and asked me to take Jack's place when he got another message to say Jack wouldn't be able to get back in time to be his second. I agreed, only to find out on the way this morning that I was the principal and I was meeting Lord Oulsnam.

Jack's men were supposed to be covering us, goodness knows what happened to them. Sam saw me go out and warned Grace. She worked out what was happening, roughly, and got her, Sam and Jamie there in time for Sam to knock Lord Oulsnam over before he could shoot me without a duel. In the process Ralph took a flesh wound to the shoulder. But Doctor Jarvie thinks he will make a full recovery."

Luke shook his head. "If I'm going to allow you to marry my sister, I want your assurances you will stop putting her in danger."

Grace spluttered next to him and Angus laughed. "Your sister has a mind of her own and she will marry where she chooses."

Luke laughed. "I couldn't be more pleased for you. I think I deserve some of the credit."

"Oh no you don't," Grace said. "Your interference had the opposite effect. I may have realised that marriage was for me after all a lot sooner without you."

Fallon shuffled in his seat. Angus held up a hand.

"As long as you've got no intention to call me out, Luke. You can take all the credit you like. Now, Mr Fallon, how did you come to the conclusion that Oulsnam was my enemy?"

Fallon exchange glances with Rory, who nodded. That was interesting, Angus was instantly on the alert.

"Is it something to do with Rory's business?"

Rory loosened his collar with a finger. "That's the whole point, Angus if I'd been completely honest with you last summer, I expect you would have realised straight away who was behind it." He paused.

Angus frowned. What on earth was Rory on about? And why was he so uncomfortable? His cheeks were bright red again. He'd grown out of his tendency to flush the colour of his hair years before, so something major must be causing it.

Rory grimaced and rubbed at his thigh. "It's not my business, Angus. My father was a brilliant seaman but not so good at commerce. A few years ago, he got into a muddle and your father helped him out. Both with an investment and guiding him into better systems of management."

"Yes, I know about that. I know I own part of the company."

"You own more than half of the company. My father made sure your father had overall control of any major decisions so he couldn't get into a mess again. He was furious with himself for nearly losing the business. So, when Oulsnam was hassling me to sell it I called on you for help, but I didn't tell you the whole truth."

"I see. That doesn't explain why Oulsnam was so determined to get hold of this particular shipping business or any shipping business."

Fallon coughed. "I can shed some light on that. With help

from your Scottish investigators, and your team of advocates, I managed to find out a lot about Lord Oulsnam's Scottish activities. I suspect that he has been smuggling items to and from France. I think he got greedy and wanted to grow the business. He needed a reputable, old established shipping company to hide his smuggling activities behind."

Angus exchanged glances with Grace.

Rory took up the story again. "I put you at risk, Angus. I believe Lord Oulsnam decided that the only way he could get the business was to eliminate you. The unfortunate family history of the Medleys is well known even in Scotland. Oulsnam probably saw his opportunity. If people realised you had been murdered, suspicion would fall neatly in another direction."

Grace tugged at his arm. "That makes sense, don't you think, Angus?"

"Yes. Although I have a feeling there's more to it."

Grace gave his arm a squeeze. Angus subsided. Was she warning him it would be better to say no more until he had spoken to Jack? If she was, she was right.

"Don't fret yourself, Rory. You weren't to know. Working as an advocate I did occasionally come across some bad characters, but someone like Oulsnam is rare." Angus squeezed Grace's hand. "Why don't we talk it through at dinner later? Rory, can you stay for a few days? There's plenty of room at Medley House. I might need your help with something."

Rory nodded eagerly. "Anything you want of me I'll willingly give you. I owe you."

"Put it down to experience. Now, I'd appreciate a few minutes alone with my intended. We have lots of arrangements to make."

Luke grinned at him, but shooed the others out. "No more than five minutes mind."

The door closed behind him. Angus leaned back and put an arm around Grace's shoulder, along the top of the sofa. He kissed the top of her head.

"Deuce take it. Even five minutes with the door closed might be too much for my self-control."

Grace laughed and ran a finger over his lips, making him shudder. She pulled him closer and kissed him in earnest.

It was several minutes before he drew the last shreds of common sense to the front of his brain and pulled away.

"Enough, Grace or I will be undressing you here and now."

She gave a deep throated chuckle and looked up at him with unfocused eyes.

"I was afraid my need for you was simply lust and I might regret it if I agreed to marry you, against all my objections to the state. Today the thought of not having you in my life was unbearable. That's when I knew, for sure, I was in love with you."

Angus shook his head. "I was so worried you would turn me down. I can't tell you how relieved I am."

He pulled her into his arms and kissed her, briefly. "Enough. I don't think we should be alone together until we're wed. How would you feel about a quiet wedding as soon as I can arrange a special licence?"

Grace gave him a dreamy smile. "That would be perfect."

Angus relaxed. "Wonderful. I'll send Hugh Masters to find out how I get one."

Grace laughed. "Ask Luke. He married Kitty with a special licence."

"That will save time. I want you all to myself as soon as we can arrange it." Angus stared manfully at the floor. Grace's smile was drawing him in.

"Why don't I come and join you at Medley House later? I'm sure your new staff are very discreet." Grace smiled up at him and grinned.

Angus groaned. "Don't tempt me, Grace. These last few weeks have taught me that the world is a much more dangerous place than I knew. We thought Hedburgh was my enemy, only to find out it was Oulsnam. I don't want to risk anything happening to me before we're wed and you finding yourself with child."

"I'm sure you're safe enough now, Angus."

"Perhaps, but I might have other enemies. Besides which, I'm not sure of Ralph's place in all of this. He might still be a threat."

"In what way? You know he was being blackmailed by Oulsnam but involved Jack so Oulsnam could be removed as a threat."

"But blackmailed for what, precisely?"

Grace's face dropped. "Oh! Do you think he might have been involved in some of the Medley string of deaths?"

"Possibly. I believed him when he said he didn't want the dukedom and all that went with it. However, he bears a grudge against the family for the way his father was treated by the old duke who employed him."

"Do you think he could have been on some sort of mission to improve the family line?

"Possibly. He was fond of William and saw him as a good option for Duke. Then William inconveniently got himself killed. I got the impression I'm still on sufferance with Ralph, even though he approves of you. I need to speak to Jack."

Grace sighed and put a hand on his arm, sending shivers of desire up and down his spine.

"Put like that, I can see your point. Whatever you do, take Luke and some of his men with you when you talk to Jack."

"Don't worry, I will. Now let's concentrate on getting this wedding organised. What about a wedding dress? How long will it take you to have one made?"

Grace gave an airy wave. "I've got so many clothes there will be something suitable in my wardrobe. To think I was seriously contemplating trying to suppress my love of fashion and wear all dark-coloured clothes."

"What on earth for?"

"I decided I needed to become a more conventional bluestocking and make my life centre around becoming a full part of that set."

Angus burst out laughing. "My adorable little bluestocking, you're not capable of being a conventional anything!"

Grace threw a cushion at his head. "Take that."

Angus caught her wrist. Desire hit him so hard the breath was squeezed out of his chest. Time for that later. The sooner they were wed the better. Arrangements had to be made.

"I have another suggestion. What would you say to sailing up to Edinburgh, if Rory can stay until after the wedding? I would love you to meet my maternal relatives. I miss them."

Grace's eyes flew to his face. "Oh Heavens, what if they don't like me and my managing ways?"

"They will love you nearly as much as I do. My mother's female relatives are terrifying. A couple of them run businesses of their own. Their last words to me before I left for London were to make sure I didn't fall for some insipid, society lass with more hair than wit. Not a description that could ever apply to you."

A grin spread over Grace's face. "They sound like my sort of women. I think I'm going to love your family."

Chapter Twenty Eight

Five days later Grace, escorted by Luke in his town carriage, arrived at the elegant, light-coloured stone building of St Georges Church, Hanover Square. They pulled up near the portico, which covered part of the pavement, supported by six Corinthian pillars.

Luke smiled at her. "Nervous? The service will soon be over."

"Why should I be nervous with Angus waiting for me?"

A grin spread across Luke's face. "The perfect man for you."

Grace laughed. "It's no thanks to you we got together. You very nearly ruined his chances with me right at the start. Let's not argue. I've always been fascinated by this church with its attempt at classical architecture. I'm glad we chose it."

Luke helped her down and into the church. Grace walked down the aisle on his arm. Considering the short notice, an impressive collection of relatives and friends had gathered. There was even a pale-looking Ralph Medley, his arm in a sling, seated near the back.

Luke whispered in her ear. "Clever of Aunt Theo to tell all the cousins your wedding was imminent, days ago. It's lovely to see them."

"Yes, it is." Grace broke into a grin.

Trust Aunt Theo to know her mind before she did. She shivered with a mixture of anticipation and the nervousness she had tried to deny. The fluttering in her stomach settled down when her gaze landed on Angus's broad back. He turned and smiled at her and her world settled into a calmer place. She smiled back, breathless at the joy shining from his eyes.

Grace took her place beside him. The words of the service she had never expected to be for her wrapped her in a blanket of happiness. Whatever problems they had in marriage, together, they would conquer them. Of that she was certain. They exchanged vows in firm voices. Angus's grin when she vowed to obey him was nearly her undoing, but she survived the service without collapsing into laughter.

They escaped, arm in arm, and climbed into Angus's new town coach. A grinning Jamie held the reins in the driver's seat, with an equally happy Sam up beside him. Grace leaned forward to wave at the guests filing out of the church behind them before they set off. Angus ran his eyes all over her cream silk dress.

"You look beautiful today, Grace. Not that you don't always look beautiful," he added, hastily. "Aren't you glad I plucked you from the ranks of the bluestocking community?"

Grace swatted at his arm. "Coxcomb. I decided it was my duty to rescue a hapless male. I couldn't back out once the immediate danger was over, now could I?"

Angus put his arm around her and pulled her close. "I'm so glad you didn't. How long does a wedding breakfast go on for? I want you all to myself at last."

Grace pulled a face. "I know. These last few days have been so frustrating. I'm not sorry to have had some time with Aunt Theo though. One of my cousins is going to stay with her for the rest of the season. Then she is renting a house in Brighton with an old friend for the summer."

"That's good. You will miss her and she you." Angus moved in his seat. "But back to this wedding breakfast. How long will my patience be tested for? If I don't get you to myself soon, I'll explode."

Grace laughed and ran a finger over his lips, making him groan. "A few hours I'm afraid."

"In that case I claim a kiss from my bride now to tide me over."

His lips found hers and Grace lost herself in a deluge of heated emotions. Then sanity returned. She pulled away and patted her hair back into shape.

"We must stop there. We'll have all night to ourselves."

"All evening if I have my way." Angus nuzzled at her neck.

Grace's back arched of its own accord. She turned her face towards him and kissed him again. "There. That really is the last kiss until we're alone."

Angus grunted. "Hmph! We'll see about that."

The coach slowed and Medley House came into view. Mrs Evans had all the servants lined up to greet them, when they entered. They walked along the line, exchanging a quick word with each servant. The ones from the orphanage were all smiling broadly and Grace smiled back at them. She turned to Angus.

"You have an impressive array of servants now. So different from the first time I came here."

"We do. We will have to decide on how to divide all the jobs needed to run a ducal household." He caught her gaze. "I'm rather hoping you will take over supervising some of the servants but I will understand if you want to break with tradition and manage the outdoor staff, leaving me with the interior ones."

They had reached the end of the line and Mrs Evans stared at them askance. Grace grinned at her.

"Don't worry, Mrs Evans. His Grace is merely funning. Of course, I will take over the running of his households. I count myself privileged to have you to work with."

Mrs Evans dipped a curtsey and gave Grace a gratified smile. "It will be my pleasure, Your Grace."

Grace drew in a sharp breath. Of course, she would be addressed as Your Grace too now.

"Mine too, Mrs Evans. It feels strange to think of myself as a duchess."

Angus put an arm around her waist, a gleeful expression on his face. "I think it's time I claimed my new duchess in public."

He bent closer and kissed her soundly, to the cheers of some of the orphanage youngsters. Their expressions soon sobered at a stern glance from Angus's new butler.

Grace laughed and pulled away. "Our guests will be arriving soon."

Mrs Evans curtsied again. "All is in readiness. I think you will be impressed."

"I'm sure it will all be magnificent, Mrs Evans," Angus said. "We had better take our places ready to receive our guests."

The next few hours passed in a blur. Eventually, Grace said a tearful farewell to Aunt Theo and her cousins. Only Luke, Rory and Ralph and Jack remained.

Jack looked at Angus then at her. "Perhaps you would like to leave us for a few moments, Your Grace."

Grace turned to Angus who grinned at her. "There is nothing

that cannot be said in front of my wife."

Jack grimaced but Angus took his arm and led him towards the library. He stopped by the door and gestured to Grace to enter first.

"I'm sorry about this, Grace, but there are things we need to settle before we set sail for Edinburgh tomorrow."

Angus called to the butler that they weren't to be disturbed and closed the door behind them. He sat down next to Jack.

"The most important thing to me now, is whether there is still a threat to our safety."

Jack scratched his chin. "Nothing is ever certain, but as far as I know you should be safe." He stared at the floor, looking shamefaced. "Apologies for leaving you at risk that day. We've found the traitors, who were in Oulsnam's pay, who delayed us. We're still investigating the rest of Oulsnam's organisation. Even if someone tries to take over his position, I can't see them risking taking you on again. Apart from anything else, Mr Brodie's company would no longer be a safe bet for their operation."

"Good. That's pretty much what I thought. Fallon's agreed to come with us, along with another new man, and act as bodyguard."

Jack nodded. "I know. We're hoping he'll help us investigate the Scottish side of Oulsnam's empire while he's in Edinburgh."

Angus's eyes narrowed. "I have no objection. Mr Fallon intends to open his own business eventually and the experience will be good for him. I'll have my legal investigators up there working with him as before. I hope his Majesty's government is going to give him some payment for this work."

Jack shifted in his seat. "We're still negotiating on that. I'm sure I can get something for him and once he's a free agent we will be wanting to put work his way."

Angus smiled at Grace. "That's all I wanted to hear. If there's anything else we need to know send a message up to us. I've included Rory in this meeting because he needs to know there may still be some danger, so he can protect himself and his future wife."

Rory grinned at him. "I hope we get a fast run up tomorrow I'm going to be in trouble. Not that I'm sorry to miss all the wedding preparations."

Angus laughed aloud. I don't envy you having the aunts helping to organise it for you. I'm terrified of what they're going to say because they've missed my wedding."

"When they meet your bride, all will be forgiven. Lord Enstone will arrange to get me transported to the docks later. We need to be ready to set off by mid-morning."

Angus turned to Ralph. "I'm glad to see you recovering, Ralph."

Ralph glanced from Angus to Grace and back again. "Thank you. Regardless of what Jack says, I'm confident you'll be safe now. I look forward to following your career as the Duke and Duchess of Evesham. Come on Jack, it's time we went."

Angus escorted them to the door leaving Grace to say good-bye to Luke. Rory tactfully slipped out of the library.

* * *

Grace found herself crying. "Oh, Luke I'm going to miss you dreadfully as well as Aunt Theo."

Luke put an arm around her shoulder. "We'll be seeing plenty of you, don't worry. Father would have been so proud and happy today. Not, I hasten to add, because you've married a Duke, but because you've married at all. He left a letter for me in which he said he was afraid he had helped to make you far too independent to ever want to marry. He felt your best chance was a reforming peer. So that you could help him influence Parliament. Angus is everything he would have wished for you."

They exchanged hugs and Grace dried her tears. "We'll be along to visit you and Kitty as soon as we're back."

"Kitty will be overjoyed to see you. You may have another niece or nephew by the time you're back. Enjoy Edinburgh." Luke kissed her forehead and slipped out of the library.

Grace curled up in the armchair nearest fire and waited for Angus to return. The door opened and her sadness at leaving her old life left her, at the joy of seeing the smile on his face.

"I don't think we'll ever know the full truth about Ralph." Angus sat on the arm of her chair. "But I believed him when he hinted that he is no threat to us today."

"I've thought about it long and hard. Ralph clearly has a strong sense of family honour, which may be a little warped out of loyalty to a father he feels was badly mistreated. Did he help some members of the Medley family, who he felt were unsuitable to be a duke, on their way? Perhaps, we will never know." She laughed. "I do know it would be sensible for you to make absolutely sure you don't do anything to upset him."

Angus gave a shout of laughter. "True, but at this moment all I care about is you. Come on let's go and get into something more comfortable."

Grace's pulse raced. "The sooner the better."

He pulled her up and they raced out of the library, hand in hand. Mrs Evans hovered near the foot of the stairs.

"I've told the staff you won't want to be disturbed after such a tiring day. Ring the bell if you want anything. Cook has a light supper ready to send up to you when you're ready." Eyes twinkling, she dipped a curtsey and slipped away.

They ran up the stairs, giggling like children. Angus stopped in front of the door to her room. He leaned so close his breath tickled her ear and a frisson of excitement ran up Grace's spine.

"If your maid is there, dismiss her. I want the privilege of undressing my wife tonight."

"You're making a rather big assumption there, aren't you?" Grace gave him a saucy smile and watched the desire flare in his eyes.

Angus tapped her on the rear. "In, strumpet. I'll go and dismiss my valet and join you in your room, if Her Grace pleases."

"Her Grace pleases very much." Grace ran the tip of her tongue over her lips.

Angus groaned and disappeared into the door next to hers.

Her maid was waiting for her with one of her new night-gowns and a silk dressing gown laid out on the bed. She was rather fond of this dress; Angus could wait a few moments more. What would this be like? Her pulse quickened. The room seemed more colourful than when she had been shown it before.

The maid gave her a beaming smile. "You look lovely in that dress, Your Grace."

"Thank you. Once you've helped me out of it you may leave me. I shan't want you again today so have the evening off. We'll need to leave early in the morning."

"Thank you, Your Grace. I'm so looking forward to going to Edinburgh."

Grace was in her shift studying the garden when the connecting door to Angus's room opened. He too was partially undressed. She caught her breath. He was magnificent. Was this really happening to her? Lud! This was better than being a bluestocking. She studied him unashamedly. The flickering light of the fire brought out a myriad of colours in the fabric of his silk banyan, thrown loosely over his open necked shirt. He closed the door and walked towards her.

Grace sighed and drew in a ragged breath, stroking her arms. Her body tingled. As Angus came closer, the light of the candles on the table by her bed threw the planes of his features into sharp relief, softened by his smile. He stopped by the bed and opened his arms. Grace walked straight into them and threw her arms around his neck. The feel of his breath on her cheek sent a wave of heat through her body. She hugged him closer and breathed in the scent of him. All tangy citrus mixed with a hint of musk and warm male.

* * *

Angus stroked Grace's back and then allowed his hands to drop lower until they rested on her buttocks. He pulled her closer so she would realise how aroused he was. Grace gasped and he loosened his hold. A bead of sweat ran down his face and he felt dizzy. His leg muscles quivered with tension. If she didn't enjoy her first experience of lovemaking, would she regret marrying him?

He lifted his head. "Grace, you do know what happens don't you? If you want to take this in stages, we can leave full loving making until another day. I want it to be special for you."

Grace's body shook. He stroked her hair. "Sweetheart, don't

worry." He stopped. The muffled noises coming from Grace couldn't be laughter, could they?

She arched her back and smiled up at him. "Angus, my friend, stop worrying. It's past time we were lovers."

Her mouth found his and opened invitingly. He deepened the kiss and tightened his hold on her until there was no space between them from shoulders to thighs. Her scent of lavender and summer flowers engulfed him. He pushed her away, breathing heavily.

"I'm feeling rather hot."

Grace gave him a sultry smile. "Why don't I undress you?"

"Yes please."

His banyan slipped to the ground easily once she untied the belt and gave it a sharp tug. Her hands explored him through his shirt sending waves of heat to his loins. He yanked the shirt out of his breeches and let her pull it over his head. He feathered kisses down her neck until he reached the material of her shift. Wordlessly, Grace lifted her arms and he pulled it over her head, gasping at the sight of her fully naked.

Her hands were at the buttons fastening his breeches. He pulled her onto the bed and kicked off his slippers. Together, they wrestled his tight-fitting breeches off. He lay back and she climbed onto the bed next to him. She ran her hands over his chest and sighed. He kissed her again and set about exploring her with gentle hands and lips. She was soon ready for him.

He entered her slowly, with every ounce of constraint he could muster. She tensed for a moment and then relaxed. She arched her back and moved against him. He closed his eyes and sensation took over. They moved together until Grace cried out and he joined her in glorious release. A sense of peace settled over him. Grace smiled. He moved to the side of her and cuddled her close until sleep claimed him.

* * *

Sometime later, Grace woke up feeling happier than she could remember. She opened her eyes and gave Angus a sleepy grin. "That was wonderful. Can we do it again?"

He gave a shout of laughter. "I was so worried you wouldn't enjoy your first time; I was like a callow youth. I needn't have worried. I might be ready for a repeat performance after we've had some supper."

"That's good." She stroked a strand of damp hair off his forehead. "I'm so glad I met you. I think I'm going to like being part of a couple."

"Enough to compensate for the legal disadvantages of the married state for women?"

Grace licked her lips. "Let me see. I think so, Husband, on one condition."

"What's that?"

"You start a Parliamentary campaign to give women their rights."

"That's something I will be glad to do. Although I warn you it might take a very long time."

She nibbled at his ear. "Oh well, I'll extract plenty of compensation from you in the meantime."

Epilogue

They leaned on the rail of the deck, eyes searching for the first sign of land. The wind tugged at Grace's hair hard enough to pull a lock free. Angus leaned over and tucked it behind her ear.

"Well, my illustrious duchess, we'll soon be back in London. What did you think of Edinburgh?"

"I loved it. The people are so friendly."

"Especially my father's old friends. They couldn't believe how knowledgeable you are on the classical world".

"They were interesting to meet, but I was thinking more of your family and their friends. If you ask me, commerce is the future. I loved hearing all about their businesses."

"I'll put you in charge of my business investments then. If I had taken more interest in the investments I inherited, I would have known I had a controlling interest in Rory's shipping firm."

"I'd like that. I'm glad you gave Rory your share as a wedding present."

"It felt the right thing to do. Rory has worked hard to make it such a success. I miss Edinburgh, but I have work to do in Parliament. We'll have to spend time on my estates too."

"If Rory will transport us, we can visit Edinburgh at least

once a year. Your family are brilliant." Grace smiled up at him. "Especially the female ones. They've given me some wonderful tips on how to manage menfolk."

"I told you my female relatives are formidable. If it hadn't been for that megalomaniac, Oulsnam, trying to kill me I might have thought of introducing you sooner. Then, perhaps, you wouldn't have kept me waiting so long for an answer."

"I definitely came away from Edinburgh reassured that you're likely to keep your promise to treat me as an equal. On the other hand, I was guarding my heart against attractive men so firmly we would never have become friends without the mystery to solve."

Angus pulled her closer and kissed her thoroughly. "Which would have been a dreadful shame."

"It would." Grace patted her stomach. "And Medley junior wouldn't be on his or her way now."

"What? Really?" Angus ran a hand through his already rumpled hair. "Are you sure? Shouldn't you be lying down?"

"I've never felt better. Don't start fussing me. I can't abide that."

"No, Grace. Of course not. I wouldn't dare." Angus captured her lips and kissed her again. Gently this time.

Grace kissed him back, with all the passion that flowed through her. "That's better."

THE END

Afterword

If you loved 'The Duke's Bluestocking', I would appreciate a review. This helps new readers find my books.

This is the fourth book in my Reluctant Bride series of stand-alone novels linked by character. I hope I've managed to do Grace justice!

Previous books, in order:
A Good Match For The Major
The Viscount's Convenient Bride
The Marquess's Christmas Runaway

Coming next - Lucy Vaughan's story. We find out why Lucy's father demanded she return home in the middle of the London season.

To find out more please visit my website at https://josiebonhamauthor.com
or follow me on social media
Facebook: @josiebonhamauthor
Twitter: @BonhamJosie
Instagram: @josiebonham

Printed in Great Britain
by Amazon

56862068R00202